The Baby Sitters

The Baby Sitters

JOHN SALISBURY

NEW YORK *1978* *Atheneum*

Library of Congress Cataloging in Publication Data

Salisbury, John.
   The baby sitters.

   I. Title.
PZ4.S1682Bab   1978   [PR6069.A474]   823'.9'14   77-88910
ISBN 0-689-10852-4

Manufactured by Halliday Lithograph Corporation,
West Hanover and Plympton, Massachusetts
First American Edition

Prologue

At 6.15 on a cloudless morning in the early summer of 1981 a man emerged from a house in Chester Place, Regent's Park. Closing the front door quietly behind him—his family were still asleep—he paused for a moment, warily.

It was a handsome, cream-washed Regency house on five floors, built in 1826 according to a design by John Nash, and adorned by plain Tuscan pilasters. Eight years ago, when this man's income had suddenly spiralled, he had paid £53,000 for a sixty-year lease: the Crown Commissioners granted no freeholds in this exclusive enclave of central London.

It was a pleasant place to live. But recently it had become less pleasant.

Wearing an old Achilles Club tracksuit and well-worn Adidas training shoes, Ellison broke into a fast trot, heading for the park. As he crossed the Outer Circle he shot a quick glance to his left.

The four men in the black Mercedes 450 SEL watched him disappear through the park gate.

Lengthening his stride and tracking round the northern rim of the Inner Circle, Ellison gazed thoughtfully towards the 145-feet-high white minaret of the Central London Mosque, a new £4 million complex with a golden dome and a cold-storage mortuary—the largest of Britain's 250 mosques and the largest in Europe. Soothed by the warm summer air fanning his lungs, Ellison began to pick up the fine lather of

sweat which kept his weight down to 162 lbs and his mind
razor sharp. No one observing the easy, fluent motion of the
runner across the dew-moist grass would have guessed that
he was beset by acute anxiety.

As he emerged from the park and inserted the key suspended round his neck in the front door, the four men in the
Mercedes watched him impassively.

He showered and shaved, viewing his reflection sceptically:
light brown hair cut short across a broad head, a flattish nose,
cold, steel-grey eyes, and a mouth which twisted at the corners
in mild mockery. He looked his age: forty-five. Having
slotted his Ronson back into its holder, he walked into the
main bedroom and pinched his wife's ear.

She groaned. "What's the time?"

"Seven."

"Were the men there, Bill?"

"Yes."

Pru Ellison abruptly sat up in bed, pulling the blankets
round her bare shoulders and shivering. Yet it was a warm
day. He sat on the edge of the bed and took her hand.

"Don't be frightened," he said gently.

"But why, Bill, why, I mean what are they doing, they've
never let you out of their sight for the past three weeks!"

"I know."

"But who are they?"

"I'm not sure—exactly."

"Bill, you're lying." Pru Ellison's eyes were wide with fear.

Breakfast was in the ground-floor kitchen. Though he
distractedly tucked away two cups of medium-blend Kenya
coffee, a bowl of Swiss muesli, two boiled eggs and a slice of
rye toast without butter, Ellison's real diet was the half-
dozen newspapers spread out on the table, which his eyes
consumed in savage, raking sweeps. At 7.25 their ten-year-
old son Christopher padded into the kitchen in his pyjamas,
hunting for Rice Krispies. He gave his father a curt nod.

As Ellison left the house punctually at 7.30, carrying a
briefcase fitted with a combination lock, the rear door of his

2

modest car, a brown Granada Ghia, already stood open for him.

"Good morning, Charlie."

"Good morning, sir."

Which was the limit Ellison imposed on their first exchange of the day, though Charlie James, a former light-heavyweight champion from the East End, was talkative by nature and liked to reminisce about the year he had spent in Parkhurst's maximum security wing for causing grievous bodily harm. Charlie had been stewarding a political meeting when it had been raided by plain-clothes agents of a shadowy, semi-official counter-subversion unit called the Internal Security Police. Although Charlie had no particular interest in sub-version, his instincts had led him to put three of the agents out of business. On Charlie's release from prison, Ellison had taken him on as chauffeur, with free accommodation on the top floor at Chester Place thrown in.

Displaying its rectangular, blue-rimmed Crown Estates Paving Commission parking permit, the Granada Ghia swung left into the Outer Circle, swept down to the Maryle-bone Road, turned east towards King's Cross, reached the Pentonville Road at 7.34, and passed down Farringdon Road under the Holborn Viaduct four minutes later. Inter-mittently Charlie scowled into his driving mirror. The large Mercedes 450 SEL glided in their wake.

By the time they turned at Ludgate Circus into Fleet Street, the heartland of the British national press, Ellison had flicked the switch of his Grundig Stenorette 2000 four times and dictated four brief, precise memoranda to his secretary. He tilted his head back against the leather seat and briefly closed his eyes. At 7.40 in the morning Fleet Street was at its quietest. The presses were silent. In twenty minutes' time the day-shift operatives would emerge from buses and tube trains to begin the work of breaking up last night's chases and melting down the stereo-plates; by 9.00 the first editions of the evening papers would be hurtling off the chutes into the vans.

The Granada cruised down Carmelite Street towards the Thames embankment, slowed, then turned tightly and descended into the underground executive car-park of Gowers House, the £10 million headquarters of the *Sunday Monitor*. Reaching the fifth floor, Ellison stepped out of the small executive lift and strode through the deserted Features Department to the glass-walled cubicle which bore his name.

On his desk lay a cluster of wire tapes put out overnight by Reuters, UP, AP, Agence France-Presse and the Press Association.

——The pound had fallen to a new low of $1.33 when the New York exchange closed last night.

——Interviewed on independent television, Prime Minister Murdoch had stressed that Britain urgently required massive economic assistance from the Arab states.

——An Arab consortium was due to announce its take-over of two London merchant banks at a press conference called for 11 am.

——A rally of the Guardians of Decency had demanded that the BBC clean house without delay.

——A junior Minister had resigned following allegations in the *Star* that he disclosed confidential information to a call-girl.

Bill Ellison winced, groaned and stared at the ceiling.

At 8.10 he picked up yesterday's *New York Times* and lit his first small cigar of the day. By 8.55 he had skimmed and gutted the essential information out of *Le Monde*, *Die Welt*, *The Economist* and *Middle East Review*, as well as a translation of the lead items in *Ha'aretz*, which the Israeli Embassy sent to him daily by special messenger.

The intercom on his desk flashed red.

"Yes, Ellison."

"Mr Ellison, the Chairman would like to see you."

"When?"

"Now—if it's convenient."

Pushing aside *Arab Business*, the *Anglo-Arab Trade Journal*, *International Affairs* and *France-Observateur*, Ellison thrust his

4

hands deep into his trouser pockets and wandered to the window. For several days he had been expecting this summons. By noon the local pubs—the Witness Box at the Temple end of Tudor Street, the Old King Lud in Ludgate Circus, the George in the Strand—would be reverberating with grapevine news of the dismissal of the most highly paid journalist in Fleet Street.

At 8.59 he stepped out of the executive lift on to the thick pile carpet of the tenth floor, a physically powerful man an inch short of six feet, wearing a slightly rumpled lightweight grey summer suit.

"Won't you please take a seat, Mr Ellison?" said the Chairman's personal secretary in her aloof manner, regally regarding him through oval spectacles studded with rhinestones. Ellison grunted, nodded, and sank into a leather chair which sighed on impact. Lord Gowers would keep him waiting for the statutory five minutes.

Beside his chair stood a smart, glass-topped coffee table supporting an alabaster ashtray and one newspaper. The decor was the message: he picked up the tabloid *Star* and flicked the pages until a headline leapt out at him in 96-point Century bold across two columns.

THE END FOR ELLISON?

Rumour has it in Fleet Street that the *Sunday Monitor*'s arrogant superstar reporter Bill Ellison is about to get the boot. Millionaire Chairman-Proprietor Lord Gowers is said to be at the end of his patience. Muckraker Ellison's obsessive probes into Arab-owned business interests have brought the *Monitor*'s advertising revenue crashing by 20 per cent (£80,000 a week). This has raised serious doubts in his Lordship's astute business mind whether Ellison's glittering reputation is really worth a salary of £25,000 a year.

Or any salary at all. The good Lord Gowers, an upstanding patriot whose business enterprise has won respect for our Nation round the world, is a comparative newcomer to the newspaper business. The *Star* offers him its humble advice. Don't be dazzled by Ellison's record as four times Journalist of the Year. Ask him a few shrewd questions. Ask him why he now spends so much of his expensive time in the company of bleeding-heart liberals, Zionists and members of a Certain Race. Ask him who is secretly subsidising his weekly outpouring of anti-patriotic filth. Ask him why he screams 'conspiracy' every time the *Star* puts its finger on corrupt politicians or BBC pinko executives who squander public money on prostitutes.

And a few more questions. If 33,000,000 Britons watch BBC television every day, why does Ellison yell every time the Guardians of Decency call for a clean-up of the Corporation? What perverted, alien interests is Ellison fronting for? And why has his wife, Headteacher Pru Ellison, been foisting porn and corruption on the 1,500 pupils of Crewe Hill comprehensive school? She calls it 'sex education'. The *Star* calls it sex subversion.

The *Star* makes this offer. If Ellison will take himself and his family out of this tormented Country within seven days, this newspaper will buy them tickets to any point on the globe.

Even Tel Aviv.

"The Chairman will see you now, Mr Ellison."

Ellison dropped the *Star* on to the glass-topped coffee table and walked through the electronically operated teak and bronze doors of the Chairman's office. Ahead of him, across twenty feet of Penthouse-Supreme deep-pile carpet, Lord Gowers sat behind an enormous desk, a gift from the grateful people of a Third World state whose Esteemed Leader had recently awarded the Gowers Construction Company a £48 million contract. A signed photograph of the Esteemed Leader stood on the desk in a gilt frame.

"Take a pew, Ellison."

Sharp, beady eyes were fixed on him from within the folds of a fleshy, irascible, blood-red face.

Ellison sat down without a word, folded his broad hands, and stared back.

"Ellison, I thought it was time you and I had a chat. To be perfectly frank, I have to be alarmed by what's happening to our advertising revenue. We're being squeezed."

"Who by?"

Gowers's signet ring flashed evasively. "That's not the point. The point, to my mind, is the figures. When I bought the *Monitor*, my investment advisers presented me with a detailed break-down of the paper's assets and liabilities. You and your Searchlight team figured in the assets column. In other words, they calculated that if you moved to a rival paper, the *Monitor*'s circulation would fall from 1.5 to 1.2 million, involving a loss in advertising revenue of £3 million a year. Want a cigar?"

"No, thank you."

"So what is the present position? Our circulation remains steady, indeed it's slowly climbing. But advertising revenue has fallen at a rate equivalent to £4 million a year. And I have been left in no doubt, by certain influential quarters, that this squeeze will continue so long as you remain on the paper."

"Which influential quarters?"

Gowers's eyes flashed angrily. "Ellison, I didn't bring you here to grant you an interview."

"Did you buy the *Monitor* to make money?"

Lord Gowers's thin mouth tightened at the thrust. Both men knew that Gowers had gobbled up the *Monitor*, a high-quality newspaper, out of hunger for prestige, influence, respectability. Had commercial profit been his main motive he would have invested in a television channel or a monopoly chain of provincial dailies.

"I didn't buy it to lose money," the Chairman snapped. He leant forward across the huge desk, jabbing the air with his glowing Havana Partagas. "Let's get this clear: you're losing me money."

"May I ask you a question?"

"Of course."

"Soon after you bought this newspaper, you made certain changes, even though the Editor, Ramsay Jordan, opposed them and I opposed them. You brought in Alistair McNairn as Chief Political Correspondent and Hubert Yorath as General Manager. Why did you do that?"

"McNairn and Yorath are both good men."

"They're good yes men. They'd both eat their own grandmother if you so much as inclined your head. Or the Government inclined its head."

"Are you suggesting that I allow the policy of this newspaper to be dictated by the Government?"

"Chairman, who's putting the screws on you?"

"I have no intention of going into that. But let me make one thing abundantly clear: it has nothing, repeat nothing, to do with the Government."

Ellison nodded. "Well, it seems that neither of us is happy with things as they stand. Jordan and I feel that the *Monitor* has become a newspaper divided against itself. Each week it speaks with two, contradictory voices. I can see only one solution."

"What?"

"You'd better fire me."

Gowers sighed, ran a hand over his polished silver hair, stood up behind his desk, thrust the wet tip of his cigar between his lips, and began to pace back and forth across the Penthouse-Supreme.

"Ellison, I'm prepared to up your salary to £30,000, plus thirty per cent of overseas syndication rights—on certain conditions."

"Jacobs has already offered me that—without conditions."

Gowers stopped dead. This was what haunted him, the prospect of Lord Jacobs, proprietor of the *Monitor*'s main "quality" rival, the *Sunday Dispatch*, scooping up Ellison's Searchlight team and 300,000 of the *Monitor*'s readers.

"Bill," Gowers said smoothly, "do you really have to spend so much time upsetting the Arabs? Aren't there other . . . subjects of greater significance?"

8

"What—faulty fire regulations in mental hospitals?"

"Bill, I wish I understood your attitude. We all know this country has got itself into the most ghastly economic pickle. We all know we can't bail ourselves out single-handed. None of us is completely happy about the present state of Arab economic penetration, but the Arabs have the surplus investment funds and beggars can't be choosers."

"Agreed."

"Then what have you been driving at? Why have you put their backs up? Do you hate Arabs?"

"No." Ellison smiled faintly. "Some of my best friends are Arabs."

"Well . . . explain."

"It's my belief that things are not quite what they seem."

"Really? That's news to me. Could you be more explicit?"

"Not at the moment."

Gowers flushed slightly and drew himself up. "Now look, Ellison, I realize you have a reputation as a dark horse until the finishing line is in sight, but I have to remind you that I am your Chairman——"

But Ellison was already moving towards the door.

"I take it I am dismissed and that your lawyers will be in touch with mine about a severance settlement."

Gowers sank into his desk chair with a haggard expression. Ellison could sense that the pressures on the Chairman amounted to more than financial ones. But what? Who?

"Bill, I'm in a position to lay on something special for you. In short, an exclusive, open-ended interview with the Prime Minister, the Home Secretary and the Foreign Secretary."

"Fine. So you want me to stay, could we get that clear?"

"Do you realize what I have just offered you?"

"Not really. It all depends on what they say. In the meantime, Chairman, to keep abreast of competition, would you be so good as to instruct your lawyers to draw up a draft contract guaranteeing me £30,000 a year and two years' salary in the event of dismissal?"

As the teak and bronze doors slid open, Lord Gowers angrily tossed his cigar end into the waste bin.

Two miles away a closed-circuit television recording machine clicked to off in a top security communications room. Later in the day a video-cassette of Ellison's interview with Gowers would be played back to three men.

At 11.20 the Granada Ghia moved out of 28 Kensington Palace Gardens, location of the Czechoslovak Embassy's Visa Department. After a three-week delay, the Czech Press Attaché had handed Ellison his visa with a warm smile.

"All the interviews you have requested with our senior ministers are of course granted, Mr Ellison. Yes, of course."

"I'm grateful."

"Not at all. *Bon voyage*. Enjoy your stay in my country."

Ellison had no desire to listen to the dreary self-justifications of Prague's Party bosses. And they knew it. Without doubt a full dossier on the career of Britain's most famous journalist had reached the Czech Ministry of the Interior. So what was their game?

His own purpose was simple: to interview Czech underground dissidents and to ram home to his three million readers the lesson of foreign domination: *It Can Happen Here*.

As Charlie took the Granada into the Bayswater Road, a primrose-yellow Lancia B 2000 coming from the direction of Notting Hill swerved, skidded and flicked the Granada's offside front mudguard.

"A bloody pussycat!" roared Charlie.

Both cars drew into the side.

The driver of the Lancia sprang out of her car with eyes blazing.

"Are you blind?" she stormed at the bemused Charlie. "You cut right across my path! Look what you've done to my car, just look!"

But Charlie could only stare spellbound at the beautiful young woman berating him, a lovely creature with auburn hair curling round her ears and a perfectly sculpted body clad in tight suede.

Her green eyes came to rest on Ellison. They were cat's eyes.

As Ellison climbed out on the pavement side, she marched round to confront him. A lethal wave of Yves Saint Laurent Y perfume hit him from five yards. He noted the high suede boots clinging to her long, exquisitely rounded thighs.

"Your driver was entirely responsible," she said.

Ellison walked forward to examine the nearside wing of the Lancia: it showed no trace of the collision beyond the faintest scratch.

He grimaced sympathetically. "Nasty."

For an instant she struggled to suppress a smile. Then, as her enticing pout regained control, she loudly demanded his name and insurance certificate, while searching for her own in a floppy Mexican leather handbag.

But what came out of her bag and into his hand was a small, mauve envelope. Sliding it into his pocket, he did his best to divert his eyes from the upward thrust of her breasts against her white, lace-trimmed blouse.

"I shall write to your mother about this," he said, and walked back to his car. Charlie, incensed by the damage to the Granada's mudguard, was about to start an argument, but a curt nod of Ellison's head silenced him.

As they moved off into the traffic, Ellison caught the expression on the girl's face; it lodged somewhere very private inside him. He opened the envelope.

Dear Bill Ellison,

I work for Bert Hoyle, Editor of the *Star*, who wrote the anonymous attack on you in today's edition. I have been assigned by Hoyle to keep track of your movements. Be careful, they are setting you up in Prague. Alter all points of contact at the last possible moment and vary all prearranged routes. Take no notes. And avoid the girls at the bar of the Park Hotel.

Hoyle is a rat on two legs. It is my ambition to work for you.

Yours,

Judy Rossiter

P.S. Please burn this after reading.

Ellison told Charlie to pull in while he bought the first editions of the evening papers outside Lancaster Gate tube station. His mouth twisted at the corners as he scanned the headlines.

——3 Million Jobless Predicted by Year's End.

——Chairman of BBC Governors Receives Deputation from Guardians of Decency.

——MP Dies. Government Majority Falls to 5.

——Arab Mission to Britain Expected to Include Top Personalities.

"Mind you, sir," Charles ruminated, "that was some bird. I reckon she got the better of you there, sir."

When Ellison drove to 10 Downing Street at 11.15 the following day, he noticed that for the first time in three weeks the black Mercedes 450 SEL was nowhere to be seen. The interview Gowers had promised had been laid on at remarkably short notice. After being kept waiting a few minutes, Ellison was ushered into the Prime Minister's first-floor study. George Murdoch was not alone. Apart from a private secretary, five other men were present.

"Ah, Ellison," Murdoch said in his bluff, homespun manner, shaking his hand. "You've met the Home Secretary?"

The Rt Hon Patrick Martindale, MP, Secretary of State for the Home Department, nodded curtly.

"And the Foreign Secretary you know well, of course."

The Rt Hon Roger Fullerton, MP, offered Ellison his hand and a shy, constrained smile.

Martindale and Fullerton were ranked number two and three in the Cabinet list. Ellison noticed that number four in the hierarchy, Walter Vandyke, Leader of the House of Commons, was not present.

Three other men stood deferentially in the background. Murdoch motioned towards them cursorily, almost as an afterthought.

"Ozanne, Lynedoch, Leech. Please sit down."

Ellison knew only one of the three by sight, the tall, stout, ruddy-faced Superintendent Stanley Leech, Commander of the new, shadowy counter-subversion unit, the Internal Security Police. The ISP was reputed to operate independently of both Scotland Yard's Special Branch and of MI5, and to be directly responsible to the Home Secretary in person. Its blue Triumph 2500 Mk 2 squad cars, with their distinctive, swishing, hissing sirens, were not often seen by day. According to the information available to Ellison, the "Leech Squad", as it was colloquially called, operated mainly by night. Its activities were rarely reported in the Press.

The other two men in the room were both civil servants and known to Ellison only by name. Geoffrey Ozanne, Under Secretary in the Home Office, and Martindale's right-hand man, enjoyed supervisory functions relating to both the police and the BBC. Kenneth Lynedoch was one of seven Under Secretaries of State in the Foreign Office, and was invested with supervisory responsibility for the FO's Middle East and Near East Departments. His chief was Roger Fullerton.

"Let's not beat about the bush, Ellison," Murdoch began. "I gather you're worried. Off the record, we're all worried. Ten minutes ago the tickertape here showed the pound down to $1.29. If there's anything you'd like to tell us, we'll listen. And if there's anything you want to know, we'll offer you what information we can. But we're off the record here and there is to be no attribution to 'highly placed sources'. Understood?"

"Perfectly, sir."

"Fire away, Ellison."

"The forthcoming Arab Mission to Britain, sir—what exactly is its purpose?"

Murdoch turned to the Foreign Secretary. "Roger, you field that one."

"The purpose," Fullerton said, "is to bail us out of our economic difficulties. In the short term."

Ellison noted a certain constraint in Fullerton's manner.

"Loans, export orders, investment pledges—that kind of thing?"

"Precisely," Fullerton said.

"And what do we offer in return, sir?"

No one spoke.

"What we offer the Arabs," Murdoch said, idly playing with a gold watch chain, "are guarantees that they won't be throwing their money down the drain."

"What kind of guarantees?"

"Stability. Long-term stability."

"Including political stability?"

Murdoch chuckled. "Unfortunately, that is not entirely in my hands. You'd better consult the Leader of the Opposition about that. Yesterday our majority in the House fell to five."

Ellison nodded sympathetically. "I'm not clear about the composition or background of the Mission, sir."

Murdoch again turned to Fullerton, who hesitated momentarily, then looked towards Kenneth Lynedoch, a thin, taut, dark-skinned man with wavy jet-black hair, a prominent nose, and eyes like pools of molten chocolate. In appearance, he could have passed for one of the Arab diplomats he dealt with daily.

"At the present time," Lynedoch said, "the actual composition of the Mission remains in doubt. But we are delighted to hear—as I'm sure Mr Ellison is—that it will be headed by His Excellency Sheikh Abdul Al-Abdullah Al-Jalah, brother of the Ruler of Kuwait."

Ellison knew—and liked—the Sheikh, who was forever dreaming of his rose garden in Ascot.

"Anyone else?"

"We have no notification," Lynedoch said crisply.

"But who does this Mission represent?" Ellison pressed. "Is it the Arab League?"

"Not exactly," Fullerton said.

"If I may intrude, sir," Lynedoch said, glancing respectfully towards Fullerton, "we are negotiating with various Arab interests who have a common interest in supporting the British economy."

"There's no deep political combination involved," added the Prime Minister. "It's strictly economic."

"Then why is the Foreign Office supporting the Arab League's boycott of British firms who trade with Israel, sir?"

Murdoch raised his bushy eyebrows a fraction and nodded to Fullerton.

"We don't *support* the boycott," Fullerton said with a pained expression.

"You endorse it, though."

"No."

"Then you connive at it."

Fullerton turned to Lynedoch.

"We have to be realistic, Mr Ellison," the Under Secretary said. "In our present economic condition we have to trade where we can on the terms offered to us. I assure you none of us likes it."

"None of us," echoed the Prime Minister. "If I may say so, Ellison, that's where we part company from you journalists. You fellows demand an ideal world. The Government must deal with the world as we find it."

"In other words, sir, if the Arabs twist our arms politically, we have to grin and bear it?"

"I really don't see why anyone should get a wasp in their knickers over the Arab Mission."

A decorous titter ran round the room like a shy mouse.

"I wondered about this new flood of Islamic propaganda at home," Ellison said.

"Flood?" interposed Home Secretary Martindale coolly. "Propaganda?"

"On the BBC; in the museums and schools. We're being suddenly bombarded by programmes lauding Arab culture, Arab art, the Moslem religion. This goes hand in hand with a mounting anti-semitism."

"Now one target at a time," Martindale said with a faint, slightly disdainful smile. "These things go in waves, you know. When the Tutankhamun exhibition came here, everyone went overboard on Egypt. Then it was Chinese civilization. At present there's an interest in Islam. You're not a cultural chauvinist, are you, Mr Ellison?"

"Probably. Who's paying for it all?"

Martindale turned to his Under Secretary. "Ozanne can probably help you on that."

"As regards the BBC," Ozanne said, "the Corporation's autonomy prevents us from inquiring into its programme policy. But if you would like to speak to the Chariman of the Governors, Sir Philip Lucas, I'm sure we can arrange it."

Martindale had appointed Lucas Chairman eighteen months earlier.

"And the schools, the museums?"

"In general, there's a good deal of Arab money around," Ozanne said. "One can't be surprised if some of it gets spent."

"But the drift of this Islamic propaganda is clearly authoritarian," Ellison said.

"My dear fellow," interjected Murdoch, "you don't seem to have much confidence in our own cultural traditions. For my own part, whenever I hear some of this Islamic hocus-pocus, I just laugh."

"And the anti-semitism?"

"Well, that's mostly in that rag the *Star*. To my mind Hoyle is a repulsive creep. Nothing I can do about it . . . free Press, eh?"

"It isn't confined to the *Star*, sir. A number of key controllers, producers and editors in the BBC have been hit by anti-semitic smears. And a number of Jews have recently been chased off the boards of companies."

Murdoch turned to Martindale. "Patrick, do you have anything on that?"

"If Arab companies exert economic pressure on British companies, the Government cannot intervene. Although we'd like to. About the BBC, I can't agree with you. The Corporation is in a hell of a mess, one wonders when these scandals will end."

"People don't seem to be able to climb into the right bed at night," Murdoch chuckled.

"You don't think, sir, that this wave of scandals, which has hit leading politicians as well, is a put-up job?"

Murdoch looked flabbergasted. "Put up? By whom? Do you have any evidence of that, Ellison?"

All six men in the room were studying Ellison intently.

"Yes."

"Then spill it, man."

"It's still very fragmentary, Prime Minister. I wondered, since Superintendent Leech is here, if he could brief me on the actual function of the Internal Security Police. A lot of rumours are flying about."

But Murdoch declined to toss the ball to Leech. "I can only respond to that question in very general terms," the Prime Minister said. "In recent months our intelligence services have become aware of a new threat to our national security. Indeed to parliamentary democracy itself. The ISP is essentially in business to meet that threat."

"From what quarters does this threat come, sir?"

"From heavily subsidized anarchist elements."

"Who's subsidizing them? Russia? China? Cuba?"

"Let's put it this way: there are certain vested interests determined that the Arab Mission to Britain shall not succeed. To get their way, they're prepared to pull the house down."

"Israel, you mean? Zionism?"

"Ellison, I'm not prepared to go further into this." Murdoch glanced pointedly at his gold watch.

"A final question, sir?"

"Go ahead."

"It's about the activities of Sir Stuart Ormskirk's Saviours of the Nation. Why are they allowed to parade in paramilitary uniforms in defiance of the 1936 law? Why do the police fail to intervene when they go on the rampage in districts inhabited by Jews, or blacks, or Asians? Why are they allowed to demonstrate within a mile of Westminster when Parliament is in session—also in defiance of the law? And is it true that they are training with a variety of weapons on Ormskirk's estate in Scotland? Two journalists who tried to find out ended up in hospital."

"That's a lot of questions."

"No, sir, it's all one question. And the question is this: why does the Home Office allow it?"

"Patrick," murmured the Prime Minister, "you'd better handle this one."

"In our opinion," Martindale said, "these thugs pose no serious threat. We think it wise to allow them to let off steam."

"Well, Ellison," Murdoch said, rising, "I hope we've set your mind at rest. We invited you here because we respect your work and we know that three million educated people tend to believe what you tell them." He chuckled. "I wish I had so much influence, what. Now: perhaps we can ask something of you in return?"

"By all means, sir—unless you want me to be Ambassador to Outer Mongolia."

Murdoch laughed heartily. They all laughed heartily.

"Well, it isn't such a bad idea. No, seriously. Your Chairman, Gowers, is a good man. He knows all about editorial freedom and he doesn't want to dictate to anyone. But frankly, Ellison, you're driving the man out of his mind. And you're not doing your country any good either—I may as well be blunt. The *Sunday Monitor* is widely read in the Middle East, you know. Ask Roger here"—he gestured towards Foreign Secretary Fullerton—"he's inundated with complaints by Arab ambassadors about your articles. They're convinced you're an Israeli agent—you know all that nonsense they go in for. There have even been hints that the whole Mission might be called off. Of course we try and tell them what a free Press means, but they don't have one themselves so they don't fully grasp the point. You get the drift of my remarks, I take it."

"Yes."

"Cool it, could you?"

They had all risen now, with the Prime Minister, and were observing Ellison intently.

"I'm sorry, sir, I can't make any promises."

At 5.45 pm three men met to study the video-tape of the morning's conversation at 10 Downing Street.

"Well?" the first man said.

"He's dangerous," said the second man.

"Very dangerous," said the third man.

The first man nodded. "Too dangerous," he said.

One

At the passenger terminal of Prague's modernized Ruzyne airport (the Red Army had found the facilities obsolete when its transport aircraft touched down on the morning of August 22, 1968), Morley lifted Ellison's suitcases out of the boot of his Volkswagen. Behind them the shadowing black Tatra 603 of the Czech State Security Service drew into the curb.

At the checking-in desk a blonde stewardess in sky-blue uniform examined Ellison's passport impassively and pressed a buzzer. Two plain-clothes agents immediately materialized behind him.

"Herr Ellison? *Geben Sie mir Ihren Pass.*"

The younger agent promptly lifted Ellison's suitcase.

Morley, Central European stringer for the *Monitor*, shrugged sympathetically. "I'll hang around till you board your plane, Bill."

Ellison shook his hand. "Thanks for all your help, Roy."

The agents led him up an escalator to a private office on the first floor. As they entered it, two guards in grey-green uniform and carrying revolvers stepped outside the door.

The senior agent scrutinized the visa in Ellison's passport: Cĕskoslovenské Vizum, with its entry stamp: Pasová Kontrola, Praha. Suddenly he shouted in broken German:

"We know perfectly well that during your visit to Czechoslovakia you have made contact with discontented elements!"

"Well . . . I did have one taxi driver who complained of arthritis in his driving arm."

"You're lying!"

"He may have been exaggerating."

"That was not what I meant, Herr Ellison!"

For fifteen minutes they grilled him. Then they went through his suitcase with sadistic refinement, leaving his Ronson razor in fragments, ripping the linings from his suits, and squeezing his toothpaste all over the floor. Hungry for hidden microfilm, they made him strip and prodded his anus with an anus-prodder.

"You won't find any discontented elements up there," he said.

Indeed all they found were his neatly written notes describing his boring interviews with Vice-Minister Harek at the Foreign Ministry, Second Secretary Balen of the Slovak CP, and Kozak, Secretary of the Writers' Union. Finally they released him, two minutes before the scheduled departure at 15.20 of flight BE 809. But he didn't hurry. Ruzyne airport control tower would have received precise instructions—that he should catch the plane or that he should not.

As it turned out, that he should catch it. The Trident's jets were already howling as he climbed the forward staircase to the first-class compartment. The blue-uniformed British stewardess threw him a reproving glance and locked the heavy fuselage door behind him before guiding him forward to the window seat he had reserved.

Between Ellison and his seat, however, an obstacle intervened; two obstacles, in fact, in the form of a pair of long and shapely legs clad in flesh-coloured nylon and exposed to the point where a short leather skirt, fringed in the wigwam mode, made a token appearance. Ellison squeezed past with an apology.

As he fastened his seat belt he was aware of sapphire-blue eyes gazing at him coolly beneath Mae West eyelashes. The long blonde hair cascading over the girl's lovely shoulders was not, he decided, her own: but whose was it?

The Trident flashed down the runway. Ellison tilted his seat to upright and closed his eyes.

"You're quite right to be afraid," the girl said. "Did you know that 61 per cent of fatal accidents take place during take-off and landing?"

Southern accent—Georgia, perhaps, or one of the Carolinas. He opened his eyes. There was more than a hint of mockery in her smile.

"Did you enjoy your trip?" she asked softly.

"Very much, thank you." He turned away towards the window. A patchwork quilt of green and brown fields was receding below the Trident's starboard wing.

"Were you in Prague on business?" she persisted.

He nodded. "Mine." He opened a newspaper.

As soon as the Fasten Seat Belts sign was extinguished she left her seat and walked elegantly up the aisle to the toilet. Lying on her seat was a green, soft-covered passport. He opened it. Name: Sally Clay Moore. Birth date, December 16, 1955. Birthplace, South Carolina. Height, 5' 7". Hair, blonde. Eyes, blue. American passports do not state the bearer's profession, but he was in little doubt that hers was the oldest in the world. The visa pages were crowded.

Five minutes later she sank into her seat with a swish of crossing thighs. A minor explosion of Yves Saint Laurent Y now mushroomed round him—it sparked a memory.

"You left your passport on the seat," he said politely.

"Did you check the visas?"

"I never look at a lady's visas."

"Shall I tell you what your eyes remind me of? Conkers. Grey conkers."

Interesting: "conkers" is not a word in the American lexicon.

Two stewardesses appeared with a drinks trolley.

"Can I get you a drink?" he asked.

"Thank you. A Bloody Mary, please."

"A Bloody Mary and a double Scotch on the rocks," he told the stewardess.

"Cheers," he said.

"Cheers, Mr Ellison."

"My apologies. I didn't realize we had met."

"You made an excellent impression on Vice-Minister Harek and Second Secretary Balen. I'm sorry State Security messed up your suits. Still, I daresay you can put it down to expenses."

A fierce anger seized him. If there was one human type which nauseated him, it was the spy. On this subject his sensitivity was acute, for the run of mankind tends to regard journalists as spies lacking the guts to carry guns.

"I gather you slept with the whole Central Committee of the Party," he said.

"No. Two were out of town." But she had flushed; he could see she was stung. "I thought," she said softly, "that the Winchester College motto is 'Manners makyth man'."

Bill Ellison gritted his teeth. "I apologize," he said.

"Thank you. I'm glad you followed my advice."

"Did I?"

"Why yes! You managed to meet the playwright Mecelka, the novelist Wieser, and the underground socialist Lesec, but Czech State Security can't prove it. You eluded them each time round."

"Then how can you prove it?"

The blue eyes regarded him steadily. "I'll tell you on one condition—that you give me a job on the Searchlight team."

He saw, now, the pale, oval face, the green eyes, and the short, curling auburn hair of the girl who had side-swiped his car with her Lancia. He glanced quickly at the lovely, slender body reclining beside his own.

"Tell me," he said. "In what manifestation are you known to Bert Hoyle: as Sally Clay Moore or as Judy Rossiter?"

"Hoyle knows me as you see me."

"Hm. I suppose I'm old-fashioned. In my day a journalist always wore his own face and his own name. And when he went to bed, or she went to bed, he was off-duty."

The stewardess brought them lunch trays: salade niçoise,

chicken Maryland, trifle, cheese. Ellison ordered two half-bottles of Claret.

"You'd better tell me how and why you foisted this extravagant false identity on Hoyle."

She spoke now as an Englishwoman.

"After I graduated from Sussex I answered an ad by a New York PR firm. They wanted a classy receptionist with a sleek appearance. I got the job. I hoped to break into journalism but the editors only laughed. 'Baby, have you ever tried interviewing a district attorney, a baseball idol or a school superintendent in Harlem with an accent like yours?' I decided to spend the six hundred dollars I'd saved on becoming an American."

"And why South Carolina?"

"Two reasons. That was where my boss in the PR firm came from——"

"He tutored you in his spare time?"

"With your permission, sir. The second reason was that flaws in a South Carolina accent are less apparent to New Yorkers than flaws in a Bronx accent."

"But why did you have to tart yourself up? I thought you were rather nice as you are."

"Did you really?"

"Well . . ."

"I'd already done the round of New York editors. I couldn't go back to them looking exactly the same. Anyway, I got a job on the *New York Sentinel*. After two years of interviewing district attorneys, baseball idols and school superintendents I decided to go home."

"But why to Hoyle?"

"I suppose you've climbed so high up the tree you can no longer see the ground. Don't you know how difficult it is to break into Fleet Street?"

"Then how did you break into Hoyle?"

"He was in New York. The Editor of the *Sentinel* gave me a glowing recommendation."

"And Hoyle also glowed a bit?"

"It's possible."

"He fixed you up with a work permit?"

Her voice dropped. "Hoyle need only pick up the phone to obtain any kind of permit."

"Tell me more about that."

"No. Not until you give me a job."

"You're really asking me to believe that you have been working for Hoyle while secretly double-crossing him?"

"Only recently."

"Why recently?"

"Because I've begun to see what's really going on."

"And what's really going on?"

"Mr Ellison, I don't have your political brain. With me, it's more instinctive . . . a feel for people and what they stand for. But I'm good at finding things out. Very good." Briefly her hand touched his sleeve. "I believe I could help you."

He turned and looked down out of the window at the brilliant-blue band of the English Channel, crowded with toy tankers and cargo boats whose motion through the water was betrayed only by slivers of white wake. He imagined the flocks of gulls hovering low over the sterns, scarcely moving a wing yet effortlessly keeping pace with the ships. He knew that if he hovered he would plunge straight into the sea, and no one would pluck him out.

He couldn't decide. He was acutely aware that the girl beside him was extraordinarily desirable and that his body ached to possess hers. But that was the worst possible reason for giving her a job; never in the entire course of his career had he allowed sex to interfere with his work.

"One thing," she said, "you ought to know. If I leave Hoyle, change my identity and move to the *Monitor* as Judy Rossiter, it has to be under deep cover. My life would be in danger."

He grinned. "Hoyle carries a gun?"

"His friends do."

"Who are they?"

"Ever heard of Spectrum Security?"

"No."

"They're the ones who follow you around in a black Mercedes 450 SEL."

"But they don't work for Hoyle."

"Of course they don't. They work for the same outfit that Holye works for."

"Which is?"

Judy Rossiter smiled. Or Sally Clay Moore smiled. "That's what I want to help you find out. That's what you've *got* to find out, and quickly."

Fifteen minutes later the Trident began its westerly run-in to Heathrow along the Thames. As the red tile roofs of the semi-detached houses rose to meet them, he fastened his seat belt and closed his eyes. A man who boards an aeroplane forty or fifty times a year is bound to run out of luck sooner or later. He liked the idea of later.

As they touched down with a mild jolt a cool, slender hand lightly brushed his own. The Trident taxied towards Terminal 2, now used by certain British Airways flights due to airport congestion.

"Please," she said.

At passport control they were bound to separate; his blue UK passport would have the edge for speed over her green American one.

"Hoyle will have sent someone to meet you, of course?"

She nodded. "When can I see you?"

"Judging on past performances—whenever you choose to."

"No. It's up to you, now."

"I'm a survivor."

"I can't win?" She smiled sadly and took a step towards him. "Want another tip free of charge? Take a taxi into London. Leave your car where it is."

He read the anxiety in her face. It was genuine anxiety. But the anxiety of a good actress is always genuine. He nodded and walked through passport control without looking round. In the baggage hall he picked up a porter and presented him with his suitcase and two pound notes. Passing through the Nothing to Declare customs area, Ellison walked warily to the flight arrivals barrier, behind which a throng of relatives and friends awaited the travellers.

His eye skimmed the crowd.

Reaching the exit to the covered overhead walkway which links Terminal 2 with its car-park, a hundred and fifty yards away, he loudly instructed his porter to wait while he made a few phone calls. As he walked rapidly away down the main concourse, a newspaper happened to slip from under his arm. Stooping to retrieve it, he turned and glanced briefly back towards the flight arrivals point.

A swarthy, muscular man in a smart brown suit and dark glasses had positioned himself close to Ellison's porter and suitcase. The man was watching him intently.

Ellison walked past the central staircase, traversed the bookstand, then descended to the ground floor at the Alitalia-Iberia reception area. Entering the covered walkway at street level, he began to run up and above the airport road system, with the redbrick control tower to his right, until he entered Terminal 2 car-park at its second level.

Reaching the third level, he turned right. His Ford Granada Ghia stood where he had left it six days ago, in the middle of Block 10.

Moving round the car, he looked through each window. Two threads of black cotton laid across the black leather seats in front had been disturbed. A sliver of fine tissue paper he had wedged in the driver's door as he closed it was now lying beneath the handbrake.

Ninety seconds later he was back in Terminal 2. He barged past a slow-moving competitor into a free phone cubicle and dialled a number. Then he checked his watch and bought a cup of espresso: he had five minutes to kill.

As the porter followed him on to the covered walkway their footsteps echoed along the corridor. Soon Ellison picked up the thread of a third pair of feet. The midway bend in the corridor offered him a momentary line of vision to his rear.

The muscular individual in the brown suit and dark glasses was now fifteen yards behind the porter. His left hand was concealed in his jacket pocket; his right hand swung free.

Reaching the second level of the car-park some ten seconds ahead of his porter, Ellison absorbed the unnatural silence in the semi-dark concrete vaults. No car moved either up or down. A knot of bewildered travellers had been denied admission and herded into a protected alcove behind the stairway and lift. As a uniformed security guard blocked his path Ellison murmured his own name and nodded towards the covered walkway behind him. Two Special Branch detectives in plain clothes unobtrusively detached themselves from the group of car-seeking travellers, their eyes fixed on Ellison.

Ellison's porter turned the corner, wheeling his trolley. "Thank you, thank you," he called impatiently, trying to push his way through to the lift. But a security guard blocked his path. "Why does it always happen to me?" the porter complained to Ellison.

Footsteps approached cautiously from the covered walkway. The muscular, swarthy man in the smart brown suit turned the corner, saw the security guards, and momentarily hesitated. Ellison's head nodded almost imperceptibly.

The two Special Branch detectives took the man in the brown suit very fast indeed and without preliminary courtesies. As one pinioned his arms the other reached under his jacket and plucked a Beretta from a shoulder holster beneath his left armpit.

Almost immediately sirens began to scream as bomb disposal units converged on the Granada Ghia on the third level, immediately above them. The passengers were herded rapidly back across the covered walkway.

In airport security they showed Ellison the device they had found in the man's pocket. It was no bigger than a pocket calculator or miniature dictaphone. Originally developed by a Mitsubishi subsidiary in Kuwait for wealthy clients in the Arabian Gulf, where summer temperatures reach 120° Fahrenheit, it enabled the owner to switch on the engine and air-conditioning of his car before he reached it. The operative range was seventy yards.

"But surely," Ellison said, "as soon as I turned the ignition key . . ."

"No, sir. The bomb wasn't wired to the ignition. When a car is left here for a number of days there's always a possibility that the staff may have to move it."

"Who is he?"

"He was carrying no identification papers at all."

"And won't talk?"

"Not a whisper."

"I'd like to have a word with him."

"They've taken him into London, sir."

"That was quick. Who's 'they'? The Special Branch?"

"I believe the Internal Security Police will handle this case, sir."

Ellison smiled grimly. "Fancy that."

"There is one small point puzzling us, sir. Can you explain why you chose to drive yourself to the airport and to leave your car unattended for six days, at a cost of £36?"

"Is that so unusual?"

"It might be unusual for a well-known personality with a chauffeur at his disposal."

Three hours later Ellison gave a Press conference at the International Press Centre in Shoe Lane. The later editions of the morning papers carried prominent headlines: BOMB ATTEMPT ON TOP JOURNALIST. Ellison's allegations were quoted verbatim:

"The attempt on my life was the work of a private murder organization called Spectrum Security. The same people have kept me under constant surveillance, round the clock, for the past five weeks. One thing is certain: Spectrum Security, and the masters it serves, are dedicated to the destruction of the free Press in this country. It is my belief that a parallel organization working a criminal prostitution racket has been responsible for framing a large number of MPs and media personalities who are outspoken liberals and democrats.

"But make no mistake. I have not run foul of the criminal underworld. I have run foul of powerful vested interests operating at a high political level.

"I call upon the Government to investigate, expose and prosecute this conspiracy. I am told that the man arrested today at Heathrow has been taken into custody by the Internal Security Police. I want to know why. I want to know who he is. And I want to know when this man will be charged.

"The general public will now know how to interpret the next attempt on my life, or on that of any other journalist who tries to find out what is happening in this country."

Two

It all seemed outrageously expensive to Mrs Laura Box, but she had never refused her niece anything, so she took a lease in her own name on the unfurnished flat in Bonham Terrace, South Kensington.

"But darling, can you afford £30 a week and £1,500 for fixtures and fittings which don't exist! And why all this secrecy? Why must the telephone be under my name and ex-directory? Are you hiding from someone, dear, some man? Of course you never tell me anything about your life, and your poor dear mother used to say the same, when she was with us."

Judy Rossiter sat in the small front room of Aunt Laura's semi-detached in Brentford.

"Auntie, you did get the cheque to send on to your solicitor?"

"Indeed I did! A most extraordinarily handsome young man came here in an Aston Martin. *So* good-looking. And who is this Mr Ellison who could write out a cheque for £2,280 on your behalf?"

"Oh . . . just an accountant in the firm."

"But what firm, darling? What is this new job of yours?"

"They do market research, Auntie. It's rather hush-hush . . . you know, industrial things."

Aunt Laura's eyes opened wider. "Oh. I see."

The cheque Aunt Laura had received was in fact drawn on

Searchlight's confidential slush fund (£20,000 per annum). This fund, out of which Judy's salary of £6,000 was also to be paid, was deposited in a bank account known only to three men: Ramsay Jordan, Editor of the *Monitor*, Bill Ellison, and Magnus Massey, Ellison's trusted colleague. They alone were authorized to sign cheques. So rigorous were the security measures surrounding Judy's incorporation in the Searchlight team, so determined was Ellison that neither Lord Gowers nor General Manager Hubert Yorath should catch wind of her existence, that her real name was concealed from Ellison's secretary Cherry and the junior member of the Searchlight staff, Joe O'Neill. To them she was simply "Alice". For Judy, Gowers House was strictly out of bounds. Phone-calls to her flat in Bonham Terrace had to be made from call-boxes; Ellison had reason to believe that all his telephone conversations were tapped—by whom, he wasn't sure. He was also working on the assumption that electronic bugs had been installed in Gowers House.

The second immediate task was to throw dust in the eyes of Bert Hoyle, editor of the *Star*. The cable that landed on Hoyle's desk was transmitted by Western Union from New York and read: "Terribly sorry sudden departure stop mother seriously ill stop hope to return soonest stop love Sally Clay Moore." Subsequently a letter handwritten in London on an American airmail form made a two-way journey across the Atlantic and informed Hoyle that the condition of Sally's mother remained critical. The letter was datelined and franked from Charleston, South Carolina.

But Ellison was not satisfied: Judy's life was now at risk. If Sally Clay Moore's sudden departure had not in itself aroused Hoyle's suspicions, Ellison's uncanny evasion of the traps set for him in Czechoslovakia undoubtedly would. Further burdens were imposed on the Searchlight slush fund. Ellison had insisted that Judy should leave in her old flat almost everything except a suitcase of clothes, which meant that the flat in Bonham Terrace had to be furnished from scratch. The wisdom of these precautions was confirmed when the caretaker reported to Sally Clay Moore's London solicitor that her old flat had been broken into but nothing stolen.

Sally's primrose Lancia B 2000, on loan from the *Star*, remained outside her old flat. Although Ellison offered to contribute towards a replacement, Judy insisted she could afford a down-payment on a red Mini Cooper with smoke-glass windows. She was particularly keen on the smoke-glass windows.

"Bill," she said on the phone, "I'm giving a house-warming party."

"Vetoed."

"With just one guest."

At 6.30 in the evening Charlie swung the Granada out of the executive car-park of Gowers House into Carmelite Street. The black Mercedes 450 SEL immediately moved into the slipstream.

"Go down the Strand," Ellison said.

"Rush hour, sir."

"I know. Go down the Strand."

Opposite the Savoy Hotel dense traffic brought them to a halt. Cars were inching forward, nose-to-tail; a U-turn would be impossible to execute quickly. Ellison glanced in Charlie's driving mirror; the Mercedes was directly behind them. A taxi with its sign illuminated, but travelling in the opposite direction, drew level with the Granada and stopped in front of a red light. Ellison waited until the amber light showed, then swiftly opened the rear door and climbed into the taxi as it was beginning to move.

"South Kensington tube station," he said.

He glanced through the rear window. The Mercedes was fighting to turn, its headlights blazing and its horn blaring, but within half a minute the taxi had lost it.

He walked the last three hundred yards to Bonham Terrace. Even Judy herself was under strict instructions never to take her Mini Cooper within detectable range of her flat.

Clutching a bottle of Moët champagne and a bunch of Dutch tulips, he pressed the bell. He struggled to control the quickening of his pulse rate, the electric physical desire she had aroused in him from the day her Lancia had so deftly side-swiped his car. The intercom crackled.

"Your boss," he said.

"Wait while I check you out in *Who's Who*."

The street door buzzed, then clicked open.

He began to climb the stairs. It wasn't only her body which disturbed him, it was equally her personality, the constant, humorous flicker in her green eyes which perpetually challenged his manhood.

She was standing in the doorway of her second-floor flat. A soft light from the hallway behind her played on her auburn hair and on the ivory skin of her bare shoulders. As he walked up to her she didn't move.

"Who are you really?" she said.

Should he kiss that delicious, pouting mouth? He wanted to. Clumsily he pushed past her, thrusting the Moët into her hands with an awkward grunt. She closed the door.

"Well," she said, "are you pleased to see the departure of Sally's Revlon Touch and Glow foundation, her Princess Galitzine eye pencil in Blue Sapphire and her Yardley lipstick in Rose Coral? Yes, *mein Herr*? But the worst abomination, don't you think, was her Ultima II Patina eye shadow in Platinum. I really do believe Clinique's Ivory Bisque suits her so much better. Yes?"

He nodded and pretended to reach for his notebook. "Would you mind repeating that?"

She poured him a Scotch and herself a Bloody Mary, then sat down on the sofa beside him and crossed her long, soft thighs—the skirt of her green velvet gown parted almost to the hip.

"Do you like boeuf bourguignon and petits pois?"

He could sense her faintly mocking green eyes playing on his face.

Bill Ellison wasn't a man who had ever given much

philosophical thought to the problem of marital fidelity. It was more instinctive, a form of stubbornness; he bore the torments of the flesh in stoical silence. When travelling abroad he had occasionally surrendered to temptation because Hong Kong or Nairobi or New York could be brushed off as a never-never land without a past and without a future, only a present. When young women "made eyes" (as he antiquatedly thought of it) at him in London he vaguely put it down to the aphrodisiac power of fame, of success—it would never have occurred to him to regard himself as a physically attractive man. Ellison had grown up in a culture where only females were supposed to be physically attractive.

"Yes," he said, "I like boeuf bourguignon and petits pois very much."

"I really do believe you're shy."

He flushed slightly and shrugged. "Well . . ." he muttered. Then he cleared his throat. "To tell you truth, I'm not quite sure of my own motives."

"In hiring me?"

"Mm."

She laughed softly. "That's something we ought to sort out without delay," she said, springing up and walking away to the kitchen.

He tilted his head back against the sofa and closed his eyes. Why resist, why sublimate his desire, when sensual release was so obviously his for the asking? Why not let those deft, cool hands unzip him; why not offer his throbbing sex to her darting tongue? Why not surrender to the embrace of that supple, pliant body with its magnificent breasts and long, soft thighs? Life is now.

"Dinner's served!" she called from the kitchen. "Will you uncork the champagne, please?"

"Of course."

He stood up and shook himself like a wet dog. If he succumbed, he would respect himself, and trust himself, less. And so would she.

35

He already had a wife. And a mistress, too: his work.
The champagne cork fizzed across the room.
"So you're good at gathering information?" he said.
"Try me and see."
"I will."

The Oxford and Cambridge Club, designed by Sir Robert and Sidney Smirke in the 1830s, at the tail end of the classical revival, stands on the south side of Pall Mall close to St James's Palace. Once a week—world peace permitting —Ellison took his young colleague Magnus Massey into the club's squash court and flayed a small rubber ball for thirty minutes until he was lathered in sweat. Conceding sixteen years to his opponent, not to mention the younger man's fluent grace about the court, his nonchalent athleticism, Ellison nevertheless enjoyed two advantages: a finely disguised drop shot into the "nick", and an inflexible will to win.

On this particular evening—five days after his return from Prague—Ellison and Massey hurried out of the showers into presentable suits and up the broad marble staircase to the bar. Within a couple of minutes the first of Ellison's dinner guests arrived.

"What will you have, Maurice?"

"Orange juice, if it's kosher."

Maurice Cohn, Head of Current Affairs, BBC Television, nodded his sad, delicate features at Magnus Massey.

"You've grown another inch," he said.

"He'll be eligible to vote soon," Ellison said.

Close on Cohn's heels came his friend Moshe Levene, a tall, willowy Old Etonian with a reputation for mischievous humour. But Ellison knew that Levene and his colleagues in the Jewish National Fund and the Board of Deputies of British Jews were now deeply anxious men.

"You're on orange juice too, Moshe?"

"Certainly. Glenfiddich. To celebrate your recent salary cut."

36

Ramsay Jordan, silver-haired Editor of the *Sunday Monitor* and Ellison's trusted associate for fifteen years, puffed into the bar.

"Where are we—Tel Aviv?"

"And they gave you a visa?" Levene said.

The last to arrive, typically, was one of those Englishmen who, even in middle age, retain a permanently boyish appearance; black hair flopping over dark eyes, an olive-tinted skin drawn smooth and unlined across sensitive features.

"What will you have, Stanford?"

"Oh . . . water with a slice of lemon, if they have it."

Everyone laughed. How Stanford Christie, Director of the Middle East Institute at Oxford University, maintained his vigour without any visible input of calories had baffled Ellison for the last twenty years.

"Well, Stanford," Levene said, "what does Bill pay you to tell him what he wants to hear?" The allusion was to Christie's part-time appointment as consultant on Middle East affairs to the *Sunday Monitor*.

Hands in pockets, square-shouldered, carelessly dressed, Ellison led his guests to a table in the quietest corner of the room.

"Where is Magnus's highchair?" Levene said.

"Well, I may as well tell you about Magnus," Ellison said, ordering the waiter to bring the four bottles of Clos de Veugeot, Domain Drouhin-Laroze, which had been un-corked, decanted and allowed half a day's breathing space in honour of the forthcoming game pie. He glanced at his young colleague, who was smiling serenely, utterly unruffled. "When I first hired him, I used to say, Magnus, where were you at nine o'clock this morning? Asleep, he'd say. And where were you at three o'clock this afternoon? Why, asleep, he'd say. Later I discovered that he walks in his sleep."

"Enigmatic," said Christie.

"Well, Bill, we have to congratulate you on your narrow

escape at the airport," said Moshe Levene. "Has the ISP named your would-be assassin yet?"

"No."

"Have charges been brought?" Christie asked.

"No."

"What do you make of it?" Cohn asked.

"I'll tell you what the Board of Deputies makes of it," Levene said grimly. "We're confronted by an imminent Arab take-over of this country. The ground has been prepared by a systematic campaign of intimidation against British Jews and their friends. Those boys will stop at nothing."

"Which boys, Moshe?" Ellison said.

"You're not going to tell us about a bunch of ex-Nazis living in Brazil?" Ramsay Jordan said.

"Listen," Levene said angrily, leaning forward across the table, "do you happen to know how many British firms have been blacklisted by the Arab League's boycott office? At the last count, two-and-a-half thousand. And what does our Foreign Office do about it? It provides the Arab League with certificates of compliance on behalf of firms which promise to sever relations with Israel. How many Jewish directors have been removed from the boards of companies under Arab pressure? At the last count, over twelve hundred. How many physical attacks have the Saviours of the Nation made on Jewish shops, businesses and even homes? We don't know—the Board of Deputies has recorded three hundred proven cases. How many Jews have lost their jobs in the mass media during the last six months? At least seventy. How many Jews are there living in this country? Half a million. How many of them are afraid? Half a million. Even the babies."

Maurice Cohn nodded sadly. "And there's more to it than that."

"A lot more," Levene added.

"After all, Bill," Cohn said, "you're not my idea of a Jew. Yet they tried to dispose of you."

"Oh, I don't know," Ellison said. "My mother's grand-mother's second cousin was one-quarter Jewish."

"You never had a mother," said Cohn. "For a thousand years water ran over a stone. And then you were born."

A small ulcer of pain stabbed Ellison. Both his parents had been drowned when he was five years old. But it was not the kind of thing he liked to discuss.

He turned to Christie. "Stanford, how do you assess the situation? Who are the boys?"

Christie, who had been pecking at his game pie, gratefully dropped his fork on to the rim of his plate.

"As you know, the Arabs began buying their way into the British economy in the early seventies. The same thing occurred in America. At first they concentrated on property companies, prestige office blocks, hotels, one or two stately homes. Then they swallowed a few merchant banks with Middle Eastern business interests. And still the oil surplus, the petrodollars, searched for sound investments. By the mid-seventies the Arabs were moving into manufacturing industries, construction, even defence plants. But we don't know the whole story because large quantities of stock have been bought by dummy companies and Swiss banks."

Ramsay Jordan turned back to Levene. "But who are the boys, Moshe? Do you mean a coordinated political con-spiracy?"

"That's exactly what I mean."

"But who?"

Levene declined to answer. His mood was grim. Ellison had a strong sense that Levene was sitting on important information.

"A conspiracy by 'the Arabs' makes no more sense than a conspiracy by 'the Jews'," Ellison said. "It merely sounds like the Protocols of the Elders of Zion in reverse. We all know that no two Arab states have remained on friendly terms for more than ten minutes."

"Tell that to the two thousand five hundred British firms

and the many American firms which have been boycotted by the Arab League," Cohn said.

"But Israel is a special case, a unique case," Christie said. "Moshe was suggesting a concerted conspiracy to take over Britain, a very different kettle of fish. I have to agree with Bill. Egypt and Syria formed a union under Nasser; then they quarrelled. Egypt and Libya were about to federate; yet within two years they were virtually at war. Iraq constantly threatens Kuwait. The Iraqi Ba'ath Party denounces the Syrian Ba'ath Party every day. At one time the Syrians were regarded as the staunchest allies of the Palestinians. Then the Syrian army intervened in Lebanon and Palestinian commandos stormed Syrian embassies round the world. Shall I continue?"

"Let's take it from this end first," suggested Ellison. He turned to Cohn. "Maurice, what the hell is really going on in the BBC?"

"Within the space of a year we've lost one managing director, two programme controllers, five editors, half a dozen producers, and probably ten journalists."

"How many were Jews?"

"Seven out of twenty-four. But don't be misled by that. Every one of those men and women had either protested against the mounting flood of Islamic propaganda over the airwaves, or shown sympathy for Israel—or, in four cases, attempted to investigate Arab economic and political penetration of this country."

Jordan shrugged. "It's much the same story in Fleet Street. I suppose you all remember the story of poor Steve Moyars? You know Steve pretty well, Stanford."

Christie nodded. "He's still out of a job."

"He worked for your great rival, the *Sunday Dispatch*, I seem to remember," Levene said to Jordan.

"Tim Powerstock, their Features Editor, assigned Steve Moyars to investigate Ormskirk's Saviours of the Nation. He was set three questions to answer: who finances the Saviours, where are they getting automatic weapons from, and why are the police never on the scene when the Saviours go on the rampage? So young Steve charged around like a bullock. One day a fellow came up to him in a pub and offered him £500 to close the investigation. Soon afterwards Steve's wife received a string of threatening letters. This was all grist to Powerstock's mill: he went to press with a banner headline and was seen walking on water down the middle of Fleet Street. A week later the *Star* printed a picture of Steve in bed with the family baby sitter. The girl had confessed to Hoyle that she worked as a secretary in Police Department F4 of the Home Office, and claimed that Steve had seduced her to obtain classified documents. Powerstock issued a denial. The ISP obtained a warrant and raided the *Dispatch*. Naturally they 'found the documents'."

"Yet they didn't prosecute the *Dispatch* under the Official Secrets Act," Ellison added. "Why? Because they knew their case would collapse in court under cross-examination."

"So?" said Moshe Levene. "Is there a conspiracy or isn't there?"

"Maurice," Ellison said to Cohn, "what is the BBC hierarchy making of all this?"

"Jack is puzzled and pained. He's no sooner investigating one scandal than the next hits him. 'Why can't they sleep with their wives?' he groans."

Cohn referred to Sir Jack Armstrong, Director-General—chief executive and top-ranking professional—of the British Broadcasting Corporation. A lean, dour Scottish Presbyterian, a public servant of outstanding rectitude, Armstrong believed that the Beeb's proper function was to ventilate "society's quarrel with itself"—in other words, he was a liberal.

"But is Jack master in his own house?" Ellison asked.

"That we don't know," Cohn said. "To know that one would have to be a member of the Committee of Management and sit in on their discussions."

"What do you make of Sir Philip Lucas?" Jordan asked Cohn.

"Well, as you know Martindale appointed him Chairman of the Governors eighteen months ago. During that time Lucas has made no public pronouncements. On the face of things, Jack Armstrong continues to enjoy the full confidence of the Governors."

"Martindale is a shit," Levene said. "I don't trust that man, and I don't trust his top aides."

Ellison grinned. "Another Delphic utterance from Moshe." He turned, summoned the waiter, and ordered coffee, brandy and cigars.

"Maurice," Christie said to Cohn, "what about Edmund Strachan, your new Managing Director of Television? Does he ever lean on you?"

"I wouldn't say so," Cohn said. "Edmund's attitude towards the Current Affairs Group is perfectly correct."

They all laughed.

"You mean he lets you do what you want," Ellison said.

"What I want to know," Cohn said, "and what I cannot discover, is who is financing all these programmes on Islamic culture, Islamic art, the Moslem religion and so on. Why is everybody learning Arabic all of a sudden?"

"The Foreign Office," Jordan said emphatically. "It's obvious. Anything to please our Arab friends. Anything to ensure that the Arab Mission plucks us from the whirlpool— and swallows us."

"You're not suggesting that the Government is involved in this conspiracy?" Cohn said.

Levene gestured in exasperation. "Maurice, you're a bright boy——"

"So he's a boy too!" Ellison laughed.

"Shut up, Bill, while I demolish your Jewish friend here. To my knowledge, huge sums of money, bribes, pay-offs, golden handshakes, are now changing hands. Blatant 'insider' deals on the stock exchange are so common they're not considered worth reporting. It stinks, I tell you!"

"Wait a minute, Moshe," Christie said. "We all know that Arab business interests have made big inroads here. We also know that the British Government turns a blind eye to certain things. But where is the conspiracy? How does it all hang together?"

"Take my word for it," said Levene.

"Moshe," Ellison said gently, "my three million readers won't buy that—much as they love you, every one of them."

Moshe Levene swilled the Cognac in his glass thoughtfully.

"Bill, if I told you the truth, you wouldn't print it."

"Why?"

"It's too hot."

"For whom?"

"For your boss, Lord Gowers, to name only one."

"Gowers doesn't vet our copy," said Jordan huffily. "If he tried to, Bill and I would walk out."

Levene sighed thoughtfully. "Very well. I'll tell you what I know. We in the Board of Deputies have been paying close attention to the careers of certain people, a group of fanatical pan-Islamic Arab chauvinists who will stop at nothing——"

At this juncture Levene fell silent. The hall porter had approached their table and was now murmuring in Ellison's ear. Ellison turned to Levene.

"Moshe, your secretary Mr Rabinowitz is downstairs and wants a word with you."

"Rabinowitz? Downstairs?"

"Apparently it's urgent."

Levene rose, tall and stooping. "Make sure Cohn doesn't drink my Cognac," he said.

He followed the hall porter out of the dining-room and down the main staircase. In the hallway below he could see no sign of Asher Rabinowitz. The second desk porter approached him.

"Mr Rabinowitz said he would wait for you outside, sir. He felt he was . . . unsuitably dressed, sir."

Levene smiled inwardly. Asher lacked all sense of sartorial convention, but he was sensitive and a word from the desk porter would have sent him scurrying out into the night. Asher was a scruff, like all his generation. Hadn't been seen in a tie since his *bar mitzvah*. Two pairs of trousers: blue jeans and blue jeans. The cool night air greeted Levene as he walked down the broad steps into Pall Mall. He scanned the pavement to right and left but he didn't see Asher Rabino-witz. Odd. He looked again. Nothing. The foreboding, the warning, might have sparked earlier in his shrewd head but for the whisky, wine and Cognac. It sparked too late. The large black Mercedes 450 SEL had already glided like a shark off the kerb and into line with the club entrance when Moshe Levene noticed the Kalashnikov sub-machine-gun protruding from the rear window. It was the last thing he was destined to notice; three cordite-filled percussion bullets primed to explode on impact entered his skull, splattering fragments of bone and brain over the walls, pillars and steps of the club. He died instantly.

A bubble of blood appeared where two words had formed on his lips.

Al-Ittihad.

Three

At 10.30 the following morning Cherry, Ellison's secretary, came through on the intercom.

"I still can't get Maurice Cohn."

"Keep trying till you do."

"Max Ucelik would like to see you if you can spare a minute."

"Send him in."

A timid knock on the door was followed by the cautious entry of a thin, pale young man with steel-rimmed spectacles and an unruly mop of brown hair. Max Ucelik worked for the *Monitor* as an assistant picture editor.

"Bill, we haven't had a chance to talk since your return from Prague."

"Take a seat, Max."

"I very much admired the piece you wrote. Irena and I both thought you drew a brilliant parallel between the tragic fate of my country and what might happen here."

"Mm."

"If I may say so, you very cleverly disguised the contacts I gave you."

"OK."

Max Ucelik flinched in the face of Ellison's brevity.

"You did meet Wieser, Lesec and Mecelka, as planned?"

"No."

"But why?"

"None of them showed up," Ellison lied.

A vein began to throb under Max's left eye. "Bill, you have never spoken to me in this tone before. Why do you look at me so coldly? When Irena and I escaped to this country in '68, you and Pru gave us a home and you paid for us to continue our studies. I owe my job on the *Monitor* to you. When you were planning your trip to Prague I naturally put all my underground contacts at your disposal. Why didn't you tell me that they had failed to show up at the appointed time and place? This is extremely worrying."

"Max, I'm pretty busy right now."

The interview was over; no one could end an interview so rapidly as Ellison. Looking hurt and alarmed, Max Ucelik left the office.

Ellison reflected for a moment on Max's manner. It tended to confirm his suspicions. Someone had tipped off both Hoyle and the Czech Embassy in London—hence Judy's prior knowledge of his plans. But Max Ucelik alone knew of his plans. And why should Max, a sincere democrat, a deeply honest young man, betray both Ellison and his underground contacts in Czechoslovakia? There could be only one reason: Max's wife Irena worked as personal assistant to the Head of Plays, BBC Television, David Gottlieb. Not only was Gottlieb a Jew, he had also pursued a policy which brought him under constant, venomous attack by Hoyle and the Guardians of Decency.

Ellison tapped the fine point of a pencil on his desk and his grey eyes set very cold. Someone had got at Max Ucelik; someone had warned him that Gottlieb was about to fall and that Irena would lose her job unless Max played ball.

The intercom buzzed.

"Yes, darling?"

"Maurice Cohn is on the line."

"Hullo, Maurice. I don't want to talk about last night. I can't."

"OK." Cohn's voice sounded faint, the voice of a man shattered to the core.

"When is your *Deadline* film on the Libyan arms deal scheduled for transmission?"

"Next Wednesday. Why?"

"You and your editor Denis Laslett made contact with a former IRA man who claimed he'd been involved in smuggling Libyan arms to Ormskirk's Saviours via Drogheda and the west coast of Scotland?"

"Correct." Cohn's tone was defensive.

"How did this story break?"

"The former IRA man wrote to me. Simple."

"Too simple. I presume he sang for a small consideration?"

"Correct."

"How much?"

"I'm not at liberty to disclose that. It's against Corporation policy."

"Has the Board of Management seen the finished film?"

"Of course."

"No objections?"

"None."

"No advance protests from the Foreign Office or the Libyan Embassy?"

"Not to my knowledge. Look, Bill," exploded Cohn, apparently close to tears, "why don't you make it your business to expose Moshe's murderers and leave me alone?"

"Maurice, don't show this film. They're setting you up. They couldn't get you with sex because you're a good family man. They couldn't involve you in a financial scandal because you're the sort of chap who tells his bank it has made a mistake in his favour."

"I don't need compliments this morning. The story holds up. We've checked every angle we can. This is how Ormskirk is getting his munitions."

"I agree."

"Then leave me alone."

"The best way to kill the truth is to peddle a bogus version of it. They're killing two birds with one stone."

"Bill, do me a favour."

"No."

"Give a simple man a simple answer. Who's 'they'? You tell me who's framing me and I'll listen."

"I don't know but——"

"Thank you, Bill."

The phone went dead in BBC, Lime Grove.

The intercom buzzed.

"Well?" Ellison snapped.

"Nothing in the world is entirely my fault," Cherry said gently.

"Sorry."

"You were due to lunch at the Brasserie du Coin with Bernie Holzheimer of the *New York Times*."

"Has he called it off?"

"No, you have. The Leader of the House of Commons wants you to lunch with him at 12.45."

In the elegant ground-floor kitchen of the Ellison residence in Chester Place, a young woman poured herself a third cup of coffee off the Scholtes gas hob and told herself it was time she got back to her law books. Jilly Thorndike, student of commercial law at the London School of Economics, had been living with the Ellisons as part-time au pair for the past six months. Her main function was to make Christopher's tea when he came home from school; she also stayed home on the rare evenings when Ellison found time to take his wife to the theatre or opera.

As she poured the coffee some of it slopped into the saucer. She stared in bewilderment at her hands: they were trembling.

Though no one spoke of it, everyone in the Ellison household now lived in the constant presence of fear.

She moved to the sink to wash up the cup. The back doorbell rang. She broke into a cold sweat even though she was expecting the milkman to call for his money.

Now come on, Jilly Thorndike.

The door of the rear lobby faced on to Albany Street. She slid the bolt back and opened the door.

For a moment—five seconds perhaps—she stood transfixed. Then she screamed.

As the Granada moved along the Strand towards Trafalgar Square, Charlie's back began to stiffen. Before he could take evasive action and head down to the Embankment, they were caught up in something they hadn't bargained for, a frenzied mass rally of Ormskirk's Saviours of the Nation.

As the loudspeakers boomed, broadcasting Ormskirk's strident denunciations of Jews, blacks, aliens, and "liberal scum", brown-shirted stewards with curving daggers in their belts prowled round the plinth of Nelson's Column searching out the "termites" who plotted to divide the Nation and sap its vitality, its will, its racial integrity. "We demand Strong Government!" screamed Ormskirk. A vast, militarized war-cry of assent echoed back from the throng.

There was scarcely a policeman in sight—merely a row of ambulances lined up in front of the National Gallery.

Charlie was now as tense as a rod. He spotted the coming attack before Ellison did. As Ellison hastily snapped shut the lock on his door, a half-dozen brown shirts converged on the Granada with livid snarls of hatred, hurling stones at the windows and kicking the side panels. The car began to rock on its axis.

As Charlie put his foot hard down on the accelerator the car shot forward, hurtling two brown shirts six feet into the air. Before the car reached the safety of Whitehall two more had been sent spinning across the road.

Max Ucelik walked out of the main entrance of Gowers House with the lunch-hour throng of secretaries, stenographers, sub-editors and reporters. The sound of the bells of St Dunstan-in-the-West pealing from Fleet Street reminded him of St Nicholas in Prague; a lump formed in his throat. For several weeks past he had been able neither to sleep nor to eat; the sight of food brought on nausea. There was one man, and only one man, to whom Max wished to turn for advice and comfort, but that one man's eyes had stared at him this morning like discs of dull metal and now Max's legs carried him, against his will, towards the ancient church of St Bride's.

As he entered the empty church he paused, sniffed the wood polish, and listened. Then he descended into the crypt.

The crypt was apparently empty. The sounds of the city above were blotted out; blanketed in silence and misery, Max waited.

Presently a man stepped out of the shadows formed by the Roman and early English walls which support the crypt. As he passed Max, the young Czech handed him a long manilla envelope.

Ellison was ten minutes late when he checked into the Members' dining-room overlooking the Thames. He found the Leader of the House, Walter Vandyke, seated at a corner table with his bright, brash young Parliamentary Private Secretary, Marshall Durban. Also at the table was Jeremy Bentley, a junior shadow minister from the Opposition front bench. Which was odd.

"Sorry I'm late, Walter."

"I'm sure you're not, Bill," smiled Vandyke with his proverbial charm. "Big Ben is running a bit fast these days."

Ellison winced and took the vacant chair. The tall, handsome and charismatic Vandyke, known to his friends as VD and to his enemies as Clap, was one of the few British politicians who commanded a wide personal following. Time after time he topped the popularity ratings in the opinion polls. He had risen to the number four spot in the Cabinet with precocious speed. Ellison found it hard to forget that when he had been a prefect at Winchester, VD had been a tiny "new man" with golden curls and a plump, peachy arse which Ellison, to his everlasting regret, had never given the thrashing it deserved. Now it was too late; and he winced.

"You'll have a lager," Vandyke said, settling the matter without consultation. "They should put you in one of those Heineken ads, Bill. After all, you reach the parts other journalists can't reach. You were first to the post with the full Profumo story, first to the post with the Nigerian arms deal, the Poulson scandal, military interrogation methods in Ulster——"

"You're composing the New Year's Honours list?"

"No." Abruptly Vandyke's debonair charm faded as he leaned forward intently across the table, dropping his rich, orator's voice. "I think you ought to know . . . some odd things are happening. Of course I can't leak to you what is said in Cabinet——"

"A Cabinet leak," Ellison said, "is something a journalist tells a minister, who then leaks it to the entire Cabinet."

Durban scowled. Ellison's notorious disrespect for politicians rankled with him.

Vandyke disregarded the jibe. "The murder of Levene came up in Cabinet this morning."

"Moshe was about to reveal something when he was called away. I made ten phone calls this morning to the Board of Deputies and the Jewish National Fund. But no one will see me. They're scared and I don't blame them. No one knew where Levene's secretary Rabinowitz was."

"He's under arrest."

"He's what!"

"Martindale reported to the Cabinet that the ISP possesses clear proof that Rabinowitz was privy to a Zionist plot to murder Levene—as an act of provocation to sabotage the Arab Mission to Britain."

"Jesus!"

"I'm not sure how much help He is going to be."

"Has the Cabinet discussed the bomb planted in the car of Britain's best-loved reporter?"

Vandyke nodded gravely. For a moment his eyes flickered away from Ellison's. "The man they arrested confessed: it was all part of the same Zionist plot. Then he committed suicide in Brixton prison."

Silence settled round the table.

"Listen, Walter, if you think *that's* going to remain off the record——"

Vandyke raised a hand. "Both stories will be in the evening papers."

"What was the Prime Minister's reaction to these revelations?"

"He played with his watch chain."

"So what the hell is going on in your Government?"

"The same," intervened Durban acidly, "as what's said to be going on inside the *Sunday Monitor*."

"OK. But don't you ever thrash these things out in Cabinet?" Ellison asked Vandyke.

"No. Murdoch won't allow it. There is an Inner Cabinet, you know, which meets in the evening."

"Are you telling me that you, Leader of the Commons and number four, are not a member of it?"

"Exactly."

"Who is?"

"Murdoch, Martindale, Fryer, Burnett, Lynedoch and Ozanne."

"Lynedoch and Ozanne! You have to be joking! They're merely civil servants of the second rank! Do you mean that Lynedoch represents the Foreign Office instead of Foreign Secretary Fullerton?"

"So it goes. What do you know about Lynedoch and Ozanne?" Vandyke asked.

"Very little." Ellison turned to Bentley. "Murdoch hinted to me at Number 10 that future political stability depended on the Leader of the Opposition—your chief. The Government's majority is down to five. What's going to happen?"

Bentley stared intently at the table cloth. "It's my belief," he said quietly, "that some kind of a deal is afoot."

"No parliamentary crises until after the Mission has come, seen and conquered?"

"Maybe. There are rumours flying about concerning a Ministry of All the Talents."

"A national coalition government?"

"Perhaps," said Bentley. "Perhaps something different. We just don't know. The normal contours of Westminster politics are changing fast. Which is why I'm sitting at this table—observed on all sides."

"Bill," said Vandyke, "it seems to me you've got some fast digging to do. We'll help you every way we can."

"In that case, I'll make a suggestion. Spend your nights in the right bed."

Durban flushed. "That's an outrageous remark! I demand that you withdraw it."

"Mr Speaker, I would like to apologize to the three Honourable Members."

"I am not offended," Vandyke said with a hard glint in his blue eyes which betrayed that he was. "We all appreciate that Bill's curtness of manner merely reflects the burden he has to bear."

"What burden?" said Ellison warily.

"The widespread prejudice that muckraking journalism, however brilliantly pursued, is not exactly the done thing for a Wykehamist with a First in modern languages at Oxford."

Bill Ellison winced. And dreamt of whacking that plump, peachy arse.

When the phone rang in the office of Bert Hoyle, Editor of the *Star*, he answered it with his usual cynical snarl. But as soon as he heard the voice on the line he leapt to his feet and stood rigid.

"According to Ucelik," the voice was saying, "Ellison suspects him of having blown his Czech friends. Now what could have put that into Ellison's head, Hoyle?"

"I . . . I've no idea."

"It can only mean, Hoyle, that Ellison knows Ucelik's network was blown from the London end. How did Ellison discover that, Hoyle?"

"He must have——"

"The American girl reporter you sent to Prague to shadow Ellison vanished soon after her return: correct?"

"She went back to America——"

"Did she, Hoyle? I doubt it."

On his way to the dented Granada Ghia, Ellison picked up a couple of evening papers.

——Levene Secretary Arrested on Murder Charge. Zionist Plot Suspected.

——Ellison Assailant Confesses to Zionist Plot, Cuts Throat in Cell.

——Leading British Publisher Sells to Arab Consortium.

——Chairman of Anglo-Israel Parliamentary Committee Denies Bribery Allegation.

Cherry came through on the car telephone.

"Your wife rang, Bill. You're to go home immediately."

Abruptly his body was bathed in a cold sweat. He knew of no one less liable to panic or call for help than Pru Ellison.

"Chester Place, Charlie. And put your foot down."

A Rover 3500 with Metropolitan Police markings was parked outside the house. He ran up the stairs to the drawing-room on the first floor.

He found Pru seated on the sofa, holding Jilly Thorndike's hand. The girl had been crying. Standing at opposite corners of the room were two uniformed policemen. Ellison read their faces at a glance and he didn't like what he read.

"What happened?"

"The kitchen-door bell rang at 9.30 this morning," Pru said in a level, controlled voice. "When Jilly opened the door she was confronted by a man wearing a black stocking over his head. He leered at her, unzipped his trousers, and displayed his erect member. Then he took a step towards her. She screamed and slammed the door."

The policeman wearing a sergeant's badge of rank nodded impassively. "My name's Calhoun," he said. "And this is Constable Straw."

"Which station are you from?"

"The one Mrs Ellison telephoned," Calhoun said curtly. "Albany Street."

"Have any similar incidents been reported to you?"

"Not recently."

"They think it's personal," Pru said.

Ellison turned to Jilly Thorndike. "You haven't jilted anyone, Jilly?"

"No," Jilly whispered, dabbing at her eyes with a wet handkerchief.

"Now you, Mrs Ellison, are presently Headteacher of Crewe Hill Comprehensive?" Calhoun said, with ponderous gravity.

"What can that have to do with it?"

"Forgive me if I'm mistaken, but haven't parents been complaining about so-called sex education courses at your school? I seem to recall that a 'blue film' gave particular offence."

"I've never seen what you call a 'blue film' in my life. Of course the Guardians of Decency kicked up, but it didn't offend the children."

"Some might disagree about that."

"What are you driving at?" Ellison said quietly.

Abruptly Calhoun's expression shed its official impartiality. A leer surfaced. "What am I driving at, Constable Straw?"

Straw grinned sycophantically. "What you are driving at, Sergeant, is that when decent people get disgusted with the filth that's going around nowadays, they may express their disgust in ways——"

"That you and I, Constable Straw, might not agree with."

"Alternatively," Ellison said, "you might."

Calhoun's mouth tightened. "There are people around

who consider themselves pretty smart, Mr Ellison. If you want my opinion, some of those people are due to come unstuck."

"Perhaps it's time you showed me your identity cards." But Ellison was under no illusion that they would oblige; clearly the ISP had penetrated the Metropolitan Police.

Calhoun smiled. Two of his front teeth were missing. "I think we ought to search this house, don't you, Constable Straw?"

"I do indeed, Sergeant Calhoun."

Ellison noticed that although neither of them appeared perceptibly to be moving, the expanse of carpet separating them from him had diminished. Evidently Pru shared his instinct, for she suddenly stood up.

"Don't you dare lay a hand on my husband!"

It was nicely done. As both Calhoun and Straw turned, anticipating an attempt by Pru to run for help, neither noticed the three short jabs Ellison gave to the small button concealed under the mantelpiece. This bell had once connected the drawing-room to the kitchen below, but the day after the Spectrum Mercedes loomed up in his life Ellison had had it re-wired—to the top floor.

Calhoun and Straw were only a few feet away from Ellison when the door opened. Both swung round. The grins were wiped from their faces by the sight of fourteen-stone Charlie, with a brass-studded knuckle duster strapped to his left hand, a tyre iron clenched in his right, and a very special light in his eye.

"Just say the word, sir."

But Ellison had no need to say the word; within seconds Calhoun and Straw were gunning out of Chester Place in their Rover 3500.

Pru put Jilly to bed with a sedative of valium.

Two hours later, a girl who was studying history at Somerville College, Oxford, heard a knock on the door of her flat in St John's Street. Casually she opened the door—then banged it shut fast.

A man wearing a black stocking over his head had exposed his genitals to her, leered, and taken a step forward.

The girl's name was Faith Ellison.

She phoned her boyfriend and asked him to come round. Then she made a pot of tea, lit a Gauloise, and returned to the book about the Hundred Years' War she had been reading. She was determined not to phone her parents.

But at 10 o'clock she did.

"I'll ring your Principal tonight," her father said. "You must move out of your flat and back into Somerville tomorrow."

"But, Daddy, it was only a small tribute to my sex appeal. Actually, I thought it was rather an impressive penis. I almost invited it in for tea."

Her father groaned. "Pru, you talk to her. It was you who brought her up as a liberated woman."

Half an hour later Pru climbed into bed beside him. "Jilly will leave and Faith will stay put," she said. "And why? Because your daughter is exactly like you—stubborn as a mule."

He grunted, turned over, and pretended to fall asleep. Over and over again he worked the two events through, and over and over again he could arrive at only one conclusion.

But it was the wrong conclusion. A trap had been set for him by a man whose intelligence equalled his own.

Four

"Irena Ucelikova?"

A slight young woman wearing a raincoat and a worried frown on her delicate Slav face was standing outside White City tube station, one hundred yards up Wood Lane from the BBC Television Centre. She peered anxiously through the smoke-tinted window of the red Mini Cooper which had screeched to a halt beside her.

"Yes, I am Irena. You are Alice?"

The driver of the car, who wore a silk scarf round her head, reached across to open the passenger door. Her green eyes were shielded by large, oval Polaroid sunglasses.

"What time do you have to be at the Acton rehearsal rooms, Irena?"

"At 9.45."

The Mini Cooper gunned off the kerb, spun into an illegal U-turn, then roared to a halt in an empty street behind the White City Stadium.

"You work for Bill, then?" Irena asked.

The girl without eyes shook her head. "I'm freelance. I do a job for Bill once every six months at the most. When he's busy."

"Oh yes, I understand. Max and I owe Bill a great deal."

"Bill's very concerned about the mounting campaign against your boss, David Gottlieb."

Irena nodded sadly. "The things they say about him are terrible."

Three years earlier Gottlieb, a brilliant young director whose productions had been acclaimed in London, Paris and New York, had been appointed Head of Plays within the BBC TV Drama Group. It was a controversial appointment, for which the Director-General, Sir Jack Armstrong, was held mainly responsible. It was a big job: with an annual output of seventy-five plays a year, and an average budget of £15,000 per play, Gottlieb's department regularly reached between four and seven million viewers through the "Thursday Play", "In the Round" and "World Theatre". And Gottlieb had lost no time in exciting controversy. Among the plays he commissioned, one explored the nocturnal activities of the Internal Security Police, a second exposed the anti-semitism of the Saviours of the Nation, a third depicted the machinations of Arab financiers, indicating Government connivance, a fourth described the effect of Moslem values on British schoolchildren. Gottlieb was now known to be planning a production which would take a swipe at the sexual hypocrisy of the Guardians of Decency.

Gottlieb's supporters supported him silently. His enemies attacked him noisily. The Guardians of Decency, a vociferous pressure group claiming half a million members, bombarded the BBC with phone-calls, telegrams, letters and petitions demanding Gottlieb's dismissal and a thorough purge of the Drama Group.

First into the attack was invariably the *Star*. It soon became evident that Bert Hoyle was laying his hands on scripts and cast-lists soon after they were mimeographed. When she had worked for Hoyle, the girl behind the wheel of the Mini Cooper had seen them lying on his desk. When she had asked him how he got hold of them he had grinned and pinched her bottom.

"Who's working for Hoyle in your department, Irena?"

Irena Ucelikova stared through the windscreen at the bleak tenement flats of the White City estate.

"Do you have a cigarette, please . . ."

"Yes, of course." Judy Rossiter reached into her bag.

"I don't smoke, but just recently . . ."

"Just recently what?"

Irena puffed at the cigarette in little, amateurish motions of distress. "I have never told anyone this . . . I could be mistaken, you see . . ."

"Scripts have been disappearing from your home?"

Irena stared at her with horror. "You knew?"

"It was written in your face. How many copies of a script do you normally take home?"

"At least three. I copy-edit one; mark up technical notes on another; and perhaps list potential actors on a third. From time to time a script vanishes from the dining-room table where I work."

"Do you have a cleaning lady?"

Irena shook her head. She was weeping now. "Only Max could take those scripts. But why? Why should he pass them to the *Star*? He despises the *Star*. It makes no sense at all."

Fifteen minutes later the Mini Cooper pulled into the forecourt of the BBC's Acton rehearsal building, the largest in the world. Judy laid a hand on Irena's.

"Don't worry. There must be some other explanation."

As Irena's slender back disappeared through the glass door Judy reached under the indicator panel and switched off the tape-recorder concealed behind the dashboard.

"How's things, Lassy?"

Denis Laslett, editor of *Deadline* (audience 4.5 million), looked up from a desk crowded with shooting scripts, correspondence and cans of film.

"Good God, it's Massey. Who let you in here?"

Ellison's colleague, all six foot three of him, sauntered round the office, followed by the enraptured gaze of Laslett's two production assistants. Nine years earlier, when Magnus Massey had been the most famous fashion photographer in the land, his gold-topped features had been idolized by millions of romantic hearts.

"Lassy, as you know I'm the busiest man in the Western world. Show me the script of your Libyan arms film."

"Fuck off."

"I could read it here."

"It's under lock and key in Maurice Cohn's office."

"Who has the key?"

"Maurice's secretary, Marianne Irving."

"I thought Maurice's secretary was called Annie Keyser."

"Annie had a baby. Seven pounds, four ounces if you must know. She decided to stick with it like any nice Jewish girl would."

"Is Marianne Irving a nice Jewish girl?"

"Go and look."

"Where did she work before?"

"What *is* this?"

"Did she work in the Beeb?"

Laslett sighed. "I don't believe so. Maurice took her on under special recommendation. By a friend."

"Name of friend?"

"No idea. Now fuck off."

"See you, then." Magnus drifted out of the office followed by two mesmerized pairs of female eyes. When he reached office H 13, Head of News and Current Affairs, he ambled in without knocking.

"Is Maurice at home?"

A middle-aged woman with short-cropped grey hair, double-lensed spectacles, and a fine display of down on her chin was observing him coldly.

"Mr Cohn is extremely busy. I can take a message."

Magnus nodded lazily. Both filing-cabinets were securely locked. And Irving herself resembled the Tower of London.

"I'll look in again later."

He walked down the corridor lost in thought. Reaching the ground floor, he took a seat in the reception area and buried himself in an evening paper. It was 5.10.

Presently the staff of the BBC's Lime Grove studios began to leave the building.

Irving emerged from the lift at 5.45. She was wearing a square-shouldered raincoat, brown woollen stockings and flat-heeled brogues. She carried an attaché case.

He folded his paper, waited five seconds, then walked out into Lime Grove. Heading for the Goldhawk Road, Irving solidly marched past a red Mini Cooper with smoke-tinted windows which was parked on a yellow line. As she did so Magnus tapped his elbow with his evening paper and a young woman got out of the car, leaving the keys in the ignition. Magnus gunned the Mini Cooper away down the one-way street, turned left at the Uxbridge Road, turned left again along the black ghetto of Devonport Road, then swung left a third time into Goldhawk Road, just as Irving and Rossiter boarded a number 88 bus. He fell in behind the bus as it moved slowly round Shepherd's Bush through the dense, rush-hour traffic.

Irving got out at Notting Hill Gate. Magnus idled the car while she trudged down Pembridge Road, followed at a distance of twenty yards by Rossiter. Branching off into Portobello Road, Irving entered one of the pretty, two-storey houses standing on the east side.

Magnus parked forty yards further down the road. Judy took the passenger seat.

"Who are you?" she said.

"The name's Carella. Steve Carella. 87th Precinct. Poissonally, I never went along with the idea of female cops. Too risky. Get themselves into all kinds of trouble." He peered into the driving mirror. "She's coming out. With the attaché case."

"And she's changed into jacket and trousers."

"She's really a man. That should send you. Out."

"Whose car is this?"

"Out."

He gunned down Portobello Road, executed three right turns, into Chepstow Villas, Chepstow Crescent and back into Pembridge Road, then idled to a crawl behind Judy as she trailed Irving back to Notting Hill Gate.

Irving hailed a taxi.

The taxi led them all the way to the Aldwych Theatre, London home of the Royal Shakespeare Company.

"It's *Othello*," Magnus said. "Call me in when the Moor takes his unfaithful wife out with a pillow. I can never have enough of it."

In the lobby Irving was met by a man of artistic and somewhat debauched appearance. He wore black velvet trousers, tight at the crotch, widely flared at the ankles, and a red velvet smoking jacket. His straw-coloured hair fell over his ears in carefully styled disarray, framing a face partly Jewish, partly Scandinavian. Judy bought a ticket at the box office and followed them into the stalls.

When the lights went up for the first interval Irving and her companion made for the stalls bar, the ugly woman firmly clutching her attaché case. Pushing through the crush in the bar they forced a path towards two men who were waiting for them with glasses of white wine. When she was within ten feet of them, Judy put a long cigarette in her mouth, tilted her chin up, and flicked her lighter. It didn't spark. She tried again, then a third time.

Minox microfilm cameras never produce a flame.

Abruptly she turned away from the group, her heart hammering, and merged back into the crowd. A fourth man, grinning broadly, displaying ragged, nicotine-stained teeth, had joined the group.

Bert Hoyle.

She forced herself to turn towards them. Irving had now opened the attaché case and was feeding Hoyle with a set of large, cardboard-backed manilla envelopes.

Hoyle's small, beady eyes, half-closed by cigarette smoke, suddenly swivelled round the room, then settled on Judy. Baffled, bemused, he stared at her.

Irving now broke away from the group of men and left the bar. Instead of heading for the Ladies, she trundled flat-footed right out of the theatre and began looking for a taxi.

The Mini Cooper was already moving as Judy jumped in, her skirt rippling up her thigh.

"Maybe she couldn't face the pillow scene," Magnus drawled, determined not to betray his interest in Judy's thigh.

"She handed over the entire contents of her case to Hoyle."

Magnus whistled.

"And in the company of guess who?"

"The President of the United States."

"Sir Philip Lucas and Edmund Strachan, Managing Director of BBC Television."

Magnus swerved to avoid a scooter and tucked in behind Irving's taxi.

"You're not doing badly for a beginner."

Her green eyes glimmered in the semi-darkness. "You'll regret that remark, Carella. I'm old enough to be your daughter."

While Magnus shadowed the taxi up the Charing Cross Road, Judy described the man with whom Irving had sat in the stalls. Rounding Cambridge Circus, the taxi threaded into the narrow streets of Soho and stopped at the corner of Old Compton Street and Dean Street. Irving climbed out.

"Shit, I can't park here."

"Just take my lovely car home to bed. Wherever your bed is. Is it a state secret?"

"Holy cow, she's going into the Lesbos Club. You can't go in there. They can smell a straight a mile away."

"Who says I'm a straight? If you want to know, Irving turns me on. If you had ankles like hers you wouldn't have to grovel for my favours."

"Need some money?"

For an answer came only the slamming of the car door. A taxi was angrily hooting at him from behind. He jerked two fingers out of the window and turned into Dean Street.

At the entrance to the Lesbos Club a middle-aged Greek in a dinner jacket asked Judy whether she was a member.

"No. I'd like to join."

"Certainly, certainly. The entrance fee is £10 and the cover charge £2."

She filled in the membership application form under the name of Tessa Herron.

"Have a nice time," the Greek said, taking her money.

He was the last man she would see.

A heavy satin curtain hung at the end of the corridor. The club room beyond it was only faintly illuminated by electric candelabra secured by plastic replicas of the naked poetess Sappho. Tables were set back in discreet alcoves along walls fluted and decorated with murals of idyllic life on the island of Lesbos. At the far end of the room an all-girl pop group dressed in unisex were alternately moaning and screeching at the couples dancing round them. A line of women sitting at the bar, some in couples, some alone, turned to look her over as she came in. She wished she was back in the car with Massey.

As her eyes accustomed themselves to the semi-darkness she spotted the short-cropped head of Irving up on a high stool towards the far end of the curving bar. The stool to her left stood vacant.

"May I?"

Marianne Irving turned slowly and examined Judy through her double lenses. Then a smile twisted the corners of her hair-fringed mouth.

"Want a drink?"

"Oh thanks. A Bloody Mary, please."

Irving snapped her short, masculine fingers at the large, butch woman bartender.

"This is my first time here, you see. I mean, so many of my friends have told me I ought to come." Judy paused. "I've been so . . . unhappy."

Irving just looked at her. "What's your name?"

"Tessa."

"Mine's Robert."

"Oh."

"You're meeting some of your friends here?"

"Later maybe. I don't know."

"Would you like to dance with me, Tessa?"

"I'd love to."

Irving rose heavily, awkwardly, and snapped a warning to the bartender to keep the two stools vacant. She put her right arm round Judy's waist and took Judy's left hand in her right. They began to shuffle. Irving was breathing heavily: the top of her head was level with Judy's eyes. At a wild guess they were doing a post-war quickstep.

Afterwards Irving collected their drinks from the bar, then led Judy by the hand to one of the tables set back in alcoves. As soon as they had sat down a pretty girl in a trouser-suit came hurrying across and stared at Judy with undisguised jealousy. Irving shooed her away with a snarl.

Her large hand found Judy's knee under the table.

"Does Tessa like Robert, mmm?"

"Oh yes, thank you, she likes him very much."

"And what does pretty Tessa do when she's not with Robert?"

Judy sighed. "This and that. I do wish I knew. I mean I just wish I knew who I really am." She turned an appealing gaze on Irving. "Can Robert understand that?"

The eyes were now moist behind the double lenses. "Is Tessa a teeny bit short of money?"

Judy nodded shyly. "Tessa's broke."

Irving's hand had worked its way under her dress and up her thigh.

"Tessa's broke," whispered Irving into her ear, "and Robert's lonely."

They held hands in the taxi all the way to Portobello Road. It was after 11 when they arrived; Judy noticed that no lights were burning in Irving's house.

A Mini Cooper was parked forty yards down the road, with its lights extinguished.

The drawing-room was handsomely furnished and lined with bookshelves, classical gramophone records, and large canvases painted in a violent, post-expressionist style. Judy estimated the insurance value of the contents of this one room at over £5,000. Many of the books were in Arabic.

"Gosh, whatever language is this?" Judy said with awe.

"Now Tessa mustn't be inquisitive, must she?"

"But Robert has such a lovely house! He must be a very important person."

Irving grinned. Her large hands hung loose at her sides; the fingers were twitching.

"Tessa's a teeny bit frightened of Robert, mmm? Tessa knows she's a naughty girl? And what happens to naughty girls, mmm?"

"They . . . they have to be . . . punished?"

"Yes!"

In the bedroom upstairs a large, two-way mirror was suspended over the double bed. Irving stood panting as the beautiful young woman peeled off her dress and then stretched out, face down, across the bed. Irving turned a switch under the mirror; a battery of 1kw bulbs flooded light onto the bed. Simultaneously there was the faint hum of a 16mm-camera from behind the mirror.

Judy Rossiter closed her eyes and clenched her hands as the first lash of the whip scalded her buttocks. She gasped. At the second stroke she cried out. At the third, she pleaded for mercy. At the fourth, she leapt off the bed.

"You're mad!"

Irving's breath was billowing from the bottom of her lungs in manic, horse-like rasps. The tiny eyes behind the double lenses were alight with sadistic joy.

"Down!"

Judy grabbed her dress, shoes and underclothes and ran for the door. With a snarl of rage and unforeseeable agility Irving bounded to block her escape. Her square, powerful hands grasped Judy's throat. Judy dropped her clothes and reached desperately for Irving's wrists. She couldn't budge them. The pressure round her throat tightened inexorably, she struggled for breath, her knees began to buckle. In desperation she hurled herself backwards, away from

Irving, on to the floor. The sudden movement threw Irving off balance; she toppled sideways; her head struck the floor with a thud. Horrified, yet driven on by fear, Judy found herself grasping the short, steely hair and banging the woman's head against the ground. At last Irving lay still. Saliva trickled from her mouth. Her spectacles lay broken on the floor.

But the eyes, larger now, opaque, unseeing, refused to close.

Trembling from head to toe, Judy pulled on her clothes. Then she tore the covers off the bed and bound Irving's arms and feet. The sheet round Irving's arms she tied to the bed-post.

Abruptly the battery of flood bulbs went out. The camera ceased to hum. The room was now in semi-darkness. Switching on the ceiling light and rapidly working through the wardrobe and chest of drawers, she came across a number of objects of interest to students of perversion, but none of interest to the *Sunday Monitor*. Except a Koran. She left the bedroom, closing the door behind her.

Cautiously she opened the front door. It was after midnight: the street outside was quiet. Almost immediately Magnus walked past her into the hallway, then smiled when he saw her dishevelled condition. She threw him a withering glance and led the way into the drawing-room. Dividing the room between them, they began systematically to search desk-drawers, bookshelves and cupboards. A small steel filing-cabinet, three feet high, twelve inches wide and fifteen inches deep, was locked. It contained fifteen shallow drawers.

He followed her up to the first-floor landing, then hung back in the shadows as she cautiously opened the bedroom door. Irving was lying on the floor, her bulging eyes still open, her breath coming in short, pained gasps. Judy covered the woman's eyes with a towel then gestured to Magnus. Standing on the bed, he reached up behind the two-way mirror, plucked a magazine holding 400 feet of 16mm film from the camera, and quietly left the room. Judy removed the towel from Irving's face and untied her hands; it would take Irving at least a quarter of an hour to free her legs.

The Mini Cooper drove out of Portobello Road at 1.30. The filing-cabinet was propped across the rear seat.

She lit a cigarette. "And they say a reporter's life is an easy one."

"Those are nasty bruises round your neck."

"And what do you do for a living?"

Five

Bill Ellison emerged from his bank in Fenchurch Street, where the Irving documents were now stored in a strong-room safe-deposit box, aware that Judy Rossiter had presented him with one of the biggest scoops in his entire career.

The core of the Irving documents consisted of memoranda on the progress of the Cohn-Laslett *Deadline* film exposing the smuggling of Libyan arms to Ormskirk's Saviours of the Nation via the Provisional IRA.

The documents showed that Bert Hoyle, Editor of the *Star*, had been instructed to approach a former IRA man, Sean Kelly, with an offer of £2,500 to hatch a bogus story —more accurately, a bogus version of the truth. Marianne Irving had then planted on Cohn's desk Kelly's offer to "come clean" for a fee of £1,000. Cohn had duly made contact with Kelly, paying over the money by instalments. Under instructions from Hoyle, Kelly had carried a recording device whenever he spoke to either Cohn or Laslett. The transcripts of these conversations, showing the black rims of Xeroxed copies, appeared in the Irving files, and they illustrated clearly how Cohn and Laslett had been compromised.

Kelly's technique, as tutored by Hoyle, had been to "reveal" aspects of the story to Cohn and Laslett and then, later, to retract them in a manner suggesting that he was too frightened of reprisals to adhere to the truth. As a result, Cohn and Laslett had frequently persuaded him to testify to facts which he was apparently denying. Cleverly edited, these transcripts, and the tapes on which they were based, could be made to present Cohn and Laslett as plain fabricators of the story.

That Hoyle intended to resort to precisely this trick was confirmed by another document in the files, a draft outline of the violently denunciatory article scheduled to appear in the *Star* the morning after *Deadline* went out to its 4.5 million viewers.

It was a frame-up. But who was involved?

Developed and blown up by Magnus, the Minox microfilm shots taken by Judy in the Aldwych Theatre bar confirmed that Irving had been in the company of Hoyle, Sir Philip Lucas, Chairman of the BBC's Governors, and Edmund Strachan, Managing Director of BBC Television. This in itself opened a can of worms. The fifth person present, the man of artistic appearance with features half Jewish, half Scandinavian, was not known by sight to Ellison.

However, there were clues.

Included in the Irving documents were two letters, one a photo-copy of a letter from Maurice Cohn to a certain Ulf Steinberg, the other a carbon copy of a letter from Steinberg to Cohn.

Writing to Steinberg, Cohn profusely thanked him for sculpting his bust, casting it in bronze, and presenting it to him without fee in honour of Cohn's appointment as Head of the Current Affairs Group. Cohn also mentioned the birth of their friendship out of a meeting at the St John's Wood Reform Synagogue.

Steinberg's letter to Cohn, written some months later, referred to the fact that Cohn was in urgent need of a reliable personal secretary. Steinberg believed he could recommend the perfect woman for the job—Marianne Irving. Efficient, reliable, and of impeccable liberal views, Steinberg explained, Irving had tragically lost her job as an editor with a London publishing firm as a result of a disastrous Lesbian affair with a secretary who became hysterical and attempted suicide. For that reason, no reference could be provided.

On the basis of the information contained in these memoranda and letters, Ellison pondered for almost an hour the most significant document of all:

From: APCR
To: BBC Guardians

I am instructed by the highest authority to provide a replacement for Cohn's secretary Keyser. Miss Irving has worked here as a translator and programme coordinator for 3 years, and was largely responsible for the successful "Milestones of Islam" series. She is efficient and devoted to our cause.

The highest authority instructs me to point out that Cohn's sexual and financial morality is such that he is not considered vulnerable to temptations to which other BBC personnel have succumbed. But the highest authority regards Cohn as naive and uncritical where his own political and racial feelings are involved. Hence the decision by the highest authority to plant a story concerning Libyan arms smuggling on his desk.

The highest authority, through an intermediary, some time ago instructed US, whose father was Jewish, to join the St John's Wood Reform Synagogue and to befriend Cohn by doing his bust in bronze for no fee. For this work US was paid £1,000 by AA on the instructions of the highest authority. US has now been urged to plant Irving on Cohn.

The highest authority has now allocated a further £3.5 million for schools radio programmes, payable by AA to us here.

Interesting. But who was APCR, the author of the memo? Who were BBC Guardians, the recipients? Ellison was prepared to guess that this was a code for Lucas, Strachan and other conspirators within the BBC hierarchy.

Irving, then, had worked for APCR, who evidently headed an organization producing Islamic programmes for BBC TV and radio. What was that organization? Irving—so her files demonstrated—was one of those people who don't readily throw away their old bank statements. The ones dating back to the time before she joined the BBC as Cohn's secretary showed that she had been receiving regular monthly payments from the "FSCR". That rang no bell in Ellison's head, though he noted the overlap between APCR and FSCR. The bank statements also showed occasional receipts of proportions which might account for the luxurious furnishing of her Portobello Road house.

Clearly the US referred to was the sculptor Ulf Steinberg. A check of that name in the *Monitor*'s press cuttings library showed a photograph of Steinberg at the opening of his retrospective exhibition at the New Mayfair Gallery—the photograph coincided with the one taken by Judy in the Aldwych Theatre bar.

But who was the "highest authority", referred to no less than six times in the memo? Clearly he pulled all the strings: APCR and his organization, the FSCR; Steinberg "through an intermediary"; and "AA", who paid over the money to Steinberg for the bust of Cohn and, on a vast scale, for the BBC's Islamic programmes.

Ellison was prepared to guess at AA: Arabair.

But how did the "highest authority" know Cohn well enough to gauge exactly his personal strengths and weaknesses? Was this the man who had masterminded the ruin of so many BBC editors and producers—and possibly of others outside the BBC, like Steve Moyars of the *Dispatch*? If so, how did he ensure they were snared in sexual or financial scandals?

Did the Government know what was going on? It was Home Secretary Martindale who had appointed Lucas as Chairman of the BBC's Governors. Was Martindale perhaps a law unto himself, playing a long-term power game at the expense of his colleagues? And what was in it for people like Lucas and Strachan? Strachan might covet Director-General Armstrong's job, but what could Lucas covet?

As he drove from his bank to Gowers House, Ellison faced one immediate, crucifying decision. He could take copies of the Irving documents to Armstrong and Cohn, thereby temporarily saving the careers of Cohn and Laslett. But Ellison's reading of the Director-General's character led him to fear that Armstrong would immediately resign with a ringing public statement of protest, leaving Martindale, Lucas and Strachan with a free hand in the Beeb.

Equally serious, the fact that the *Monitor* had lifted the Irving documents would inevitably come out in the wash. A prosecution for theft would put Ellison on the defensive; it would blow Judy's cover; and it would lead the conspiracy— whatever its identity and ultimate aim—to take vigorous action. None of which suited Bill Ellison. He needed time.

The three men convened hurriedly in a large, North London house set back behind tall trees in a spacious garden decorated with exotic tropical plants. Security precautions, as always, were massive: while two Mercedes 450 SELs prowled the street outside, Triumphs of the Leech Squad discreetly patrolled the neighbourhood.

"When were the documents taken from Irving?" the first man demanded in a cool, gentle voice.

"At approximately 1 o'clock this morning," the second man replied. "This is an unprecedented disaster," he added.

"And how were they taken?"

"According to Irving, she picked up a girl in the Lesbos Club. When they got home the girl turned nasty, attacked Irving, bound her hands and feet, then ransacked the house. Irving is convinced that the girl had an accomplice waiting outside, almost certainly a man—the girl could not have lifted the filing-cabinet by herself."

"A highly skilled operation," the third man commented grimly. "Has Irving described this girl's appearance?"

"Yes: very pretty, with auburn hair and green eyes, about 5′ 7″ tall. Probable measurements, 37-22-36. This description

74

coincides closely with that of a young woman seen earlier in the evening by Hoyle in the bar of the Aldwych Theatre. Hoyle believes she may have been using a Minox microfilm camera disguised as a cigarette lighter."

The first man cursed softly, in Arabic. The gentleness of his manner did not mask the smouldering anger in his dark eyes. He turned to the second man.

"How does this physical description compare with that of the girl who left the *Star* soon after shadowing Ellison in Czechoslovakia?"

"Height and measurements are very similar. Hair, eyes and accent are different—Sally Clay Moore came from South Carolina."

"You're sure of that?" the first man said sarcastically.

"Well, Hoyle——"

"Is a toad. Have we any evidence that Ellison is now employing a girl on his investigating staff?"

"None. All probes have proved negative," the second man said. "But I have ordered a raid on the *Monitor* tonight—we might turn up something."

"What about the *Sunday Dispatch*?" the third man said irritably. "Ever since we fixed Steve Moyars, Powerstock has redoubled his efforts."

The first man smiled faintly. "Powerstock is one of nature's silver medallists. Ellison is in a class of his own."

"In that case," the third man said, "we must at all costs prevent him from publishing these documents in the *Monitor*. Gowers must be given a final ultimatum."

But the first man shook his head dismissively. "Ellison will be in no hurry to publish. Only the whole truth interests him. He never shows his hand until he holds the ace."

"He must be exterminated," the second man said.

"No. The risk is too great now. That botched job at Heathrow airport was a disaster. He set a trap and Spectrum walked right into it. And the result? Ellison made hay—he practically took out a national life insurance cover on the strength of it. No, I will pursue other methods with Ellison."

75

"And Irving?" the second man inquired.

"Her house shall be kept under surveillance during the next thirty-six hours. If Ellison took those documents, he won't be able to resist returning to study the aftermath. As soon as we have confirmation, Irving will be murdered by Zionist terrorists."

Abruptly the first man stood up. The other two men immediately sprang to their feet.

"Remember!" the first man said quietly. "The idea of *jihad*, of holy war, is now a reality; it governs our entire policy towards the infidel world. The time of the *hudna*, of the armistice, is over; we are powerful now, and we are ready. In pursuit of the *jihad* we will use every method—for the sake of Allah. Praise be to Allah!"

"Praise be to Allah!"

"Victory to Al-Ittihad! *Asabiyya!*"

"*Asabiyya!*"

Removing their shoes, the three men sank to their knees on Baghdad prayer rugs.

Sad as all three of the Chester Place Ellisons were to see Jilly Thorndike pack her bags and leave, they could scarcely blame her. Ellison himself was well aware that the same thing —or worse—might happen again. Fearing an attempt to kidnap Christopher, he traded on an old friendship with Superintendent Edgar Bradlaw of Scotland Yard's Special Branch. Bradlaw promised to keep the house under observation round the clock.

Pru didn't want Christopher to be alone in the house when he came home from school, so the task of finding a replacement for Jilly Thorndike assumed an extreme urgency. A vague memory took her to the desk drawer where she stored the business cards which flooded through the letter-box: plumbers, electricians, radio cabs, 24-hour emergency services, Chinese meals on wheels. Her memory proved correct: about a week earlier an impressively lavish brochure had arrived from an agency called Relief, Ltd. It offered reliable, qualified home-help of all kinds, including cleaners, baby sitters and au pairs. References would be provided. Pru dialled the number given and spoke to a Miss Eltenbridge, who was both sympathetic and helpful. Two girls arrived for interview within a couple of hours. Pru opted for a very bright and pretty German girl who came from a solid Hamburg family and spoke excellent English. She made an instant hit with Christopher.

Monika Bauer moved in the following day.

Joe O'Neill, twenty-eight years of age, thick-set, bearded, the son of a Belfast shipyard welder, an ambitious journalist with a training in chartered accountancy, was studying with absorbed interest the contents of Collins's antique shop-window at the head of Portobello Road. Joe was tired, stiff and hungry—he had been driving past Marianne Irving's house at ten-minute intervals since 3 am, when he had relieved Magnus Massey. He had abandoned this tactic, parked his Allegro in Pembridge Square, and taken up his present position at 7.51, when an electric milk cart had shunted into sight and deposited a single pint of milk on Marianne Irving's doorstep.

All her curtains remained drawn. Joe wanted to see who collected the milk from the doorstep.

But no one did. And so he waited, rocking from foot to foot, cursing his lot.

At 9.13 a blue Triumph 2500 Mk 2, of the kind used by the Internal Security Police, drew up outside Irving's house. Two uniformed policemen got out, rang the bell, then entered the house by forcing the lock. Within five minutes an ambulance turned into Portobello Road, passed Joe, and parked behind the Triumph. A stretcher was carried inside.

Ten minutes later the stretcher reappeared, supporting a body completely covered by a sheet. O'Neill raised Massey's Nikon F2A, a camera equipped with AI-automatic indexing and Aperture Direct Readout, and focused the 300mm 5.6f stop lens.

Returning to Pembridge Square, O'Neill unlocked the door of his Allegro and inserted the key in the ignition. It was then that he noticed a white card resting on the dashboard *inside* the car. It contained two printed words.

Spectrum Security.

In the top left-hand corner his name had been written in capitals.

An older, more cautious man might have left his car where it stood. But Joe O'Neill was neither old nor cautious— merely stung in the depths of his pride that he, the observer, had been so easily observed.

He turned the ignition key.

The engine came to life quite normally.

When he reached the fifth floor of Gowers House, he found Ellison and Massey sifting the shambles of scattered papers and ransacked files which had confronted Ellison on arrival at 7.50. Ellison gestured; the three men left the office, which Ellison suspected had been bugged with the connivance of General Manager Hubert Yorath, and wandered into the open spaces of the Features floor. As usual they muttered rather than spoke, tapping their feet. Ellison now called himself the Fred Astaire of Fleet Street.

"Irving was carried out of her house, stone dead, at 9.30," O'Neill disclosed, with the muted gleam of triumph he betrayed whenever he told his boss something he didn't already know. "It's all in there," he added casually, handing Massey the Nikon camera.

"How do you know it was Irving on the stretcher, Joe? It could have been her cat."

O'Neill flushed, bit his lip, turned on his heel and stomped away. He was damned if he would say anything about the Spectrum card on his dashboard. Magnus regarded Ellison reprovingly: he disliked his habit of needling Joe and he was deeply shaken by his decision to let Cohn and Laslett hang themselves.

"How many times have we warned them?" Ellison growled. "How many times have we asked to see that fucking film?"

Massey shrugged. "It's your decision."

At 8.45 that evening Ellison tuned his 22-inch Sony into BBC1 and sat back in mounting gloom as *Deadline*'s "scoop" unfolded on the screen. Half an hour later Magnus turned up with the first edition of tomorrow's *Star*.

On the front page a 144-point bold headline was capitalized across five tabloid columns:

BBC1: CHANNEL OF DECEIT

Beneath this, a sub-headline in 54-point upper and lower case announced: "Bogus Irish Witness Exposes *Deadline* Fraud".

Having picked off Cohn and Laslett as men prepared to pay heavily for information they knew to be false, Hoyle turned his guns on the Director-General: "Was Sir Jack privy to this whole filthy Zionist intrigue?" screamed Hoyle. "Why has he so stubbornly ignored the proven Zionist links of the Jew-subversive Cohn?"

And then a neat twist which caught Ellison half by surprise: "Why did the Director-General flout the advice of the Foreign Office to scrap the film?" But the Irving documents proved that the Foreign Office had deliberately kept silent.

"Well, at least they can't prove to themselves that we know anything about it."

Magnus, who had been sprawling in a chair, hands cupped behind his blond head, long legs folded at the ankles, tossed him a cardboard-backed manilla envelope, $10\frac{1}{2}''$ by $8\frac{1}{2}''$.

"Take a look at these blow-ups."

Ellison studied O'Neill's photographs of Irving's body being carried out of the house to the ambulance. Suddenly he dropped them.

"Shit."

Magnus nodded. "Someone was photographing Joe from the top floor of the house."

Six

Magnus Massey checked his watch, then continued to study the tapes chugging off the news agency wire machines:

——The Foreign Office had been swamped by diplomatic protests from the Arab states.

——A Foreign Office spokesman had issued a statement of regret.

——The Prime Minister himself had described the *Deadline* film as a calculated sabotage of the forthcoming Arab Mission.

——Chairman Lucas has promised a full inquiry. But Director-General Armstrong, Maurice Cohn, and Denis Laslett were unavailable for comment.

——An Arab League Press conference in London was set for 11.30.

——Cohn's secretary had been found dead in her London house. Documents stolen from her were "thought" to incriminate Cohn: a police spokesman had hinted at foul play by Zionist elements . . .

Massey's Aston Martin DB6 emerged from the executive car-park of Gowers House and turned its nose towards Green Street, Mayfair, the London headquarters of the Arab League. It was immediately picked up by a Mercedes 450 SEL.

In the pubs of Fleet Street there were still many journalists who refused to take seriously this tall, athletic young man whose face was that of a romantic poet drifting to perdition. They remembered the time, eight or nine years previously, when Magnus's name had been linked to the tall, wafer-thin models Claire Boothroyd and Kicky Rapp whose gorgeous gowns and haughty, impassive stares he had photographed against chic Cockney backdrops: Covent Garden, Tower Hill, the Docks. He had even starred in a film himself, called *Close-Up*. It had flopped; as co-producer Magnus had lost £50,000. Sulking, Magnus had withdrawn to meditate in a fisherman's cottage on Skye. Emissaries from *Harper's & Queen*, *Vogue*, *19*, *Mademoiselle* and *Elle*, tipped off by Magnus's PR firm, had travelled north to discover that the hermit was disgusted by jet-set affluence and shallow materialism. So avidly did the readers of these magazines lap it up, that Magnus's temperamental disappearances became an annual event, and every year millions of young women stampeded to discover whether this time he was utterly alone with Claire Boothroyd or utterly alone with Kicky Rapp. Photographs containing the answer were invariably shot against a romantic background of sand, sea, rock and wind-swept sky: most of them were taken by Magnus himself, with the help of a tripod and a delayed-action shutter.

Then, one summer, he really did disappear. For several months there was no trace of him until a female graduate student spotted him—incredibly—in the Reading Room of the British Museum. All attempts by his agent and PR consultants to lure him out failed. When they heard that he had begun to write about political and historical topics they laughed sourly.

One day he walked into Bill Ellison's office clutching a pile of essays, and asked for a job.

"Apply to the fashion editor," Ellison suggested.

For half an hour the tall young photographer explained to the famous journalist the significance of the English Revolution of 1640, the Great Reform Act, Marx and Che Guevara.

"Try the colour magazine, Massey. If you've got a

nice snapshot of Oliver Cromwell they might use it."

Magnus nodded gravely, a little sadly. "Nice of you to listen, all the same. I like your work."

It was a year later that Ellison again came across Massey. General Arik Sharon had just forced a bridgehead across the Suez Canal and was thrusting his armour towards Cairo. Ellison and three fellow-correspondents accredited to Zahal were flat on their faces behind an Israeli Centurion tank at the height of an Egyptian artillery bombardment when bumping across the Sinai desert came an old jeep carrying a tall, blond photographer armed with a Nikon whose 500mm lens was aimed at the Egyptian gun and tank emplacements. Ignoring the warning shouts of the Israeli officers, Massey's jeep drove recklessly on and would no doubt have over-run the enemy positions if an Israeli sergeant hadn't put a bullet through the jeep's offside front tyre.

For twenty-four hours the Israelis held Magnus in detention: it took all of Ellison's influence to persuade them that he wasn't a spy. Only after Zahal's Military Intelligence had developed the photographs in his camera were the negatives reluctantly returned to him. After one glance at them Ellison offered to buy the lot. Magnus smiled gently.

"They're for my own story." His tone of voice was almost apologetic.

"*Harper's* or *Mademoiselle*?"

"No idea. Haven't sold it yet."

"By the time you do, the Yom Kippur war will be forgotten."

Ellison was wrong. Magnus's story and photographs were published the following Sunday by the *Monitor*'s great rival, the *Sunday Dispatch*. The story was as good as the pictures. Ellison's own report was put in the shade. Ellison wasn't accustomed to being put in the shade, and he didn't like it. He offered Magnus a job.

"Sorry. I'm under a year's contract."

"Break it."

"They've been very decent to me."

"Whatever they're giving you, I'll top it by £5,000."

Magnus smiled. "It's my old Scottish nanny, you see. She'd turn in her grave if I broke a contract."

At their late-Victorian, red-brick house in Green Street, Mayfair, the staff of the Arab League greeted accredited journalists with Turkish coffee, delicious almond cakes and mimeographed statements headed "Not to be released before 1300 hours". Magnus was immediately struck by the mood of jubilation. Even the representatives of the *Jewish Chronicle* and the *Jerusalem Post* were courteously received instead of being, as was now customary, thrown down the front steps. (Magnus could remember the time, not so long ago, when every journalist would have walked out of a Press conference if a colleague had been excluded—alas, no longer.)

As the throng of reporters crushed into the small conference room, Bernie Holzheimer of the *New York Times* playfully elbowed Magnus in the kidneys.

"They seem to be celebrating," he murmured. "I thought they were supposed to be outraged."

During the two years since Holzheimer had moved to the New York paper's London bureau, he and Magnus had developed a mutual professional respect which, as Bernie once put it, threatened to "degenerate into friendship". Despite his deceptive aura of boyish innocence—the world beyond Brooklyn never ceased to astonish him—Bernie enjoyed access to sources of information unavailable to Ellison and Massey. More than once the Searchlight team had benefited from a slyly delivered Holzheimer tip-off originating in the State Department's Bureau of Intelligence and Research, an outfit with a modest budget of $12 million.

"There are two problems, Massive," Holzheimer said quietly as the reporters waited for the Press conference to begin. "The first is the White House and the National Security Council. They know what's happening over here, but they don't want to know."

Magnus shrugged. "More than fifty per cent of American oil is now imported."

"Correct. Politics is no longer about offending sheikhs."

"What's the second problem?"

"Your own government—I haven't had a straight answer from the Foreign Office to a single question I've put since I've been here."

"They're scared too."

"More than scared, Massive. If they *wanted* American intervention they'd get to work scaring the hell out of American public opinion."

"By means of unidentifiable leaks to Bernard F. Holzheimer?"

"I'm modest. I was in Washington three weeks ago. I had three separate 'background' briefings—unquotable. Two came from State's Bureau of Intelligence and Research, one from the Near East Bureau. The message was the same: the cryptanalysts have broken a code operating between certain Arab capitals."

"Whose code?"

Holzheimer glanced casually at their closest neighbours. His voice was barely above a whisper.

"Al-Ittihad's."

"Spell it."

"Tell Ellison this: time is short."

"You could publish."

"I could also lose my sources."

The Arab League spokesmen now took their places on a raised dais. First to the microphones was Mamoun Abdul Shukhairy, First Secretary of the Libyan Embassy, a man of massive physique who wore a smart brown business suit and a brilliantly laundered white shirt.

"On behalf of the Arab Republic of Libya and its great leader President Muammar Gaddafi," he shouted, "I wish to express the indignation felt by all Arab peoples, and by all progressive humanity, in the face of recent Zionist calumnies, fabrications and insults."

And so on. Questions from the floor were few and low-keyed; most of the reporters present accepted that *Deadline* had fallen flat on its face, and many of them were prepared to believe that even a colleague of Cohn's proven integrity might have stumbled into the old trap of "fabricating the truth". Shukhairy had an easy ride. His broad, heavy features began to beam with satisfaction.

Until Timothy Powerstock asked his first question.

The small, densely packed room was suddenly charged with an electric tension.

Powerstock headed the *Sunday Dispatch*'s counterpart to Ellison's Searchlight team. As such he was Ellison's principal Fleet Street rival. Not an enemy, like Hoyle, but a rival. Both men shared the same ideals. The two Sunday newspapers fought, week by week, for the same middle-class "quality" readership; people who were prepared to pay 25p for a 72-page paper in three sections (front, review, and business), plus a colour magazine; readers who so attracted advertisers that advertising accounted for sixty per cent of the total revenue of both papers. In this battle the *Monitor* held a clear lead: its circulation stood at 1.5 million compared to the *Dispatch*'s 0.9 million. The *Monitor*'s weekly advertising revenue topped £400,000, while the *Dispatch*'s stuck at £225,000.

In the mind of the *Dispatch*'s proprietor, Lord Jacobs, this gap could be explained in almost one word: Ellison. Time and again Jacobs had prayed that Ellison's silences and evasions were the mark of genuine ignorance or apathy; time and again Ellison had finally scaled the wall against which Powerstock had been ramming his head. Twice a year Jacobs invited Ellison to lunch at the Ritz. Twice a year he increased his offer. Twice a year Ellison thanked him and promised to think it over.

Powerstock's voice was now raised: "Mr Shukhairy, I put it to you that Cohn and Laslett have been framed by the enemies of British democracy working in collusion with certain Foreign Office officials and the Arab League."

Bernie Holzheimer nudged Magnus. "Does Tim know something," he murmured, "that I don't know?"

Shukhairy's face was suffused with rage. Every Arab on the dais had jumped indignantly to his feet.

"You're adding insult to injury!" shouted the Libyan diplomat. "But I am not surprised, Mr Powerstock. It is a matter of common knowledge that your paper is now entirely under Zionist control."

"How do you explain the fact," Powerstock persisted, "that Cohn's secretary, Marianne Irving, was found dead yesterday morning, apparently murdered? Perhaps she knew too much, Mr Shukhairy."

The Arab seized his chance; he had been quick to spot that Powerstock was shooting in the dark.

"Perhaps she did know too much, Mr Powerstock. Ask Mr Cohn about that. Ask Mr Cohn who murdered her and why."

The Arabs on the dais smiled in relief and delight.

Holzheimer tried a question about the Arab boycott of firms trading with Israel, but the tension had ebbed now and soon the journalists were shuffling towards the door, where pretty Arab girls presented them with lavish leather folders containing an armoury of brochures, statements and statistics lauding Anglo-Arab trade, loans and investments.

But the well-manicured hand which lightly touched Magnus's sleeve as he made for the door was a man's hand.

"My dear Mr Massey, could I borrow a moment of your precious time?"

Magnus knew Nashat Al-Khatib by sight and reputation only. Born in Jeddah of a rich Saudi merchant family, educated at Harrow and Trinity College, Cambridge, invariably dressed in brightly coloured blazers with dazzling silk scarves at his neck, not to mention two-tone shoes with high platform heels, Nashat Al-Khatib was a byword for lavish hospitality. Equally at home in Claridge's and the Playboy Club, at Ascot and the Covent Garden opera, he also possessed other, more substantial claims to consideration:

——President of the Anglo-Arab Chamber of Commerce.

——Managing Director of Arabair.

Nashat Al-Khatib was smiling in the friendliest manner.

"Mr Shukhairy and I are most anxious to snatch a few minutes of your precious time."

"Fine. Here?"

"I think not. Suppose we meet in my office in Piccadilly in half an hour's time."

"Fine."

Magnus's cool manner belied his inner interest. For almost two months he, Ellison and O'Neill had been zeroing in on Arabair and its related companies. It was as a result of these investigations that Spectrum Security had suddenly surfaced, like a black shark; it was as a result of these investigations that acute pressure had been brought to bear on Lord Gowers by the withdrawal of advertising revenue; it was as a result of these investigations that Ellison had been invited to 10 Downing Street and found a bomb planted in his car.

The *Monitor*'s consultant on Middle East affairs, Ellison's friend Stanford Christie, had told them enough about the careers of Nashat Al-Khatib and Mamoun Abdul Shukhairy to convince the Searchlight team that these two Arabs were key figures in the conspiracy. According to Christie, both men enjoyed a close working relationship with Kenneth Lynedoch, Under Secretary at the Foreign Office with responsibility for the Middle East and Near East Departments—one of the two civil servants who, according to Walter Vandyke, sat in on meetings of the Inner Cabinet. Beyond that the trail faded into thick undergrowth, though Foreign Office collusion in the Cohn-Laslett fiasco suggested a possible link between these two Arabs and the conspirators exposed by the Irving documents.

Suggested. No proof.

The Arabair offices stretched for thirty opulent yards along the south side of Piccadilly between Duke Street St James's and St James's Church. The ground-floor exterior had been decorated in grained Egyptian marble from Aswan and smoky-brown plate glass. The display window contained not only models of Arabair's McDonnell Douglas DC-10

30 CF carriers, each capable of freighting 64,860 kilos over an inter-continental range, but also pyramids, sphinxes and posters advertising Islamic cultural events in London.

Magnus walked into the lushly furnished reception hall of Arabair and was immediately greeted by one of the ten pretty air hostesses in salmon-pink uniforms who decorated the room. Ten mascaraed pairs of eyes fluttered in his direction.

"Mr Massey? Mr Nashat Al-Khatib is expecting you."

On the first floor the Managing Director was waiting to receive him at the small private lift. "Will you have tea or coffee? I don't believe you've met my friend, Mr Mamoun Abdul Shukhairy."

The Libyan diplomat shook his hand sullenly. "You asked no questions at today's Press conference, Mr Massey. Or did Mr Powerstock steal your thunder?"

"Those are very pretty girls you have downstairs," Magnus said to Khatib.

"Hospitality is a sound investment. Speaking of pretty girls, I understand Mr Ellison has recently recruited into his team a beautiful young lady with auburn hair."

"It's news to me. I've never known him employ a woman."

"A false report, you think?"

"Has to be. If ever there was a male chauvinist pig, it's Ellison. Does it matter so much?"

"No, no, not at all. We are merely curious to know who murdered Marianne Irving. Aren't you?"

"Fairly."

"Mr Massey, in recent weeks you and your colleague Mr O'Neill have been taking an unusual interest in our business here. You have also paid visits to the Samarkand Trading Company in Cannon Street and the merchant bank of Howles, Cramp and Roope in Moorgate. I am told that you and your admirable range of cameras have been seen in the vicinity of Ferndale airport in Essex, out of which our fleet of DC-10s operate. You were observed in conversation with an official of Customs and Excise in a pub. Mr O'Neill has called on several of the British firms whose exports we transport to the Middle East. Now why?"

Magnus was gazing thoughtfully at a large, framed poster on the wall. It depicted three girls in salmon-pink uniforms checking freight being loaded aboard an Arabair DC-10: very pretty girls, too, with beguiling smiles.

"Nice ad, that. Who was the photographer?"

Nashat Al-Khatib shrugged impatiently. "I have no idea. The advertising agency handles such details."

"Sure. Who are they?"

"Mr Massey, let us be serious. Am I to understand that you do not regard Arabair as strictly a business concern?"

"Is it?"

"Of course, of course."

"According to the files in Companies House, you and Mr Shukhairy here are directors of both Arabair and Samarkand, as well as Howles, Cramp and Roope."

"So?"

"All seven listed directors of Arabair are Arabs, five of them apparently resident in various Middle East countries."

"Certainly. Arabair is registered outside of Britain. It is wholly Arab-owned."

"Quite. But who are the shareholders?"

"Arabs, of course."

"But who?"

"It's in the folder in Companies House."

"I'm afraid not. The Companies Act doesn't require companies registered overseas to list their shareholders."

"Quite true. That slipped my mind. Arabair has many shareholders and I . . ."

"Even though it's a private company with only a hundred shares?"

"I don't have a list of shareholders."

"Who does?"

"You can write to our Head Office in Amman."

"Is it in Amman? I noticed that the Articles of Association

in the file are covered with official Jordanian registration stamps, but that was twelve years ago."

"Yes, of course, write to Amman, PO Box 662. Nothing has changed."

Massey knew that Nashat Al-Khatib was lying. Paget, the *Monitor*'s stringer in Amman, had been instructed to look up the registration and had discovered two things. Arabair's original four Jordanian shareholders and directors had been bought out three years ago, and shortly thereafter registration had been withdrawn. But where had it been transferred to?

"I also wondered about the Samarkand Trading Company," Massey drawled softly. "Arabair holds a fifty-five per cent stake in Samarkand. But since we don't know who owns Arabair, we don't know who owns Samarkand either."

Shukhairy glowered darkly. "It is of no significance except to Zionist intriguers."

"No, no, Mamoun, Mr Massey is puzzled and we must help him. We have nothing to hide, absolutely nothing."

"If you're helping me," smiled Magnus lazily, "I'd hate to be around when you're trying to be unhelpful."

Nashat Al-Khatib flashed a bright Harrow-and-Trinity smile. "You're not a Marxist, surely, Mr Massey. Private ownership doesn't offend you ideologically, I suppose?"

"Now take Howles, Cramp and Roope, the merchant bank: three Arab directors, including your good selves, and five British."

"Quite so."

"Nominal capital value, £34.5 million."

"Excellent memory."

"How are the shares divided? That does slip my memory."

"Fifty-five thousand shares are owned by a British consortium headed by City gentlemen of unimpeachable reputation. And that gives them a controlling interest."

"Does it?"

"Why, yes. Fifty-five per cent."

"And who owns the rest?"

"Ten per cent belong to Samarkand. Thirty-five per cent to the Swiss Bank of Hauptmann."

"Address, Talackerstrasse, Zurich."

He saw Khatib flinch. He knew that the Arab had been twisting the facts so palpably as to rule out any possibility of an honest error. The British consortium's shareholding was confined, in fact, to "B" shares which carried no voting rights at all. This left the controlling interest in the hands of the "minority" shareholders, Samarkand and Hauptmann. But Hauptmann was no gnome of Zurich; Hauptmann was a holding company wholly owned by the Trans-Arabian Bank of Tripoli.

Which, in Ellison's view, was the crucial force across the whole spectrum of operations. The evidence—impossible to glean from records available in Britain—had already cost more than £1,000.

And Freddie Nash his life.

The *Monitor*'s stringer in Cairo, on receiving a coded Telex message from Ellison, had flown to Beirut, spent $80 on acquiring a forged Libyan visa, then caught the next flight to Tripoli with the idea in his head that Trans-Arabian had been taken over by a pan-Islamic movement with limitless funds and dreams of world conquest. Conversations with the few battered Western newsmen who had survived under Gadaffi's austere, no-drink, no-girls curfew regime had led him to Telex an excited message to London. On leaving the hotel in mid-afternoon Freddie Nash had disappeared without trace.

According to Ellison's sources in the currency market, the Trans-Arabian Bank had given the push to a recent series of disastrous runs on sterling. The sterling liabilities of British banks to Arab interests stood in excess of £3,900 million. To keep this money in sterling, the Treasury had guaranteed the Arabs against falls in the parity of the pound as measured against a basket of currencies. Yet sudden, drastic withdrawals of short-term money had nevertheless taken place, causing a flight from the pound, a further drain on the Bank of England's foreign currency reserves, and a general paralysis of confidence. In Ellison's view, the Trans-Arabian had a single objective—to prostrate Britain at the feet of the forthcoming Arab Mission.

Magnus was twiddling a red, felt-tipped pen and gazing at the three salmon-pink girls hanging on the wall.

"About a hundred and fifty British firms export their goods through Arabair, right?"

"Approximately."

"Do you offer them any particular incentives?"

"Efficiency."

"I gather that the Samarkand Trading Company not only acts as agent but pays the British firms in full as soon as the exports are delivered to your bonded warehouses at Ferndale airport. Now that *is* attractive, gentlemen—no uncertainties, no delays, no bad debts."

"That is what I call efficiency, Mr Massey."

"And payment is arranged through Howles, Cramp and Roope? Where the pill is sweetened, to my naive mind, quite sensationally. Yes?"

Khatib and Shukhairy were watching him intently. The Managing Director's office was very quiet—the traffic of Piccadilly was completely muffled by double-glazing.

"I thought," Magnus said mildly, "that you had nothing to hide."

"Quite so."

"Yet I appear to be interviewing myself."

"I am told that is a technique that Mr Ellison is famous for."

Magnus shrugged. "Would you care to confirm or deny that Howles, Cramp and Roope is guaranteeing your British clients a fixed exchange rate above the market value of sterling?"

"It's possible."

"And you call that efficiency, no doubt?"

"What would you call it, Mr Massey?"

"To qualify for the benefits of all this efficiency, your

British client firms have to meet certain conditions?"

"Do they?"

"Yes or no?"

"I can't imagine what you have in mind."

The conditions Magnus had in mind were four: no trading with Israel; no Jewish directors; no advertising in the *Sunday Monitor* or *Sunday Dispatch*; and a sizeable donation to the Saviours of the Nation. A brash young executive, exultant about the tax-free bonus of £2,500 nestling in his bank, and thoroughly thawed by the fifth double Scotch Magnus had poured down his throat, had revealed a further condition— that the British client firm must contract its transport and warehouse security to an outfit recommended by Samarkand and Arabair.

An outfit called Spectrum Security.

Magnus now sensed that Nashat Al-Khatib was anxious to bring the interview to a close. He decided on one final throw. The key memorandum in the Irving documents had contained the sentence: "Highest authority has instructed payment of an additional £3.5 million by AA for schools radio." In Ellison's view, AA could well refer to Arabair.

"A small detail . . ." Magnus murmured.

"Yes, of course."

"How much did the 'Milestones of Islam' series on BBC Television cost you? More than the extra £3.5 million you're sending the FSCR for schools broadcasts?"

Both Arabs froze. The blood rushed to Shukhairy's face. "We have nothing to do with the FSCR!" he snapped. "Nothing! It's a Zionist fabrication!"

Instantly recognizing Shukhairy's mistake, Nashat Al-Khatib intervened smoothly. "I personally have never heard of the FSCR, Mr Massey. What is it?"

Magnus rose from his chair. "It has been a pleasure, gentlemen."

As he left the office there were no handshakes.

Seven

"Bill, Irena Ucelikova has been in touch. She's in quite a state. It sounds as if David Gottlieb has been hit."

"Another sexual frame-up?"

"Almost certainly."

"Then get to him, Judy. I badly need a break on these sex cases. And I'm in a hurry."

"Message received."

"But, Judy . . ."

"Yes, chief?"

"Well . . . I've always . . . you know, there have to be limits in journalism."

"Are there?"

"I suppose your generation——"

"You didn't complain when I came up with the Irving documents."

"Well . . ."

She laughed. "You're very sweet. And who would guess that you're quite clever too?"

Judy Rossiter took care to arrive four minutes late for her lunch appointment at the White Tower with David Gottlieb and Irena Ucelikova. The entrance she had planned had its effect; it was only on a second "take" that Irena recognized the lovely girl in green suede and white puffed sleeves gliding towards their table. Rising to take the hand of "Alice Pryor", David Gottlieb made no effort to mask the impact of her large, high breasts and long, slender legs.

94

Irena stammered the introductions.

The fragrance of Alliage perfume drifted across the table.

It took Judy Rossiter thirty seconds to confirm that Gottlieb was highly susceptible to a pretty woman's flattery. He talked about himself almost without interruption through the taramasalata and the kebab. He was delighted when she, as hostess, begged him to choose and taste the wine. And when she told him that he was the most talented and original theatre director of his generation, his modest denial carried no conviction.

Irena might as well not have been at the table—his eyes never left Judy Rossiter.

Over coffee Judy began to steer the conversation towards the mounting storm over the play *Guardian of Decency*. Gottlieb responded with machine-gun volleys against "fools and fascists". Gazing at him dewy-eyed, Judy nodded in constant agreement, the curled tips of her auburn hair flicking round her ears to caress her cheek.

"And there's some fuss about an actress called Kitty Summerbee?"

Abruptly Gottlieb's relaxed self-assurance vanished. His mouth tightened.

"Who told you about that?"

His gaze, hard and threatening, was fixed on Irena.

Judy's gentle hand quickly fastened round his wrist.

"But, David, don't be so silly, *everyone's* talking about it. The wildest, craziest rumours are flying around."

"I thought you were writing about my work for *Plays and Players*."

"I am. Just that."

"Then we don't need to discuss idle gossip."

"Sorry. I won't say another word. But it's entirely your fault."

"Oh; why?"

"Because if you weren't so talented and attractive, women wouldn't be so helplessly fascinated by your private life."

"Rubbish." He looked delighted. His good humour

returned. "So you want to tape an interview with me? Why don't you come to my place tomorrow evening?"

"Fine."

When she tried to pay the bill he wouldn't hear of it.

The following evening she parked the red Mini Cooper in Holland Park, then took a taxi to Lansdowne Crescent, where he was living alone in a smart but soulless service flat.

"Oh David, I'm so sorry I'm late. The traffic!"

He tried, but failed, to conceal his erotic interest as she peeled off her light raincoat to reveal a tight-fitting beige silk dress with a short, flared skirt buttoned down the front. The bottom two buttons had not been fastened; as she sank into a sofa the fine silk glided up a long expanse of thigh clad in black fishnet stocking. Extracting her Grundig Stenorette 2002 from its case, she beckoned him to the sofa beside her.

For thirty minutes Gottlieb spoke with fluency and wit about the play *Guardian of Decency* and about his own vision of the social function of television drama. The play exposed the hypocrisy of a suburban vigilante who constantly bombarded the BBC with protests about "filth", but himself had a clandestine affair with an under-age girl whom he finally murdered on a lonely path to avoid a scandal.

"Marvellous," she said, replacing the recorder in its case.

"Quite a lot of things about you are also rather marvellous, Alice."

"Really? Like what, for example?"

"Like your breasts. Like your legs. Like your mouth."

"Oh dear, it's beginning to sound like the wolf and Little Red Riding Hood." She put her hand on his knee. "David, do tell me: why are you living here all alone? I mean a man like you could have any woman he wanted."

His eyes sparked with pleasure. "Any woman?"

"Almost," she whispered.

He caught her chin between his fingers. "I am in fact married to the actress Fay Towers."

"Do you still love her?"

He nodded. "I do. But it all went wrong as soon as the

kids came. Fay became restless when she began to realize she'd sacrificed her career. And of course she blamed me. She started to mix with the wildest harpies of the women's lib movement. Then she told me to go."

"And your children?"

Gottlieb looked pained. "I think Jewish fathers find it particularly hard to be separated from their children."

"But you still see them?"

"They come here on alternate weekends. That's how the whole Kitty Summerbee business started."

"Well, I wouldn't *dream* of asking about *that*. Not after last time."

He smiled and lifted her chin. "You're jealous?" Her green eyes gazed steadily into his. "Why is green always associated with jealousy?" he said.

"I wouldn't know," she pouted.

"Are you hungry?"

"Oh yes!"

"Kiss me."

"No."

They dined down the road in the Artiste Assoiffé. Halfway through the first carafe of red wine Gottlieb began to unbend about his private life; halfway through the second, he became confessional.

"I used to sit in the flat on Saturday evenings, when the children were staying. Then suddenly I couldn't stand it, telling them infantile stories and pretending I was mummy. So I began asking people whether they knew of a reliable baby sitter. As it turned out, I found one through an agency who sent me their brochure." He laughed. "Maybe they employ detectives to trace broken marriages."

"Maybe they do. What was the agency called?"

"Relief. So this girl turned up: Pat." He shrugged. "I was short of a woman. She was a woman."

"Don't expect me to applaud that remark."

"Well, I felt very lonely. We began to see each other during the week. You're very beautiful, aren't you, Alice?"

"Thank you."

"Anyway, there it was, a low-keyed affair. Then one evening, after we'd been to the cinema, she invited me back to her place. I met her flatmate."

David Gottlieb stopped abruptly.

Judy Rossiter lit a cigarette. "Where did Pat live?"

"In Phillimore Avenue. Number 18."

"And the flatmate?"

Gottlieb sighed. "That was Kitty Summerbee. A stunningly lovely girl. An actress out of work."

"Of whom there are many."

"Kitty had worked in provincial rep, mainly at the Nottingham Playhouse, plus one or two TV slots. But for the last two years her agent hadn't found her a single job."

"Out of sight, out of mind."

"Right. Especially in the theatre."

"You decided you preferred Kitty to Pat?"

"Yes. Ten men out of ten would have agreed. Different league. She became an addiction to me, a drug."

"And she knew it?"

"Oh yes. One evening she was at my place and picked up a script of *Guardian of Decency*. She sat down and read it. Then she said——"

Gottlieb stopped.

"What did she say?"

"Never mind. I'm talking too much."

"It's late, David. I must go home and write my article."

"Come home with me, Alice. Please."

"Only if you promise to be good."

As soon as the flat door had closed behind them she pressed him against the wall and reached into his trousers. He groaned and closed his eyes as she brought him up, swollen and throbbing, into her hand. Greedily he clutched at her breasts, then pulled up the skirt of her dress, kneading the soft flesh above the tops of her stockings and biting his fingers into her buttocks. Her hot tongue teased his tip——

maddened, he threw her across the bed and tore off his own clothes. Her thighs, decorated by black fishnet stockings and a red garter belt, locked round his as he drove into her, her hips goading him rhythmically towards an explosive climax that he struggled in vain to control and delay. His head fell forward on to the pillow beside hers.

"Don't judge me," he murmured.

"Why not?"

"I can do better."

"Prove it."

Already her fingertips were provoking his testicles while her tongue flickered, long and wet, inside his mouth. When she rolled him on to his back his fuse was already burning; he reached up for the big breasts swaying above his face and glowed with pleasure as he saw the fine curve of her hips and thighs thrusting down. Her mouth was slightly open, her cheeks flushed, her green eyes alight with triumph and mockery. It was the mockery, the fine shading of humiliation, which brought him up and on towards his second orgasm.

Abruptly she withdrew. Her mouth had folded into a pout. "I'm jealous," she said.

He smiled and caught her swollen nipples between his knuckles. "Of Kitty?"

"You're still seeing her!"

"Come here."

Deftly she swayed out of his reach. "Not till you tell me about that bitch."

He stretched out a hand to the bedside table and lit two cigarettes.

"Kitty read the script and demanded the part of the under-age girl whom the vigilante finally murders. I saw at once she could do it; Kitty has the nymphet look, adolescent, sluttish. The author, the director, the Casting Department and I went through *Spotlight* and narrowed the field to a short list of six actresses with baby doll faces. We held auditions. Kitty came. I thought she was the best. The author wasn't sure; the director, Chris Carrington, was against her. The next day I told Chris I wanted to direct this play myself."

"And Kitty got the part?"

"Yes. I sent the cast list to the Artists' Contracts Department, where they decide the fee to be offered to each actor or his agent. I was amazed when they told me Kitty was too expensive. I spoke to the Head of Contracts. He couldn't explain it: even though Kitty had been out of work for two years, her agent was demanding £300 for a small part. Do you know what the Equity minimum rate is?"

"No."

"£148 for a minimum of eight rehearsal days plus one day's shooting within a period of fourteen days."

"She wanted double the minimum."

"Well of course I thought it must be her agent. I rang Kitty and tried to explain the facts of life. She knew them. She was cold and unyielding. The play needed her and I needed her: pay up. I then offered to pay her £150 out of my own pocket if she would agree to accept £150 from the Beeb. She agreed. As you may know, nowadays the Casting Department automatically sends its cast lists to Equity. At the end of the first week's rehearsals an Equity rep rang Contracts to complain that Kitty's subscription had lapsed two years ago. Apparently she promised to pay the £24 she owed—there's a fixed rate for all actors earning less than £2,500 a year. We went into production, the film was canned. Equity began to blow nasty: she still hadn't paid her subscription. They came to me—Irena, actually, I was away—with the astonishing story that I was going to pay her subscription. Kitty had told them so."

"And you did?"

"I didn't have much alternative."

"But you went on seeing Kitty?"

"I . . . she dropped me."

Judy Rossiter smiled. "Good," she whispered as her loins began to coax him back to an erection. David Gottlieb closed his eyes and moaned with pleasure; these were delights he had never known before.

Presently he fell asleep . . . beside the best actress he had ever set eyes on.

But the best actress he had ever set eyes on had two things in common with Joe O'Neill: youth and impetuousness. From Holland Park she drove straight to Kensington High Street, snatched a parking space into which another car was waiting to reverse, flashed an apologetic smile at the maddened driver, and walked the last three hundred yards to Phillimore Avenue, wearing a headscarf and dark glasses.

The apartment block where Gottlieb had met his doom stood in a quiet residential street behind Kensington Public Library. She mounted the steps of number 18 and examined the name plates. There were no names.

The front door was locked.

"Did you want something?"

She turned quickly. A man with massive shoulders and the face of a prize-fighter had climbed out of a black Mercedes 450 SEL. His small eyes burnt through her like laser beams.

"I think that's my business," she said.

"Is it?"

For a moment she thought he was about to strike her. But the large, calloused hand that reached out was quite gentle as it lifted her dark glasses then eased the scarf from over her hair. He smiled. "Nice."

She walked away with as much dignity as she could muster but her heart was hammering and a cold dew of fear had seeped into her marrow.

Ellison reached Chester Place at 8.55, five minutes before *Guardian of Decency* was due to go out over BBC1. But he hadn't the heart to watch it. In his hand he held the first edition of tomorrow's *Star*:

BUT WHO IS THE REAL HYPOCRITE?
BBC's Gottlieb In Sex Scandal.

Extending across two columns was a photograph of Gottlieb ravishing Kitty Summerbee in a king-size bed. Caption: "This is the Jew Director Who Exposes Sexual Hypocrisy." The point of the anatomy at which Gottlieb and Summerbee were locked had been pasted out with a white panel: "We are a family newspaper."

Hoyle began with a summary of the play, *Guardian of Decency*. But what of Gottlieb's own behaviour? Having abandoned his wife and children, he had seduced his baby sitter, then moved on to her flatmate, awarding her a plum part despite the superior claims of five other actresses. To make sure she got the part, Gottlieb had taken over the direction of the play himself, paid half of Summerbee's inflated fee, and then settled her Equity dues.

When approached by the *Star*, Kitty Summerbee had confessed: "It's true I twisted Gottlieb round my little finger. I needed the part. If I had wanted to play Othello David would have said yes. He's completely unscrupulous. I'm disgusted and disillusioned. I agree it's high time the BBC was cleaned out."

Pru came into Ellison's study. "You look whacked, darling." He showed her the *Star*. "Oh God," she groaned, "why can't they be more careful?"

"Man is frail."

"Any news of poor Maurice Cohn?"

"A five-man Board of Inquiry has found Cohn and Laslett guilty of 'unprofessional conduct' and of allowing 'personal bias' to over-ride the 'respect for truth expected at all staff levels in the Current Affairs Group'. The vote was four to one; only Jack Armstrong dissented. Lucas and Strachan voted with the majority."

"Can anything be done . . . to help?"

"No."

She bent and kissed him. "Don't stay up too late, Bill. You're very short of sleep."

Twenty minutes later there was a timid tap on his door followed by the entry of Monika Bauer, carrying a tea tray. She was wearing a tight turtle sweater and tight Levis, but her smile wasn't at all tight.

"A nightcap for the master of the house?"

"Very kind of you, Monika. Actually I usually have something a bit stronger . . . as you can see." He gestured ruefully towards the half-empty whisky bottle on his desk. "So how's your language course going?" he asked.

"Don't speak of it!" As she raised her hands in a gesture of mock despair her full breasts lifted sweetly. "I'm lazy," she added, "and stupid."

She poured him a cup of tea, then sat down. For the first time he absorbed the full power of her physical attraction.

"I have discovered that you are a very important man," she said.

"Who told you that?"

She laughed. "Christopher."

"Then it must be true."

"He says you are having a great struggle against some very bad men and that they tried to kill you. Did they really try to kill you?"

"Yes."

"But how awful! And who are these wicked men, do you know their names?"

"No, and I'm unlikely to find out."

"You like Mozart?"

"I've never met him."

She laughed. "If you will come to my room I will let you hear my beautiful new stereo."

"I'd love to. But not tonight."

When Monika had gone to bed he went into the sitting-room and lifted the flap of Pru's desk. The lavish brochure was lying on top of a pile of business cards. As he picked it up

Ellison's eyes were like grey stones washed by a millennium of tides.

Monika Bauer had come from an agency called Relief, Ltd, of New Bond Street.

So had Steve Moyars's baby sitter.

So had David Gottlieb's.

As Ellison closed the flap of the desk the phone rang. It was Magnus.

"Maurice Cohn threw himself from the top floor of Lime Grove early this evening. When the ambulance reached Hammersmith Hospital he was already dead."

Eight

Joe O'Neill, known to himself as Dogsbody, walked down City Road from Old Street tube station and into the ugly building called Companies House. A commissionaire searched his briefcase at the door. Turning off the main hallway into the index room, O'Neill parked himself behind a Bell & Howell SR-VII electronic scanner covering the letters A to F, observed the long lists of white-printed names flash across the black screen, and noted down the six-figure reference number of Relief, Ltd. Finding no reference to Spectrum Security, he crossed the road to Pembroke House, where business names other than those of limited companies are registered. Again he drew a blank.

According to the Companies Act of 1916, "Registration is required whenever business is being carried on . . . in names other than those of the proprietors." He doubted whether Spectrum was run by a Mr Spectrum; Joe also had reason to doubt whether failure to register was Spectrum's most serious violation of the law.

Back in Companies House, he paid 5p, filled in a slip, took it to the reading room to be time-stamped, and was given a red plastic tab indicating his seat number. Fifteen minutes later a woman brought him an envelope containing 105mm × 148mm blue diazo microfiche slips duplicated from 16mm-microfilm of the Relief, Ltd company file. He slotted the first microfiche into the huge NCR Reader in front of him, adjusted the hold and focus, and began to read off a 24× magnification.

Joe O'Neill longed for a scoop, a breakthrough which would wipe the perpetual, cold scepticism out of Bill Ellison's hard, grey eyes.

In its Articles of Association, Relief listed a wide range of activities including provision of home help, au pairs, baby sitters, cleaners, as well as guides, hostesses, escorts and couriers, arranging social introductions, and running a model agency. The accounts were missing and Joe swore loud enough to draw a reproving glance from his neighbour. He filled in a complaint slip then returned to the NCR Reader. Only two directors were listed: F. Eltenbridge (sex not revealed, occupation "company director", former names blank); and F. Cain (ditto). The company's nominal capital of 100 £1 shares was divided between them 99 to 1. The "usual residential address" of F. Eltenbridge was given as 14 Rosedale Avenue, NW1, and of F. Cain as 18 Freemont Street, W10. Instead of Relief's actual business address in New Bond Street a nominal registered address was given, that of a City agency specializing in registrations.

Joe O'Neill leant back and groaned. It took no great leap of the imagination to visualize Ellison skimming his notes:

"Great, Joe. Now tell me something."

He walked out of Companies House and took the tube at Old Street. Number 18 Freemont Street had vanished. The local newsagent assured him it had been demolished five years earlier to make way for council flats. As for 14 Rosedale Avenue, it did exist, but housed a harassed woman with a clutch of howling children pulling at her skirts—he was hardly surprised when she didn't own up to the name F. Eltenbridge, company director. The house next door was teeming with squatters who mistook Joe for a bailiff.

O'Neill emitted an oath peculiar to Belfast's Shankill Road. OK, cowboy, you ride down New Bond Street, burst in on Eltenbridge and Cain, thrust your felt-tipped pen into their villainous guts, and snarl, "Spill it, baby."

And Ellison fires you.

*   *   *

Stanford Christie, the *Monitor*'s consultant on Middle East affairs, came on the line from Oxford.

"Bill, something urgent. Rupin wants us to meet him at the Embassy at 3.30."

"I'll see you then, Stanford."

At the entrance to Kensington Palace Gardens, once called Millionaires' Row, the Granada was flagged down behind a barrier. The duty guard phoned through to the Embassy to check that the visitor was a welcome one. Presently the barrier was raised.

The Israeli Embassy had for some time past been protected against terrorist attacks by an iron grille, six feet high, tipped with spikes. Ellison pressed the button. The intercom crackled. "Yes, who you, what want?" rasped a hoarse voice . . . could have been an Arab.

"Bill Ellison to see Solomon Rupin."

"Wait."

He waited. A buzzer buzzed. Monitored, as he knew, by closed-circuit television, he walked towards a massive steel door which swung open as he reached it. The janitor who met him inside the small lobby was wearing a loose jacket which bulged suggestively over his right armpit. A left-handed Arab, then: a typical Israeli.

"I fought my way in," Ellison said, taking Solomon Rupin's hand as he entered a small, spartan office lined with maps of an Israel considerably more extensive than Ellison thought justified. But he hadn't come to argue about frontiers in the Sinai desert.

He exchanged nods with Stanford Christie, the absence of a handshake being a measure of their friendship, and their culture. Neither man could bring himself to speak of Maurice Cohn.

"I have something extremely serious to report to you," Rupin said, gesturing Ellison into an empty chair.

"Well, Solomon, you're scarcely a star of light entertainment even in the best of times."

Short, stocky, balding, Solomon Rupin was known to the

diplomatic community as First Secretary; to Ellison he was also known as principal agent in Britain of the most ruthless of Israel's five intelligence agencies, Ha-Mossad—officially, the Institute for Information. Together with Agaf Modi'in (known as Aman), the intelligence bureau of the armed forces (Zahal), Ha-Mossad shared responsibility for Israel's intelligence and espionage operations abroad. It was Ha-Mossad's specialist squads which had abducted Adolf Eichmann from Argentina in 1960. Following the massacre of Israeli athletes at the Munich Olympics in 1972, Ha-Mossad's hit team had struck back at Black September, infiltrating Beirut from the sea, bursting into an apartment block, and shooting down Abu Youssef, Kemal Adwan and the PLO poet Kamal Nasser.

Ellison knew from Rupin that in recent months Ha-Mossad's European operations centre in Brussels, highly alarmed by developments in Britain, had infiltrated a number of deep-cover agents across the Channel. So seriously was the danger of a pro-Arab coup in Britain taken by Jerusalem, that these agents were poised to strike immediately Israel's top-level Committee for Security gave the order. But the briefing was clear: on no account strike at the limbs until you have located the head.

Ha-Mossad had not located the head. No one had.

Rupin leant forward over his cluttered desk, grim-faced, pushing aside airmail editions of *Ha'aretz*, the *Jerusalem Post* and *Al Kuds*, a pro-PLO Arab-language daily published in East Jerusalem. Rupin spoke fluent Arabic.

"Al-Ittihad," he said quietly.

"Meaning?"

"Meaning 'Unity'," Christie said.

"For some time," Rupin said, "our intelligence units operating in Tripoli, Jeddah and Baghdad have been compiling profiles of Nashat Al-Khatib and Mamoun Abdul Shukhairy. Both of these men are directors of the Trans-Arabian Bank of Tripoli; and that bank, we are now convinced, is controlled by Al-Ittihad."

"Is it a religious sect?"

Ellison masked a quick leap in his interest—Al-Ittihad was the name that Bernie Holzheimer of the *New York Times* had mentioned, without further explanation, to Magnus.

"It is a ruthless conspiracy combining a fanatical belief in Islam's mission to dominate the world with the most modern techniques of gangster terrorism."

Rupin banged his desk in frustration: scepticism was writ large on the faces of his two English guests.

"Stanford, you don't look convinced," Ellison said.

"Every informed graduate student has known about Al-Ittihad for the past fifty years. Originally it was an Arab response to the Balfour Declaration and the British policy of creating a Jewish National Home in Palestine. It became a focus for idealistic young Arabs who felt bitter and helpless. But according to my information Al-Ittihad was killed stone dead by Nasser. As you know, the only Arab word for unity he recognized was 'Nasser'."

"That is exactly what we in Israel thought," said Rupin emphatically. "Our attention was distracted by three major wars in seventeen years, by Soviet tanks, MIGs and Katyusha rockets. We failed to notice that Al-Ittihad had been reborn on the Arab oil boom. A new Al-Ittihad: not a society of penniless young idealists, but a criminal syndicate controlled by mature men with limitless funds at their disposal—ruthless zealots whose appetite for power has been whetted by the dramatic collapse of the British economy. All right! Don't believe me! But if you don't wake up soon it will be too late!"

Christie sighed and shrugged. "The trouble with Ha-Mossad is the trouble with all intelligence and espionage agencies: they are obsessed by plots and conspiracies."

"Wait a minute, Stanford," said Ellison. "Something damned odd is happening in this country."

"It's not odd at all. We have merely been subjected to commercial and political blackmail. Nashat Al-Khatib is a genius at washing money, flouting currency regulations and disguising the flow of huge funds from one country to another. He is powerfully placed: Managing Director of Arabair and President of the Anglo-Arab Chamber of Commerce. He can dictate terms. Shukhairy, as First Secretary in the Libyan Embassy, handles liaison with the Foreign Office where Lynedoch and a handful of officials are convinced that if we don't play ball we'll go under. I have no doubt that money is flowing out of Arabair in all directions: scores of trade union leaders, dons, experts, scientists, journalists, media men and MPs are being paid fat consultancy fees to toe the line. And if Nashat Al-Khatib has hired a call-girl racket and a gangster outfit called Spectrum to help his work along, that should surprise none of us." Stanford Christie smiled his donnish smile. "But I could be wrong."

Ellison smiled too. Ever since the two men had met twenty years ago in Beirut, he had always liked that streak of scholarly caution in Christie. Second Secretary (Information) in the British Embassy, Avenue de Paris, Ras Beirut, and a bachelor at that time, Christie had impressed Ellison with his mordant wit and deep knowledge of Arab society; the petty gossip and intrigues which preoccupied most diplomats merely exasperated him. Ellison hadn't been surprised when, eleven years ago, Christie had abandoned the diplomatic service for the groves of Academe. Soon afterwards he had married.

"I assume," Ellison said to Rupin, "that Al-Ittihad was the fatal word on Moshe Levene's lips when he died?"

A spasm of acute pain crossed Rupin's features. But he merely shrugged his broad shoulders. "I have no idea."

"Personally," Christie said, "I have little doubt that Moshe was involved with Ha-Mossad's intelligence apparatus. He frequently visited Oxford to talk to Israeli scholars at the Middle East Institute."

"Then why has Solomon held back on this information for so long?"

"Moshe was exceeding his brief. Don't you recall how hesitant he was?"

Ellison nodded. "And suspicious of the *Monitor*, too."

"Since *you* mention it, yes."

Ellison was brooding about the key memorandum in the Irving documents. Its cryptic ciphers moved kaleidoscopically through his brain cells. Who was the author of the memo, who was APCR? Massey's interview with Shukhairy and Nashat Al-Khatib had virtually clinched Ellison's hunch that the AA referred to in the memo was Arabair—it was Arabair which, on the instructions of the "highest authority", had funded the BBC's Islamic programmes. But who had produced the films for television, the recordings for radio? According to the memo, Irving herself had worked on one of the series, "Milestones of Islam". Her bank statements showed that she had been on the payroll of the FSCR, but what was it?

"What do you think of the FSCR?" he said casually to Christie.

"The what?"

"You're supposed to be the expert. I thought you knew every Islamic front inside out."

"I take it you're referring to the Foundation for the Study of Comparative Religions at Oxford?"

"Correct. Who runs it?"

"A shit."

"Is that his name, Stanford?"

"His name is Hugh Swinburne."

"A don?"

"*Professor* Swinburne," said Christie caustically.

"Professor of what?"

"Of venom."

Ellison winked at Rupin. "This is what is known as objective reporting. Professor of what, Stanford?"

"He is Arnold Professor of Comparative Religions."

The ratchet clicked in Ellison's head: *APCR*, the author of the Irving memorandum.

"And why do you like him so much, Stanford?"

"Because he has demanded my resignation as Director of

the Middle East Institute more often than I can remember. He denounces me as a Zionist agent."

"Maybe he's right. Are these denunciations verbal or written?"

"Both."

"When did they start?"

"God knows—as soon as I became Director of the Middle East Institute and started bringing Israelis and Palestinians together in a constructive dialogue. Swinburne's a classic case of a scholar corrupted by political ambition. Years ago he wrote two well regarded books: one on the Sufi mystic strain in Islam, the other on the rise of Indra as king of the gods. Since then . . . nothing but intrigue."

"When did he become Director of the FSCR?"

"When the FSCR was first set up, in 1975."

"It *is* an Islamic front, presumably?"

"It's a small house in Norham Road occupied by a toad with dreams of becoming a frog."

"How is it financed?"

"I believe the University makes a small contribution. As a matter of fact, I recently persuaded Council to slash the FSCR's grant by half. I thought it was time I gave Swinburne a taste of his own medicine."

"Who are the FSCR's trustees?"

"No idea."

Solomon Rupin exploded with impatience. "We are wasting time, my friends! Forget about these petty university squabbles; focus your attention on the leadership of Al-Ittihad in Britain."

But Bill Ellison was doing precisely that.

"I don't like that glint in Solomon's eye," Christie said. "It's his High Noon look."

Rupin struck the wall with his fist, causing the outsize maps of Greater Israel to vibrate. "You goyim always insist that we Jews should survive by being Christians!"

Joe O'Neill was in the *Monitor*'s press-cuttings library, carefully sifting every recorded speech made by Professor Hugh Swinburne during the past ten years. The notes Joe was taking were based on a single question Ellison had instructed him to bear in mind. Joe didn't understand the logic behind the question, but that in itself was not unusual. As far as he was concerned, Ellison's devious mind was a place where the sun never shone.

When he took his notes to Ellison, his boss read them intently. Then he looked up impassively.

"Thanks, Joe. As usual, you've brought me bad news."

Some sixty miles away, in the Blenheim-Woodstock countryside north of Oxford, Magnus's 500mm lens was focusing on a palatial imitation of a late-Georgian house designed in the style of Robert Adam and set in five acres of wooded garden. Magnus estimated its value at £150,000.

According to the local publican, Professor Hugh Swinburne had built it three years ago.

"Oh yes, the professor has a lot of visitors, you know, but mostly at night."

Driving to the Garrick Club to lunch with the Director-General of the BBC, Ellison listened to the Arab string music wailing out of Radio 2. He switched wavelength and found himself in the middle of lesson 8 of "Basic Arabic of the Arabian Gulf".

"Please don't trouble yourself: *la tit'eb nafsek*. I'll repeat that useful phrase: *la tit'eb nafsek*. Write it down, please. *Iktibli yah, min fadhlek*. That means, 'write it down, please'."

"Not today," Ellison muttered, switching off.

What should he do about Max Ucelik? He felt affection for Max; he didn't want to hurt Irena either. Had not E. M. Forster said that he hoped he would choose his friends rather than his country if the dilemma ever confronted him? And a wife was more than a friend. Besides, Ellison lacked proof. Any attempt to fire Max would involve intervention by the

National Union of Journalists and a full-scale inquiry. Ellison saw no way of proving his case without bringing Judy in as a witness; he was determined to avoid that at all costs.

And Monika Bauer? A spy, a seductress, in his own home? Probably. He saw now how he had been deceived by the carefully contrived coincidence of his daughter Faith suffering indecent exposure on the same day as Jilly Thorndike. Ellison had examined Monika's room and found nothing of interest, no hidden 16mm cameras. He had also checked his clothes and shoes for miniature transmitter bugs: again, nothing. As a precaution he had put a lock on his wardrobe door with a thread of fine cotton inside which snapped whenever the door was opened.

In the Garrick Club bar, the tall, gaunt, angular figure of Sir Jack Armstrong, a veritable spire of Scottish rectitude, greeted him without a smile. Armstrong had never been known to smile. They moved straight to a corner table in the dining-room overlooking Garrick Street. Sir Jack didn't drink either.

"I see David Gottlieb has been suspended pending an inquiry," Ellison said.

"That is correct."

"I supposed he's doomed?"

"I wouldn't wish to prejudge the issue."

"You're not the easiest man in the world to interview, Jack."

"I never give interviews, Ellison. Since this meeting was at your suggestion, I assumed you had something to tell me."

"OK: Cohn and Laslett were framed."

"Evidence?"

"If I gave you the evidence, you'd resign. I don't want you to resign."

"To my mind that implies the allegation that my superiors in the Corporation were involved."

"Yes."

Armstrong inhaled his soup by a process of long-distance suction. "I would like to see this evidence, Ellison. You perhaps forget that the Scots are not only prigs of moral rectitude, but also endowed with a certain native cunning."

"In other words, this evidence might not entirely surprise you?"

"You haven't told me what it is."

"Oh come on, Jack, if we don't pull our fingers out we're going to have the British Brainwashing Corporation."

"To answer your hypothetical question, but off the record: no, it might not altogether surprise me."

"Do you have any allies left among the Governors or on the Committee of Management?"

"Naturally I cannot discuss my superiors or my colleagues."

"Yes or no?"

"A few. Not many. I seem to be giving an interview."

"Jack, I'm prepared to let you see the Marianne Irving documents in my bank. But I can't let them out and I must ask you not to disclose my knowledge of the affair."

"This would have been more timely, don't you think, before the *Deadline* film went out?"

The remark stung; it reopened the wound of Ellison's guilt. He had just attended the *shiva* for Maurice Cohn, the Jewish prayer meeting to comfort the bereaved, and the look in the eyes of Maurice's widow Sarah haunted him. Animal instinct lured him towards a sharp rejoinder—that any professional worthy of the name should have spotted the Libyan arms film for what it was. But he bit back the remark.

"Why is the Beeb buying up all this Islamic stuff, Jack?"

"Pressures. It's very cheap, of course."

"It doesn't look cheap: the visual material on television I would describe as lavish."

"Quite so. It's subsidized."

"Who produces it?"

"It is the policy of the Governors that the production agency shall not be disclosed. I am bound by that decision."

"If I headed for Oxford would I be on the wrong track?"

"You may be wasting your time, Bill." A ghost of a smile. "But it may also be time well wasted."

"Swinburne?"

"Same reply."

At 10.15 on Saturday evening the Ellison family sat down, in the company of eighteen million other Britons, to watch the weekly TV satire programme, *Believe It or Not*. In Ellison's view, only two factors kept *Believe It or Not* on the air: with eighteen million viewers it topped the peak-hour ratings; and Sir Jack Armstrong. Every week the Guardians of Decency bombarded the BBC with protests; and every week the Corporation's Director of Public Affairs, Paul Verschoyle, declined to comment. Questions were asked in Parliament by outraged backbenchers. Tight-lipped, Home Secretary Martindale merely served up the standard comment about the BBC's autonomy; but no one could doubt, from the tone of his remarks, that *Believe It or Not* was detested on the Government front bench.

No sooner had the compère, Roy Winter, made his solemn, long-nosed appearance on the screen than the nation was emotionally sliced right down the middle.

"Greetings, fellow slaves. This week we expose another terrorist plot against the Master Race. A filthy Zionist intrigue was hatched right here in the Beeb by the late Mad Maurice Coon, Head of Current Buns, and Denis the Menace Laslett, now having an affair in Tel Aviv with ninety-six-year-old Golda My Ear. The whole nasty idea was to fuddle fifty million Aryans and their Arab blood brothers into believing that Libyan safety belts were reaching Sir Stuart Gaschamber's male models via the leprechauns of Drogheda. To prove to you that Coon and Lassy would stop at nothing to poison your minds, we now show you the incriminating evidence."

Image on screen: an Arab sheikh feeling up a bunny girl in the Playboy Club.

Winter: "Sorry, slaves, Bert Hoyle must have sent us the wrong one from his family album."

On camera: a familiar *Believe It or Not* character, Sheikh Abdul Bin-Grab:

"Hilloo, Islam!"

Three seconds for laughter.

"Go on, then, call me a liar! Insult the piss-lovin' Arab pipples . . ."

Christopher Ellison fell out of his chair.

Roy Winter on screen: "And now, sheikhs, an appeal for nationwide bigotry from the leaders of the Guardians of Decency, Bishop Bonfire and Lady Meg Thumb-Screw."

Five minutes later, Winter returned to the Maurice Cohn theme: "And who did murder frail, lovely, seven-stone Marianne Irving? Who stole fifteen rolls of largely unused toilet paper from her handbag? Although this matter is now *sub judice*, which means under the carpet, we name the guilty men!"

The screen went blank. Then a caption appeared: "Do not Adjust your Minds. Normal Lies will be Resumed as soon as Parliament is Dissolved."

Sheikh Abdul Bin-Grab: "So fuck off."

As usual, the satirical content of *Believe It or Not*, which dominated the programme, was offset by a "straight" documentary episode. Ellison sat up fast when he saw that Winter had with him in the studio Marshall Durban, MP, Walter Vandyke's PPS and closest political disciple.

"Marshall Durban, I want to discuss the non-existent Internal Security Police with you. I ask you frankly, is this not the moment when a sensible, power-crazy politician like yourself beats a retreat to the men's loo?"

Brash, confident, polished, Durban leant forward towards the camera: "I believe," he said, "that the public is increasingly disturbed by the activities of the ISP. In other words, it's time the Government came clean."

"I thought you were a member of the Government," Winter said.

Durban smiled urbanely, determined not to allow Winter to rattle him. "Technically," he said, "more than a hundred

MPs are members of the administration. It's my belief that not more than a half-dozen of them know the truth about the ISP."

"And is your glamorous chief, Walter Clap Vandyke, one of the half-dozen?"

"Absolutely not."

"But I was told that Clap is Leader of the House of Cards."

"Let's get one thing clear," Durban said. "If the ISP is acting beyond the law, then Parliament, with public support, must call it to account. And those responsible."

"Frankly," said Winter, "I am outraged by your filthy insinuations. Clearly it's time you and Clap were ruined. To ruin you, we're going to show some film."

"Why is Durban sticking his neck out like this?" whispered Pru Ellison.

"It's political suicide. Walter must be getting pretty desperate."

The film on the screen showed a woman talking straight to the camera. To conceal her identity, she wore a hood. As a member of the National Council for Civil Liberties, she had been arrested in the dead of night by four Leech Squad agents, denied access to her lawyer, and held for three weeks in a rat-infested cell until she "confessed" that Zionist agents had bribed her to undermine the coming Arab Mission. A Catholic priest who had preached against Islamic brain-washing of British children told of a similar experience; he bared his back to reveal livid weals and scars. A trade unionist, who had led a delegation of workers to protest against the take-over of their firm by an Arab consortium, testified how he had been arrested at night by the ISP and strapped to a red-hot central-heating radiator until he too signed a confession that he was a Zionist agent.

End of film sequence.

"Don't tell me you swallow all this Zionist propaganda," Winter said to Durban.

"I believe these things are happening every day—and every night. And I want to know why."

"OK, Aryans, we now bring you the man himself, frail, lovely seven-stone Superintendent Stanley Leech, seen here behind his desk in ISP Control, Whitehall."

Rubicund, relaxed, benevolent, Leech smiled paternally into the camera. Although the interviewer remained off-camera, Ellison immediately recognized the voice of Denis Laslett. Evidently this film had sat in the can for several weeks until Armstrong had finally given the go-ahead.

Laslett: "Superintendent Leech, do you deny that the Internal Security Police uses torture as a method of extracting information and bogus confessions?"

Leech: "I do. I deny it absolutely. These allegations are part of a systematic campaign of hatred against British institutions by professional disrupters and saboteurs. A skilfully coordinated campaign, I might add."

Laslett: "So in your opinion these witnesses are lying?"

Florid and genial in his blue uniform, with its silver laurel-leaf lapels, its impressive ribbons of honour across the chest, Leech settled back in his chair.

Leech: "Well, young man, I don't know where you found these people, or how you found them, but I do know this: if any incident such as the ones described came to my attention, the officers responsible would be out of the ISP within the hour."

Laslett: "Superintendent, do you believe a Jew should enjoy the same rights as any other British citizen?"

Leech blinked. Then he panicked. His eyes darted round in search of an escape. This in itself made sensational television. Every second of silence was worth a dozen words. Then rage consumed his face.

Leech: "Turn the camera off! Turn it off!"

Laslett (quietly): "If you insist."

Leech: "Is it off now, is it off? Is it still running?"

Laslett: "No."

The camera was still running.

Leech: "I should never have let you filthy Jew scum in here! I warn you, you mother-fucking anarchist, I'll have your dirty, circumcized prick pickled in vinegar!"

CUT.

Roy Winter on-screen: "Believe it or not, slaves. By the way, you may wonder who made that film, and you may wonder how Vinegar Leech and his friends set about getting him pickled. The name is Denis Laslett, editor of last week's *Deadline* film which turned out to be a fabrication. Or was it? Was it perhaps a frame-up? Put away those sawn-off shot guns, Aryans and Arabs, there's no perhaps about it. That's why frail, lovely, seven-stone Marianne Irving was battered to death: she knew too much.

"Believe it or not. Goodnight, slaves."

Ellison turned on the sitting-room lights and gently led his son up to bed. A few minutes later the front-door bell rang.

It was Magnus Massey.

Three hours earlier Magnus had parked his Aston Martin DB6 outside the loading bay of platform 8 at King's Cross. It was here that vans carrying the first editions of the Sunday papers unloaded on to the trains bound for Scotland and the North. In Denes Buffet Magnus had passed a pound note to a friendly porter; five minutes later the porter had returned with three copies of the *Sunday Star*.

"VANDYKE AIDE IN SEX AND BRIBERY SCANDAL."

Immediately beneath the banner headline was a photograph five inches high and sensational even by the *Star*'s standards. It depicted a naked Marshall Durban, MP, in bed with two beautiful girls, one of whom was offering herself on hands and knees as Durban penetrated her from behind, while the other caressed his testicles. As usual, a white panel had been pasted over the inner action zone.

According to Bert Hoyle, Durban had seduced his baby sitter, Mary Wilkinson, when he learnt that her flatmate, Sally Shields, worked as a stenographer in ISP Control. Durban had approached Sally on behalf of a group of Jewish businessmen with an offer of £10,000 for personal information about senior ISP officers which could be exploited for purposes of blackmail. Both Mary and Sally had been hypnotized by the vast sum of money involved, and when Durban had demanded, in passing, that he wanted them both in the same bed at the same time, they had decided to humour him.

Durban, Hoyle reported indignantly, had then advanced the sum of £1,000 in cash. Sally Shields had subsequently fed him with tit-bits of idle gossip and Durban had grown exasperated. So, too, had his Jewish masters. After a further £1,000 had failed to produce any sign of decadence or corruption among "the fine, dedicated, upstanding patriots who lead the ISP" (as Hoyle put it), Durban had angrily broken off relations.

The girls had then repented and taken their dreadful story to the *Star*.

But how, exactly, they managed to bring a clear-image photograph of Durban in bed with them both, Hoyle didn't specify.

Magnus drove straight to the Durbans' flat in Victoria. It was 9.15 when he rang the bell. Polly Durban, a cheerful, lively girl whom he'd met twice before, opened the door.

"Is Marshall at home, Polly?"

"Why no, he's at Television Centre. Didn't you know—he's appearing with Roy Winter on *Believe It or Not*."

"I might have guessed."

"Well come in, Magnus."

"What's Marshall going to talk about?"

"The ISP."

"It figures."

"What on earth are you talking about?"

"Polly, do you have a baby sitter?"

"Not at the moment. Like to volunteer? The last girl suddenly vanished."

"Mary Wilkinson?"

"How did you know?"

"How did you find her in the first place?"

"From a friend, I think. No, I'm a liar: from an agency."

"Called?"

"Gosh . . . it was a short name, one word . . ."

"Did the name begin with R?"

"Relief! That's it, Relief."

"Did they send you a brochure?"

"Yes, quite a lavish job. I remember it came by post a couple of days after poor Angela was knocked down by a car."

"Angela was your previous baby sitter?"

"She was riding her bicycle down Great Portland Street when she was hit from behind. She's still in plaster from head to toe . . . they say she may never be able to walk again."

"Did the car stop?"

"Did it hell! The bastard."

"I suppose Angela never saw it?"

"A pedestrian did. He stopped to help poor Angela. It was a black Mercedes 450 SEL."

"Polly, I'm going to give you some advice. You may have a crowd of journalists ringing your bell tonight and——"

"Of course we shall. Marshall's going to be quite a sensation on the box, I can assure you."

"No, Polly, there's something else, something . . . not so good. If you're sensible, you won't answer the door or the phone. And you'll call your husband and advise him to stay away from here for a couple of days."

"My dear Magnus, you must be mad! Publicity is the food of life to Marshall."

Magnus hesitated, sighed and extracted a copy of the *Sunday Star* from the pocket of his leather jacket.

"Don't believe a word of it," he said.

Polly Durban stared at the front-page photograph.

"That's . . . that's . . . I mean . . ." Numbed with shock she turned slowly to Magnus. But Magnus had gone.

He drove straight to the BBC Television Centre at Wood Lane. A dozen other reporters were on hand, clamouring to interview Durban, only five minutes before the show went on the air. Magnus stayed to watch the show in the reception hall, then drove to Chester Place.

"That stupid, fucking, arrogant twit!" exploded Ellison. "Do you know what he said to me at the Commons when I made a comment about everyone sleeping in the right bed? 'That's an outrageous remark!' he said. 'I demand that you withdraw it.' "

"Bad blow for Walter Vandyke."

"Yes . . . I see Hoyle makes that point very neatly: 'Marshall Durban's beliefs, like his style, are closely modelled on those of his blue-eyed hero, Walter Vandyke, Leader of the Commons.' "

"The call girls, by the way, came from Relief. I spoke to Polly. It seems that a Spectrum Mercedes deliberately put in a hit-and-run on their regular baby sitter."

Ellison's eyes were like stones. "You know something, Massive? Somewhere, behind all this, is a very clever man. And I mean to find him."

Nine

Joe O'Neill took the lift to the sixth floor of 59 Haymarket. In the Central Register of Charities he found half a dozen girls working in an office filled with steel racks carrying folders bound in dark red webbing. He plucked out the relevant folder and looked up the registration number of the Foundation for the Study of Comparative Religions. As a basis for comparison he also noted the number of the Hopetoun Foundation Trust Fund. He filled in a blue form and handed it to one of the girls; within a few minutes she brought him both files and a nice, if brief, smile.

The financial operations of Hopetoun Foundation Trust Fund, whose governing instrument was a trust deed under the will of the First Viscount Hopetoun, were set out with exemplary clarity:

Cash receipts under the Fund		£661,600
Income Tax Refunded (Schedule A) ...		£393,543
Interest on Loans Less Income		
Tax (Schedule E)...........................		£179,617
	Total	£1,234,760
Payments:		
Grants for benevolent and		
research purposes (Schedule B)		£985,805
Research awards and other grants		
(Schedule C)..................................		£85,289
Administration Expenses (salaries		
of staff, advisory fees, etc.)		£51,821
	Total	£1,122,915

The Hopetoun returns, furthermore, itemized in scrupulous detail who received the grants, and the amount allocated to each project.

O'Neill opened the FSCR file.

The FSCR's application in 1975 for registration as a charity under the Act of 1960 listed no permanent endowment whatever. The Foundation's balance-sheet was sketchily itemized on the Charity Commissioners' Standard Form of Account, a fact which assumed added significance when Joe compared the FSCR's stated income with that of the Hopetoun Foundation Trust Fund:

Hopetoun: approx £1.25 million

FSCR: approx £13.75 million

Yet, by British standards, the Hopetoun was a giant. Indeed the average income of British grant-making trusts was a mere £20,000 per annum.

If the FSCR had no permanent endowment, where the hell was it getting £13.75 million a year? The Standard Form neither asked this question nor received an answer. But it did ask the nature of the benefits for which grants were made, and the number of recipients. The latter question had been completely ignored.

Joe asked to speak to the Supervisor.

She was most helpful. The Charity Commissioners, as she explained, were more interested in a trust's expenditure than in its sources of income.

"But they haven't attempted to itemize their expenditure," he protested.

"That, too, is largely a matter for the discretion of the Commissioners. As long as they consider that the trust is being properly run——"

"And would the names of the trustees affect their judgment of that?"

She smiled. "Well, I suppose it might."

"Thanks."

Bearded and triumphant, O'Neill burst into Ellison's office and banged his notes on the desk.

"Guess who the trustees of the FSCR are!"

Again Ellison felt the almost irresistible itch to tease Joe. With difficulty he suppressed the impulse. Magnus was right: it was time he made Joe feel good.

"Is this a big story you're bringing me, Joe?"

"Lynedoch, Ozanne, Lucas and Strachan. That sounds big to me!"

Ellison whistled. "Top officials in the Foreign Office, the Home Office and the BBC are running this racket on Arabair's money! Jesus! No wonder Swinburne's £150,000 country mansion sees a lot of visitors at night!" He plucked the *BBC Handbook* off his shelves. "The Beeb's entire range of educational broadcasting currently costs some £7 million a year. That pays for over 3,100 broadcasts to schools on radio and television, plus about half that number of adult education programmes. Where does the money come from?"

"Licence fees."

"How has the Beeb maintained a constant level of output at a constant level of expenditure over a period when costs have escalated by fifty per cent? Shall I tell you how? By buying pre-packaged material on the cheap. But it isn't cheap material, it's lavish, all this pan-Islamic stuff. So?"

"So it's subsidized."

"Correct. According to your notes the FSCR admits to having spent £13.75 million on 'educational purposes' in a single year—which is almost double the Beeb's entire educational budget."

"In Companies House the Arabair accounts are prefaced by a summarized balance sheet: turnover, operating profit, taxation, net profit. But there is no reference to charitable contributions."

"They're fudging their accounts."

"Inland Revenue would know."

"They should know. They can authorize tax refunds to a charity only on the basis of itemized sources of revenue."

Joe seized the phone and called the Information Service of Inland Revenue at Somerset House.

"How do I get to examine the tax returns of a specific charity and three specific businesses?"

"Are you an accredited official of these organizations?"

"I'm a journalist."

"In that case, sir, you don't."

"But that's ridiculous! The public has a right to know!"

"All tax returns are strictly confidential, sir."

Joe banged down the phone. "This bloody country!"

"If you want information handed to you on a plate," Ellison said, "go and work in the United States. You could pick up this phone now, dial the White House, describe yourself as Mr Ali Baba of Main Street, and demand a statement of the President's personal assets. Within seconds a computer with a voice like Marilyn Monroe would have told you the answer. Joe, go and find something about the *Star* I don't know."

"What's the *Star* got to do with the FSCR?"

"That's what I want you to find out. Oh . . . Joe."

"Yes, boss?"

"That was nice work." Joe O'Neill beamed. "Tell Cherry to give you a chocolate biscuit."

Sitting in Patrick's New Bond Street unisex hairdressing salon, Magnus Massey waited impatiently for his £11 wash, trim and blow—the last relic of his unregenerate past. He discarded *Playboy* and picked up *Penthouse*. He discarded *Penthouse* and picked up *Dildo*. Here the porn ran harder. Being sentimental, he personally liked it soft.

He turned the page.

What held his interest in this particular photograph? It was a full-page, salacious view of three naked girls and their pussies. They were spreadeagled across the wing of a DC-10, the visible portion of whose fuselage showed the lettering, ARABA . . . Magnus recognized the three girls. They were the same models who had featured, fully clothed in salmon-pink uniforms, in the advertisement he had seen on the wall of Nashat Al-Khatib's office.

To Magnus's expert eye, the internal evidence was clear: the two photographs had been taken using the same plane on the same day, but not by the same photographer.

On leaving Patrick's, washed, trimmed and blown, he made a few phone calls. After two misses he scored a hit: the Thomas Parnell Agency handled the Arabair account. Fortunately, Adrian Drysdale, executive director of Thomas Parnell, was someone for whom Magnus had done occasional contract work in the past.

"How about lunch today?" Magnus suggested.

"I'd have to break an engagement."

"Fine. I'll book a table at the Victor Hugo for 12.30."

Drysdale arrived at 12.40. Magnus waved towards the other chair.

"The Arabair account is quite a fat one, I suppose?"

Drysdale shot his stiff cuffs, lit a cigarette with a gold-plated lighter and said, "What's it to you, Massive? Looking for work?"

"What will you drink?"

"Dry Martini."

"That was a pretty ad you did for Arabair—three pink hostesses checking cargo for a DC-10 with a forklift truck in the background hoisting a crate into the plane's vagina."

Drysdale laughed. "We didn't want the girls; freight planes don't carry 'em. But Nashat Al-Khatib insisted."

"So you cut a corner off your code and complied? Arabair were giving you the maximum 17.5 per cent discount on the media space you bought—and there was going to be a lot of space. Right?"

"You used to be so nice, Massive, when you were ignorant."

"Who was your photographer?"

"Ed Pollock."

"You supplied the models, of course?"

"Naturally. What *is* this?"

Magnus placed the copy of *Dildo*, open at the relevant page, across Drysdale's knife and fork. The advertising executive stared at it for several seconds.

"Shit. But this is outrageous!"

"Same models. Everyone in the business will assume you're pushing this porn as a form of down-market advertising."

"And we paid for the girls' time!" Drysdale motioned to the balding French waiter. "Where's your phone here?"

"Hold it, Adrian. Don't phone Nashat Al-Khatib—not yet. This thing's got other aspects. Phone the models and ask them who took the pictures. Clearly it wasn't Ed Pollock. Someone got to those girls with fistfuls of green paper."

Drysdale nodded sourly and disappeared into the phone cubicle. When he returned to the table five minutes later he looked grim.

"I got through to two of the bitches. They both swear they don't know the photographer's name. They describe him as a short, runty fellow with a bent back, a nasty leer and a Cockney accent."

"What did he pay?"

"One hundred to each of them, *sur le champ*."

"Then he was subsidized. When's your next appointment?"

"2.15."

"Let's skip the lunch."

Magnus placated the hurt feelings of the manager with a £5 note for the food they hadn't eaten. "Your hospitality is prodigious," Drysdale remarked as Magnus hustled him into a taxi. In Dean Street, Soho, Magnus led the way up a linoleum-covered staircase which reeked of cigarette butts into a small, seedy office also reeking of cigarette butts.

"Mr Silvers?"

"So what?"

The editor of *Dildo* was critically overweight and wheezed instead of breathing. He didn't look pleased to see them; he didn't look as if he wanted to see anyone, ever.

Magnus showed him the photo. "Who took it, Mr Silvers?"

"That's my business. I have no idea who took it."

"At the time that picture was taken," Drysdale said, "those models were on contract to my agency. We were paying them."

"Prove it in court, mister."

Silvers knew perfectly well that no reputable agency would risk publicity of that sort.

"Just give us the name of the photographer and you're out of it," Magnus said.

Silvers sighed and gestured towards the piles of photographs and proofs overflowing his ash-covered desk.

"Gentlemen, I want no trouble. It's killing me keeping all this filth afloat, believe me. People threaten me round the clock. The printer threatens me, the Guardians of Decency threaten me, my wife threatens me, my son is a junkie though I brought him up right. A lot of reputable photographers bring their stuff here: I give away their names, I go out of business."

"There's another way you can go out of business," Drysdale said. "This issue of *Dildo* carries full-page ads by Yoshiba cars, Simmel's watches and Brinley's men's wear. We handle all those accounts."

Silvers sighed again, wheezed, heaved himself in a torment of quivering flesh from his chair, and twiddled the combination of a small steel safe. He extracted a cheap, cardboard-bound ledger, licked his finger, and flipped the grease-stained pages. Then he pointed to a name and address. Magnus also noted down the phone number.

"Say nothing," he warned.

"You do have to be joking, mister," Silvers wheezed. "If Micky Kolarcz ever found out Solly Silvers had shopped his name, keeek . . ." He gestured expressively at the folds of his neck.

"Tough character?"

"He has friends. Go careful, mister."

Joe O'Neill was deep into the *Newspaper Press Directory*, the *Directory of Directors*, the *Business Who's Who*, *Who's Who in Finance*, and the *Company Directory*. The more he pondered the board of directors of Allied Newspapers, proprietors of the

Star, the more convinced he became that Professor Hugh Swinburne's Foundation for the Study of Comparative Religions was exercising a controlling influence. The three youngest directors who had recently been appointed to the Board had no visible experience of newspaper publishing, but all three had graduated from Oxford with Honours Degrees in Comparative Religions—Swinburne's subject. No less suggestive was the sudden appearance on Allied's publications list of a number of specialist magazines with titles like the *Ecumenical*, *Islam Quarterly*, *Arab Arts Review*, and *Koran Studies*.

O'Neill's training as a chartered accountant led him to ponder something else which nine journalists out of ten would have passed over. The *Star*'s circulation was given as 2,435,618. The stated advertising rate per column centimetre was £14.50. That figured. What didn't figure was how a tabloid could demand £9,350 for a full-page advertisement —about 180 per cent of the normal going rate.

Flipping through back numbers of the *Star*, he studied the full-page ads with mounting understanding. The majority of them were non-commercial. How could the Guardians of Decency afford to spend £9,350 a week reiterating its ten-point programme to cleanse the nation? Either the Guardians were massively underwritten or the *Star* was offering them a privileged page-rate. Another weekly full-page feature was a list of Islamic events currently available to the public in museums, mosques, galleries and cinemas—and on the BBC. At the foot of the page a single word appeared: "Advertisement".

Joe O'Neill seized the phone, rang the *Star*, and asked for the Advertising Department.

"Yes, can I help you?" a girl said.

"Is it too late to make a change in next week's Islamic events ad?" he asked.

"Oh. Wait a minute please . . . Are you ringing from the Foundation, then?"

"Yes."

"I'll just find Mr Tracy. He handles the FSCR account. Hold on, then . . ."

O'Neill banged down the phone and somersaulted into Ellison's office. Ellison listened, absorbed.

"The FSCR floods the Beeb with Islamic propaganda," Joe was saying. "It controls the *Star*'s anti-semitic campaign through Allied Newspapers. It also subsidizes the Guardians and the Islamic blitzkrieg. And who's masterminding the whole thing? Professor Hugh Swinburne. Go and see him, Bill, confront him."

"No."

"Want me to?"

"He'd merely be interviewing *you*."

Joe O'Neill stormed up to the Old King Lud in Ludgate Circus and ordered a double whisky. An hour later his Allegro fizzed on to the M40. By-passing High Wycombe and scaling the Chilterns, he touched 90 mph, consuming adrenalin faster than petrol. He crossed Magdalen Bridge a mere seventy-five minutes after leaving Gowers House.

He parked in St Aldate's and walked through the main gate of Christ Church, averting his head as he passed the porter's lodge. Circling Tom Quad anti-clockwise, he checked the name plates at the foot of each staircase, then marched into Peckwater quadrangle. Though tempted to drive straight to the Foundation's headquarters in Norham Road, he had decided that Swinburne was more likely to have lunch in college.

Eventually he found the professor's name at the bottom of a staircase in Peckwater.

He hesitated. Why hesitate?

An undergraduate in a commoner's gown glanced at him with faint contempt, then ran up the wooden staircase.

A door slammed.

O'Neill climbed to the second floor and knocked on Swinburne's door. A short bark came in answer. He opened the door. At the far end of a large, elegantly furnished study, a round, pink, Father Christmas of a man in a Harris tweed suit was staring at him from behind a desk.

"Professor Swinburne?"

"Well?"

"Could you spare me half an hour?"

"No. What's your business?"

"My name's Joe O'Neill. I'm a reporter."

"Where are you from? The *Oxford Mail*?"

"The *Sunday Monitor*."

"Well, why the hell didn't you phone my secretary and make an appointment? I've got a tutorial in ten minutes' time."

"Maybe I could call back."

Swinburne rose from behind his desk and strutted to the fireplace, with his thumbs tucked into his waistcoat pockets. He lit a pipe.

"What did you want to know?"

"Principally, about the FSCR."

"Then look it up in the *Directory of Grant-Making Trusts*."

"I'm puzzled where £13.75 million a year comes from. And how £13.75 million a year is spent."

"Hm. Anything else?"

"I see that three of your former pupils are now directors of Allied Newspapers. Do you deny that your Foundation pays for the weekly full-page ads the Guardians of Decency take in the *Star*, and for the weekly announcements of Islamic events? Would you confirm that the Foundation is financing educational films and then selling them at below cost to the BBC? There's also one further question."

"I'm listening."

"How did it come about that Marianne Irving, who had previously worked for you, was recommended to Maurice Cohn by Ulf Steinberg? Who is the 'highest authority' who masterminded that operation?"

Swinburne chuckled serenely, shrouding himself in aromatic tobacco smoke.

"How long have you been a reporter?"

"Well . . ." O'Neill flushed, painfully aware that he had delivered a prosecutor's impassioned oration and fallen into the trap predicted by Ellison.

"Who's your immediate superior at the *Monitor*?"

"Bill Ellison."

"I suppose he might have had the courtesy to consult me personally. I'm not a desk sergeant in a police station."

Criticism of his boss tended to rob Joe O'Neill of his judgment.

"Actually, I came here off my own bat."

"Ah. AWOL. I've got an hour free before dinner this evening. You'll find me at the Foundation in Norham Road. Six o'clock?"

"Thank you, sir."

There was a knock at the door. An undergraduate poked his head inside. O'Neill descended the staircase and walked through Tom Quad into St Aldate's. Passing the main post office he hesitated; he knew he ought to put a call through to the *Monitor*, but he didn't relish the prospect. If Ellison took the call there would be hell to pay. In for a penny, in for a pound.

He parked the Allegro in Norham Road at 5.55. Finding the front door of the modest, red brick house open, he rang the bell and walked into the hallway. The walls were hung with paintings, drawings and photographs of all the world's principal deities, prophets, and messiahs. A middle-aged woman emerged from an office and confronted him coolly.

"Can I help you?"

"I have an appointment with Professor Swinburne. My name's O'Neill."

"Ah, yes. Professor Swinburne sends his apologies. He misread his diary. Would you like to meet him here at 9.30 tomorrow morning?"

"Thanks," O'Neill sighed wearily.

As he climbed into the Allegro he was in two minds whether to drive back to London for the night or to find a hotel in Oxford. With petrol at £1.15 a gallon he wasn't going to save money either way. He decided to look for a hotel.

As soon as he pushed the gear lever into first and let out

the clutch, the Allegro began to shudder and hobble. A flat tyre was all he needed to complete a wonderful day. He walked to the rear of the car and bent down to examine his rear offside tyre.

Three men got out of the black Mercedes 450 SEL which had glided in behind him.

Ten

The House of Commons is served by four bars: the Smoking
Room (MPs only); the Strangers' Bar (which outsiders can
enter at the invitation of an MP); Annie's (where MPs and
journalists meet on equal terms); and the Press bar (which
MPs enter only at the invitation of an accredited journalist).
Ellison liked Annie's. But Walter Vandyke, as usual, preferred
the Strangers'.

Vandyke had brought Durban along—a haggard, deflated
Marshall Durban.

"You warned us," Vandyke said quickly, as if to close the
subject. "However, I want you to know that Marshall stays
on as my PPS. I'm determined to save his career even if I
can't save his marriage."

"Polly took it badly then?"

Durban nodded, eyes downcast.

"What's the Murdoch line?" Ellison asked Vandyke.

"I was called in to the Inner Cabinet last night and
roasted. Naturally I counter-attacked. I asked them to come
clean about Operation Talent."

"What is it?"

"In strictest confidence, Bill: I have been approached by a
senior officer in the Ministry of Defence. This man claims to
have knowledge of a top-secret document which is nothing
short of a blue-print for a future state of emergency. Very
nasty, too. That's all I know."

"You didn't see the document?"

"No. Impossible, apparently."

"Who was the officer?"

"Sorry, Bill. He risked . . . a good deal in approaching me at all."

"What did Murdoch and Martindale say when you mentioned Operation Talent?"

"They predictably disclaimed all knowledge of it. They then demanded to know who had leaked it to me—Burnett, the Parliamentary Under Secretary for the Army, seemed particularly interested in that aspect."

"So you bluffed?"

"I said rumours were flying about the corridors and lobbies. Murdoch then threw a left hook: if I found myself out of sympathy with Government policy, I could always resign. Naturally I didn't fall for it. I reminded him that the Cabinet was no longer making policy and that I had a right to know what policy was. We reached stalemate."

Durban raised his heavy head and sunken eyes. "Bill, you were right and I was a damned fool. I want you to investigate those people who framed me."

Bill Ellison smiled.

It was the second time in three days that Magnus Massey had grown a tail.

Magnus's gift for spotting and throwing off shadowers was second to none. When it suited him he would turn north to the M1, or west to the M4, cruising along the motorway gently until he reached an exit feed-off. He would then draw on to the soft shoulder and wait, leaving the Spectrum Mercedes with no alternative but to draw in behind him. Magnus had picked up his stop-start technique from professional sprint cycling. From a standing start the £15,000 Aston Martin, with its V8 engine fitted with four overhead camshafts, could reach 60 mph in 6.2 seconds, compared to the 9.1 seconds required by the 4.5 litre Mercedes. At top speed the Aston Martin's 150 mph gave it a 19 mph advantage.

He picked up his shadow in the driving mirror as soon as he turned off Carmelite Street on to the Embankment. Changing course, he struck north-west towards the Edgware Road, turning right into Frampton Street, and right again into Penfold Street, with the Mercedes glued to his tail.

At the junction of Penfold and Church Street the traffic crossing his path enjoyed precedence. He waited until a heavy container truck coming from his right was within twenty yards of the junction, then released his clutch fast. The truck screamed on its klaxon as it missed him by inches. By the time the Mercedes had forced its way across Church Street, Magnus already held a seventy-yard lead and was turning into his target, an M & L garage, one of the very few in London whose entrance and exit are sited on different streets. As the Mercedes drew level with the Frampton Street entrance barrier, Magnus had already paid his 20p to the drowsy Pakistani cashier and the exit gate was rising to release him into Salisbury Street. He executed two quick turns, hit 50 mph before reaching Lisson Grove—and was clear.

Twenty minutes later the Aston Martin DB6 passed Tower Hill and Tower Hamlets and headed towards Limehouse. In the bad old days the editors of glossy magazines had despatched him in a chauffeured Rolls to photograph Claire Boothroyd and Kicky Rapp, those fragile giraffes, against a little earthy East End "colour": gnarled and stunted ex-dockers selling whelks and eels from barrows; cloth-capped, workless men gazing into an empty future outside the pubs of the Commercial and West India Dock Roads. And street urchins; the editors were very fond of dirty street urchins.

According to the address reluctantly surrendered by the porn merchant Silvers, Micky Kolarcz lived in Narrow Street, which runs beside the north bank of the Thames from the Grand Union Canal to the point where the river bends south into Limehouse Reach towards the West India Docks. Magnus approached from Commercial Road, turning right at the Christopher Wren parish church of St Anne into Three Colt Street.

The number he wanted was one of a row of former ware-house buildings recently converted into smart pads by people with money. On the Narrow Street side the red brick of the houses had been sooted brown but at the rear, over-hanging the river, were modern balconies and huge studio windows.

He spent half an hour exploring the road system.

The following day a small Bedford truck arrived in Narrow Street at 7 am and pulled off into a short cul-de-sac called Ropemakers' Fields, directly opposite the row of houses numbering from 78 to 94. It was a protected spot: virtually no cars would pass down Ropemakers' Fields, for nothing lay beyond it except the Black Horse pub and a patch of open ground surrounded by iron railings.

A tall, strapping fellow with blond hair got out of the truck, placed red and white warning cones around the triangle, then unloaded a 2.0 KVA generator, a heavy-duty driller, and a rammer. These articles he had acquired from a hire shop for £9.60, £7.20 and £10.50 respectively. The cones could be hired only by the week, at 40p each. A pick and spade also lay in the back of the truck.

He went about his work slowly, in no hurry to wake the neighbourhood with his drill, and pausing often to admire the residents' cars parked in the lay-by immediately in front of the houses.

The bit of his driller had been wrecking the road surface for twenty minutes when a girl came out of the door he was watching and double-locked it with a mortice key. She was instantly recognizable as one of the three models in the Arabair advertisement displayed in Nashat Al-Khatib's office. No wonder Drysdale had been able to trace only two of the models—Kolarcz had swallowed the other. She threw a brief, somewhat sullen glance at the road-driller then drove away in a two-seater Datsun 260Z.

The line of parked cars opposite him was thinning out now as the residents headed into town. He had long since laid his bet on a Ford Mustang Mach 1 with a left-hand drive.

Children were tumbling out of the council flats on their way to school. A few of the bolder ones tossed him disparaging remarks. Maybe the hole he had made in the road didn't look all that convincing; he wondered when he would strike a gas or water main.

Micky Kolarcz emerged at 10.15, a short, bent, stunted figure in a long leather coat, humping some pretty camera equipment which he loaded into the back of the Mustang. The car drowned the noise of the drill as it roared away up Narrow Street, towards the City.

By noon a weary Massey had filled in his hole and rammed it into amateurish order. He was thirsty now and the Black Horse beckoned, but he wanted out. By 12.20 the Bedford truck had departed.

At 8.15 the following morning Kolarcz's pretty model girl emerged from the house in Narrow Street and locked the front door. As she drove away in her Datsun a red Mini Cooper with smoke-glass windows hustled out of Ropemakers' Fields in pursuit. The two small cars crossed the Grand Union Canal nose to tail, followed Narrow Street into a sharp right then a sharp left, and began to gather speed along a straight stretch devoid of houses and fenced in on both sides by corrugated iron sheets.

A deserted stretch of road. By this time the Mini was hooting angrily and flashing its headlights as it tried to overtake the Datsun with only a few inches to spare. Fearing an impending collision, the girl in the Datsun slammed on her brakes, swerved, spun right round, and came to rest against the iron sheeting. Her small black handbag had hurtled off the front passenger seat, spewing its contents on to the floor. Shaken but unhurt, Kolarcz's mistress sat pale and dazed behind her wheel, too stunned to notice the Aston Martin DB6 which now glided in behind her.

The driver of the Mini Cooper, a very lovely young woman with auburn hair and blazing eyes, had pulled open the door of the Datsun and was shouting furiously.

"What's the matter with you? Don't you know how to drive? Look what you've done to my car! I suppose you think you own the whole bloody road or something!"

"But it was you who——"

"I've got a good mind to give you the belting you deserve. This isn't stock-car racing, you know . . ."

And so it went on. Kolarcz's girl sat shaking, her eyes riveted on her manic protagonist whose unreasoning fury constantly threatened to break into physical violence.

Quietly, unnoticed, Magnus's long arm had slipped through the open nearside window of the Datsun and grasped a bunch of keys lying on the floor beside her small black handbag.

Ten seconds later the keys were back where he had found them.

"So what's the trouble?" he said soothingly.

Both girls turned towards him and began to speak at once.

"Neither of your cars is damaged so why don't you both forget it."

The young woman with auburn hair stalked angrily back to her Mini Cooper, snarled her engine, and roared away towards the Highway.

He smiled gently. "You OK?"

Almost in tears, the girl in the Datsun nodded and slowly began to retrieve the contents of her bag from the floor. Her house keys felt slightly sticky, as if they had been pressed into wax, but she was much too shaken to give it a second thought.

Half an hour later Judy Rossiter drove cautiously up Narrow Street. Magnus's main fear had been that Kolarcz's mistress would creep back home and sedate herself. But there was no sign of the Datsun.

In Cairn & Bayliss, master locksmiths of Brewer Street, Magnus Massey was always a welcome visitor. Old Bayliss glanced up from his cutting machine.

"And what can we do for you, sir?"

Magnus gestured and Bayliss led the way into the back

room where he opened the flat tobacco tin that Magnus drew from his pocket and examined the two indentations in the wax.

"I'm in a hurry," Magnus said.

"Give me an hour, then."

"Another thing. I may run into a safe. I need a specialist."

Bayliss appraised him thoughtfully. "Key or combination?"

"I've no idea."

"What's the risk?"

"The place will be empty."

"And if you're surprised?"

"I'm prepared to pay over the odds. I need a man within a couple of hours."

Bayliss raised his eyebrows. "Three hundred."

"That's high."

"If this chap gets nicked, he goes back with five previous convictions."

Magnus then drove to the bank where the Searchlight slush fund account was held, drawable only on his own signature, Ellison's, or Jordan's. When he returned to the locksmith's, old Bayliss had a message for him.

"A lady rang, sir. The message is 'all clear since 10.30'."

Magnus handed over the £300, plus payment for the newly cut keys, a Chubb and an Ingersoll, then drove back to Limehouse. In the parish church of St Anne he saw a young man in the back pew, kneeling forward, apparently lost in prayer and piety. A large leather holdall protruded from under the pew. Magnus momentarily hesitated—he had expected the traditional old lag with a cloth cap and a face like creased parchment. But when he rubbed each ear in turn, the young man sat up and pulled up each sock in turn. Magnus was shocked: five convictions and the face of a cherub.

In Barleycorn Way he pulled in behind the Mini Cooper.

"I do anysink for zoo, darlink," she said, "but zeating here I no get any yunker."

He left the Aston Martin and led the young man up

Narrow Street. It was now 12.15 and there was mounting activity round the Black Horse pub. It was a risk he would have to take; there was no knowing when Kolarcz would return. And Kolarcz had friends. "Go careful, mister," Silvers had warned.

The keys turned sweetly in the front door.

"Best turn it from inside and leave it in the lock," the young man murmured. "You get a bit of warning that way."

They worked their way up the house, rapidly scanning each room in turn. The whole interior had been removed and replaced by a modernistic elevation of open-plan rooms linked by a central spiral staircase wrapped round an immense steel tube. Thousands of pounds had gone into it.

As he had expected, the studio was situated on the top floor, with a huge plate-glass window overlooking the Thames, Scandinavian furniture on tubular steel frames, and sanded floorboards polished to a high gloss. An adjoining door was locked. This had to be Kolarcz's dark room.

As soon as he had examined the lock the young fellow began to chatter—apparently it focused his concentration and maybe calmed his nerves. Out of his holdall came "fellers" (skeleton keys), a vernio gauge, a loop of 13-amp fuse wire and a jemmy carrying a wide range of interchangeable steel components.

"What you 'ave 'ere is the upright two-bolt mortice approved to British Standard BS 3621. It's a 76mm job with a 'ardened plate to resist drillin'."

As he sprang the lock the panel of wood housing it splintered. Magnus found the light switch. The walls of the dark room were lined with steel racks packed with canisters of 16mm-film, Nikon and Leica cameras, 1kw flood bulbs and infra-red equipment.

"How long will that safe take you?"

The young fellow laughed. "If that's a safe, mate, I'm a kangaroo. Your bloke ain't afraid o' burglary, 'e's runnin' scared o' flames. That's a fire protection cabinet. Look, no plates weldin' it down. At 440 kilos, the two strongest men in the world could lift it easy. I did a Chubb TDR safe recently, six-lever lock, no way. Tried oxy-acetylene and off came the outer skin. But those jobs are cast in a solid bell. Ruin any electromagnetic drill, the bits just 'eat up. Now look at this combination: five dials, right? Five is a 'ard day's night. But put your ear in and you find two of 'em are dummies, only three ratchets are operatin'. We're after a three-figure code, right?"

While he chattered he worked with an intense, almost desperate concentration. Sweat poured down his face. Fifteen minutes later the heavy door of the cabinet, with its tongue and groove closure, swung open.

"Thanks."

"Anythin' else?"

"Nothing else." He let the young man out of the house into Narrow Street, then re-locked the front door and began shifting the contents of the cabinet and the canisters of developed film from the dark room to the ground-floor hallway. Finally he left the house and walked back to Barleycorn Way.

The Mini Cooper purred to a halt in front of the house.

"Stay behind the wheel with your engine on while I load the stuff into the back seat and boot. And if I say go, go."

"Yes, cap'n."

He had almost finished the job when an E-type Jaguar parked in front of the Mini. The driver observed them with curiosity, then went into the adjoining house. The two journalists offered a short prayer of thanks for the lack of neighbourly feeling among the middle classes.

Magnus nodded. "Take it away."

The Mini vanished towards the Highway. It was only 1.30.

He didn't trust everyone in the *Monitor*'s dark room and preferred to work in his own. He worked round the clock, with only a four-hour break for sleep, transferring un-developed film from the spools to casettes, immersing them in developing fluid, draining out the developer and pouring in stop and fixer solution, washing and hanging the negatives in his drying cabinet, then cutting them to make contact sheets. He printed two copies of each picture on to Ilfospeed paper. But most of Kolarcz's negatives had already been developed, and many of them printed. Where necessary, Magnus made extra prints.

The written material in Kolarcz's files, of which there was a fair amount, also had to be photocopied. Avoiding the *Monitor*'s Xerox machines and the agencies, for reasons of security, he purchased two hundred 5p pieces from his bank and took the documents to his public library where he hammered away for several hours, smilingly making way for readers who wished to defraud authors by copying portions of their books.

Ellison studied the Kolarcz files behind the locked door of an office which his Fenchurch Street bank manager always made available to him on request. The two men had shared a room and certain ideals at Oxford.

Later the same day he shook off his Spectrum cover and made his way to Bonham Terrace.

"Hullo, stranger," Judy murmured, kissing him tenderly on the mouth.

"Take your hands off my father," Magnus said, observing this from a sofa.

"OK, Massey, just leave my niece in the condition in which you found her. Where's the brandy? Don't you know how to receive a man with a house and car?" He poked Magnus in the ribs and sat down beside him. "So how did a dumb-head like you figure out that this Kolarcz creature was Relief's photographer in residence?"

"I was having my hair cut."

"Well, I don't like long explanations. I notice this worm runs four bank accounts, two of them illegal, in New York and Zurich, with total assets in excess of £60,000."

"Mm," Judy said, wide-eyed. "It would take you all of two years to earn that."

He glowered at her. She was so utterly, irresistibly lovely. He ached to possess her; for a moment the sight of Massey's long legs sprawling out of the sofa and halfway across the room was quite intolerable.

"What surprised me," Magnus was saying, "was that collection of photographs taken at 18 Phillimore Avenue on 16mm film. I half expected the good guys, the Moyars, Durbans and Gottliebs and all the other democrats who went down the proverbial vagina, but that rogue's gallery of anti-semites and fascists is quite something: Hoyle, Leech, Lucas, Swinburne, six MPs, two generals, four bankers, a brace of Arab businessmen . . ."

"Blackmail," Ellison said. "Just in case they step out of line. By a process of elimination we can infer who's big."

"We can hardly assume all the others have used the girls," said Judy.

"Agreed. But we now have added confirmation that Leech, Lucas and Swinburne aren't at the top. Magnus, it's time we had a chat with Kolarcz."

"I've had one. I was afraid he might panic, so I promised to return all his negatives and prints within forty-eight hours, to sustain his cover."

"Was he frightened?"

"Terrified."

"Can I make a suggestion?" Judy said.

"No," Ellison said. "What is it?"

"We've opened the door into Relief. But we still need to know who calls the tune. So we'd better walk through the door."

"How?"

"Take Kolarcz by the scruff of the neck and threaten him that unless he plays ball the *Monitor* will publish all his muck with a covering article claiming he sold it to us for £25,000. That would be his death sentence."

"And what does playing ball mean?" Magnus asked.

"Now wait a minute," Ellison said. "Don't be offended if I remind you, Judy, that the *Monitor* is not the *Star*. And I'm not in the blackmail business either."

Judy blushed. "You can bluff."

"But what does playing ball *mean*?" Magnus persisted.

"It means me."

Ellison rose from his chair and walked slowly to the other end of the room. "No," he said. "No."

"But I don't mind, Bill!"

"Maybe you ought to mind," he muttered, looking away from her.

"How do you think I got the Gottlieb story?" she said angrily. "And the Irving files, too."

"Yes, Judy, sure," said Magnus gently, "but Gottlieb's a nice guy, I mean . . ."

"Either you want to get this story or you don't!"

"Listen, Judy," Ellison said, "even if we leave feelings out of it, the fact remains they have now sighted you twice: in the Aldwych, and outside 18 Phillimore Avenue—with Irving's description of you confirming their identikit. You wouldn't come out alive."

"The girl they sighted isn't the one they'll see."

Ellison turned to Massey. "Magnus, support me."

"I support you. These people are killers, Judy."

"And you're a couple of wets!"

Eleven

Despite a second attempt to persuade Walter Vandyke to divulge the name of the senior army officer who had confided to him the existence of Operation Talent, the Leader of the Commons was adamant: he couldn't jeopardize a brave man's life.

Ellison asked Cherry to compile a list of the private addresses—where they could be traced—of twenty-five senior officers currently working in the Ministry of Defence. He then sent each a brief letter requesting an interview, off the record, on "general questions of policy". The following day Ramsay Jordan received a stinging reprimand from Giles Burnett, MP, Parliamentary Under Secretary for the Army. Jordan was reminded in swingeing terms that interviews on matters of policy were the prerogative of the civilian authorities, namely Burnett himself and his immediate superior, the Secretary of State for Defence. This call was immediately followed by one from the Secretary of the D-Notice Committee, a voluntary body set up by the newspaper industry to protect itself against prosecution. Jordan was warned that the publication of any unauthorized interview with any officer would incur prosecution under Section 2 of the Official Secrets Act.

"Kind of you to remind me," Jordan said. He put down the phone and turned to Ellison. "Next move?"

"We wait."

"For blustering abuse? This letter has just arrived—take a look." He handed Ellison an envelope.

Ellison extracted a sheet of crested War Office notepaper from the envelope.

The Editor,
Sunday Monitor.

Sir,

I am writing to inform you that I consider the note I received today from your correspondent, Ellison, nothing short of a damned impertinence. An Editor of your experience should know that this Country has benefited from civilian rule since the time of Oliver Cromwell. Unlike certain American generals whose combat service is restricted to "leaking" to journalists, I have never confused a soldier with a gossip. If your man Ellison were a member of White's, where I lunch daily, I would take the opportunity of giving him my version of a raspberry.

I have the honour to be, Sir, your obedient servant,
John Winstanley, KBE, DSO, MC
Lieutenant-General

Ellison flicked his lighter, held the letter to the flame, and dropped the ashes in to Jordan's waste-bin.

"I didn't imagine you'd react that strongly, Bill."

"Ramsay, you're slowing up."

A quick check in *Who's Who* informed him that Winstanley had served as a subaltern in the Normandy landings, taken part in the defence of Hill 60 in Korea, and subsequently served as company and battalion commander in Cyprus and Nigeria. After commanding a brigade in Aden he had returned to the Army Staff College at Camberley. Following a stint in Ulster, he had been appointed Director of the Military Assistance Office of the Chief of the General Staff's Office at the Ministry of Defence.

It was now 1.30. He took the lift to the executive car-park.

"Find me some dense traffic, Charlie. Head in the general direction of St James's."

"Will do, sir."

The taxi to which he rapidly transferred in the Strand reached White's Club at 1.55. The shadowing Mercedes had fought its way through a tight U-turn but the taxi had a start and a £5 note had done the rest.

Ellison approached the club's porter. "Kindly give this note to General Winstanley, would you?"

The porter returned a few minutes later. "The General asks you to come through to the smoking-room, sir."

Winstanley was sitting alone with a newspaper in the quietest corner of the room. He was wearing a regimental tie beneath his stiffly starched white collar.

"Sit down, then," he gruffed, examining Ellison with two beady eyes. "Too young for the war, were you?"

"Bad timing."

"National Service?"

"I seem to recall."

"Regiment?"

"Royal West Kent, seconded to the Parachute Regiment."

The General's bushy white eyebrows lifted, creasing the red tan of his forehead.

"Paras, eh? Ever heard a shot fired in anger?"

"It was quite noisy in Malaya."

"Then you ought to know better!" Winstanley snapped, raising his voice several decibels. "Putty-fingered muck-raker! Thought I'd tell you, face to face."

With that the General rose majestically to his feet, jerked back his shoulders, flattened his stomach, and marched briskly out of the smoking-room.

Ellison pocketed the crumpled sheet of paper which had landed in his lap, counted to twenty, then left the Club and hailed a taxi.

He unfolded the note:

"Sunday next, 2 pm. Use hired car. From Abergavenny take A465 to Llanvihangel Crucorney; B4423 to Capel-y-ffin; then bear left along metalled track following tributary of the Afon Honddu, passing ruined monastery and wooden shrine with inscription, Peace to the Wayfarer through the

Blood of Jesus. Cottage is up mountain track from white metal gate with black hinges. Commit this to memory and destroy. On no account keep rendez-vous if followed."

The chances were a hundred to one against that his meeting with Winstanley in White's would go unobserved in certain quarters. And it didn't. As evidence of this a dramatic change took place in the landscape surrounding Chester Place.

The Spectrum Mercedes 450 SEL disappeared.

It was replaced by a blue Triumph 2500 Mk 2 of the Internal Security Police.

This was the first recorded instance that the Leech Squad had so blatantly showed its hand in broad daylight. Indeed Ellison became the first national figure to be honoured by undisguised, round-the-clock ISP surveillance.

The mesh was tightening. Somewhere Searchlight's investigations were beginning to hurt.

A letter arrived through the post in a large pica typeface. "You have a week to leave the country. If you don't we will send you O'Neill by registered post. Piece by piece. After that, look to your family. Spectrum Security." No contact phone number was provided; the letter had been posted in Central London.

On the Saturday, Ellison and his son left Chester Place at 9.30 and walked across Regent's Park to Lord's Cricket Ground, a mile away. Two Leech Squad plain-clothes agents followed them on foot, chattering into walkie-talkie sets linking them to ISP Triumphs prowling the perimeter of the park.

Christopher continually pressed his father to explain why he had been mad enough to give away his two "rover" tickets for the second test match of the 1981 series between England and Australia. As a member of the Marylebone Cricket Club, Ellison carried a red card entitling him to enter Lord's for any match and to buy two daily rover tickets for a test match. Christopher was to have one and

Magnus the other—a prospect which had filled the boy with ecstasy for several weeks.

"We probably won't even get in," he moaned. "There's bound to be a queue a mile long."

But they did get in at the East Gate turnstiles in St John's Wood Road, where Ellison bought two tickets for the public stands. So did the two ISP agents shadowing them. Having hired a couple of seat cushions, he led Christopher round the east end of the ground past the nursery nets, where the England batsmen were warming up for their second innings. At the sight of his heroes in the flesh, only a few yards away, Christopher shed his anxieties.

From the public stands they enjoyed a view straight down the wicket towards the Pavilion as the England batsmen hobbled towards a miserable score of fifty-seven runs for the loss of three wickets at the lunch interval. Even the ISP agents seated in the row behind them seemed gloomy as the Australian fast bowlers unleashed their bouncers and yelled in coarse triumph as the ball flew off the bat to slip. At 1.30 the green-capped Aussies strode happily into the Pavilion as the dazed crowd of thirty thousand made for the bars and toilets.

To hold their unreserved seats, the Ellisons left behind them their Thermos flask and picnic hamper. As he had anticipated, only one of the two agents followed them down to the concourse leading to the toilets beneath the Grand Stand on the north side.

It was in the gents' urinal that Ellison produced from his wallet one of the rover tickets he had pretended to have given away, and told the astonished Christopher what he must do with it.

The agent was waiting close to the urinal exit.

"I'm going to fight for a beer," Ellison said loudly. "Why don't you go and take a look in the Museum behind the Pavilion? I'll pick you up in fifteen minutes."

The boy shrugged and vanished. Ellison joined the throng clamouring for plastic pints of beer at the Cricketer's Bar. His shadow, of course, stuck with him.

Fifteen minutes later Ellison entered the Museum, where he failed to find his son. Bright boy. Looking worried, Ellison then disappeared into the Pavilion, a holy of holies strictly reserved for members of the MCC and their guests. Stuck at the door, the Spectrum agent began to chatter into his walkie-talkie. His face was bitten by anxiety.

Ellison traversed the crowded Long Room, mounted the broad staircase which players descend on their way to the wicket, passed the England dressing-room on the first floor, and walked out of the Pavilion across the bridge connecting it to "Q" Stand—also reserved for members and their guests.

Magnus and Christopher winked at him as he passed the "Q" Stand bar. He had given Magnus the other rover ticket the day before.

Within thirty seconds of entering the Pavilion he was down the spiral staircase of "Q" Stand and into the crowded concourse. Fifty paces carried him to the Grace Gates (entry for members only) and out into St John's Wood Road.

"You're half a minute late," she said, gliding the Mini Cooper back into the traffic. "I had to promise a policeman unheard-of favours."

"Drop me at Maida Vale tube station."

"Why don't I take you all the way to Ladbroke Grove?"

"You're not the sort of woman I can afford to be seen with."

"Swine. It's all Monika Bauer now, eh? Playing with fire."

"This isn't the motorway. One thing I don't need now is to get stopped for speeding."

Coming off the Metropolitan Line train at Ladbroke Grove, he fumbled for his ticket until every other alighting passenger had passed him. Most of them were black: there were no blacks in the Leech squad.

He hired an Austin 2200 from a small mews garage. It had to be in his own name—he had never carried false papers and he never would. The risk was there but it was unavoidable.

By late afternoon he had covered a hundred and forty-four

miles and was approaching Abergavenny. He pulled off the road at a phone-box, consulted his Automobile Association Guidebook, and phoned through to the three-star Angel Hotel.

"Yes, sir, we have a room. What is the name, please?"

"R. M. Minors."

He dined off fish and chips out of a paper bag, drove past the Angel Hotel in Cross Street, parked in a quiet street a quarter of a mile away, then walked back to the hotel and paid in advance for his room.

"Will you be having dinner, sir?"

"No dinner."

He was given room 4 on the first floor, overlooking the Cross Street entrance to the hotel, which suited him very well. A short reconnoitre revealed a useful line of retreat down the back stairs and through the rear entrance to the car-park. He then locked his door, removed the trilby hat and dark glasses that Judy had thoughtfully packed for him, and fell into a deep sleep. The Welsh air was very sweet and he hadn't slept properly for over a month.

The dawn chorus woke him: it was 4.30. He had slept for ten hours. If he left now the desk clerk might remember him. He shaved, showered, dressed and calculated his chances. He reckoned he had a full day to play with. Unless his luck ran out.

Unless he was walking into a trap.

Who was the "highest authority" referred to in the Swinburne memo? Martindale? Ozanne? Lynedoch? But why focus on obvious villains? Walter Vandyke, perhaps? Ellison's mind was racked by total suspicion. Neither Vandyke nor Armstrong had been dismissed. Either of them could be playing a subtle game behind an impeccable democratic façade . . .

By 5.30 his mind had run out of practical thoughts and had nowhere to go except to Joe O'Neill and to the menace hanging over his family. On Monday he would have to phone Joe's parents in Belfast and report that their only son, their white hope, was now under death sentence. "We know he's like a son to you, Mr Ellison," Joe's mum had said on the phone a few days ago. "He thinks the world of you and we know you won't let the boy down." How could he tell them that he was prepared to have Joe cut up like beef if it was the price of hunting down the men behind Al-Ittihad's conspiracy to destroy British democracy?

With time to kill he bought a batch of Sunday papers but found the *Sunday Monitor* unobtainable.

"That's four weeks running we've had no delivery," the newsagent complained.

Parking his car in a secluded country lane, Ellison reflected gloomily on the sudden succession of crises that had resulted in a shortfall of between 200,000 and 400,000 copies of the *Monitor*. On one occasion the cashiers had declared a go-slow in support of a grievance; when the casual workers employed in the publishing room received no pay they stopped work. The presses had to be stopped. Three weeks ago an unusual sequence of paper breaks had hit the huge Nohab-Ampress presses. Two weeks ago not one but two casters in the foundry had suffered from metal floods, with the flongs jammed tight and no stereo-plates coming out. One week ago the linotype operators had called a chapel meeting at a crucial hour of the evening to discuss piece-work rates. Ramsay Jordan had consulted the Imperial Father of the NGA Chapels, the senior union official in the composing room, and had received the impression that saboteurs were at work. Ellison himself was in no doubt that Hubert Yorath, the General Manager and a pro-Government man, was steadily applying pressure on Gowers to fire the Searchlight team.

He opened the *Dispatch*:

The rout of the BBC was now almost complete. Gottlieb had been dismissed, *Believe It or Not* was being taken off the air, and Armstrong's own position was now regarded as precarious. Chairman of the Governors Lucas had publicly recommended that the External Services should be hived off from the Corporation—in Ellison's opinion they would then become no more than the Government's propaganda agency.

Ormskirk's Saviours of the Nation had gone on the rampage in Leeds while the police stood by: the style of it suggested a pogrom. Was Sir Stuart Ormskirk the "highest authority"? In London four noted defence lawyers, members of the National Council for Civil Liberties, had been arrested by the ISP and held without bail. In a major speech, Prime Minister Murdoch had presented the forthcoming Arab Mission as the key to Britain's economic salvation. Home Secretary Martindale, speaking during a by-election campaign, had gone so far as to hint that parliamentary government might not survive the national crisis.

A speech by Walter Vandyke in Leeds had been disrupted by organized hooligans chanting "Jew boy, out!"

The General had provided Ellison with precise route instructions but he decided to deviate from them: what had been prudent in Czechoslovakia was prudent in the Black Mountain country of Wales. Instead of taking the A465 to Llanvihangel Crucorney to the north of Abergavenny, he drove north-west along the A40 to Llangrwyne, overshot the inconspicuous turning he was looking for, doubled back at Cwrt-y-gollen army camp, found his turning, then followed a winding road often no wider than a single car and bounded by high hedges. Periodically he checked his watch and stopped to scan the V-neck of sky formed by the convergence ahead of him of two flanking ranges of hills. He didn't know exactly what he was looking for but when he first caught sight of the helicopter, about a mile to the north-east, he knew that he had been wise to deviate from the General's recommended route.

Pulling off the road and behind a barn, he took his binoculars from the glove box. The forty-foot-long utility helicopter was cruising at about 160 mph at an altitude, he estimated, of fifteen hundred feet. As it circled over the Llanvihangel Crucorney road junction it shed pace and he had leisure to identify it as an army five-seater Aérospatiale/

Westland Gazelle AH Mk 1, a craft possessing considerable stamina over a cruising range of four hundred miles and blind-flying instrumentation that made it notably effective in mountainous country subject to low cloud and mist.

So he was expected. But by whom? The Gazelle was now lost to sight behind the hills. He drove on.

The B4423 took him through Forestry Commission country. Trees shielded the narrow road and the last of the bluebells carpeted the rich pastures flanking the clear waters of the Afon Honddu. But the country ahead of him would become increasingly desolate and his own position helplessly exposed. Tension was now localized at the base of Ellison's neck; he knew the Westland Gazelle would take him from behind.

It did. Seven miles short of Capel-y-ffin the valley broadened. He saw nothing in his mirror but heard a shattering roar and felt the car tossing about like a leaf in the wind. He braked and simultaneously opened the offside door, hurling himself clear of the car and into a gully. For perhaps twenty seconds the helicopter hovered above him, hammering him into the dry mud, then rapidly gained altitude and soared up between the mountain ranges in the direction of Capel-y-ffin.

Nursing a bruised shoulder, Ellison drove on.

At Capel-y-ffin he followed the directions he had committed to memory, forking left along a narrow metalled track, passing the ruined monastery and the wooden shrine —"Peace to the Wayfarer through the Blood of Jesus"—and finally halting outside a white gate with black hinges. It was a lonely spot. The helicopter was now hovering five hundred feet above him.

A dirt track took him up a steep incline to an isolated cottage standing on the open hillside with sheep grazing up to the walls. A battered old Morris 1000 station wagon parked outside the front door had evidently gone to sleep long ago.

The General was waiting for him. Dressed in a soiled

white shirt and baggy grey flannels, he beckoned Ellison inside with a curt gesture. "Next time, follow my directions to the letter. Saves a lot of fuss."

"Is it your toy, the Westland Gazelle?"

"Three reliable fellows. Coffee or something stronger? They say you were playing the fool." He led the way into a primitive kitchen equipped with a Calor gas ring and a water pump. "Shambles," the General muttered with a vague gesture. "It'll be like Latin America soon . . . Perónism . . . a coup every other week . . . corporals dressing up as generals . . ." A big black kettle began to hiss on the ring. "Which school?"

"Winchester."

"That's the place where they don't play games."

"Somebody should tell them."

The General chuckled and poured hot water over instant coffee, then slopped in a huge dollop of Scotch. "Cheers," he grunted, bending his legs and groping under an ancient Welsh dresser. Ellison watched him lever up a tile and extract a waterproof plastic bin-bag, an exertion which brought the blood to his face. Clutching the treasure, Winstanley shuffled into the sitting-room in carpet slippers and baggy tweed trousers, then plonked himself down in the only chair.

"Have a pew," he grunted, gesturing vaguely. Ellison drew a white wooden chair from the wall and sat on it. He heard a crack and his head struck the stone floor.

"Thought they taught you how to fall in the paras," Winstanley commented, tenderly picking up the white chair and fitting the two broken cross-struts back into the rear leg sockets. "Keep meaning to get the damned thing mended. Headache, old boy? I may have some aspirin."

Cautiously Ellison eased himself on to the only other chair in the room, an unpainted stool. Winstanley was still clutching the plastic bag.

"Kafka saw it all, ahead of his time. People think soldiers can't read. I've spent years killing my fellow men, now I'm beginning to wonder why."

He tossed the bag to Ellison. Inside it was a fat document: "TOP SECRET: OPERATION TALENT". Beneath the title were the words: "Access Restricted under the Official Secrets Act to Ten Persons Designated by the Prime Minister". But the ten persons were not named.

Ellison flipped the first page:

PREAMBLE: Operation Talent is a contingency plan for the dissolution of Parliament and the declaration of a State of Emergency in the event of a national crisis.

A national crisis shall be any state of affairs which, in the opinion of HM Government, poses a threat to the security of the Realm, to the stability of society, to law and order, and to the ability of the Government to govern.

The dissolution of Parliament shall be *sine die*. No general election shall follow.

A State of Emergency shall be a period characterized by executive rule without reference to the legislature (dissolved). Legislation shall be by executive fiat and decree.

The executive shall have power to suspend traditional constitutional guarantees and liberties, as well as statutes.

Security measures shall include the suspension of habeas corpus. Internment without legal representation or trial in designated internment camps (Shetland Islands, West Yorkshire) shall extend for a maximum of five years.

Special Tribunals shall be empowered to impose the death penalty for crimes against the State.

Under a State of Emergency the Government shall immediately undertake the following measures: (1) to ban all political parties and meetings; (2) to dissolve all trade unions and business confederations, and to replace them with organizations responsible to the Minister of Economic Coordination; (3) to dissolve all voluntary associations of a political or civil libertarian character; (4) to bring all media, including the BBC and the Press, under the direct control of the Minister of National Guidance; (5) to censor all printed material and to ban the following publications (list follows).

A new category of second-class citizens shall be created, to include all subjects of African, Asian or Jewish stock (definition follows). Second-class citizens shall not be entitled to own any business enterprise, land or residence, and shall be subject to deportation from these shores at the discretion of the Home Secretary.

The instruments of authority, law and order under the State of Emergency shall include: the Internal Security Police; the Armed Forces; the Saviours of the Nation (para-military).

AUTHORITY

Supreme and absolute power shall be vested in the SUPREME EXECUTIVE COUNCIL, which shall consist of three members.

LEADER: (Designated)

1st Deputy Leader: (Designated)

2nd Deputy Leader: (Designated)

All decisions of the Supreme Executive Council shall be binding on the Government.

GOVERNMENT

The Government shall be known as the MINISTRY OF ALL THE TALENTS. Its members shall be drawn from all spheres of national life.

Composition (provisional):

Prime Minister, Rt Hon George Murdoch; Deputy PM and Home Secretary, Rt Hon Patrick Martindale; Foreign Secretary, Cyril Quilley . . .

Ellison read down the list of future Ministers of All the Talents. The present Leader of the Opposition was to be Chancellor of the Exchequer; the fascist Sir Stuart Ormskirk, leader of the Saviours, was to be Minister of National Guidance; Sir Philip Lucas, Minister of Information; Professor Hugh Swinburne, Minister of National Culture;

Superintendent Stanley Leech, Minister of Justice; Edmund Strachan, Minister of National Resources; Bert Hoyle, Minister of Communications; Lord Gowers, Minister of Economic Coordination.

"Jesus," Ellison muttered. So that was Gowers's game—no wonder he wanted to play ball with the Inner Cabinet! This was the glittering prize for all of them!

Lady Meg Ormond-Clubb, President of the Guardians of Decency, was to be the Minister of National Morality.

Ellison then came to a long list, over three hundred names, of those who were to be arrested and detained without trial in an internment camp. They included Sir Jack Armstrong, Roger Fullerton (the present Foreign Secretary), MPs like Durban and Bentley, Lord Jacobs and Timothy Powerstock of the *Sunday Dispatch*, Denis Laslett, David Gottlieb and Roy Winter (all formerly of the BBC)—Cohn's name, like Moshe Levene's, had been inked out following his death—Superintendent Edgar Bradlaw of the Special Branch (on whose protection the Ellison family now depended), Stanford Christie and a number of other dons and writers.

Ellison noticed that Magnus Massey's name appeared on this list but not his own, which was puzzling. He soon found the answer.

"Death List. The following shall be shot dead by the ISP while resisting or evading arrest: Walter Vandyke, Bill Ellison . . ." Ten names appeared on the list.

So that's your ambition, Gowers . . .

General Winstanley was watching him intently, pulling on a briar pipe.

"Who are the three members of the Supreme Council and why aren't they named?" Ellison asked.

"I've no idea. Security, presumably."

"I notice that neither Kenneth Lynedoch nor Geoffrey Ozanne figures in the list of Ministers."

"I thought you might spot that."

"It's damned dark in here, General. I'd like to read this outside . . ."

Winstanley's hand shot out demandingly. "Let's have it, then. No, not the document, man."

"You want my car keys?"

"I'm not worried about that, my Westland Gazelle wouldn't let you get far. It's your microfilm camera I'm interested in."

Ellison sighed. "Presumably you have no objection if I take notes?"

"Every objection. No notes. Commit it to memory—you do have a prodigious memory, don't you?" The General's eyes twinkled.

"Is this a schoolboy battle of wits, Winstanley, or are we both in business to save our country from fascism and foreign domination?"

The General sat very still in his armchair—only the vibrating hands betrayed the wound to his dignity. Ellison was not inclined to break the silence. Tilting *Operation Talent* towards the small window, he began to study it afresh.

"Fair comment," Winstanley eventually grunted.

"I suppose this document *might* be authentic," Ellison said drily.

"That remark is not appreciated."

"I assume these plans are periodically reviewed in the Ministry of Defence?"

"Correct."

"Who attends the conferences?"

"Martindale; Burnett, my immediate civilian superior; Vice-Chief of the General Staff Sir Harry Travers-Bellings; Superintendent Leech; from time to time Sir Stuart Ormskirk . . ."

"Who else?"

Suddenly the helicopter swooped out of the descending mists and roared low over the cottage, shaking the rafters. Ellison didn't believe in coincidences. The clouds were closing in now, drifting down from the twin peaks of Waun Fach and Pen-y-Gader-fawr to blot out the skyline of the Fwddog Ridge which rose up sheer behind the cottage. They

were hemmed in by mountains on every side; Ellison knew
that the narrow valley road was the only way in and the
only way out. The General now sat rigid in his chair, his
forehead suddenly layered in sweat.

"How sure are you that no one followed you here,
Ellison?"

"Quite sure."

"Let's hope you are right."

"Who else attends these conferences, General?"

Though midsummer, it was almost dark in the small
sitting-room. Winstanley rose, found matches, and lit an
oil-lamp with an unsteady hand.

"The fact is . . . these meetings are invariably monitored
on two-way radio, you follow? One of three men listens
in . . ."

"Three? You mean you've heard three different voices at
one time or another?"

"Correct."

"And they comment, give guidance?"

"Stronger than that: they command."

"Can you identify any of these voices?"

"I . . . I believe not."

"You hesitated."

"It would be speculation."

"But the voices are clearly English?"

"Oh yes."

"Is it your impression that any of those physically
attending these conferences in the Ministry know these voices?"

"Yes, Martindale."

"Only Martindale?"

"Possibly Burnett. Possibly. One of the voices, you see . . .
Put it this way: two of the voices refer to the 'Leader'. The
third voice does not."

"He *is* the Leader?"

"My strong impression, yes. A gentle, educated voice . . .
but authoritative. A soldier smells authority like a dog smells
a bone."

"Has the name Al-Ittihad ever been mentioned?"

"No."

"I assume the exact date for Operation Talent has been set?"

The helicopter again emerged out of the enclosing mists, hovering less than a hundred feet over the cottage so that the china and glass shook and Ellison felt himself being pressed into the floor. Winstanley tried to speak but the noise was deafening. Finally, after a full minute of torment, the helicopter lifted away.

"Sorry, old man, that's a signal. Adequate surveillance is no longer possible. You'll have to go."

"An Aérospatiale/Westland Gazelle AH Mk 1 carries blind-flying instrumentation."

The General ignored the remark as if he hadn't heard it. "Tell you what, Ellison, if you want to hear the rest, come back half an hour after dawn: 5 am. I have to leave at 6 to be at my desk by 9."

At the door he gently eased *Operation Talent* from Ellison's hand. "Drive carefully."

He took a room in a poky hotel in Crickhowell. His alarm woke him at 4 o'clock. By 4.15 he was on the road. Two miles down the A40 he turned off it at Llangrwyne and pointed his nose up into the Black Mountains. A pink glow had begun to expand across the horizon; it was a fine summer morning.

He rolled down the car window, now, and listened intently for the throb of the helicopter which he was sure would pick him up from his rear. But the bracing silence of the hour after dawn was unbroken except for the occasional screech of a buzzard, the bleating of a sheep. By the time he turned on to the B4423 he had begun to conclude that the Gazelle was out of the game. He would soon know why.

At the white gate with black hinges he turned up towards the cottage. Only the blazing upper arc of the sun was visible above the mountain ridge to the east, but he had a clear view of the cottage from the gate and of the Morris station wagon parked in front of it.

He knocked on the front door, waited, then knocked again, loudly. The curtains of the sitting-room were drawn. He tried the door. It opened. He flashed his torch round the empty kitchen, then bent his head to enter the sitting-room.

The first object his torch picked up was a white chair lying on its side in the middle of the room. He shifted the beam—two shoes were suspended some fifteen inches above the floor.

General Winstanley was hanging from a meat hook in the central beam. A dim quarter-light illuminated the purple, swollen, distorted face, the twisted mouth covered in bile, the eyes glassy and desperate.

Ellison drew the curtain. The room was undisturbed—there was no sign of a struggle, of violence. A sheet of paper lay on the table. The message was short: "I have betrayed my oath of allegiance. I embrace my fate. Winstanley." Ellison had, of course, destroyed the crumpled note which the General had tossed into his lap in White's, but from what he could remember the handwriting was similar—small, neat, spidery. He searched the room for a specimen of handwriting but found none.

He returned to the kitchen and lifted the loose tile beneath the Welsh dresser. His hand made contact with the waterproof bag. He brought it up into the light; *Operation Talent* was now in his possession.

He was already a hundred yards from the cottage when a grain of doubt began to surface. He braked and reversed the Austin back up the hill. The source of his doubt refused to identify itself, so obscurely was it locked into a shifting backcloth of images.

He forced himself back into the sitting-room, fighting off the nausea rising in his stomach at the sight of the General hanging from the meat hook. He allowed his torch beam to roam the room, hoping that his eye would unlock his mind.

Then he saw it.

The chair. The chair lying on its side at the General's feet, apparently kicked away from under him, was the white chair with two broken struts which had collapsed as soon as Ellison had sat on it the previous afternoon. And Winstanley was well aware that it wouldn't carry a man's weight.

Ellison knelt to examine the white chair lying on its side. Both struts remained in their leg sockets. No one had stood on that chair.

He walked to the door of the cottage and regarded the Black Mountains thoughtfully.

The General had been murdered. Then why had the cottage not been ransacked in the search for *Operation Talent*? Because, obviously, they wanted it to look like suicide. No doubt a search had taken place but revealed nothing—and they would assume, he suddenly realized, that Ellison had departed the previous evening with a microfilm of the document.

In all probability Winstanley had briefed his helicopter crew that he was expecting a visitor who was to be warned off if shadowed. But there was no reason to believe that the General had been so imprudent as to reveal the visitor's identity. Thus the helicopter, on sighting Ellison's car in the early afternoon, had been able to transmit to ISP Control one item of information only: the car's registration number. On a Sunday afternoon the national Vehicle Licence Office in Swansea was closed; it would take a local ISP squad a couple of hours to gain access to the filing system. The London garage to which the car belonged was also closed on a Sunday evening, involving further delays in tracing the proprietor and checking the car hire documents. Ellison reckoned that ISP Control would not have positively identified him as Winstanley's visitor until 8 or 9 on Saturday evening.

Leech would not have entrusted a job of this delicacy to a local ISP unit. A crack elimination squad would have been despatched from London. Winstanley had no doubt been alive and well in his bed until midnight.

Had Winstanley informed the Gazelle crew that his visitor

would be returning shortly after dawn? Ellison had no way of knowing . . .

He took his binoculars from the Austin 2200 and scanned the surrounding mountains. All he saw was scattered sheep. No sign or sound of the helicopter. Yet instinct instructed him that his movements had been constantly monitored and that the trap was about to be sprung on him with *Operation Talent* in his possession. When he came to trial—if he came to trial—the outraged public would be told how an unscrupulous journalist had hounded an honourable officer to the point of suicide.

The car was now out of the question. Whichever of the two valley roads he chose, north to Hay-on-Wye or south to Llanvihangel Crucorney, unmarked squad cars of the ISP would be waiting for him.

He studied his Ordnance Survey map. Five miles to the west lay Talgarth and the A479, but those were no ordinary five miles; two totally exposed mountain ridges, the Fwddog and the Gader, and an intervening valley river lay between him and Talgarth. Time and the terrain were both against him. But there was no alternative.

It was now 5.20. Removing his small overnight grip from the car, he placed *Operation Talent* inside it and started to make tracks up the Fwddog Ridge, periodically scanning the skylines through binoculars. The temperature dropped as he climbed. Cresting the Fwddog, he began to run through short heather across its gently sloping back and down into the valley of the Grwyne Fawr where a reservoir glinted like black steel below him. Directly ahead, beyond the valley, the higher Gader Ridge rose up, dark and imperious. The morning sun had not yet struck its lower slopes.

His first presentiment of the helicopter was a distant murmur, deepening as it approached, then culminating in a sustained angry snarl. He guessed that it was now hovering directly above the General's cottage and that within minutes the fact of his escape on foot would become apparent to the Gazelle's crew. He had barely reached the sanctuary of the pine trees clustered at one end of the reservoir when the helicopter soared up above the Fwddog Ridge behind him and began to describe wide arcs across the valley, constantly revolving through 360°, then swooping hawk-like over the copse where Ellison lay motionless, face-down. He held his breath; it was not a voluntary act.

He waited. Even after the Gazelle's engine had faded away over the Gader peaks he made no move. The valley he was now in, culminating as it did in thick woodlands, offered a tempting line of retreat, whereas the Gader Ridge promised only a painful climb and merciless exposure to the sky as the sun rose to illuminate the whole of the east face. But the valley carried him in the wrong direction; at its mouth the squad cars would be waiting.

His guess that the Westland Gazelle would return one more time, to scan the Gader Ridge and probe the valley floor, proved correct; and he thanked God that the crew were too lazy to ground their machine and search the copse on foot. As soon as the irate pulse of the engine faded down the valley he picked up his grip and began to climb rapidly. Within minutes his body was soaked in sweat; the sheep observed his laboured passage with glassy nonchalance.

He saw the helicopter once more, as he was descending the Ridge towards Talgarth. He threw himself flat in the heather, tucking the binocular lenses under his body and pressing his face into the ground. But the Gazelle was now circling without conviction; it approached no closer than half a mile before it whined away to the south.

When he reached Talgarth it was 8.45. People glanced at the dishevelled stranger with distant curiosity and he decided not to inquire about a local taxi service. He passed a bus stop but gave that a miss too. Ten minutes later an empty furniture-van bound for Builth Wells, in central Wales, offered him a lift. He took it.

"Had a break-down, did you?" the driver asked in a lilting Welsh accent.

Ellison nodded. He noticed that the muscular young

fellow was scanning him with something more than curiosity.

"You'll think I'm mad, but I know your face. Been on the telly, have you?"

Ellison laughed drily. "I flog insurance."

"You do? Then you won't be able to tell me why we haven't seen the *Sunday Monitor* up here these last few weeks?"

Tensing, Ellison glanced at the speedometer; the van was now topping fifty. The driver chuckled: "I wouldn't jump out at this speed, Mr Ellison. On the run, are you?"

"Just so."

"Looking for a quiet way back to London?"

"Preferably through the Midlands."

The driver removed his right hand from the wheel and extended it: "Emrys Jones at your service, sir."

"What can I pay you, Mr Jones?"

"The price of the petrol. No—say no more. We're not blind round here, you know. My father still works down the pit in Merthyr. Only the other day he said, 'They'll kill that Ellison soon enough.'"

"'They'?"

The young driver's face was set rigid with anger; he gripped the wheel so tightly that his knuckles were white. "The lying bastards who run this country."

Twelve

At 5.30 on a fine midsummer morning, at the moment Ellison
was forced to abandon his hired car outside the General's
cottage and to hoof it, an Aston Martin DB6 glided into the
deserted car-park of the Sanderton Golf Club. Two men and
a woman got out. The driver of the car lifted a leather golf-
bag from the boot while the second man, short and stunted
in physique, emerged carrying two Leicas and a camera bag.
His quick, shifty eyes scurried over the empty clubhouse like
frightened mice.

Judy Rossiter had already undergone a radical change of
appearance. Her auburn hair had been died raven black and
worked into a mass of fluffy Afro curls; her eyebrows and
pubic hair had also changed colour. Brown-tinted contact
lenses now masked her green eyes while skilfully applied eye-
shadow and cosmetics altered her complexion and the
apparent contours of her face.

Magnus selected the sixteenth hole as one whose fairway
was shielded on both sides by rows of elms and oaks. The
light was perfect, bright, even, devoid of shadow-casting sun
rays—the time of day most precious to professional photographers. Watching Judy remove her flimsy cotton dress
(she wore no bra or underpants) Magnus witnessed for the
first time her naked body in its lithe, supple perfection:
large, high, delicately sculpted breasts; rounded shoulders
and arms layered with a satin sheen of firm flesh; a slender,
elastic waist; powerful hips which promised a challenging
contest in the battle of love; and long, tapering thighs whose

easy, seductive movements suggested a latent muscular power. And he could well imagine this self-assured young woman taunting a man to prove himself by forcing them apart.

She smiled at him, a muted, cat-like smile, which acknowledged how badly he wanted her, not for her body alone but also, as with Bill Ellison, for the quick, clever, audacious personality which commanded the body. For a moment Magnus experienced an acute frustration. To want a woman who might be beyond his reach, his claim, was a novel and disturbing sensation for Magnus Massey.

Judy tucked her left hand into the golfing glove he provided, climbed on to the raised tee, braced her legs on her two-inch heels, and swung a number 1 driver through a pretty, graceful arc which sent her breasts dancing.

"You look just like a pro," he said.

"Pass me my score card, caddie."

"Hole in one?"

"Not your one, poof."

While Micky Kolarcz bent, crouched and hopped around his model like the hunchback of Notre Dame, Magnus tutored Judy to brace her legs straight as she bent to thrust the ball and tee into the ground. Kolarcz's Leica came up underneath her to catch the hang of her breasts as she stretched down.

"Now rest the club head on the ground, let the shaft run straight up between your legs—and pout."

Further up the fairway Kolarcz snapped her from behind as she bent, straight-legged again, in search of a ball evidently lost in the rough. On the sixteenth green Magnus put her through a wide range of provocative horizontal poses as she gauged the lie between her ball and the hole. Finally he persuaded her to swing a number 8 iron into a deep bunker and to grimace prettily as the flying sand descended on her head, shoulders and breasts.

"You swine, I'm covered in it."

As she climbed out of the bunker, threatening to clout him

with the iron, he caught sight of two members of the ground staff moving up the adjoining fairway in an electric cart.

"Time to go."

Driving back to London through Surrey suburbia, Magnus again pressed the unhappy Kolarcz to reveal who ran Relief, Ltd.

"I told ya—Florence Eltenbridge."

"What's her real name?"

"Aw, come on."

"Who's F. Cain?"

"Her 'usband. Frank."

"Where do they live?"

"They don't tell me more than they need to."

"So you've met Frank Cain?"

"I didn't say so."

"He scares you, Micky."

Kolarcz said nothing. His wet lips trembled.

"Cain runs Spectrum, is that it?"

"Never 'eard of it."

"Even though the whole security network round 18 Phillimore Avenue is provided by Spectrum? Even though you've personally fitted and serviced the 16mm cameras in the Relief flats? Never heard of Spectrum?"

"You're a fuckin' idiot, Massey. You'll lose that gold block o' yours if you go pokin' round Frank Cain."

"Now tell me what Nashat Al-Khatib means to you."

"Who's 'e?"

"The boss of the outfit you and your current girl-friend did an ad. for. It's called Arabair. You may recall travelling to Ferndale airport to shoot a bit of porn, using an Arabair DC-10 as a prop. Does that jog your foggy memory, Micky?"

"I don't mix much with those Arab characters."

"You just take their money—we noticed that you have over £60,000 stashed away in various accounts."

"Well, I get my wages from Florence, don't I?"

"But who does she get hers from?"

"From clients, of course. Listen: Nashat takes care every bleedin' Arab businessman and diplomat who needs a bit of pussy gets it from Relief. Arabair and Samarkand pay Florence fantastic retainers to make sure their clients get the best, quickest, right? That's business to my mind."

"And is framing a lot of MPs and media people also 'business'?"

"Don't ask me, Massey. I just do what I'm told."

"Who chooses the targets, Micky?"

"No idea."

"Who's the contact man between Relief and the ultimate boss?"

"No idea." Kolarcz picked at his nose. Magnus had begun to notice his habit of picking his nose whenever he told a lie.

"Is it Ulf Steinberg, Micky?"

Hunched low in the car, terrified that they would be picked up by a Spectrum Mercedes, Kolarcz shrugged.

"Never 'eard of 'im, 'onest."

Micky Kolarcz was still picking his nose.

Ellison drove up to Oxford in mid-afternoon with a double purpose: to talk to Stanford Christie and Solomon Rupin, and to look in on the dress rehearsal of the OUDS production of Hamlet at the Playhouse Theatre. Faith Ellison, a young amateur actress of great promise, was playing Ophelia.

"And negelecting her work into the bargain, I expect."

"Nonsense, Bill," said Christie's wife Margaret, a handsome woman who was slotting the lunch plates into the dishwasher when Ellison arrived. "You know perfectly well that Faith gets splendid praise from all her tutors."

"Well she's damned well going to be off-stage during her final year."

"Bill, you've no idea how absolutely heartbreaking she is as Ophelia."

"Whose heart does she break: the audience's or the director's?"

"Oh Bill, you're such a cynic."

"Margaret's helping out with the stage costumes," Christie said.

"And the first night is tomorrow?"

"Yes, June 13. Are you sure you can't stay for it? We could easily give you a bed," Margaret Christie said.

"I wish I could."

"Well, you men are going to have to do without me, I'm due at the Playhouse twenty minutes ago. Stanford, there's coffee on the stove—it's just possible your guests may not be content with a slice of lemon in hot water." She winked long eyelashes at Ellison and Rupin, gathered her bag, and hurried from the Park Town house. A moment later Ellison heard the sound of a sports car gunning away.

Ellison rarely saw Stanford's wife during his visits to Oxford, and he sensed that the solid, settled existence of a don didn't entirely satisfy her. Faith, who knew the Christies quite well now, believed that Margaret was having an affair in London and that Stanford, a shy introverted man, bore the knowledge of this in stoical silence. It was not an area of life that either Christie or Ellison would be inclined to discuss.

"I need to take a leak, Stanford."

"Upstairs, first on the left."

Finding the door of Christie's study half-open, Ellison went to the handsome Georgian window and looked down to the road where the two ISP Triumphs were drawn up, one behind his own Granada and the other behind the Israeli Embassy's massive, armour-plated Buick. He had always enjoyed browsing in Christie's study—other men's books held a peculiar fascination and there were perhaps five hundred titles on the shelves he would have liked to read, had he the time. On his way out he paused to admire the collection of pictures on the walls, many of them photographs taken by Christie himself during his travels. Of the mosques, minarets and palaces confronting him, Ellison could name about half by sight; the other half depressed him. Once again he promised himself a sabbatical leave of absence.

"That's some tank you've brought with you, Solomon," he commented, rejoining the others in the drawing-room.

"Everywhere I go, it's the Mitla Pass," said the Israeli diplomat. Rupin liked to remind his flabby English friends that he had been one of Tal's tank commanders during the brilliant Sinai campaign of 1967.

Christie apologized for the mass of papers strewn across the tables and floor; it was exam time.

"Then we mustn't keep you," said Ellison.

"We now know the composition of the Arab Mission to Britain," Rupin announced.

"Really? None of the news agencies has reported it to my knowledge," Ellison said.

"This is a news agency called Ha-Mossad," Christie said, winking slyly.

"The titular leader will be Sheikh Abdul Al-Abdullah Al-Jalah, Deputy Ruler of Kuwait," Rupin said.

"I was told that at 10 Downing Street several weeks ago," Ellison said. "He'll go down well at the Palace. Nice fellow. You're not suggesting he's involved with Al-Ittihad, Solomon? Or has Ha-Mossad had second thoughts about Al-Ittihad?"

"The Sheikh is merely the front man. He is most probably unaware that he is being manipulated. We agree with you: he is a man of integrity. But the same cannot be said of his number two, Isa bin Sulman Al-Rashib, Deputy Minister of Oil and Economic Development of Libya."

Christie nodded sombrely. "Al-Rashib is dangerous. A Gaddafi protégé. He not only controls Arna, the Libyan news agency, but he may well be connected with the Trans-Arabian Bank."

"Thank you, Stanford," Rupin said with more than a hint of sarcasm. "It is always pleasant to see a scholar blinking in the strong light of reality."

"Yes, but——"

"No 'buts' when you hear the name of number three:

Yusuf Hashim Yacoub, Director General of the Iraqi Ministry of Cultural Development."

"Jesus," Christie muttered. "I suppose you realize that Yacoub's real job is Director of the Ba'ath Party's Revolutionary Command Council's Intelligence Section. I knew him years ago when he was an obscure technician working for the Iraq Petroleum Company—at that time British-owned. Yacoub became involved in politics after the fall of Aref in '65 and soon emerged as a ruthless, cold-blooded killer. He controls the notorious Squad 9 of the Baghdad police."

"He also stage-managed the public hangings of Jews in Baghdad," Rupin added. "Yacoub was responsible for the bizarre attempt on the life of the Kurdish leader Barzani."

"The occasion when seven messengers were despatched to Barzani bearing gifts, each messenger a walking stick of dynamite?" Ellison asked.

"Precisely. The fuses were detonated by remote control: miraculously Barzani survived while the seven messengers were blown to bits."

"Yes, charming."

"Al-Rashib and Yacoub have been identified by our intelligence cadres as leading Zamils of Al-Ittihad."

"Zamils?"

"It's classical Arabic for brother or companion," Christie explained. "Quite different in tone from Rafiq, which signifies a comrade in the Marxist sense, or the Ikhwan of the Moslem Brotherhood in Egypt. It has always been a tradition in Al-Ittihad to endow its leaders with the names of historic Arab-Islamic buildings, often a mosque. The names usually have a geographical significance peculiar to the particular Zamil—where he was born or where he operates. The names thereby express not only *wataniyya*, which means loyalty to the specific country of one's birth, but also *qaumiyya*, which signifies loyalty to the whole Arab nation."

"Exactly," Rupin said. "According to our information,

Al-Rashib is known within Al-Ittihad as Zamil Umayyad and——"

"But he's a Libyan," Ellison objected.

"He was born in Damascus. Yacoub is designated Zamil Kadhimiya, after the great mosque in Baghdad."

"Are Nashat Al-Khatib and Mamoun Abdul Shukhairy also Zamils?"

"We assume so. But we don't have the names."

"Would it be conceivable for non-Arabs to be formally accepted into the leadership of Al-Ittihad as Zamils?"

Rupin shrugged. "Possibly not."

"It's extremely unlikely," Christie said. "Al-Ittihad has always been fiercely jealous of its Arab identity. What I want to know is why you two characters are suddenly shadowed in broad daylight by the ISP."

"It's just conceivable," Rupin said mischievously, "that Bill knows more about that than I do."

"Give me the back of a postage stamp and I'll write down what I know," Ellison said.

Christie and Rupin exchanged sceptical glances.

"Bill, I have told you a good deal," Rupin said angrily. "I think you owe me something in return."

"According to Bert Hoyle, I'm on the Ha-Mossad payroll. According to me, I'm not."

"But we are fighting a common battle!"

Ellison laid a hand on the Israeli's shoulder—he very rarely touched a member of his own sex. "You're one of the best, Solomon. Just leave me to do things my own way, eh?"
He turned to Christie. "Stanford, you were in the diplomatic service with Lynedoch and Ozanne——"

"A long time ago," Christie pointed out.

"But Lynedoch has attended conferences at your Middle East Institute."

"Not since the anti-semitic campaign began. The last time we met we had a flaming row—he virtually accused me of being an agent of Ha-Mossad through the Hebrew University."

"It's rumoured that both Lynedoch and Ozanne are Moslem converts."

"I've heard that too. Difficult to confirm; the biographical directories are silent on that subject. What one can say is that both are ambitious men with a wide range of contacts in the Middle East."

"And presumably they're on intimate terms with Al-Rashib and Yacoub, the two leading Zamils of the forth-coming Arab Mission?"

"I'm sure, yes."

"Of course Lynedoch bears a remarkable physical resemblance to an Arab. Touch of the tar brush?"

Christie quivered in reaction; his normally placid eyes were suddenly fired with anger. "And I suppose all Jews have hooked noses?"

"Well . . ."

"Beneath that liberal veneer, Bill, there's an ugly cancer of racism in you. I've noticed it before. Your vocabulary is littered with the offensive phrases by which we demonstrated our superiority in the heyday of the Empire."

"Point taken. I'll make an effort. What puzzles me is why Ozanne chose to transfer from the Foreign to the Home Office at precisely the moment Martindale became Home Secretary."

"The answer is implicit in the question," Rupin said. "Ozanne is the link man between the pro-Arab foreign policy and the anti-semitic domestic policy."

"Any news of young Joe O'Neill?" Christie asked Ellison.

"None. His car was found abandoned in Carfax."

"No anonymous threats following his disappearance?"

Ellison nodded. "I'm afraid so."

"Terrible, terrible," Rupin muttered. "In this country!"

Shortly afterwards Christie wryly gestured towards his piles of unmarked exam papers. While Rupin went upstairs, Ellison indicated a framed portrait of a lady on the drawing-room mantelpiece.

"I've always assumed that's your mother, Stanford."

"Yes. She died in California three years ago."

"I'm sorry . . . I suppose you didn't see much of her after she and your father were divorced?"

"A few visits each way . . . all rather . . . painful. I'm afraid my father's life as an oil-engineer in Iraq didn't suit my mother . . . it was fairly rough out there in those days. I notice you never talk of your own parents, Bill. I've known you for twenty years and I don't even know whether they're alive or dead."

"They were both drowned in a fishing boat off the west coast of Scotland when I was five. I was brought up by an aunt and uncle who didn't want me . . . and that, no doubt, is why I am what I am."

"You're not so bad, really. You feel guilty about young O'Neill?"

"I couldn't stop goading him."

"And it leaves you pretty short-staffed. Just Massey?"

"Well, Magnus is worth three."

Charlie opened the rear door of the Granada as Ellison emerged from Christie's house.

"The Playhouse Theatre, sir?"

"No, London, Charlie."

"Your daughter will be disappointed, sir."

"There are worse things in life than disappointment."

"Yes, sir."

When Ellison reached Gowers House shortly after 5 pm, he found Jordan and Massey anxiously studying tear-offs from the Associated Press wire-machine.

"Take a look at these," Jordan said grimly.

The Government was rushing two bills through Parliament on a three-line whip and under the guillotine. Yet the Opposition front bench was offering no serious opposition—only a beleaguered band of back-benchers from both sides of the House had vainly protested.

The first bill, the Internal Security Act, introduced a long list of novel crimes, including "actions prejudicial to the national interest", "collaboration with foreign Powers hostile to this country", "incitement to social unrest", and "assembly calculated to propagandize ideas undermining public order".

"Jesus Christ, that can mean anything."

"And everything," Jordan muttered.

The second bill, the Public Information Act, forbade the media to "disseminate doctrines or information liable to undermine public confidence in the Government". The enforcement of this provision, as with the Internal Security Act, was now entrusted to the Internal Security Police. Henceforward the ISP would be entitled to seize copies of newspapers as they came off the presses and to seal the presses if an apparent violation of the Public Information Act came to light. The onus would then be on the Editor to prove in court that he had not violated the Act.

"Why the hell has all this shit suddenly rained down on us?" Jordan wanted to know.

"I suggest we take a stroll down to the river."

"I'm pretty——" But Jordan caught the look in Ellison's eye. "Give me five minutes."

As the three men walked down Carmelite Street towards the Thames, two plain-clothes ISP agents climbed out of their Triumph 2500 Mk 2, and tailed them at a distance of fifty or sixty yards. Presently Massey noticed a shadow on the pavement; a friendly-looking Alsatian was trotting along immediately behind them. Stooping to fondle the dog with reassuring murmurs, Magnus explored the leather strap round its neck until his hand found a small, stainless steel pendant concealed under the thick fur. Checking their stride, Ellison and Jordan had turned.

"Greetings, Islam," Magnus said softly, holding the pendant close to his mouth. Sixty yards away the two ISP agents halted in their tracks, quivering with rage. Then one of them whistled sharply and the Alsatian immediately bounded back towards them.

"And where will this end?" Jordan groaned.

"That was what I wanted to tell you, Ramsay. It will end

in two words: Operation Talent. And I'm sorry to add a third word which is worse news than we thought."

"What?"

"Gowers."

Summoned by Lord Gowers, Ellison insisted on taking Jordan with him to the tenth floor as a witness. The Chairman's normal smoothness of manner had noticeably evaporated.

"I'm told you have in your possession *Operation Talent*, Ellison."

"Are you?"

"The Home Secretary asks me to point out that under the Official Secrets Act you are not entitled to possess that document."

"The Official Secrets Act is a law passed by Parliament. The authors of *Operation Talent* are themselves in violation of the law. I expect them to be brought to trial in due course."

"Let's get one thing straight, Ellison: no reference to *Operation Talent* shall appear in the *Sunday Monitor*."

"A copy of the document is now in the possession of the *New York Times*. If any accident should befall me, it would automatically be published in the next day's issue."

"You did that!"

"We also intend to publish an editorial written by Jordan blasting the Internal Security Act and the Public Information Act."

"I forbid it!"

"If you do, every journalist on this paper—minus McNairn and a handful of stooges—will come out on strike. In short, we'll close you down."

"Ellison, you're fired!" yelled Gowers.

"Fine. I'll write a piece for next Sunday's *Dispatch*. Jacobs will be delighted to expose your political ambitions, not to mention your inability to run a newspaper. As for your patrons in the Government, they won't be pleased, will they? They'll think you bungled . . ."

Ellison had reached the door.

"Now, Ellison, wait . . ."

"For what?"

"We're all reasonable men . . ."

In a large north London house, set back behind a row of trees in a spacious garden decorated with exotic tropical plants, three men convened. These three were destined to constitute the Supreme Executive Council of the United Kingdom, and thus to dictate policy to the Ministry of All the Talents.

But only one of them was named in the document now in Ellison's possession, *Operation Talent*.

"The first item for discussion is the new legislation," the first man said quietly.

"The quick passage of the bills through the House of Sheep is assured," the second man reported. "We have the official Opposition in the bag. On the Government front bench, only Vandyke and Fullerton have protested vigorously to Murdoch. But Fullerton is nothing; he will not make a fuss in public. Vandyke will: he intends to vote in the No lobby."

"Then Murdoch must fire him," the third man said.

"No. I have instructed Murdoch to allow Vandyke to break the three-line whip," the first man said. "Vandyke remains the greatest obstacle to our cause; I do not intend him to resign in glory, I do not intend to let him stomp the country rousing the people. I intend that he shall be morally disgraced, ruined, and that his fall, when it comes, shall be catastrophic."

"Murdoch won't like it," the second man said.

"Murdoch! That bag of hay! We'll get rid of Murdoch three weeks after we take power."

"We must also consider the crisis precipitated by Ellison's

visit to the Jew-shit General Winstanley," the third man said.

"Yes," the first man said thoughtfully, "I have ordered Leech to execute the two agents who allowed Ellison to slip the net. *Pour encourager les autres.*"

"Unless we stop Ellison through Gowers," the third man said, "the whole country will know about Operation Talent next Sunday."

"The whole country will not know about it. Has the whole country been told about the Irving documents? No. Why? Because Ellison always plays a waiting game."

"But this is a scoop which any journalist—"

"Ellison is not 'any journalist'. Journalists are scum. Ellison is a uniquely dangerous intellect. So long as the whole truth eludes him he will publish nothing of importance."

"Judging from Nashat Al-Khatib's conversation with Massey, and from what O'Neill blurted out to Swinburne, Ellison is breathing right down our necks," the third man said. "On top of that, he now possesses *Operation Talent.*"

The first man shook his head. "Until Ellison penetrates my own identity he will remain baffled and silent. He is looking for the spider at the heart of the web. He won't find it."

"But we know that the auburn-haired girl was sighted a third time, on this occasion outside 18 Phillimore Avenue. There can no longer be any doubt that she works for Ellison, and there can be no doubt that he has detected the crucial role of Relief in your operations."

"Yes, he knows the question. But he remains a long way from the answer."

"And O'Neill?"

"I have instructed Frank Cain to implement our threat. Do not imagine, my friends, that I underestimate Ellison. I am not taken in by that bluff, innocent homespun manner of his. In times of national emergency, on the brink of disaster, the damp, soporific British soil invariably throws up men of Ellison's calibre—dedicated, ruthless, devious, willing to sacrifice friends, colleagues and family in defence of the nation."

The second and third men murmured in polite agreement, disciplined as they were to accept the strict hierarchy of command within Al-Ittihad. To judge from the remote light in the first man's eyes, his mind had wandered far away, to some distant land. Then a curious, twisted smile passed across his features.

"It was Englishmen like Ellison who tortured and murdered my father. In the name of what? In the name of an arrogant, idolatrous, smug, Jew-loving democracy, in the name of an insidious cancer called 'freedom'. And I mean to pay them back. Ellison will not stand in my way."

He rose. The other two men followed immediately.

"Praise be to Allah!"

"Praise be to Allah!" they echoed.

"Victory to Al-Ittihad. *Asabiyya!*"

The three men removed their shoes and fell on their knees in prayer.

Thirteen

Micky Kolarcz led Judy Rossiter into Florence Eltenbridge's New Bond Street office with the fawning obsequiousness of a Uriah Heep. The two women studied one another through a long, insolent silence; the one young and beautiful, her hair dyed raven black and worked into a mass of fluffy Afro curls, her eyes darkened to brown by tinted contact lenses; the other handsome, heavily made-up, fashionably dressed and probably in her early forties. Seated behind a small antique desk and a radiating heavy perfume, Florence Eltenbridge slowly inserted a Sobranie in a slender ivory holder, lit it with an onyx desk lighter, and examined Judy from head to toe as smoke drifted from her nostrils. She then nodded, almost imperceptibly:

"Take it all off, dear."

Judy immediately pigeonholed the accent: East End working class in origin, smoothed by an elocution course, then salted by showbiz twang.

Judy let her frock fall to the floor.

Eltenbridge's heavily jewelled hands folded together. Her long, mascaraed eyelashes dipped appreciatively.

"Show me the shots, Micky."

Kolarcz laid the photographs taken at Sanderton Golf Club on the desk. Eltenbridge turned them over with a faint smile.

"Not bad for a beginner," she said to Judy. "You *are* a beginner, I take it?"

"I need a break, Miss Eltenbridge."

"References?"

"No. I like to keep my tail clean."

"You're wanted by the police?"

"Not in this country."

"Where?"

"Hong Kong. I was Girl Friday to a man who makes wooden toys with hollowed-out insides."

"Identification?"

Judy produced her driving licence, which carried the suburban address of her aunt, Laura Box.

"Passport?"

"It was impounded in Hong Kong."

"How did you get out?"

"The captain of a Greek freighter decided he needed a navigator."

"And you met Micky in the Playboy Club?"

"You could put it that way."

Eltenbridge flicked a glance at Kolarcz. "Is she good in bed?"

"She's special, Flo. Quality product. A two-year-old filly—don't race 'er too 'ard."

"You'll take 10 per cent of her earnings here and no more. Is that understood? Now, Judy, what do you know about this agency?"

"Only what Micky has told me."

"Are you discreet? Many of our clients are important men."

"All men think they're important, Miss Eltenbridge,"

Eltenbridge smiled appreciatively. "Some of them become talkative."

"I'm not thinking of writing my memoirs."

"Sensible. One of our girls had precisely that idea. She approached a Sunday newspaper and fell under a tube train on her way home."

"I'll remember that."

"Do. We're not Samaritans here. I'm prepared to take you on probation."

"Thank you. Could we discuss money?"

"We'll discuss money when we've seen you perform."

"Micky's seen me perform, haven't you, Micky?"

Florence Eltenbridge stubbed out her Sobranie in two vicious jabs. "Let's get one thing clear, Judy. Micky's a photographer. Period. He doesn't decide policy here."

"Sorry, Miss Eltenbridge. The only thing that interests me is money. A lot of it. I'm worth a lot of it and I'm going to get a lot of it. If you don't agree, I've enjoyed meeting you."

Eltenbridge's gaze once again topped and tailed her.

"I'll start you at £40 for a full day, £20 for three hours or under."

Judy smiled sarcastically. "Is that the going rate now for one-armed dishwashers?"

"What did you have in mind?"

"Fifty an hour."

"Take her out of here, Micky."

"Now Judy," pleaded Kolarcz, "yer gotta be reasonable, I mean Flo's offer was only starters, wasn't it, Flo . . ."

But Judy Rossiter was already on her way to the door.

"Wait," said Eltenbridge. "I'll start you at forty an hour."

Kolarcz drove Judy straight to Wallis's in Knightsbridge, where he had been authorized to spend £500 on Eltenbridge's account.

"Jeez, I don't get the 'ang of yer. Almost blew the 'ole thing. Nobody pushes Flo around."

"Dwarf, you're a twit. If I'd accepted her first offer I'd have gone straight under a tube train."

A long morning and five stunning creations later, he drove her to 18 Phillimore Avenue. As Kolarcz pulled his Mustang Mach 1 in on to a yellow line, she spotted a black Mercedes 450 SEL parked forty yards up the street. The rear door opened: one of the four men sitting inside got out and watched them intently as Kolarcz led her to the front door.

It was the Spectrum agent who had confronted her on the doorstep ten days earlier.

Kolarcz pressed the bottom bell. "Yer don't get a key 'ere," he muttered. "No one gets a key, not even me. Always ring the bell, right?"

The electric door-release hummed and they walked into the front hall.

"You'd better meet the boys," Kolarcz said, leading her into a small porter's office and introducing her to two young men dressed in smart blue suits and discreet silk ties. Both "porters" looked as if they could put away King Kong inside the distance.

"Judy, meet Eric and Benny. If yer ever need 'elp——"

"Or friendly advice," grinned Benny.

"——there's a bell inside your flat."

"A friend in need is a friend indeed," Eric added with a wink.

On the first floor Micky unlocked a varnished door and presented her with a duplicate key. The flat was large and luxuriously furnished, with deep-pile carpets, brocaded neo-Regency furniture, muted lighting, a cocktail cabinet, a stereo and colour television, a gleaming bathroom in green enamel with matching tiles, and a vast bed over which hung a highly polished two-way mirror. She noticed a second bedroom.

"Who's my flatmate?"

"You're on your own."

Kolarcz drew her attention to a pretty wall-lamp positioned above the bed. Beneath it was a chrome fitting containing two switches. The switch on the right operated the lamp and could be turned to any of three positions: medium, high, and off.

"If the client wants to see the action in the mirror, yer turn to 'igh and the flood bulbs come on automatically. If 'e prefers the dark, which is rare, very rare, yer switch to off and the infra-red is automatically activated. The second switch activates the camera, which 'as a ten-minute run. Now watch me: my big finger goes on to the light switch and who's gonna notice my thumb turnin' the camera switch? It's all one movement, see? Go on, try it. You'll 'ave a client tonight, all right, but my guess is it won't be a switch job."

Judy nodded and beckoned him silently to the bathroom where she turned on both taps full blast and closed the door to intensify the echo. She seized Kolarcz by the lapels of his leather jacket and pushed his crippled back against the basin. He struggled pathetically, but she held him easily.

"Now get this clear, you worm, whoever comes here tonight gets the switch. Tomorrow morning you'll take the magazine out of the camera and straight to Massey. And just in case you get any ideas about shopping me to Eltenbridge, don't forget we have your death certificate set up in galley proof at the *Monitor*."

He whimpered pathetically; a trickle of saliva ran down his unshaven chin. "The boys . . . Eric and Benny . . . they'd never let me get away with it."

"Rubbish. They can't risk opening magazines of 16mm film. You have the run of this place and you know it."

Kolarcz slunk away into a pale summer evening.

Ten minutes later the phone emitted a delicate chime.

"Judy? This is Florence. Have you settled in?"

"It's lovely, Miss Eltenbridge, just beautiful."

"You'll receive your first client at 8 o'clock. He was extremely interested by your golf course photos—they set his imagination alight."

"What's his handicap?"

Eltenbridge laughed, a brief, mechanical, humourless laugh. "He has several. Mr Harris is a very distinguished man. He must remain anonymous. But his tastes are eccentric and he becomes talkative when excited. Whatever he tells you, forget. Understood?"

"Understood."

"This is not a switch job, Judy. Did Micky explain?"

"He did."

"Look your nicest, then, Judy."

A few minutes before 8 her intercom buzzed. Benny was on the line. "Mr 'Arris is on 'is way up, Judy."

"Thanks, Benny."

She opened the door of her flat and stood poised, beautiful, enticing, cool in a sky-blue silk gown slit, oriental style, up both sides of the skirt almost to the hip. The pale light glowed off the milky curves of her full breasts.

The man who came out of the lift halted stiffly and stared at her. He was dressed in a black coat, striped trousers, and a black Homburg hat. He wore dark glasses and carried a rolled umbrella in one hand and a briefcase in the other.

"Mr Harris?" A seductive smile wafted across her oval face.

Without a word, he walked stiffly past her, flicking the steel tip of his umbrella up the slit of her dress and into the soft flesh of her thigh. She winced: that could leave an ugly bruise. She wasn't in a hurry to become shop-soiled.

He turned like a ramrod in the centre of the white, deep-pile carpet, tossed his Homburg to her like a discus, then let his overcoat fall to the floor. Meekly she knelt at his feet, her breasts dipping and parting, and picked up the coat; as she did so the crook of his umbrella curled round the back of her neck and she was forced forward, prostrate. She rolled slowly on to her back, lifting her knees so that the blue silk of her dress slid sleekly up her legs, exposing the swell of her thigh where her red garter belt tautly held her flesh-coloured stockings.

"Brute," she moaned, twisting her body on the floor as the tip of his umbrella prodded her stomach.

"Champagne," he snapped. It was the first word he had uttered.

She brought a bottle of Moët from the kitchen ice-box, eased the cork forward, then fired it over his head.

"You realize I don't drink," he said, drinking. "It's against the Faith."

Her eyes widened in innocence: "You're a Hindu, Mr Harris?" She moved close to him, her left hand holding her champagne glass, her right insolently unzipping his flies and bringing his small, stiffening penis out into the room. He stood rigid, enraged and delighted, as she turned deftly, picked up his Homburg, and hung it over his 45° erection.

He slapped her across the face. She recoiled. "Oh."

He flung the hat away and removed his dark glasses.

"Do you know who I am—slut?"

She nodded slowly, mischievously. His pallid skin was stretched tightly across prominent cheek bones and his mouth was permanently compressed into a thin pencil line.

"Who am I?"

"Why, you're the famous Mr Harris. You empty the waste-paperbaskets in a back-street betting shop."

"Insolent bitch, you'll regret that!"

"Want to play golf? Winner takes all?"

She peeled off her dress and tossed it over his head. He snarled and tore it away. His eyes were livid with a cruel, aggressive lust.

A brand new golf ball was gleaming on the mantelpiece. She let it fall to the carpet, picked up his umbrella and turned it upside down. The man was breathing more heavily now.

"On your back," she commanded.

He went down like a toy soldier. She unbuckled his trousers and pulled them from his legs, then seized his ankles and stretched them wide apart. She struck the ball hard with the umbrella handle; it skimmed across the carpet into his scrotum. His whole body vibrated. The penis swelled.

"Hole in one," she said. "Your turn."

She stretched herself out on her back, arms and legs spreadeagled. His hands shook with excitement as he took the umbrella and aimed the ball at her vulva. It was a feeble, half-cock shot which trickled weakly up her thigh.

"Ha! Beaten!" She sat up, smiling in triumph. "Console yourself in champagne, Mr Harris, while I prepare the bed for your final humiliation."

But he came after her, panting, and threw her down on the bed. His moist hands began to plunder her breasts.

"Mercy."

"Again. Beg!"

"Mercy!"

He knelt over her, tearing off his upper garments, gazing in mounting excitement at their reflection in the huge, curved mirror suspended above the bed. She reached swiftly for the two switches: a battery of 1-kw bulbs flooded them in a harsh, uncompromising light. The hum of the camera was scarcely audible—it might have been the refrigerator in the kitchen. The light goaded him to a frenzy.

"Slut! Whore! Filth! Don't you recognize one of the chosen?"

"Forgive me."

He descended on her and she braced herself for the horror of the moment when he would penetrate her. His sour breath scorched her face while his talon-like hands clawed across her body.

"Who am I? Be honoured, bitch, to serve one of the elect, one of the elite, brought forth by Allah to purge this corrupt and decadent land of dung and dross! Feel now, now, now! the terrible sword of Al-Ittihad burning you in punishment for your sins, your slavish whoring, for the eternal curse of being a woman!"

"Oh, oh, oh!—you are the one and only Leader."

"No!" His face came over hers, pulsing with sexual pleasure and rage, his climax surging from its throbbing prison. "No! It is blasphemy for any woman, high or low, to speak of the leader, of Zamil Al-Alhambra! Repent! Repent! Grovel!"

For a moment she braced her arms and pushed him up, away, taunting him. "There is no man who could resist me, not even this great Arab."

He exploded inside her, his mouth open, his tongue flecked with white, his eyes bulging. Then his whole body collapsed on top of hers and his head fell forward on to the pillow.

"Zamil Al-Alhambra is not an Arab, little woman. A mother is nothing, only an instrument. The father is genesis."

Micky Kolarcz appeared at 10.30 the following morning, bent, ashen, terrified. He removed the magazine from the camera, replaced it, shot her a venomous glance (which she returned in double measure), and departed, carrying the incriminating evidence in his big camera bag.

A quarter of an hour later the phone chimed prettily. It was Eltenbridge.

"Mr Harris was well pleased, Judy. He's very anxious to see you again."

"Fine."

"I suppose he talked his usual nonsense?"

"It was certainly nonsense to me. He seemed to think he was an Arab sheikh or maybe a Hindu prince, I couldn't get it. I guess he has no head for champagne."

"Or women."

Shortly afterwards Judy Rossiter took the lift to the ground floor, smiled coolly at Benny and Eric, and heard the front door of 18 Phillimore Avenue click fast behind her.

The rear door of the Mercedes opened. The Spectrum agent who had intercepted her two weeks ago climbed out.

"Excuse me, miss."

Her spine stiffened. "Yes?"

"Haven't I seen you before?"

She returned his stare and waited till his eyes flickered down. "If you try to proposition me ever again, you'll be on Miss Eltenbridge's carpet. What's your name?"

"Cliff," he mumbled.

"Cliff *what*?"

"Cliff North. Honest, I wasn't tryin' . . ."

"Very sensible of you, Cliff." She turned on her heel and walked swiftly towards Kensington High Street, where she hailed a taxi. Three hours after she reached her flat the phone rang.

"How's Alice?"

She immediately sensed the constraint, the embarrassment in Ellison's voice. It triggered an immense, vibrating aggression within her—that smug liberal hypocrite would shelter behind his moral code while taking full advantage of her talents.

"Well, have you seen the film?" she snapped.

"We . . . naturally . . . just enough for purposes of identification . . ."

"OK, you're a frightfully nice fellow, Ellison, very Winchester and Oxford. You really ought to be a vegetarian."

"Judy, it was your idea . . ."

"Am I old enough to be told who my client was?"

"You didn't recognize him?"

"Where would we poor tarts be without your encyclopaedic brain?"

"Judy, perhaps I should come and see you . . ."

"Who the fuck was it?"

"Geoffrey Ozanne, Under Secretary of State at the Home Office."

"Thanks. Now I'll tell you what he said to me. One, that he is a member of the elite, the elect, chosen by Allah to cleanse this country of people like you—and I wish him luck, by the way."

"Did he mention Al-Ittihad?"

"Yes, sir."

"Did he claim to be the supreme leader?"

"On the contrary. The supreme leader goes by the name of Zamil Al-Alhambra."

Ellison whistled.

"Did I just tell you something you wanted to know?" she said sarcastically.

"Yes."

"Here comes the third thing. I'll quote verbatim and leave it to greater minds to interpret: 'Zamil Al-Alhambra is not an Arab, little woman. A mother is nothing, only an instrument. The father is genesis."

"He said *that*!"

"Ellison, I should have your salary."

On the top floor of the London Library, in St James's Square, Ellison received the usual mild electric shock and uttered his usual expletive as he pulled the light cord. For half an hour he prowled along the metal racks of the Islamic section, plucking out religious histories and works of reference, examining illustrations and occasionally taking a note. He was reminded of the astonishingly rapid penetration of South-Western Europe by the Arab armies in the early eighth century—an advance finally halted by Charles Martel at the battle of Tours in 732. By that time the name of the prophet-son of Arabia, joined with the name of Almighty Allah, was being called five times a day from scores of minarets in the Iberian Peninsula.

Climbing into the back seat of the Granada Ghia, Ellison had reason to ponder the historical resonance of his car's brand name—it was in eighth-century Granada that the victorious Arabs had built a vast palatial mosque to symbolize the triumph of Islam.

The name of the mosque was Al-Alhambra.

Fourteen

The chauffeur-driven Silver Cloud Rolls-Royce drifted silently up Lisson Grove and Grove End Road into the quiet residential streets of St John's Wood. In the back seat, fanned by discreet air-conditioning, Judy Rossiter sat beside Florence Eltenbridge. Wearing sapphire earrings, a clutch of peridot and emerald rings on her fingers, a broad-brimmed straw hat and a creation by Cardin in shot silk, Eltenbridge was dressed for Ascot, where her three-year-old horse, Escort, was due to compete in the Gold Cup. Racing metaphors were much on her mind.

"You're a promising filly, Judy, and I'm taking you to the scene of the big prize money." Momentarily the older woman's white-gloved hand gripped her wrist. "Be cool, be smart, obey orders and don't overreach yourself."

"What's it worth, Miss Eltenbridge?"

Eltenbridge shot her a glance beneath false eyelashes a quarter of an inch long. "It's always money with you."

"What else is there in life?"

"Nothing. And how does a woman get it?"

"How?"

"She keeps her cunt open and her mouth closed."

Judy giggled. "Not like your Monika."

The straw hat turned sharply. "Monika who?"

"I don't know her second name. German girl. I met her a couple of weeks ago at a party. She was plastered."

"And?"

"She bragged about working for Relief. She had some unbelievable story about au pairing for a famous journalist as a cover for spying on him."

"Really? Who is the journalist?"

"Don't ask me, I don't read newspapers."

"But she mentioned his name to you?"

"Oh yes. She was pissed out of her mind. Where are we going?"

The Silver Cloud swept past St John's Wood Reform Synagogue: Maurice Cohn's synagogue; Ulf Steinberg's synagogue.

"You are to meet a very distinguished gentleman, a sculptor of some note. You are to become Mr Steinberg's model and assistant—like clay in his hands. You will be involved in an operation of great importance."

"Sounds like money," Judy said cheerfully.

In a large, light-filled penthouse studio whose walls were covered with valuable paintings and exotic tropical plants, the sculptor came forward to greet them. He kissed Eltenbridge's hand, then Judy's. Something inside her trembled, wavered, as he smilingly looked her over. She remembered that debauched face, half-Jewish, half-Scandinavian, from the Aldwych Theatre.

"Charming! So this is she. *Charmante. Ravissante.*" He turned back to Eltenbridge. "And you, my dear, they'll have to give you the Gold Cup, and not your horse."

It was then that Judy noticed the other woman.

She was reclining, motionless, beside one of Steinberg's fibre-glass sculptures—a naked Nubian girl reaching up with tautened breasts and thighs to net a basketball. This woman, too, was clearly dressed for Ascot. Her physical resemblance to Eltenbridge was unmistakable: they had to be sisters.

The woman smiled drily at Judy. "Take off your rags, dear." Her voice was veneered with a theatrical gloss.

Judy slid out of her dress.

In the silence which followed something—a relationship,

a hierarchy—became apparent. Eltenbridge was offering her; Steinberg was accepting her; the other woman was weighing the decision. Finally she nodded.

"Good. Promising."

Then, peremptorily, she summoned Eltenbridge out to the waiting Rolls. Steinberg hurried after her, oozing obsequious charm. When he returned a few minutes later he threw up his hands in mock disappointment.

"Oh dear, you've got dressed."

"Whatever you say."

"Ah, how I envy them Ascot: the champagne, the strawberries, the people, such lovely people, such elegance—but I hate horses."

"Who was that lady?"

His eyebrows arched with a hint of remonstrance. "A friend, my dear, a friend."

She turned away to the gallery of fibre-glass and plastic resin sculptures surrounding her—Pop and Op in style, derivative, vulgar, always erotic: slave girls being ravished by minotaurs wearing Papal mitres, naked girls kneeling to support glass coffee tables, hermaphrodite youths masturbating one another on Honda motorcycles . . .

"Wow!" she said, bright-eyed.

He bowed. "One must live, dear. But one must also confess that work of this kind is not my first love. I am at heart a man of the theatre, always, always."

"As a stage designer? I'm sorry, I ought to have known."

"Ah, but you are too young, too young. That was long ago. Now how do I see you . . . yes, yes, I have it! As queen of the gladiators, mistress of the martial arts! Come, come."

Tittering with joy, he led her down into a bedroom on the floor below, opened a Chippendale chest, and excitedly flung items of clothing on to the bed: a G-string; thigh-high boots with heels spurred in burnished steel; an armour corset cut to prop up her naked breasts; and an eagle-crested helmet.

"I shall be waiting," he said intently.

She climbed the richly carpeted stairs and walked into the

studio, into the compass of his saturnine smile. The beauty of his muscles, the tautness of his long limbs surprised her as she approached the chair in which he was reclining naked, the chair in which the nameless lady had sat. Spreading her legs to straddle his thighs and sinking her loins down to receive his huge spire, she felt his hands clasping her waist with silent, assured power. Three times in rapid succession she let him goad her on to orgasm, registering his mastery by arrogantly withholding his own.

Finally her head fell forward on his shoulder.

Effortlessly he lifted her up into his arms and carried her back to the bedroom below. Spreading her limp, spent body across the bed, he removed her gladiatorial garments, lifted the covers to her chin, turned out the light and closed the door.

"Sleep," he said.

She heard the swish of a shower in the adjoining bathroom, then the closing of a door and his soft footfall ascending to the studio above. Flicking the light switch above her head, she studied her reflection in the large, two-way mirror suspended over the bed. The dual switch panel in the wall resembled exactly the ones Kolarcz had installed at 18 Phillimore Avenue. So.

Quickly, quietly, she went through the wardrobe and the drawers of the Chippendale chest. The top drawer was packed with a woman's things, pairs of stockings, bras, garter belts, bottles of perfume, a velvet evening bag, costume jewellery, lipsticks, eyelashes, skin lotions, nail varnish . . . At the bottom of the drawer her hand found a few slips of paper. She drew them out: two were the stubs of theatre tickets, which she tossed back, but the third one was something else. She slipped it deep into the lining pocket of her handbag, lay back on the bed and closed her eyes.

Presently the sculptor brought her black coffee.

"We haven't done much work today, I'm afraid," she apologized.

"Tomorrow, tomorrow. A distinguished client is due here

for a sitting, my dear, and today is perhaps not the day to introduce you."

"Oh. Why?" she pouted.

"You look a little . . . a little . . ."

"Ravished?"

"I would not have used that word, my dear. But come up to the studio when you're dressed so I can ask you whether you recognise this man."

When she entered the studio Steinberg smiled and pulled back the polythene sheet which was draped over a clay bust on a pedestal.

"Of course it's far from finished," he said.

"It is somehow familiar . . . No, I can't get it."

"You will, you will," he said, courteously conducting her to the front door where a taxi was already waiting.

"18 Phillimore Avenue," she told the driver.

As the taxi turned off Baker Street into the Marylebone Road, she paid the driver off. As soon as it was out of sight, she hailed another cab and drove to within three hundred yards of her flat in Bonham Terrace. It was during this second lap of her journey that she examined the slip of paper she had taken from the Chippendale chest in Steinberg's bedroom.

Ellison rang through an hour after she arrived home.

"Any news?"

"Is being screwed by Ulf Steinberg news?"

"Look, Judy . . . I . . . perhaps you ought to——"

"There was a woman there. She's the spitting image of Eltenbridge, she could even be a twin. Theatrical voice. The signal was clear: she was calling the tune. Steinberg declined to divulge her name. One of the drawers in the bedroom was full of a woman's stuff——"

"The same woman's?"

"I can't be sure. I found a few theatre stubs and something else which might or might not interest you. It's an Oxford City ticket for a parking offence committed in Beaumont Street."

"Date?"

"June 12."

"Registration number of the car?"

Judy read it to him.

"There's one other thing. Steinberg said his first love was the theatre—stage design—but he hadn't done any for years. Does that ring any bells?"

"Darling, you're wonderful. Take it easy."

In recent years car registration records had been centralized at the Department of the Environment's Vehicle Licensing Centre in Swansea. Although these records were normally closed to the general public, solicitors, journalists and private detectives habitually gained access to registration information through contacts in the police or the Centre itself. In normal times Ellison would have sent a Telex request from the *Monitor*'s wire room to Gareth Williams of the *South Wales Evening Post*. But union rules insisted that Telex messages be transmitted by professional telecommunicators, and Ellison no longer knew whom he could trust. A direct phone-call, even from a call-box, was hazardous at the receiving end; cables and telegrams were now systematically scrutinized by the Government; and first-class mail, the safest method, was too slow. Ellison sent Cherry up the road to the Swansea paper's London office in Bouverie Street; within ten minutes a phone call went through from Alan Davies to Gareth Williams, without mention of Ellison's name.

Ellison returned to the press-cuttings library and re-examined the clippings on Ulf Steinberg. But there was nothing earlier than 1970—the old clippings had been thrown out to make space. He descended to the Arts Department on the third floor and went in search of the paper's veteran theatre critic, Moses Montgomery.

"He's in bed," a girl told him.

"Ill?"

"He works at night, doesn't he?" she said with disdain. "He never comes in till mid-afternoon."

"Give me his phone number."

"He never takes calls in the morning. He leaves the phone off the hook."

"Then give me his address."

"Ooh, I don't think I could do that."

A pillar of revolving address cards stood on her desk. He twirled them round until he found Montgomery's address and number.

"Ooh, you have got a cheek," the girl said. "Who are you, anyway?"

"Anton Chekhov."

"How do you spell that?"

He drove to a block of flats in Battersea and routed Montgomery out of bed.

"Good God," said the old critic, opening the door in his pyjamas, "I must be a person of greater consequence than I had imagined."

"Moses, you know I can't resist a pretty face. Make some coffee and tell me about Ulf Steinberg's career in the theatre. If possible, pursue the two activities simultaneously."

Montgomery stretched, yawned, ran a hand through his tousled white hair, and groaned. "Who?"

"Ulf Steinberg, the sculptor. I believe he did stage designs in the sixties."

"Ah, yes, Steinberg."

Ellison followed Montgomery into the kitchen, where the critic experienced some difficulty in locating the sink. "Plush stuff, bright and vulgar, drawing-room comedies and French farces. Horrible."

"Did Steinberg work for a number of theatres or just one? The water will come out, by the way, when you turn the tap anti-clockwise."

"Always the Pavilion Theatre, on Shaftesbury Avenue."

"You might still have some of the programmes?"

Montgomery sighed. "Do you want the coffee or the programmes?"

"The programmes."

Montgomery shuffled into a small study where theatre programmes extended along four shelves. After much fumbling and muttering, he came up with two dozen Pavilion programmes dating back to the sixties. The only photographs they contained, Ellison noted with disappointment, were of leading actors and actresses.

"Thanks, Moses. I think I hear the kettle boiling in the kitchen."

Ellison spent a quarter of an hour noting down credits and productions.

"Moses, this fellow Conrad Styles, who was General Manager of the Pavilion at that time—is he still there?"

"Indeed not. There was a small scandal, you know."

"What kind of scandal?"

"Better get that from him."

"Where do I find him?"

"He's an associate administrative director at the National. Back on his feet."

"A friend of yours?"

"You won't have had time to notice, but I have panned the National's last three productions."

"Moses, you should have consulted me before doing that." He found the phone and dialled the National Theatre. A secretary informed him that Mr Styles was unavailable—he was attending a rehearsal in the Lyttelton auditorium.

"Page him for me, could you? It's urgent."

"What was the name, please?"

"Bill Ellison, of the *Sunday Monitor*."

"All Press inquiries are referred to——"

"Kindly tell Mr Styles I'm not interested in the National, I'm interested in the nation. It's very urgent."

Ellison waited ten minutes until Conrad Styles finally came on the line. He sounded out of breath, overweight, and in a bad temper. The National was still losing half a million a year and there had been hoarse cries in Parliament for a wielding of the axe.

"Mr Styles, I'd be grateful if you could tell me one or two

203

things about the Pavilion Theatre's productions in the sixties."

"Jesus Christ! I thought it was urgent! We're three days behind schedule on *Coriolanus*, we have a go-slow by stage hands, we have a revolving stage which refuses to revolve and . . . Fucking journalists!"

"I suppose you're aware of the political forces which would like to close the National and leave it like an empty mausoleum. Or maybe convert it into a mosque?"

Styles grunted. "What can that have to do with the Pavilion in the sixties?"

"Everything. I notice that in twelve out of twelve Pavilion productions where Ulf Steinberg designed the sets, the costumes were designed by Rose Weber."

"Indeed they were." Styles's voice was bitter.

"Was it coincidence they always worked together?"

"Was it coincidence that Macbeth and Lady Macbeth always worked together? Don't play cat and mouse with me, Ellison. Montgomery must have told you that story. In between panning our productions."

"No. He advised me to get it straight from you."

"When I was at school they taught me that newspapers have press-cutting libraries."

"I'm afraid a lot of the pre-1970 stuff has been thrown out."

"You may recall the Frank Young case. Frank Young was sentenced at the Old Bailey in 1969 for living off immoral earnings and extortion—he was a protection racketeer on a big scale. He and his underlings were suspected of several gangland murders but no one dared squeal. Young got ten years. Three of his accomplices got lighter sentences. One of them was a woman, Young's mistress. It was she who had organized the prostitution side—I believe she got seven years."

A ratchet clicked in Ellison's head. "Elizabeth Lyons?"

"The same."

"Steinberg and Weber were involved?"

"Steinberg and Weber were named by three prosecution

204

witnesses, young actresses who had worked at the Pavilion in small parts but couldn't find steady work. Each testified that Rose Weber had offered to find them regular work, then introduced them to Elizabeth Lyons, who promptly propositioned them. Two were sufficiently desperate to accept. Both recalled that Ulf Steinberg had enjoyed *droit de seigneur*, otherwise known as first dip, with the full connivance of the women Weber and Lyons."

"Even though Weber was Steinberg's mistress?"

"Absolutely. Now I'll tell you why I lost my job. The third actress was revolted by the proposition and came straight to me, as General Manager. As far as I can recall, she wanted Weber whipped from Drury Lane to Piccadilly Circus."

"And you told her to forget the whole thing?"

"I didn't want a scandal. But then Young was arrested and it all came out in the wash. Actors Equity depicted me as little short of a white slave trader."

"Steinberg and Weber weren't prosecuted?"

"The Crown found no evidence they had taken money; the gain dimension, necessary in law, was missing. Weber claimed in court that she had taken pity on the girls and introduced them to her sister as a friendly gesture."

"Weber and Lyons were sisters?"

"Of course. Weber was Rose's stage name—pronounced Vay-bur. What's your interest, anyway?"

"Mr Styles, I'm very grateful to you. Mention this conversation to no one, not even your wife. To *no one*. For you it's quite simply a matter of life or death."

There was silence at the other end of the phone. "My God," Conrad Styles whispered.

"St Catherine's House at the bottom of Kingsway," Ellison told Charlie.

"Will do, sir."

Ellison and Massey had both made fruitless checks in the

Register of Births, Deaths and Marriages, but now Ellison felt he had something to get his teeth into. Working on the hypothesis that Florence Eltenbridge, Director of Relief, Ltd, was in reality Elizabeth Lyons, and that her sister Rose Weber was the other woman Judy had met at Steinberg's house, he began to work through the red, leather-bound Birth indexes, beginning in 1933.

He found an Elizabeth Lyons born in 1936; and a Margaret Rose Lyons born in 1937. Both births had been registered at the same East London register office.

He then moved to the green Marriage indexes and discovered that an Elizabeth Lyons had married a Frank Young in 1975, the year in which—according to the *Monitor*'s press clippings library—the racketeer Frank Young had come out of jail.

No one called Frank Cain had married either a Florence Eltenbridge or an Elizabeth Lyons during the period in question.

Ellison filed three application forms, one for the Young–Lyons marriage, one for the birth of Elizabeth Lyons, and one for the birth of Margaret Rose Lyons. He wrote out a cheque for £7.50 and was told to expect duplicates of the certificates through the post within two days. Members of the public were no longer permitted to make their own searches of the original certificates—too many passports had been forged that way. Now the Register kept a record of all applications for a search.

Ellison then began a long arduous search for the marriage of Rose Weber, checking under both "W" and "L" for Lyons. As he sweated and grinded back over a period of twenty-five years he lifted down and replaced on the shelves two hundred heavy volumes, four per year under S–Z (P—Z before 1971) and four per year under L–R (G–O before 1971). He found nothing.

Neither Rose Weber nor Margaret Rose Lyons had married. Yet Ellison had a feeling that they had. The Register, of course, covered only marriages in England and Wales.

The Scottish records were held in Edinburgh, the Nevada records in Nevada, and the Tibetan records (presumably) in Tibet. It was lawful to be married in Tibet or in a submarine sitting on the ocean bed.

Ellison now turned to a different line of inquiry. He wanted to trace the birth certificates of three men—the three men who, in his view, were only a few weeks away from assuming absolute power in Britain as members of the Supreme Executive Council. The index search did not take him long, for the years of their births were recorded in *Who's Who*.

One man's birth had been registered in Canterbury.

One man's birth had been registered in Andover.

One man's birth had not been registered at all.

Ellison knew that on the seventh floor of St Catherine's House there exists a room which records the births of British subjects registered with British consulates overseas. But in that room the search has to be undertaken by a registrar official; and, since the indexes are arranged by country, no search can be undertaken unless the applicant knows the country in which the birth was registered.

Ellison didn't know.

He banged in application forms for the birth certificates of the two other men.

The certificates arrived two days later. Some of them.

Instead of the birth certificates of the men born near Canterbury and Andover, he received a standard printed note announcing that the certificates could not be located, although the search would continue. A coincidence? Ellison doubted it. Someone was throwing dust in his eyes.

On the other hand the birth certificates of Elizabeth Lyons and Margaret Rose Lyons confirmed that they were born of the same parents. Equally interesting, their mother's maiden name had been Eltenbridge. (The practice of including the mother's maiden name on birth certificates dated from the September Quarter of 1911.) Ellison had never really doubted they were sisters, so obviously were they named after two other sisters—little princesses whose father had ascended the throne as George VI shortly before the Lyons girls were born.

Ellison now knew:

(1) that Frank Cain, boss of Spectrum, and Florence Eltenbridge, Director of Relief, were in reality the racketeers Frank Young and Elizabeth Lyons. They had married after Young had served six of his ten years in Parkhurst.

(2) Rose Weber's real name was Margaret Rose Lyons, sister of the woman now calling herself Eltenbridge, and very probably the woman Judy had seen in Steinberg's house.

When Ellison returned to the Features Department in Gowers House, Cherry gave him a sealed envelope sent down by hand from the *South Wales Evening Post*'s office in Bouverie Street.

He opened it and smiled grimly. The car which had picked up a parking ticket on June 12 in Beaumont Street, Oxford, was a white Porsche registered under the name of Rose Weber. Her address was given as 18 St Mark's Road, W10. Ellison knew that area of North Kensington well; the first forty-odd houses in St Mark's Road had been pulled down years ago to make way for a new primary school.

It was this woman who had been calling the tune in Steinberg's house, according to Judy. Where did her power lie? And why did she continue to disguise her true identity and address?

Ellison lit a small cigar and gazed out of the window. Ice-cold logic drove him to a single conclusion until his head ached from the futile effort to reject it.

It was now that Ellison had to exert every available ounce of experience and self-discipline to restrain himself from confronting his suspects or placing them under physical surveillance. He could, for example, confront Ozanne or Leech with the compromising photographs taken at 18 Phillimore Avenue. Fatal. They would understand better than the subterranean Kolarcz how far a paper like the *Monitor* could go. He would merely succeed in blowing the present state of his knowledge and thereby slam the door in his own face. Magnus was an expert surveillance photographer but, according to Judy, Steinberg's house in St John's Wood was screened, round the clock, by Spectrum's Mercedes. Ellison needed an up-to-date photograph of Rose Weber; but Judy's life already hung by a thread, and to ask her to attempt a Minox "lighter" shot of Weber when next she visited Steinberg was tantamount to snapping that thread.

In the end his only weapon was his own gift for gathering and analyzing circumstantial evidence. He now had enough to guess the identity of Zamil Al-Alhambra. But to prove his case he needed more.

Fifteen

Parking her Ford Escort in Chester Place, Pru Ellison found her son sitting on the doorstep, leaning against a large parcel.

"Darling, whatever are you doing out here?"

He grimaced. "There's no one in. I do wish you'd let me have a key."

The Ellisons had decided, in present circumstances, that it was too risky to let a ten-year-old carry the keys to the front door.

"But where's Monika?"

"Don't ask me."

"What's this parcel?"

"A bomb, of course. I found it here."

Nervously she examined it. It was quite a large parcel, between three and four cubic feet in volume, and beneath the securely fastened wrapping she could feel the outlines of a wooden crate.

She opened the front door, hurried to the kitchen, put bread in the toaster and cheese on the table, then climbed the three floors to Monika Bauer's room. It was empty. Everything—clothes, personal effects, suitcases—had gone. There was no note of explanation.

Urging Christopher to eat the toast and cheese, she left the house on foot, crossing the Outer Circle into Regent's Park, where a couple of young gardeners had been at work for some weeks, apparently erecting protective wire fencing round the trees bordering on the road.

"A large parcel has come," she said.

The Special Branch detective nodded. "We've been over it. There's no bomb."

"Oh . . . But it looks . . . odd."

"If you want us to open it, Mrs Ellison, we'll open it."

"I'd better consult my husband."

"Your au pair left. In a taxi. I expect you've gathered that."

"Thank you. You're . . . a great comfort to us. I don't suppose you'd both like a cup of tea?"

"We'd love one, Mrs Ellison, but Superintendent Bradlaw is like Big Brother: he's always watching us."

With some difficulty she heaved the parcel up into the front hallway; it must have weighed twenty pounds.

"They say it isn't a bomb," she told Christopher, slicing potatoes and throwing them into the chip pan.

"Then let's open it."

"It happens to be addressed to your father."

"Has Monika gone for ever?"

"It certainly looks like it. I'm afraid it's too late to ring the agency tonight. Oh, damn, damn, damn."

"I know why she left in a hurry."

"Why?"

"Because she was spying on Dad. She was always creeping about and wearing no clothes."

Ellison arrived home at 7.30.

"Hi, Dad," chirped Christopher, "Monika's gone with all her things and I had to sit on the doorstep for over an hour until Mum came and there's this parcel for you, the men in the park say it isn't a bomb, they've checked it, so why don't you open it?"

Ellison glanced at the parcel. "Later," he said casually. "Now you push off to bed."

"I want to see what's in the parcel."

"You can see in the morning."

"I bet it is a bomb after all." The boy was pale with fear.

Pru intervened quickly. "Christopher darling, why don't

you have a bath and a quick look at television and——"

"And Mum will come with you," Ellison added.

Ellison waited until he heard the bath water stop running and Christopher's noisy immersion. Then he took a pair of wire-cutters and sliced through the thick twine binding the parcel. He ripped off the brown wrapping-paper and came to a wooden crate heavily nailed down. Neither the paper nor the crate itself carried any description of the sender. Gently he tipped the crate over and listened; it sounded as if there was padding, probably straw, but something had definitely moved, something solid and heavy. He inserted a screwdriver under the top planks and eased the $1\frac{1}{2}$-inch-long nails out, one by one. The first of the four planks came away; beneath it he found a wad of straw which had been wetted and packed solid inside the crate. He thrust the blade of his screwdriver down into the wad but made no progress. He began to ease off the second plank.

He heard Christopher climbing out of the bath on the second floor, then two high-pitched voices rising in argument. He stopped work and replaced the first plank. A moment later Christopher appeared in his dressing-gown at the head of the stairs with Pru pulling at his elbow. Two frightened faces stared down at him.

Ellison tried to smile. "Whatever it is, it isn't a bomb. It seems to be the antique glass vase I bought last week at Sotheby's auction. Why don't you go and watch the box and I'll bring it up."

Relief spread over the boy's face. But not over Pru's. She knew that Sotheby's would put their name on the parcel; she also knew they wouldn't plonk a valuable antique on the doorstep. She led Christopher away to the sitting-room.

Sweat was running down Ellison's face, neck and body and his heart was hammering against his rib cage. He removed the third plank and started on the fourth.

No need: you're only playing for time.

He dug his screwdriver blade into the still damp straw, levered, dug again, excavating it into chunks, pulling it out with his hands. He noticed that his hands and fingers were becoming sticky, slimy, and that a dark red-brown viscous stain was spreading through the lower layers of straw. He thrust his hand deeper, felt something hard against his knuckle, bone meeting bone, recoiled, probed again, and sank into a mucous mush of severed membranes and arteries.

He turned away as his acidified lunch rose from the pit of his stomach and splattered on to the carpet.

He closed his eyes, counted to ten, wiped the vomit from his mouth with his sleeve, then thrust his hand down into the bottom of the crate, fastened his fingers round matted hair—and pulled.

He feared, above all, the staring, anguished, accusing eyes. But there were none. Only empty sockets of gore. As he raised the head the jaw sagged and the tongueless mouth lolled open.

He let Joe O'Neill fall back into the crate, covered the head with straw, piled the loose planks on top, opened the front door, lifted the crate, carried it down to the basement well, came up again, closed the door, filled two pails with hot water and grabbed a couple of rags in the kitchen, returned to the front hall, and attempted to soak the vomit, straw and blood off the carpet. He had barely cleaned up the mess when Christopher reappeared at the head of the stairs.

"It was two dozen bottles of wine, mostly broken. Now go to bed, Christopher."

Half an hour after Bradlaw's Special Branch men had taken the crate away, the Ellisons, man and wife, sat together in the kitchen avoiding one another's eyes. Pru was in tears.

"You're a good man, Bill, but a terribly destructive one. There's nobody you wouldn't sacrifice, is there, in your pursuit of an abstraction."

"Perhaps we could have this conversation some other time."

"Really? After they send us Christopher's head in a box?" Sobbing, she ran from the room.

Shortly before midnight he heard Charlie's soft but unsteady footfall mounting the stairs. Ellison came to the door of his study and beckoned his chauffeur inside.

"Plastered?"

"Well, sir, I've had a few but——"

"Wine or spirits?"

"Claret, sir. I'm very partial to claret."

"Go to the kitchen and drink two pints of water. I mean two pints. Then come straight back here."

Ellison unlocked his small Chubb safe and extracted £200 in bank notes.

At 12.20 the acrid, putrescent stench which had arisen out of the crate welled up again in his stomach. He spent a quarter of an hour retching fitfully in the bathroom, then dragged himself to the phone in the sitting-room, gritted his teeth, and dialled 0232, followed by a number in Belfast.

Twenty minutes later he put down the receiver, poured himself a brandy, and collapsed into a chair. For a while he stared at a light-bulb. Then he walked quietly into the bedroom.

Pru was lying awake. He sat down on the bed and took her limp, cold hand.

"How long before your school term ends at Crewe Hill?"

"Ten days. Why?"

"Because you're going to make a call to the Chairman of the School Governors and another to your Deputy Head right now."

Soon after three o'clock the phone rang.

"Ellison speaking."

"Daddy, it's Faith. I know it's awful to wake you at this time but——"

"You didn't wake me, darling. Has Charlie arrived?"

"He certainly has. With two appalling thugs carrying Berettas. You might have warned me."

"Faith, people listen to our conversations."

"But what's happening, Daddy? Charlie insists I pack all my clothes and——"

"Please do exactly as he says, darling."

"But Julian and I were going walking in the Lake District."

"Faith, all our lives are now in imminent danger. The four of us are catching El Al Flight LY 316 to Tel Aviv at 3 o'clock tomorrow afternoon."

"But . . ."

"No buts. Charlie and his nasties will drive you straight to Heathrow. We'll meet you in Terminal 3 at 1.30."

"I feel like a prisoner in my own flat!"

"You are a prisoner. And let me assure you, darling, that you could be a prisoner in hands a lot less friendly. A crate was delivered to this house today. When your mother got home she found Christopher sitting on the doorstep, leaning against it."

"It wasn't a bomb!"

"No, Faith. It was the severed head of Joe O'Neill."

Sixteen

The convoy swept along the M40 towards Oxford, the Israeli Embassy's armour-plated Buick in the lead, Ellison's Granada behind, and two Triumphs of the Leech Squad bringing up the rear, their beacons flashing and their sirens hissing.

Ellison was seated beside Solomon Rupin in the Buick.

"Your family arrived safely at 20.35 and were taken straight to one of our Tel Aviv apartments where they will be protected round the clock."

"I'm very grateful, Solomon."

"I gather you left the El Al flight at Rome and caught the first plane back to London."

"I didn't want to take any chances at Heathrow. The ISP have agents stationed at every departure gate now."

"Very sensible. A message flashed to the control tower, the El Al flight is ordered to delay its departure, the Leech Squad goes aboard and discovers that your family are loaded with hashish . . . bingo!" Rupin snapped his fingers with dreadful finality. "That's the word, isn't it: 'bingo'?"

"Well . . ."

"I received a message from Jerusalem this morning. The British Government is expected to break off diplomatic relations with Israel the day after tomorrow."

"To coincide with the arrival of the Arab Mission? You'll have to leave, then?"

Solomon Rupin allowed himself a rare, faint smile. "In theory."

"Tell me more about Michael Ben-Dor, to whose lectures you are so mysteriously dragging me."

"Ben-Dor is Professor of Arabic in the Hebrew University's Institute of Asian and African Studies. For many years he and Stanford Christie have been responsible for the joint study programme between the Hebrew University and the Middle East Institute."

"But who is Ben-Dor really?"

Rupin shot him a reproving glance.

The four cars drew to a halt in front of Stanford Christie's Park Town home shortly before 9 am. Pulling a lock of black hair out of his eyes, Christie surveyed the cavalcade, then gestured towards another Leech Squad car parked up the road.

"You too?" Ellison said.

"Ever since Michael arrived. I suspect it may become a permanent feature of this landscape."

He led the way into the dining-room where a splendid breakfast, calculated not to offend kosher tastes, was spread across the table. Ellison shook hands with Ben-Dor, a frail, bespectacled scholar with long black hair and a bushy beard.

"Who's the girl, Stanford?" Ellison asked, as a handsome young woman bustled back to the kitchen.

"What? Oh, Teresa. Margaret's been away most of the week, so she found Teresa to help out while Michael's staying. Spanish girl, doesn't speak much English, very nice."

Teresa returned, carrying a jug of steaming coffee, and flashed each man a seductive smile. Ellison, Rupin and Ben-Dor tucked into the boiled eggs and toast with relish, but their host, as usual, merely pecked at his food.

At 9.15 they set out for the Middle East Institute in two cars, Christie and Ben-Dor in Christie's, Ellison and Rupin in Ellison's. Threading their way down Carfax and the

Broad, they became increasingly aware that Ben-Dor's scheduled lecture had precipitated a massive demonstration of opposition. Hundreds of banners and placards denouncing "Israeli Aggression" and "Zionist Imperialism" greeted them as they came within view of the Institute.

"There aren't enough police out to hold that mob back for long," Ellison said.

"Naturally," Rupin said bitterly.

City police guided them into the Institute's car-park, then ushered them into the lecture hall by a rear entrance. While Christie led Ben-Dor up on to the lecture platform, Ellison and Rupin took their places in the second row of the audience, behind a distinguished group of Oxford academics wearing gowns and mortar boards.

The Fleet Street Press was also represented in strength. Ellison and Timothy Powerstock exchanged sardonic glances. Bernie Holzheimer of the *New York Times* made a face, as if to say, "What's happening here?—don't tell me, I know." In the front row of the Press section Ellison spotted the puffy, flushed, cynical features of Bert Hoyle, licking his drooping lower lip in anticipation of the mayhem ahead.

When Stanford Christie rose, pale and tense, and took the microphone to introduce his distinguished guest, an orchestrated barrage of hisses rose from the students packed into the rear of the hall.

"I am convinced," Christie began, "that it is our sacred duty, here in this Institute, to maintain an open dialogue."

"Not with racists!" came a shout from the back.

"During the ten years that I have been Director of this Institute, it has opened its doors to scholars and students of every nationality, every race, every religion, and every belief. And it will continue to do so. We have many friends in the Arab world who recognize——"

At this point the noise from the back reached such a level that Christie could no longer be heard. It was now that the small, pink, Father Christmas-like figure of Professor Hugh Swinburne rose majestically from the front row, wrapped the folds of his black gown around him, and stalked out of the hall to deafening applause from the back.

The first rotten egg splattered on the projection screen behind Christie's head. The second caught him on the shoulder. The ominous, bullet-like rattle of metal ball bearings hitting the stage brought the meeting to a close. Screaming students were now storming forward towards the platform.

Bert Hoyle was grinning from ear to ear.

"Let's go." Ellison and Rupin fought their way through the chaotic throng and out of the rear entrance into the car-park, hard on the heels of Christie and Ben-Dor. A glance towards the entrance of the car-park was enough to convince them that they stood no chance of making a getaway on wheels. A police officer hustled them out of a door in the car-park wall and into a patrol car.

Christie was ashen-faced. "Michael, I don't know how to apologize . . ."

But the thin, wiry Israeli professor was smiling serenely. "I was so sure this would happen that I didn't even bother to prepare the lecture. We'll all go for a walk in the Meadows before lunch and recover our composure. Yes?"

Ten minutes after they reached Park Town a call came through from the City police to inform them that both Christie's car and Ellison's had been overturned and set on fire in the Institute car-park.

Ellison broke the news to an outraged Charlie and told his chauffeur to take the first train back to London.

The Meadows were still soft from an early morning rain shower. In the distance, skimming over the invisible sunken band of the river, boats were pirouetting under bright-coloured sails. As the four men squelched across the wet turf Ellison noticed that the two ISP agents pursuing them kept closing the gap in worried, almost frantic, bursts.

He also noticed that both the Israelis had deliberately confined the conversation to trivialities.

As they halted on the water's edge in a mire of mud and

cow pat, the black-bearded Ben-Dor smiled enigmatically behind his wire-rimmed spectacles and extracted a small, stainless-steel transmitter from his trouser pocket.

"It's manufactured by a Mitsubishi subsidiary in Spain," he explained dispassionately. "I found it concealed in the sole of my shoe last night." He glanced slyly at Christie. "Stanford, kindly remove your left shoe."

"A bout of summer 'flu is all I need to complete my day," Christie grumbled, reluctantly complying.

With several swift and practised strokes of a hunting-knife blade, Ben-Dor cleanly scythed the leather heel from Christie's shoe. An identical transmitter fell into his hand. "Just so," he murmured, holding the second transmitter below the surface of the river. "What brought those ISP goons to within twenty yards of us was the progressive shortening of this bug's range by the wet grass."

Turning, Ellison noticed that the two agents had now sullenly withdrawn to a distance of a hundred yards, where they were reporting anxiously into their walkie-talkie.

"If I were you, Stanford," he said, "I'd give the lovely Teresa her marching orders as soon as we get home."

"But Margaret found her!"

"Margaret may think so. But how did she find her?"

"From an agency, I believe. They sent a brochure through the post."

"Exactly. The agency found *you*."

Ben-Dor was studying Ellison with interest. "Solomon sometimes complains that you tell him less then he tells you. I'm well aware that your knowledge of this conspiracy exceeds our own in vital respects. Frankly, you could head any intelligence agency in the world."

"I'm not sure Bill will be entirely flattered to hear that," Christie said. "He suffers from the delusion that he's an honest man."

But Ellison's thoughts were elsewhere: he was no longer in any doubt that Professor Michael Ben-Dor was Ha-Mossad's Chief of European Operations.

"Since Solomon last discussed our penetration of Al-Ittihad with you," Ben-Dor said, "new information has reached us. Have you ever visited the State of Qatar?"

"The oil-rich blob on the Arabian Gulf? Yes, twice."

"About six months ago, a member of the Ruler's Council gave a small dinner-party in his palace in Doha. One of his guests was referred to as Sheikh Abdul Issa Attiqi. It emerged that Attiqi owns a large estate and palace in the northern deserts of Qatar. A contact within the Qatar Petroleum Company later revealed that for many years a vast royalty has been paid in to Attiqi's Swiss bank account."

"OK."

"However . . . there are one or two odd things about Sheikh Abdul Issa Attiqi. Throughout dinner he wore a mask over his face, with slits at the eyes and mouth. And although he spoke perfect Arabic in the local dialect, he pronounced the names of British politicians as only an Englishman could pronounce them. Nor does he appear in the Qatar phone-book. In your country one expects important people's phone numbers to be unlisted, but not in Qatar, where every aristocrat, including all three hundred members of the ruling family, takes great pride in publicly listing five or ten phone numbers—front gate, drawing-room, office, kitchen, stables, swimming-pool and bedroom."

"Anything else?"

"Yes. Two days after this dinner, Sheikh Abdul Issa Attiqi reappeared in the same house, the same palace, in Doha. Again he wore a mask. Then several other guests arrived. They went into private conclave for five hours behind locked doors."

"You're going to tell me who the other guests were?"

"They included the two most powerful representatives of Al-Ittihad in the forthcoming Arab Mission to Britain: Al-Rashib and Yacoub."

"What did they discuss?"

"We don't know."

"Your source was the wrong side of the locked doors?"

"Our source is of no interest to you."

"On the contrary: you have offered only one slender item of evidence to suggest that Sheikh Abdul Issa Attiqi is not a Qatari but an Englishman—his way of pronouncing the names of British politicians. I'd like to know whether your source was qualified to make that judgment."

"Our source has been a student in both England and America."

"Hm."

"He's not convinced," Rupin shrugged. "He's never convinced."

"Then we must convince him," Ben-Dor said calmly. "On the day following the conference behind locked doors, Sheikh Abdul Issa Attiqi complained to our source that the rampant Islamic chauvinism of Al-Ittihad had prevented it from taking any Englishman fully into its confidence. And this, apparently, was hindering the Arab cause in Britain."

"You've convinced me," Ellison said sharply. "You've also confirmed my guess as to your source."

Ben-Dor and Rupin stared at him aghast.

"In the popular imagination," Ellison went on, "an Israeli agent is a brave Jew in a frogsuit who slips up a deserted Arab beach in dead of night. In practice, not so. Ever since the Jews were kicked out of the Arab countries, you have had to rely on Arabs living in territory occupied by Israel—and their far-flung Palestinian relations who work as engineers, advisers and civil servants in a wide range of Arab states. Now I happen to know well that honourable old gentleman Saddam Nureddin, former Jordanian Governor of Jerusalem, to whom so many West Bank Arabs still bring their grievances and tales of torture. I also know that the Israeli Government values Nureddin as an Arab one can do business with. Can it be a coincidence, I ask myself, that his son Badr Nureddin, who was educated in England and America, has for the last three years been working as a senior technical adviser to the Ruler of Qatar? And that, of course, is why the mysterious Sheikh Abdul Issa Attiqi fed him a package of disinformation—in the expectation that it would filter through to Ha-Mossad via his father. Yes?"

Michael Ben-Dor slowly raised his eyes from the patch of mud he had been studying with total concentration.

"Bingo," he said.

Ellison turned to Christie. "Why do these Zahal tank commanders keep using that word?"

"My conscience is clear," Ben-Dor said. "Only God can keep secrets from the Devil."

"And my feet are cold," Christie said, leading the way back across the Meadows.

And then, abruptly, he stopped. "Bill, I have never been a gossipmonger?"

"No one could dispute it, Stanford."

"Idle tittle-tattle has always repelled me. And yet, in view of this remarkable story Michael has told us, I think I ought, in all conscience, to report something I heard fifteen years ago, when I was still in the FO. I had been posted to Bahrain, where I ran into an Arab woman who was teaching in a girls' secondary school. She told me that she had been born in Qatar but had chosen to study and work in Bahrain where female emancipation is much more advanced than in other Gulf states. She then asked me whether I knew Kenneth Lynedoch. I said, 'Of course, we served together in Baghdad.' This woman smiled, hesitated, and then said: 'Kenneth is my half-brother.' "

Solomon Rupin emitted a resounding exclamation in Hebrew.

"The gist of her story," Christie continued, squelching his cold feet in the soggy turf, "was this. While working in Doha, Lynedoch's father had had an affair with a Qatari woman related distantly to the Ruler. When the woman became pregnant, it was arranged that she should be sent to England, where she duly gave birth to Kenneth Lynedoch. Kenneth's father insisted on bringing him up in England, and browbeat his English wife into allowing Kenneth to be registered as her own child. The actual mother returned to Qatar."

"Where she later married and gave birth to the school-teacher you met in Bahrain?" Ellison asked.

"Yes. Kenneth, apparently, suffered dreadfully at his prep school on account of his Arab appearance; it reached such a point that his father decided to tell him the truth. Several years later, as a young man, Kenneth set out for Qatar to discover his real mother. And did. He was warmly welcomed by the ruling family, learnt fluent Arabic, became a secret Moslem, adopted the Arab cause, and established a second home in Qatar."

"But managed to conceal all this in England?" Ben-Dor asked.

"Oh yes. It was all news to me. I doubt whether he would have been able to enter the Diplomatic Service otherwise."

"And the school-teacher who told you all this—what was her family name?" Ellison asked.

Slowly Christie pulled a lock of hair back from his forehead. "Attiqi. Until today I had never really believed her story."

When they got back to the Park Town house there was a general soaking of feet in hot water and a generous distribution of dry socks and shoes by Christie, whose feet were fortunately larger than those of his guests.

The Spanish girl Teresa had laid out a splendid salad lunch—her eyes, teeth and buttocks flashed in a continuous semaphore of seduction.

"I'll settle with her later," Christie muttered.

"That's a nice car you've lost, Bill," Rupin said.

"Lord Gowers has lost it. Besides, Pru's Ford Escort now stands idle. It's not beneath my dignity, though it may be beneath Charlie's. What about you, Stanford—will Margaret let you borrow her Porsche?"

"Never. I can walk."

After lunch Ellison took himself to the first floor for a leak. The door of Christie's study stood ajar. As he opened it the girl Teresa, who was bending over the papers on Christie's desk, looked up, flustered.

"Somewhere must be a pen," she smiled, blushing and

guiltily beating a retreat. He glanced appreciatively at the books and pictures on the wall then followed her out.

At 3.15 the Israeli Embassy Buick set out for London, tracked by two ISP squad cars. As soon as they turned on to the northern by-pass Ben-Dor motioned to Rupin and Ellison to remove the shoes that Christie had lent them. Extracting his lethal snap hunting-knife from his pocket, he began to slit the soles.

Ellison knew the Israeli was wasting his time, but said nothing.

Ellison reached the house in Chester Place an hour and a half later. Instinctively he listened for his son's stampede of greeting as he opened the door, but there was only silence.

Seventeen

At the *Monitor* there was an air of expectancy, of final crisis:
the Arab Mission was due to arrive at Heathrow at 11.35
GMT. Entering Gowers House at 7.58, Ellison went straight
to the News Department where he watched a battery of wire-
machines tapping out their messages at the behest of
invisible hands.

```
ZCZC LUA262 121905 ULR 197
OO LCO NMX HKG NHB LTA LUP
XKX K
PIXFILE 10/12
MANAGING EDITORS/PICTURE EDITORS: THE FOLLOWING
NEWSPICTURES HAVE MOVED ON THE UP TELEPHOTO/
UNIFAX NETWORK SINCE 0015 GMT:
BAGHDAD: YUSUF HASHIM YACOUB, DIRECTOR GENERAL OF
MINISTRY OF CULTURAL DEVELOPMENT, LEAVING FOR
LONDON VIA KUWAIT
TRIPOLI: ISA BIN SULMAN AL-RASHIB, DEPUTY MINISTER OF
OIL AND ECONOMIC DEVELOPMENT, TAKES LEAVE OF COL
GADDAFI BEFORE DEPARTING FOR LONDON VIA KUWAIT
ABU DHABI: BRITISH PARLIAMENTARY DELEGATION LEADER
CYRIL QUILLEY RECEIVED BY RULER
```

Ellison wandered into the wire room where the Mufax
monitor machines were registering pictures of various
members of the Mission picked up by high-frequency

226

telephone signal. He studied them thoughtfully. The Telex machines were spluttering a continuous series of excited messages from the *Monitor*'s own correspondents in the Middle East. In the News Department reporters arrived and departed with new assignments, each linked to the Mission's highly planned schedule during its first seventy-two hours on British soil. In the Business News and Advertising Departments the desks were strewn with galley proofs of lucrative supplements advertising the commercial glories and political stability of the leading Arab states. In the bench foundry operators were needle-drilling, or routing, the picture plates to provide a clearer impression on the flongs.

When Ellison reached his office he found a message from Ramsay Jordan directing him to contact the Editor immediately. He flicked his intercom.

"Bill, the Foreign Office has restricted us to one Press pass for the airport."

"That's shit. Have you checked with other papers?"

"Yes. Full quota all round—except us and the *Dispatch*."

"Try the Head of the FO's News Department."

"He's unavailable. His deputy is unavailable. The tea boy is unavailable."

"And the one pass goes to McNairn?"

"It's already in his pocket."

He dialled 9, then the home number of Walter Vandyke.

"Bill Ellison here. Do me a favour and get Roger Fullerton at his home number. Tell him the *Monitor* has been restricted to one Press pass for the airport, and that all normal channels of protest are unavailable. I'm at the *Monitor*, extension 457."

Five minutes later his phone rang.

"This is Roger Fullerton."

"Foreign Secretary, we're being shut out. It has to be deliberate."

"How many passes do you want?"

"Two more—in my name and Magnus Massey's."

"They'll be waiting for you at Heathrow."

"With respect, Foreign Secretary, they'll be mislaid until the Mission has arrived and departed."

A pause.

"I suggest you present yourself at my private secretary's office at 9.45. There's room in my car."

"Thank you, sir, I'm most grateful."

As the official convoy of black saloons swept over the Chiswick flyover towards the M4, heavily flanked by police outriders, Roger Fullerton, MP, Secretary of State for Foreign and Commonwealth Affairs, listed at number three in the Cabinet hierarchy, below Murdoch and Martindale, sat stiff and erect, maintaining the silence for which he was renowned. Beside him, his Parliamentary Private Secretary sat in respectful imitation.

"A busy time ahead of you, sir." Ellison finally ventured.

Fullerton grunted politely. Magnus was gazing with rapt attention at the rooftops of Brentford passing below the flyover.

"But not for long, perhaps," Ellison pressed. "Could you confirm or deny reports that you are shortly to be replaced by Quilley?"

He referred to one of the leading pro-Arabists on the Government benches, Cyril Quilley, MP, Chairman of the Commons Committee on Foreign Policy, Chairman of the Inter-Party Middle East Council of the House of Commons, and a director of several banks and businesses linked to Arab interests.

"No comment."

"In my opinion, you are the sole guarantee of the FO's integrity."

Fullerton shot him a glance. "Kind of you to say so. Naturally, I can't agree."

"We're off the record, sir."

"Ellison, I offered you a lift not an interview."

"Epitaph."

"Meaning?"

"We haven't long, have we? Three weeks, two? Don't

they discuss Operation Talent in full Cabinet? For God's sake, sir, come out into the open."

"I'm not an orator."

Ellison smiled inwardly. He knew that the barb was directed at Walter Vandyke, whose flamboyant appeals to the people violated Fullerton's instinctive preference for elitist government. Yet he also knew that Fullerton was deeply attached to parliamentary democracy.

"Of course," Ellison said, "if Quilley takes over the FO, he won't run the show. He'll be merely a front."

"Can't comment."

"For Kenneth Lynedoch."

The convoy of official cars was now filtering off the motorway, slowing its pace as it passed through a series of heavily manned check-points. The airport was less than a mile away.

Ellison went in again. "Am I correct that a British subject with a British father but a foreign mother would not be admitted to the diplomatic service?"

"Policy on that is flexible. It's a matter of discretion in each case." Fullerton's impassive features now registered a flicker of interest. "Why do you ask?"

"I'd like to check Lynedoch's file in the FO's Personnel Operations Department."

"Ha! No chance."

"But if you yourself were to request it?"

A pained grimace slowly twisted the Foreign Secretary's dignified features. "The only man with access to Lynedoch's file is Kenneth Lynedoch."

The saloon drew to a halt outside Terminal 3 and was immediately engulfed by obsequious officials and anxious security officers. Ellison and Massey murmured their thanks, displayed their passes, and were conducted into the Press room adjoining the VIP lounge, outside which a fleet of Cadillacs awaited the Mission. Security was massive: the perimeters of the airport were guarded by military detachments, including tanks. Someone was trying to imply an acute terrorist threat to the Mission, and so coax the public deeper into an acceptance of the coming State of Emergency.

The VIP and Press lounges were decorated with the flags of the Arab League nations. Kaffiyeh and dishdashas mingled with the formal morning dress of the non-Arab diplomatic corps: ambassadors had been instructed to arrive more than an hour before the Middle East Airlines Boeing 747 was due to land.

Ostracized on all sides, by diplomats and reporters alike, Ellison and Massey slowly pushed through the throng, noting the pattern of invitations and non-invitations. Alistair McNairn, chief political correspondent of the *Sunday Monitor*, shot Ellison a startled and venemous glance. The eyes of the Rt Hon Patrick Martindale, as they settled on Ellison, were frozen in hatred. Ozanne, Lucas, Strachan, Burnett, Fryer, Shukhairy, Nashat Al-Khatib, Superintendent Stanley Leech and Professor Hugh Swinburne all carried the smug, arrogant air of men within a stone's throw of absolute power. Ellison winked when his eye met Bert Hoyle's.

"Nice demo your friends laid on at Oxford," he said.

Massey and Ellison collided in a corner.

"Who's missing, then? Vandyke; Armstrong, of course; and who else?"

"Gowers."

"Exactly my impression. They've scuttled the old bastard."

It was then that Ellison began to edge towards his target—a slender, dapper, middle-aged man in morning dress, working his way towards the end of the line of foreign diplomats. His jet-black hair was brushed straight back from the olive skin of his forehead in a polished sheen, adding force to the jutting hook of his large nose. The superficial ease and charm of a diplomat's smile failed to mask the deeper map of ruthless calculation etched in sharp grooves round the tight mouth and sharp brown eyes.

Ellison edged closer.

The man exchanged a word with an Arab diplomat and then, momentarily alone, dabbed at his face with a silk handkerchief.

"Zamil Al-Alhambra."

Kenneth Lynedoch swung sharply on his heel and stared at Ellison.

"My name is Ellison. I believe we met at 10 Downing Street."

Lynedoch glanced sideways, then flicked his head. Ellison followed him out of the VIP lounge on to the red carpet laid to welcome the Mission.

"You wish to speak to me, Mr Ellison?"

"What was your mother's name?"

"Is that your business?"

"You're a public official, a servant of the Crown, and a diplomat. Was your mother a British subject or not?"

"Why did you first address me by an Arab title?"

"What made you so sure I was addressing you?"

"Instinct. And you were staring at me."

"When did you last visit Qatar?"

"Eight or nine weeks ago. Why?"

"I have no more questions."

At 10.30 a Concorde from Bahrain touched down, disgorging fifteen MPs of the Inter-Party Middle East Council, led by the fat, jovial Cyril Quilley. Facing banks of microphones and cameras, Quilley painted a glowing prospect for Arab-British cooperation—"provided we clean house and put down the saboteurs".

At 11.20 Heathrow Control Tower froze all outward-bound planes in their loading bays and stacked half a dozen incoming flights at five thousand feet over the Thames Estuary. In the VIP lounge men began to straighten their ties nervously and to flick specks of ash off their dark coats. The Prime Minister led his entourage to the end of the red carpet.

Ten miles away, in Hyde Park, a Royal Artillery battery boomed into a nineteen-salvo (called a nineteen-gun) salute.

As the giant Boeing 747 turned majestically on its axis, ladders were rushed to the exits. The rear door opened instantly, disgorging Arab reporters who stampeded towards the front ladder where security guards linked arms and forced the jostling journalists back.

First to emerge from the high door of the Boeing was the leader of the Mission, His Excellency Sheikh Abdul Al-Abdullah Al-Jalah, Deputy Ruler of Kuwait, brother of the Ruler, and a man of modest wealth variously estimated at between £200 million and £350 million. He and Murdoch embraced in the Arab style, a two-handed clasp followed by a kiss on each cheek. Then came the hard core of the Mission:

Isa bin Sulman Al-Rashib. Libyan. A Zamil of Al-Ittihad.

Yusuf Hashim Yacoub. Iraqi. A Zamil of Al-Ittihad.

Jamal Al-Din Al-Bakrir. Libyan. President of the Trans-Arabian Bank, which almost certainly owned Howles, Cramp and Roope, together with Samarkand and Arabair. Financial fountainhead of Al-Ittihad. A Zamil of Al-Ittihad.

Then junior members of the mission, followed by the poker-faced hit-men of Yacoub's killer outfit, Squad 9, Baghdad, Ishmail Aziz and Tariq Kazzar.

As the platitudinous speeches droned to a close, Ellison felt a hand pluck at his elbow. It was Fullerton's PPS.

"The Foreign Secretary wants you to meet His Excellency," he whispered. They pushed through the throng.

"I believe Your Excellency knows Bill Ellison," Fullerton said.

The Sheikh's benevolent features broke into a broad smile as he pumped Ellison's hand.

"You have been away from Kuwait too long, Bill. I fear our hospitality must be at fault, what?"

"Very nice to see you again, sir."

"Bill, I will confide in you and I beg the Foreign Secretary to close his distinguished ears. There is one thing I cannot wait to see——"

"Your rose garden at Ascot? I remember calling on Your Excellency in Kuwait when you were Governor of the National Bank. Although it was a scorching November day, you baffled me by complaining about the frost."

"Ha, ha, I remember your face!"

"It transpired that every morning you listened to the BBC's weather reports for the south-east of England. Your roses were in peril."

"Well, there you are, the secret is out. The Arab Mission is led by a surrogate Englishman. The Arabs are outwitted again."

He roared with laughter. The cordon of tight, anxious faces round them tittered nervously, then slid back into expressions of fury and exasperation.

"Very well, Bill," boomed the Sheikh, "one weekend soon you will visit me at Ascot, eat Shish Taouk, and praise my roses in terms to flatter the ego of a prince."

It was then that Fullerton struck—this tight, stiff, introverted, secretive politician, knowing that his own career was at an end, put Ellison beyond reach of assassination in two sentences.

"We must hope, Your Excellency, that Ellison remains alive to accept your invitation. There has been a recent attempt on his life and a junior colleague of his was murdered only last week."

The Sheikh's face clouded; slowly he scanned the circle of tense official scowls surrounding him.

"I trust," he said with emphasis, "that no effort will be spared in bringing the killers to justice. And you, Bill, must bring to Ascot your wife and children whom my own dear wife is so anxious to meet."

"Ellison's family have gone to Israel, Your Excellency," Lynedoch said quickly.

"They are no doubt visiting the Holy Places," the Sheikh snapped back and strode majestically towards the exit followed by a milling throng of retainers.

It was a nice moment. But for how long could the influence of the Mission's solitary figurehead outweigh the massive, disciplined and fanatical drive for power of Al-Ittihad?

Having taken over the top three floors of the Arab-owned Dorchester Hotel, overlooking Hyde Park, the Mission embarked on a splendid succession of official banquets and receptions. Grenadier Guards, Life Guards and Horse Guards were drawn up in dazzling arrays of burnished brass and steel. In the course of a dinner at Buckingham Palace, Sheikh Abdul Al-Abdullah Al-Jalah presented the Sovereign with a gift, his two-year-old colt Neptune, out of the famous Cormorant by the magnificent Arc de Triomphe winner Morning Shadow (stud price £2 million). The horse was not actually led in under the chandeliers due to lack of toilet training.

At Lancaster House the Prime Minister played host to the Mission at a splendid, televised dinner. The Lord Mayor of London dramatized the business community's enthusiasm with a spectacular feast at the Mansion House. The wines uncorked for that occasion were selected not merely from the vintage years of France's finest vineyards but—consummate tact—from only those vineyards recently acquired by Arab investors.

The guest-lists for these affairs were printed each morning in the newspapers. Ellison studied them with interest.

So, too, did Lord Gowers.

The summons to the tenth-floor office reached Jordan and Ellison three days after the Mission's arrival in Britain. A light lunch was served in the Chairman's private dining-room in which hung two Picassos, a Monet and a Braque—the latter unaccountably upside down.

The Chairman came straight to the point over cold vichyssoise.

"Do you know what people say to me, Ellison? They say: 'What has become of that great liberal paper, the *Sunday Monitor*? What has happened to Britain's greatest journalist, Bill Ellison? Why so much silence?' Why don't you hit the bastards where they deserve to be hit? Here! Here!"

The Chairman was stabbing his index finger into his solar plexus in a cold fury. Jordan stared at him in astonishment; Ellison, with cynical interest. He said nothing.

"It has come to my attention," Gowers continued, with a fixed, obsessive gaze, "that this whole building is honeycombed with bugs. From top to bottom! Bugs! Why wasn't this reported to me? Who do they think I am, eh?"

Ellison and Jordan watched him, intently.

"Now, gentlemen, let's get one thing straight. I want this paper to speak out. This filthy excrescence of crooks that calls itself a government, while planning to subvert our historic liberties, is going to discover what I'm made of. Next Sunday my construction company will strip the whole building. And more than walls will be stripped. As of today, Yorath and McNairn are fired—they're nothing but Murdoch's yes men and Arab agents. Understood?"

The waiter brought grilled salmon and a light Alsatian wine.

"Now, as to policy. We must give Walter Vandyke a boost. He's the man to save this nation, understood? Commission a series of articles by Walter immediately. And send a man to Israel to interview their Prime Minister. Right? Now, Bill, how can we get Operation Talent into the paper, advise me."

"Jews are a good thing now?" Ellison said quietly.

Gowers nodded gravely. "Where would music, literature and science be without them?"

"Is that so? Ramsay, we should really follow that up."

"One other thing, gentlemen: I want a feature piece next Sunday on Gowers's crusade to save British democracy. Bill, you'll write it."

Ellison wiped his mouth with a starched napkin of the best Irish linen. "Kind of you to give us a lead, Chairman."

Ramsay Jordan stared at Ellison in astonishment. Was he taking tranquillizers or something?

The BBC launched a three-week festival of Islamic music, art and religious instruction. The Sheikh was conducted round Television Centre by Sir Philip Lucas and Edmund

Strachan, with the Director General conspicuously absent. The Sheikh then journeyed to Oxford to lay the foundation stone of Al-Jalah College, a new graduate centre intended to eclipse Wolfson College, the life's dream of a British Jew. At the ceremony it was announced that the first President of Al-Jalah College would be Professor Hugh Swinburne.

Interviewed in Oxford, a leading member of the Mission, Yusuf Hashim Yacoub, praised the continuing occupation of the Middle East Institute and described its Director, Stanford Christie, as a "tool of Zionist racism". In a series of daily attacks, Bert Hoyle of the *Star* linked Christie to Ellison, Rupin, Ben-Dor and "Ha-Mossad's terror apparatus in Britain". By this time diplomatic relations with Israel had been broken off, as predicted; Rupin and Ben-Dor were expelled from the country at six hours' notice.

Ellison didn't expect them to be away for long.

The Mission embarked on a vast tour of factories, docks, mines, North Sea oil-rigs, nuclear power plants, and defence installations. Ministers, MPs, businessmen, trade union leaders, journalists and television crews followed the Mission everywhere with sycophantic devotion. Each day Isa bin Sulman Al-Rashib announced a new loan, a new export order, a new construction contract: the wires hummed with beguiling news of petrodollars, loans to support sterling, new jobs, and universal prosperity.

Ormskirk's para-military Saviours of the Nation paraded down Whitehall to the Cenotaph, wearing brown shirts and sub-machine guns. The Sheikh was persuaded to take the salute. A menacing note was now creeping into the speeches of Yusuf Hashim Yacoub and Isa bin Sulman Al-Rashib— apparently the package had its price: evidence of internal discipline and an end to the divisive, chaotic, anarchistic charade conducted in Parliament.

"We have less than three weeks now," Vandyke told Ellison.

*   *   *

Ellison played a card he could play only so often.

Noon. As the first office workers threaded their way into St James's Park with their sandwiches, two men stood in front of the pond, a few hundred yards from Horse Guards' Parade and the Foreign Office, throwing chunks of stale Hovis to the ducks.

"You're falling short," Ellison said. "Unless you hit the water the pigeons and tits get it."

"Failing nerve," said Jack Knight.

Knight was the sort of man you pass without noticing in the street: hair, skin, shirt and suit receded into a pale lifelessness. He would have blended into any street-corner betting shop, fag-end in mouth, eyes half closed against the smoke, bad cough. The Inland Revenue and Social Security files showed that Knight worked for Section F4 (public order, firearms) of the Home Office's Police Department. The files were not wrong; but nor were they altogether right.

For fifteen years Jack Knight had tracked down foreign agents operating on British soil: Eastern bloc diplomats, members of trade delegations, and the British officials who had been bribed or blackmailed into working as deep-cover moles and sleepers for foreign powers. He had believed in his work, he had pursued it with skill and total dedication. And then, one day, he had realized that he had been liking his work less and less.

Since Patrick Martindale became Home Secretary; since Geoffrey Ozanne transferred from the Foreign to the Home Office. Since the birth of the Leech Squad.

Looking back, Knight realized how the work of the Security Service, known as MI5, had been subtly transformed. Foreign agents were no longer the principal targets. The machinery of surveillance was now focused almost exclusively on critics of the Government, on British citizens exercising democratic rights which Knight had always regarded as a sacred national heritage.

Knight had taken himself off one Sunday to Brighton beach. He stared at the waves rolling up on to the sand, at the thin, shifting line which marked the farthest point where this fat, ugly, carbohydrate-filled people could paddle without getting their knees wet. His people. And he watched the children at play: horrible, noisy kids with rotten teeth and an addiction to television rubbish—tomorrow's people. Jack Knight felt a strong anger rising in his throat. He wasn't too sure of the exact dates, the historic milestones of this island's liberty, but he remembered the smell of carbolic soap in a primary-school classroom in rural Somerset.

By the time he caught the electric train back to London, Jack Knight had decided to put his life on the line. Not quixotically, not flamboyantly, but shrewdly, patiently.

Knight and Ellison were getting to the end of the stale Hovis.

"How's things between you and Sergei Tretiakov?" Ellison said.

Both men understood the rules of the game. As they talked they were under constant observation. The Leech Squad allowed Knight to fertilize his friendship with Ellison and to foster the journalist's trust by feeding him small morsels of information. In return Knight had to take something back to Superintendent Stanley Leech.

Leech thought he was getting the better of the deal.

Ellison held a different opinion.

"That would depend," Knight said, "on what you can give me."

Sergei Tretiakov, Second Secretary at the Soviet Embassy, was the KGB's principal agent responsible for the surveillance of anti-Soviet émigrés in Britain. His bitter rival within the Soviet intelligence *apparat* in London was First Secretary Dmitri Zarobin. Within the vast, deceptively monolithic empire of the KGB burned the same departmental rivalries which divided the CIA and the FBI in America, MI5 (counter-intelligence and internal security) and the SIS (overseas intelligence) in Britain. Zarobin's job, essentially, was to penetrate British institutions with Soviet agents and to recruit by blackmail or bribery British citizens as deep-cover moles and sleepers—the same function undertaken by the CIA and the SIS in Eastern Europe. But Tretiakov's role corresponded to Jack Knight's: internal security at home. Over several years the two men had developed a wary, foxy dialogue of trade-offs in information. Knight would "sell" Tretiakov news of the anti-Soviet exile activity in Britain, in return for which Tretiakov would "deliver" Zarobin's espionage agents into Knight's hands.

Ellison tossed a piece of bread far into the pond; he didn't like pigeons or tits. "Well?"

"They want to know why you threw Lynedoch so much fresh meat. And where you bought it."

"Pure speculation."

"Why Lynedoch?"

"His role sticks out a mile."

"Why the interest in his mother?"

"His birth certificate has vanished from the Register. You'll find only his father's name in the directories. Suppose his mother was an Arab. Consider the implications."

"But what put you on to that line of thought?"

"Native intelligence."

"I feel very dead. Sell me a source, any source."

"Foreign Secretary Fullerton has been trying to probe Lynedoch's background but can't get hold of his file from the Personnel Operations Department. Someone tipped him off that Lynedoch's mother was an Arab."

Knight's shoulders relaxed slightly. "I'll buy that. What can Tretiakov do for you?"

"A line to Kim Philby in Moscow."

Knight's eyebrows lifted a fraction. In the MI5 man's private lexicon of dishonour, the British diplomat and journalist, who had worked for over twenty years as a Soviet agent before defecting to Russia in 1963, figured among the most detested names.

"What makes you so sure Philby is behind Tretiakov rather than Zarobin?"

"The Ministry of All the Talents won't suit the Russians.

Once in power they'll embark on heavy re-armament, military conscription, an end to détente."

"Philby might welcome that—as a prelude to a left-wing revolution here."

"Kim doesn't regard the wretched British as worthy of Communism. His sole concern is the defence of Soviet state power."

"You know him better than I do," Knight said acidly.

It was true: in the early sixties both Ellison and Philby had been stationed in Beirut, the one writing for the *Sunday Monitor*, the other for the *Observer*.

"It's important, Jack."

"I can try."

Parents and children were crowding into the London Planetarium on a Saturday morning when Magnus Massey slipped into the back row and sat down next to the bent, dwarf figure of Micky Kolarcz.

"What's up, reptile?"

In the darkness, offset only by the stellar glow of the dome above them, Kolarcz threw him a twisted, sneering grin.

"I need bread," he snarled hoarsely.

In short, he was ready to shop Judy to Eltenbridge unless the *Monitor* paid him ransom money. The triumphal procession of the Arab Mission round Britain, and the *Monitor*'s continuing failure to publish anything about Relief's operations, had worked Kolarcz into a truculent, avaricious frame of mind. He wanted £10,000 on the nail. And behind Kolarcz's truculence was an acute, nagging fear—that Judy would be blown in any case and that retribution would flow down to Narrow Street in the small hours of the night in the shape of a black Mercedes 450 SEL.

For half an hour the two hissed threats and counter-threats, their voices periodically rising to the point where spectators sitting in front of them turned and angrily "ssshed" at them.

Finally Magnus realized that he had to look beyond logic. Judy's life was at stake; it was a life that deserved better support than a simultaneous equation.

On the following Monday he visited the bank which held the Searchlight slush fund and withdrew the first of the £500 cash payments he had promised to deliver to Kolarcz each week. He was confident he had purchased Judy's continuing cover.

He would have been less confident if he had asked himself why one of the parents seated in front of him in the Planetarium had merely leant back in his seat while other fathers were angrily hushing the two men engaged in argument. In the darkness he had failed to recognize Ernie Jacks, chief feature writer for the *Star*, Bert Hoyle's right-hand man.

Eighteen

At the entrance to the forecourt of the British Musuem in Great Russell Street Ellison flashed his Reading Room admission card to the blue-uniformed commissionaire, the chain was lifted, and Pru's little Ford Escort slipped into a parking space. It was exactly 9.00 am, an hour before visitors, other than accredited library readers, are granted admission. By the time the ISP agents tracking Ellison had argued their way into the forecourt, past the commissionaire stationed in the main doorway and, finally, past the commissionaire guarding the entrance to the great, domed Reading Room, Ellison had walked through the building, past the State Papers Room, and out of the rear entrance into Montague Place.

He hailed a taxi and disappeared.

It was a typical prep school at the fag-end of the summer term: small boys in grey shorts and blue blazers, a tall chapel spire, spacious games fields, an atmosphere of timeless immunity to the winds of change buffeting the outer world. The Bursar, a retired infantry officer, blew pipe-smoke in Ellison's face and affected an air of condescension which failed to mask his rampant curiosity.

"We're off the record, of course."

Ellison repressed a smile. "Absolutely, Major."

"I've looked up the registers for the mid-thirties. He was a pupil here from 1935 to 1939. Bright boy, 'A' stream, according to his reports, but useless at games and liable to funk a tackle. That's off the record, by the way."

"Of course. Any trace of his mother's maiden name?"

"The mother? Good Lord, no. Fathers pay fees."

"But when the boy was admitted, the school presumably saw his birth certificate?"

"Merely to check his age. We don't keep birth certificates."

"Where did the boy live during the school holidays?"

"No idea."

"Perhaps you have a record of where his school reports were sent?"

The Bursar rummaged through the crumpled file of yellowing paper.

"Hmm . . . Here we are—to his uncle, in Cheltenham. There's a note here: father abroad and on the move . . . uncle *in loco parentis*."

"Father's brother or mother's?"

"Father's: same name."

"Is there any record of why the boy left in 1939? He was still short of public-school age."

"Hm, you're probing into a rather private area there. According to the book, you know, I shouldn't be telling you anything. Can't claim I always see eye to eye with the *Monitor* . . . what's that fellow Gowers like? . . . bit of a social upstart, isn't he?"

"He pays my salary."

"These days one must take the hay where one finds it, what?" The Bursar banged the bowl of his pipe on the desk and shook a wad of wet, evil-smelling tobacco into the metal waste-paper bin. "This would be in the strictest confidence?"

"Of course."

"Between you, me and these four walls, the boy was plucked out of school early in the Michaelmas Term of 1939." He threw Ellison a look of deep complicity, the complicity of men who knew their history. "War had begun. Hm."

"This is hardly a spot to attract the Luftwaffe."

"Hm. Not the point. Father was on the other side, you see."

"In Germany?"

"Somewhere in the Middle East. I have only these records to go by, you understand. I don't want to be quoted."

"Is there anyone alive who taught here at that time, anyone who would have known the boy personally?"

"Harold Taylor. Lives near Dorking. Close to eighty but sharp as a knife—always comes down for Speech Day, this place is in his bones. He's a widower; we pay him a modest pension."

"Perhaps I could have his address?"

"It's against the rules."

"I'd gladly pay for a phone call to clear it with him."

"He doesn't believe in phones. Bit of a recluse. I'll write to him, if you like, and let you know when I get an answer." The Bursar rose, intimating that the interview was over. Outside, in the cloisters, a bell was ringing and small feet were scurrying.

Ellison, too, stood up, and offered his hand.

"Very kind of you, Major. Don't worry about Mr Taylor, I have a deadline and I usually find that old men have forgotten more than they ever knew."

The Bursar opened the door for him, took a few steps out into the quadrangle, and pointed him in the direction of the main gate, sixty yards away.

"Thanks so much, Major."

The door closed behind him. Ellison turned sharply to his left, away from the main gate, and positioned himself behind one of the cloister pillars. A moment later the Bursar burst out of his office, carrying Ellison's briefcase, looked about him, then made off rapidly in the direction of the main gate.

Ellison walked into the office, leaving the door open, and slid his finger into the Bursar's leather-bound addressbook at "T". Then he stationed himself just outside the door and waited for the Bursar to return.

"You didn't happen to have seen a black briefcase, Major?"

*   *   *

"My dear Walter!" effused Ulf Steinberg in greeting as a manservant conducted Walter Vandyke into his penthouse studio. "I am so delighted you could squeeze a precious hour out of your crowded schedule. Yours is a portrait which simply insists on being finished."

But the Leader of the Commons paid no attention to his own clay bust. His gaze swivelled between a fibre-glass composition and its immobile human model.

"Which girl is real, Ulf?"

The composition depicted a lovely girl gladiator, proud, arrogant and triumphant, straddling a prostrate City banker whose penis raged upwards in helpless lust. The model, clad in high boots, an armour corset thrusting up against her large, naked breasts, and an eagle-crested helmet, sustained her frozen poise without fluttering an eyelash.

"She is bewitched," smiled Steinberg. "Only a great man's kiss can release her from the spell."

But Vandyke laughed shyly and sank into the chair placed for him under the huge plate-glass window. The 16mm camera concealed in the ceiling behind a barrage of spot-lights turned in vain.

Judy Rossiter stood up and smiled at Vandyke. Steinberg affected an introduction. "When I told her you were coming today, Walter, she accused me of pulling her leg. I fear you are little short of a god to a whole generation."

As Vandyke absorbed this compliment with a modest smile, the manservant returned with coffee, brandy, cigars and Turkish delight, while Judy, still half-naked, busied herself combing Vandyke's hair and massaging cold cream into his face and neck. As her breasts moved within inches of his face he closed his eyes—then opened them.

For an hour Steinberg worked on the clay bust with total concentration. And yet, when Vandyke rose an hour later to meet an official luncheon appointment, the bust had progressed very little; Steinberg was in no hurry.

"Now, Walter, promise to come back soon."

"Things are pretty hectic at the moment."

"Oh you must," cooed Judy, "I can't wait to see you in bronze."

Vandyke allowed his eyes to settle on her for a moment. Then he was gone.

Steinberg winked, threw off his clothes, and stretched himself impiously in the chair recently vacated by the white hope of Britain's democrats. His great, erect penis summoned her; as she straddled his legs and sank her loins down, instantly triggering his first orgasm, the woman walked in.

"Was Vandyke hooked?" Rose Weber said.

"Mr Taylor?"

A tall, sprightly old man stood in the cottage doorway examining Ellison with sharp, quizzical eyes.

"I'm Bill Ellison, of the *Sunday Monitor*."

"Well, I'll be damned. Come in, come in, the place is squalid, old men don't get visitors in our atomized, insensitized society. Don't tell me they want to build a motorway through this cottage. Oh, yes, a girl was raped near here last week. I'm a prime suspect, is that it?"

Ellison asked him whether he remembered the boy.

"Him! Of course I do. Sit down." He plucked a cat off the chair. "Him, eh?" He chuckled. "Oh yes, oh yes. A bright boy, of course, but never happy, never fitted in, they ragged him constantly. Touch of the tar brush, you know. Boys are very cruel, they never miss a thing. At night, you know, he used to talk in his sleep, well a lot of boys do that—but not in Arabic."

"I suppose he picked it up during the school holidays?"

"In the cradle."

"His mother was Arab?"

"In 1935 the Head kindly allocated to me the unpaid, unsung job of filtering admissions applications."

"You saw the boy's birth certificate?"

"Yes. The birth was registered at the British Consulate in Qatar. Of his mother he never spoke in my hearing, except

246

once, when provoked beyond endurance by the racist taunts of the ghastly little snobs one finds in every prep school."

"What did he say?"

"He said: 'My mother is a noblewoman. She's the cousin of a king.' "

"I don't suppose you remember her name from the birth certificate?"

Harold Taylor looked hard at Ellison. "Ever heard of inflation? You will, when you're on a pension."

"Mr Taylor, if you want payment for this interview, I'll write you out a cheque here and now."

"How much is it worth?"

"Would a hundred pounds do?"

Harold Taylor chuckled grimly. "I'm not an ass, you're on to something. How long has this country got, eh, two weeks, ten days?"

"Perhaps you'd like to name a price, Mr Taylor."

"Five thousand pounds."

Ellison wrote out the cheque and handed it to Harold Taylor. The old man's hand shook as he took it.

"My God . . . my God . . . so that's it, eh?" Slowly he shredded the cheque into tiny particles. "Him, eh? That boy . . . You know something? It doesn't surprise me." Harold Taylor leaned back in his chair, his finger-tips lightly touching, the mists of time past and time half-forgotten passing across his lean face like autumn clouds. "What you have to remember is that people were much more intolerant at that time . . . nowadays they fit the hole to the peg, but not in those days . . . he was a liar, too, a fantasist, very common symptom of insecurity, what they call alienation today . . . when he told them his mother was the cousin of a king the other boys laughed and stuck a chamber-pot over his head . . ."

"The father never came to the school?"

"The father? Good Lord no. Never set foot in this country during the last thirty years of his life. As far as I know."

"He took his leave in the Middle East?"

"Leave? What leave?"

"From the Iraq Petroleum Company. He worked as an engineer in the Kirkuk oil-fields."

Harold Taylor chuckled. "Rubbish. How could he work for a British company when there was a warrant out for his arrest?"

"Please go on."

"You *are* in the dark. Now why did I tear up that cheque? There are twenty countries in the world I have always wanted to visit . . . China . . . India . . . The father, you see, had served under Allenby in Palestine. He met T. E. Lawrence, caught the bug, and made contact with the secret Arab societies that the Turks had attempted to suppress: the Fetah in Syria and the Ahad in southern Iraq, whose leader Sayid Taleb had been imprisoned by the British. Later the father joined the British Mandate administration under Lord Samuel. As an Arab agent. Our intelligence boys got on to him during the riots against Jewish immigration. Evidently he was tipped off in the nick of time—he was well connected, by then, King Abdullah of Jordan may have interceded . . . Anyway, he got away, went underground, dedicated his life to the Arab cause . . . Amman, Baghdad, Cairo, always on the move, always protected by a secret Arab brotherhood."

"What was the brotherhood called?"

"No idea."

"How did you learn all this?"

"From the brother, of course, the boy's uncle. Poured his heart out to me one Speech Day. He had to keep reaching in his own pocket, you see, to keep the boy at the school."

"If the mother was a cousin of the Ruler of Qatar, there must have been money. Why the problem with the school fees?"

"Exactly. That was what made the uncle so bitter. Oil money. But the father often refused to fork out . . . said he didn't want his son educated in Britain . . ."

"Then why did he send the boy back at the end of the summer holidays?"

"Exactly. Exactly. Perverse. Having it both ways. It's a

form of schizophrenia very common in traitors, I'm told."

"Why was the boy taken out of school ahead of time, in 1939?"

"So you know that?"

"The school bursar told me."

"Ah. Of course, hm. It was all hushed up, of course. Agony for the uncle, agony—his own brother siding with the Axis in the Middle East. Anything to get the British out. He was mixed up with the Grand Mufti of Jerusalem, you know, and I've been told he played a key role in the pro-Nazi revolt in Baghdad, when would that have been?"

"1941. Did the boy spend the war years with his father?"

"We don't know. Almost certainly."

"Doesn't it strike you as strange, Mr Taylor, that our agents didn't pick the father up? Qatar was a British Protectorate."

Taylor chuckled. "Obviously you have a higher opinion of British Intelligence than I do. What you've got to remember is that the father adopted his wife's family name and lived under the protection of the Ruler. I daresay our boys turned a blind eye . . ."

"What *was* the mother's name, Mr Taylor?" Ellison said sharply.

Harold Taylor screwed up his forehead and flicked his fingers impatiently, summoning an elusive memory. "Damn. Damn. I had it in my head half an hour ago . . . if you hadn't written out that absurd cheque I wouldn't have lost my concentration. The name began with 'A' . . ." He smiled. "That's not much help, is it? Want some tea, by the way? You must think me exceedingly inhospitable. Since my wife died, I'm afraid . . . After the war the boy went up to Oxford, where he read Arabic. He took First Class Honours, I read it in *The Times* lists. Well, he was always very *bright*, but twisted, you know . . ."

"What *was* the mother's name, Mr Taylor?"

Suddenly Harold Taylor's gaze was fixed intently, almost desperately, on the wall.

"Attiqi. Attiqi. Attiqi." He sighed, relaxed, smiled. "You must have thought I was a fraud."

"You mentioned the uncle several times, Mr Taylor. I wonder whether he's still alive."

The old schoolmaster chuckled. "One of the benefits of retirement, you know, is reading four morning papers from cover to cover."

"The uncle died?"

"He was murdered. Thieves broke into his house in Cheltenham and put him away with a sawn-off shotgun. He was my age, exactly; strange coincidence."

"When did this occur?"

"Now you're asking. Two or three years ago. Perhaps more."

Ellison rose to leave. "Mr Taylor, I want to thank you, and to congratulate you on your prodigious memory. May I advise you, in the strongest possible terms, to tell no one about our interview."

Harold Taylor chuckled. "Want a scoop, do you?"

"Let me put it to you this way, Mr Taylor: you have been overlooked. The boy's uncle was not overlooked."

The old schoolmaster had turned pale.

Magnus Massey now had his finger pressed continuously on the front-door bell. He had been ringing it for the past five minutes. Finally the electric door-catch buzzed and he swiftly climbed the stairs. He scarcely recognized the Judy Rossiter he found sprawled across a sofa—apathetic, lifeless, her face pinched and frightened, her eyes glazed and distracted. Gently he bent over her, felt her pulse and pulled up her eyelids to examine the pupils.

"Heroin?" he murmured.

"Fuck off."

"Did Steinberg push it on you?"

"Show me your prick, debs' delight . . . if you've got one . . ." Her voice was husky, bronchial, and her words were slurred. "Always . . . suspected you were a poof, Massey."

Four hours later the Aston Martin DB6 was snarling up the narrow, winding mountain roads of Snowdonia. Judy was asleep in the front seat; she had slept throughout the journey. And when the long silence of the engine finally awoke her, as it awakens babies, she found herself in Magnus's arms and looking down two thousand feet of sheep-dotted mountainside to the sparkling blue of the Irish Sea. The island of Anglesey lay like a fine pencil stroke on the horizon. She blinked several times and drew in the fresh mountain air.

"I've been kidnapped by a poof!"

He carried her inside the stone cottage, laid her on the double bed, chased out a nest of field mice, hauled on the well rope, and put a kettle to boil on the Calor gas ring.

An hour later he told her they were going for a walk.

"No . . . my head."

"It wasn't a suggestion, it was an order."

She clung tightly to his arm for support and balance as they walked two miles across the mountain to fetch eggs, milk, cheese and bread from the nearest farm. Gradually the colour was restored to Judy's cheeks; her eyes were beginning to focus. He pointed out the peak of Snowdon to the south-east.

When they got back to the cottage she fell into a deep sleep. She slept for fourteen hours. He made himself a cheese omelette, toast and coffee, watched the sun sink towards Ireland, then stretched himself out under the stars, covered by only a light blanket. He wondered where Ellison was and fell asleep.

At eight the next morning she emerged, blinking, into the bright mountain sunlight and found Magnus reading in a deckchair. He filled her with coffee and boiled eggs, tested her focus by moving his index finger in front of her eyes, then led her up to a ridge overlooking a small lake, a glimmering coin of water surrounded on all sides by near-vertical mountain walls.

"Looks cold," she said.

"It is cold." Taking her hand, he began the descent along sheep tracks he knew well. When they reached the shingle bordering the lake she knelt and dipped her finger-tips in the water.

"Ow! Icy!"

"I daresay," he murmured, laying his shirt, trousers and underpants on the dry shingle, "that the Rossiters have been living in a suburban semi-detached since the Norman Conquest."

"Why, you bloody snob!"

He smiled and dived into the water, naked, moving effortlessly out into the lake with long, slow, powerful motions of his arms and legs. He turned, treading water, just as she, naked, hurled herself into the water with a scream. She began to swim out from the shore towards him. He dived beneath the surface, then moved swiftly up, as her shadow passed over him, to take her by the ankles.

"Jaws!"

She screamed. And went under.

He brought her up, a prisoner in his arms, gasping. The hilltops turned over. Again he took her under, then stretched himself out on the still surface of the lake, paddling gently with his feet, cradling the young woman who lay on top of him, inert, waterlogged and relaxed.

The double-headed creature glided into the shore, gently, peacefully, then lay still on the shingle, warming itself under the sun. Slowly its two heads and four legs began to writhe and pulse, as if fired by solar energy. It rolled over and over, the smooth pebbles bruising its skin, then began to toss and plunge, locked together at its two mouths and two loins, its moans and sighs unheard on the mountain tops, its rising ecstasy witnessed only by the occasional, perplexed stare of a sheep or ram. The two tossing heads broke apart now, leaving the creature locked only at one point of fire, its flanks quivering and plunging with a relentless, synchronized urgency, faster and faster, driven on by a love all the more

252

beautiful for the long delay in its consummation. At the moment of release, of fulfilment, the female head tilted back and a long, ecstatic cry echoed round the mountain walls.

Then the creature lay still on the warm shingle.

Four hours later, as the Aston Martin roared down the fast lane of the M1 towards London, she lifted her head from his shoulder and told him how Steinberg was attempting to compromise Walter Vandyke.

"You mean VD comes to Steinberg's studio for sittings!"

"He certainly does. And what am I supposed to do? If I seduce him I ruin the white hope of British democracy, and if I don't, that woman who runs Steinberg will want to know why. She watches me like a hawk."

Magnus was tempted to pull Judy out of the whole Relief business there and then. For how long would £500 a week keep Kolarcz sweet? But to do that he ought first to consult Ellison, who had temporarily vanished in pursuit of a quarry known only to himself.

"I suppose we could warn VD," Judy suggested.

"Too risky. He's quite capable of making a public speech about it."

They drove on in silence. Her head fell back on his shoulder.

"Magnus, thank you . . ."

"It was my pleasure."

She smiled wryly. "Past tense, eh?"

Magnus's foot eased off the accelerator as the Aston Martin glided off the motorway into the northern suburbs of London. "Why do you think Steinberg fed you all that stuff, Judy?"

"The dope? He uses it himself. Maybe it was some kind of test."

"Well, you failed it. Next time, say no."

Nineteen

A light drizzle of rain was falling as Ellison came off the train at Canterbury. His taxi took him past Howe Barracks, since 1966 the home of the newly amalgamated Queen's Regiment. Familiar, and faintly nostalgic, terrain. Twenty-seven years earlier Ellison had idled his way through twelve weeks of National Service basic training bullshit half a mile down the hill from Howe, in Wemyss Barracks, at that time headquarters of the Home Counties Brigade.

It was 7.15 when his taxi stopped in front of a large, Alpine-style bungalow in a quiet suburban street on the outskirts of Canterbury. As he paid off the cab he prayed the Brigadier would be at home—the risk of approaching him on duty in Howe Barracks had been too great.

The front-door bell chimed discreetly. It was opened by a youthful-looking man wearing a crown and three pips on the epaulette of his khaki jersey.

"Brigadier Tyson?"

"Yes."

Silently Ellison handed him his Press card, intently studying the Brigadier's reaction. Tyson examined the card for longer than was necessary.

"I'm sorry, Mr Ellison, but every CO is under strict instructions from the War Office to show you the door."

"Since General Winstanley's suicide?"

"Correct."

"He didn't commit suicide. He was murdered by the ISP."

The Brigadier was still standing on the doorstep. "I'm not prepared to discuss that with you. Or anything else."

"I believe you served, as a subaltern, with the Medway Regiment in the Canal Zone in 1951–2."

"Well?" Tyson said coolly.

"It's absolutely imperative that I learn who was responsible for the succession of disasters which befell the Medways at the village of Al Ain."

"It may be imperative for you, Mr Ellison, but not for me."

"Of course, Brigadier. For soldiers there's always a proper time to die in defence of their country—but it's never now."

The deliberately calculated thrust was one of the oldest weapons in his armoury: with a bishop, challenge his piety; with a politician, challenge his popularity; with a civil servant, challenge his incorruptibility; with a soldier, challenge his courage.

"You'd better come in."

Brigadier Tyson led the way into the sitting-room, turfed out two teenage boys who were watching television, and closed the door.

"I may as well tell you that Winstanley was an officer who commanded universal respect and affection. It is my understanding that you drove him to suicide by pursuing him to Wales and extracting top secret information from him in an unguarded moment."

"He was murdered. I found his body."

"Then why didn't you come forward as a witness at the inquest?"

"This is why." Ellison took a photocopy of *Operation Talent* from his briefcase and handed it to the Brigadier. For five minutes Tyson studied it with an expression increasingly grim. Then he handed it back.

"Why do you show this to me?"

"Because I want you to tell me what really happened to the Medways at the southern end of the Canal Zone."

"But that was twenty-eight years ago!"

"Brigadier, the position of Leader in the Supreme Executive Council is marked 'designated'. Yes?"

"Well?"

"It is my guess that the man who will fill that post served with you in the Medways."

"Who?"

Ellison told him.

Tyson stood up abruptly, turned his back on Ellison, and reached for a packet of cigarettes on the mantelpiece.

"Jesus Christ," he muttered, "it figures. It does figure."

"Because he was already an Arab agent twenty-eight years ago?"

Tyson poured two stiff drinks and sank back into his chair. "Very well, I'll tell you what I know."

Magnus Massey lay in a ditch opposite the main gate of Professor Hugh Swinburne's replica of a late-Georgian mansion in the Woodstock-Blenheim region north of Oxford. Three previous surveillance vigils after nightfall had yielded no dividends to his infra-red lens.

At 8.45 a large black Cadillac, with curtains drawn over the rear windows, came to a halt before the electronically operated gates. The gates opened, but not before Magnus had noted down the registration number as being Nashat Al-Khatib's.

Two hours later the Cadillac turned out of the gates and swept down the road in the Oxford-London direction, passing a lay-by where a Ford Cortina was parked with its lights extinguished.

Magnus picked up the Cadillac as it was approaching Oxford's northern by-pass. In which direction would it turn at the roundabout?

"You recall the situation," Brigadier Tyson was saying. "Ever since we granted the Egyptians independence in '36 they had been telling us to get our troops the hell out. Between '51 and July '54, fifty-three of our men were killed in the Canal Zone. From Port Said to Ismailia and down to Suez we were harassed by an auxiliary force of guerrillas put into the field by the Minister of the Interior, Fuad Serag El Din. The Bulak Nizzam, those thugs were called. At the southern end of the Sweetwater Canal, which runs parallel to the Canal proper, was a water-filtration plant on which we absolutely depended. The Medways were guarding it under constant sniper fire from the village of Al Ain. Then the order came through to bulldoze eight two-storey brick houses in Al Ain, with the result that all hell broke loose. We had an officer shot through the head and a soldier through the face. Time and again our patrols walked into well-planned ambushes. Clearly the Bulak Nizzam were breaking our codes, even when we changed them. On January 3, 1952, four of our officers and two men were hit. It was the last straw. The Intelligence boys moved in and began a massive inquiry. We were paraded at short notice while they ripped through our kit, our lockers, our mattresses and then up our arses. I remember the humiliation of it. Oddly enough, we all suspected him, perhaps unfairly: obvious touch of the tar brush and fluent in Arabic. There was never any formal notification of his arrest, he just vanished. Nothing was said. And the Bulak Nizzam stopped breaking our codes."

"And that's all you know? No charges, no court martial?"

"When I achieved field officer rank some years later, certain skeletons swept under the Regimental carpet were revealed to me. No concrete evidence was found, no call-signs, codes, ciphers or radio frequencies sewn into the lining of his kit. He was always a clever bugger. And of course he denied it all."

"So they had to let him go?"

"A National Serviceman, you see, only a month or two short of his demob. Same old story: anything to prevent a scandal, a loss of face. He was, of course, quietly removed from the Reserve list."

"You'd think a dossier like that would go to every government department."

"You would, wouldn't you," said the Brigadier grimly.

When Judy Rossiter arrived at Ulf Steinberg's house the following morning, the sculptor's manservant conducted her up to the studio without a word.

Two people were waiting for her: Steinberg and the woman who so closely resembled Florence Eltenbridge, a woman whose name Ellison had been careful not to impart to Judy. Immediately she recognized that something was wrong.

"Oh Ulf, I'm so sorry, that dope you fed me just blew my mind, I had to get away—why did you *do* it to me?"

They stared at her in silence. Then the woman nodded and Steinberg pressed a bell in the wall. Almost immediately the studio door opened and two Spectrum guards entered, dragging a sack covered in dark, russet-brown stains. They dumped the sack at Judy's feet.

Out of it slid the broken, tortured corpse of Micky Kolarcz.

"And now," the woman said, "show us the green eyes beneath your contact lenses, Miss Rossiter."

At 9.15 Ellison walked into Ramsay Jordan's office, accompanied by Richard Smallhouse, the new General Manager whom Jordan had wooed from the *Sunday Dispatch* with a £5,000 salary boost after Gowers had fired Yorath.

"Glad to see all the plaster off the walls, Ramsay. How many bugs were found?"

"Twenty-five. Three in your office alone."

"Ramsay, I want an editorial conference called for 3.30. Yourself, myself, Richard, Magnus, period. Make sure that the Printer and the NGA, SLADE and NUJ Fathers of Chapel are available for consultation. Tell Gowers we'll be calling on him at 6.30—if he has a previous appointment, he'd better cancel it."

"Anything else, boss?" the Editor said with a wry smile.

"Yes. Inform Gowers that I'm taking over his entire office suite for the next ten days. I want three camp-beds up there, a cook and a half-dozen ex-CID security guards. They should be hired from an outfit called Anvil: I got the name from Superintendent Edgar Bradlaw and double-checked with Jack Knight."

Jordan was beaming. "When do we go to press?"

"On Sunday week—which gives us nine short days."

"And what's the story?"

"It's X-certificate, Ramsay."

On his way back to his office Ellison called in on the wire room where the ticker-tapes were just announcing the resignation of Roger Fullerton as Foreign Secretary, and his replacement by Cyril Quilley.

"In other words, by Kenneth Lynedoch," Ellison thought. How long would Vandyke last?

When he returned to his office he found Massey waiting for him.

"I thought you might have joined the *Dispatch*," Magnus said, poking Ellison in the ribs. "Want some news?"

"Only if you can spare the time."

"I shadowed Nashat Al-Khatib's car out of Swinburne's place last night. Guess where it went and who got out of it."

As Ellison silently reached for a scratch pad and a pencil, the corners of his mouth curled down grimly. He scribbled a name on the paper.

Magnus whistled. "Holy cow! You *knew*!"

"Magnus, the fact that we can now confirm it on the basis of physical observation means more to me than I can tell you. For one thing, it means that I'm not out of my tiny Chinese mind."

The intercom buzzed.

"Yes, darling?"

"Bill, there's a young woman on the line to you. She says her name is Judy. She . . . she sounds like Alice . . ."

Ellison had turned pale. Gesturing to Magnus to pick up the extension, he lifted the phone.

"Ellison speaking," he said cautiously.

"Hullo, Bill, it's Judy. How's things?" a bright voice said.

Ellison and Massey exchanged glances.

"Judy who?" Ellison said.

"Hey, how many Judys are working for you nowadays? This one is called Rossiter. Where have you been?"

"I'm afraid I don't remember your name. Perhaps you could jog my memory."

"You have eyes like grey conkers."

"Where are you now, Judy, and who are you with?"

"I was just feeling out of touch, Bill. Are you any nearer home base yet?"

"No . . . Listen, Judy, feel free to tell them everything you know. Everything."

But Judy did not reply. A man's voice came on the line, cold, clinical, precise. "No, Mr Ellison, we are interested in what *you* know. Remember what happened to O'Neill. And consider how much more vulnerable a young woman is. It requires only one small movement to ruin a pretty face for ever—as a start, you understand. Now talk, Ellison."

"OK, I'll talk. Ring me back." Ellison replaced the receiver. He flicked the intercom and asked for Ramsay Jordan. "Ramsay? I want Max Ucelik suspended on full pay pending an inquiry. Get him out of the building by noon. I'll square things with the NUJ FOC myself."

"You think Max shopped her?" Magnus said.

"No. I kept him on because the evidence against him involved Judy as a witness. But now she's blown and I want this building as clean as I can get it."

Magnus recognized that Ellison's tough, pragmatic manner was merely a characteristic response to deep pain and guilt.

"At least she warned us. She's got guts," Magnus said.

"Indeed she has. The one phone number they don't know is your own because it's not only ex-directory but listed with the Post Office accounts department under the name of your obliging Canadian cousin. If she had called you at home you could easily have spilled the beans."

"I'm going to try and get her back."

"You're what! If you imagine that Bradlaw or Knight stand the slightest chance of tracing——"

"There's another way," Magnus said quietly.

They met in the Garrick Club at 12.45. Tall, thin, aloof, gaunt in his rectitude, the Director-General of the BBC stood alone and ostracized in the club bar, awaiting his guest. As soon as Ellison arrived, Armstrong led him downstairs to a corner table in the dining-room.

"Well, Jack?"

"I shall tender my resignation tomorrow."

"Kind of you to let me know."

"The gesture is not one of courtesy."

"What, then?"

Across London, the muezzins were chanting electronically from the minarets of the new mosques, summoning the faithful to kneel and pray, and reminding them of the five sacred commandments of Islam. A great celebration had been in progress, proclaimed across the air waves and on gigantic hoardings in every main street, ever since the Islamic year 1400 of the *Hegira* calendar had begun in 1979. To honour the event, the Islamic Council, directed from Jeddah in Saudi Arabia, had invested millions of pounds in a vast Moslem festival—in every supermarket records, cassettes and booklets bearing sacred readings from the Koran were being distributed free, along with Green Crescent stamps.

"Yesterday," Armstrong was saying in his stiff, clipped Edinburgh brogue, "Lucas presented me with a verbal ultimatum from Martindale—nothing written down on paper, you understand. Unless I resign the Government will cut the TV licence fees: from £25 to £21 for colour, from £12

261

to £10 for monochrome. That would represent a fall in revenue of some £60 million a year, almost twenty per cent of the Corporation's budget. It would involve the loss of fifteen hundred jobs out of fifteen thousand on the programme, technical and executive side; and a further thousand out of twelve thousand on the manual, secretarial, clerical and catering side. The Charter, as you know, forbids a deficit of over £10 million."

"It's bluff."

"It may be bluff. But they have rendered my position impossible by filtering this message through to every corner of the Corporation. Every producer, editor, cameraman, technician, secretary and stage-hand now associates my name with a threat to their livelihood. And these days . . ."

"There is no work anywhere else. Clever. At a stroke they have turned the unions against you. Even so, you stay."

Armstrong cleared his throat awkwardly while his long bony fingers made war on one another, a constant, nerve-racking snapping of the knuckles. The bushy eyebrows lifted. "For how long, Ellison?"

"For nine days."

"Why?"

Ellison told him why.

On his return to the *Monitor*, Cherry handed him a plain, sealed envelope, delivered an hour earlier by hand. He ripped it open: like every communication she let him touch, it had been run through the letter-bomb scanner. Solomon Rupin and Michael Ben-Dor were back in town, living under false identities at an address in Golders Green. They had one item of information: Badr Nureddin, Ha-Mossad's source in Qatar, had been ripped in half by sub-machine gun fire while leaving the Ruler's palace in Doha.

"Fancy that," he muttered.

Twenty

At 3.30 the most critical editorial conference in the history of the *Sunday Monitor* convened in Ramsay Jordan's office. The walls had been stripped of plaster, the floorboards taken up and the telephone dismantled, along with all other electrical equipment. Anyone entering the room was obliged to exchange his shoes for slippers in the locker room; all clothing was searched by a former CID security guard from Anvil.

"How many words do you need?" Jordan asked Ellison.

"Forty thousand."

Jordan and Smallhouse exchanged glances.

"That's eight full pages in 9-point if your display takes up twenty-five per cent," Jordan said.

"It will. The pictures are important and pictures we do have. There's an eight-page supplement advertising the glories of Kuwait due for Sunday week, right?"

"Hands off," Smallhouse said. "It's worth £50,000 in advertising revenue."

"We'll jettison Kuwait for the final edition—London and the Home Counties. That's half a million copies out of a total run of 1.5 million."

"Which means," Smallhouse said, "that on the Monday we have to pay back close to £17,000 in advertising revenue. These pages are gold, Bill: two-thirds of them are either straight commercial advertising or text sponsored and paid for by the Government of Kuwait."

"What I don't follow," Jordan said, "is why we lose it only in the final edition."

"Because the eight pages I have in mind will only go into the final edition. We have to bluff them and bluff them very hard right up to the hour before midnight. And that, incidentally, is the title Magnus and I have settled on: *The Hour Before Midnight*. Any objections?"

"I like it," Jordan said.

"Consider all recent experience," Ellison continued. "The law now permits the Leech Squad to seize random copies from the presses, even before they creep up the igranic wires into the publishing room. And seize them they do. If we put this thing into the early editions for Scotland, the North and the Midlands, fifty squad cars will surround the building and another fifty will make a dash for Euston, King's Cross, Paddington and Waterloo to snatch the bundles off the trains. They'll close us down. By midnight the Leech Squad gets bored and sleepy. They slump in their Triumphs soaking whisky out of paper cups. Then they lurch off home."

"We'll still be running risks," Smallhouse said. "Every one of the twenty-one London-area wholesalers we deal with collects from our chutes in their own vans. The cat will be out of the bag soon enough."

"Don't I know it. Even if we're lucky, very lucky and very clever, between about 4 am and 7 am ISP cars will be hitting six hundred direct-account distribution points and God knows how many newsagents and street vendors. We'll lose a lot of copies. But we'll go on printing until they seal the presses. You'll make a prior deal with the Chapel Fathers, Richard, and at 4 am every man in this building will go on to two hundred per cent overtime rate."

"And how do you intend to set these forty thousand words into print?"

"That's what we've got to decide. It's my belief that no one outside the composing room need set eyes on this stuff until 11 on the Saturday night. You can mould the flongs, cast the plates in the foundry, and set the presses running within sixty minutes."

"Yes," Jordan said, "but that still leaves the crunch in the composing room. I need hardly remind you that if we attempted to set up one word, never mind forty thousand words in type ourselves, the unions would close us down within five minutes."

"That had occurred to me. After all, I've been working in newspapers for all of three days."

"Sorry."

"Ramsay, you've got the Printer and the three FOCs standing by?" Jordan nodded. "We know them all well. Personally, I trust them all. And if we don't, we're fucked. Any reservations?"

"None," Jordan said.

"None," Smallhouse said.

Jordan flicked his intercom and asked his secretary to invite the four men into his office.

Presently Stan Gilbert, the Printer in overall charge of the composing-room staff, entered the office, followed by the Father of the NUJ Chapel, representing the journalists, the Imperial Father of the NGA Chapels, representing workers in the composing room, the foundry, the machine-room and the publishing room, and the SLADE FOC, representing the process department, where picture plates are made.

"Gentlemen," Jordan said, "we have reached a very grave hour in the history of our country, and a very challenging hour in the history of this newspaper. On Sunday week we intend to publish facts unknown to all but a small and ruthless clique. The fate of our democracy may depend upon these facts reaching the public. To achieve this, your support and loyalty are indispensable. It is no exaggeration to say that any one of you can walk out of here, make a single phone-call to Whitehall, and bury British liberty, perhaps for ever. If any of you finds such a burden of responsibility insupportable, please say so now."

There was a long silence in the small, crowded office. Then the Printer, Stan Gilbert, slowly filling his pipe from an oilcloth tobacco pouch, shyly offered his hand to Ellison.

"Nice work, Bill."

The ice was broken. By spontaneous common accord, in a moment of deep, unspoken emotion, every man in the office shook the hand of every other man. It was the moment, week after depressing week, that they had all been waiting for.

Ramsay Jordan nodded to Ellison. "Bill, it's all yours."

They all turned to Ellison. And as they did so the realization sank into everyone present that they were looking at a man approaching the limit of his physical and emotional resources. It seemed, then, as he briefly turned away and gazed down out of the window at the two Leech Squad Triumphs parked in Carmelite Street, that he might not make it. It was the Printer, Stan Gilbert, who, in his own way, once again eased the situation.

"Of course," he chuckled, blowing pipe-smoke into the air, "I never believe a word of what Bill writes. Can't imagine why so many people take him seriously."

Ellison turned from the window with a faint smile.

"Fuck off, Stan."

"Well," Gilbert said, glancing at the FOCs, "a remark like that and I think we have to call the men out." He winked. "Now you'll be wanting to set up all this nonsense at night, right? How many words and how many blocks?"

"Forty thousand words and some thirty blocks."

Gilbert whistled. "That will mean laying on a night shift Tuesday, Wednesday and Thursday, with Friday night for re-setting." He turned to the Father of the NGA Chapels. "Harry, what's the minimum we can use—five linotype operators, four time-hands to set up the formes, and one case-hand to set up the headlines by hand?"

"We might make it."

Gilbert turned to the SLADE FOC. "An overseer plus four, Frank?"

"Hard going with thirty blocks. We'll have a go."

"We leave it to you gentlemen to select your operatives," Jordan said. "I suggest we draw up short lists here and now; these men must be chosen with extreme care."

"And that means," interposed Ellison, "operatives of proven democratic convictions, operatives of proven reliability, operatives whose private lives make them unlikely targets for blackmail or bribery. Fortunately we don't print a daily paper in this building, so the production rooms are quiet at night. The operatives you select must divulge to no one what they are doing."

"Now wait a minute," said Harry, the NGA FOC, whose hackles had been visibly rising. "I can't accept these remarks. What you're asking us to do is to side with the Management against our own members."

Sensing that Ellison was about to explode, Jordan quickly intervened.

"On the contrary, Harry. Security is a problem in all departments and at all levels. Need I remind you that we have only recently fired our own General Manager, Yorath, because we knew him to be a Government agent? You know as well as I do that this paper has suffered from sabotage week after week."

Harry subsided. "Fair enough," he muttered.

Ellison turned to the NUJ FOC.

"Terry, I hope you'll buy this—we're cutting out the regular proof-readers entirely. Every galley-proof will go straight to the Chairman's office where I will correct it personally. This means, Harry, that your compositors on the stone and your linotype operators will have to break the rules by accepting corrections of literals, etcetera, in my hand."

"That won't be easy to sell. As you know, the readers are pretty paranoid already."

"There's still one problem," Stan Gilbert said. "We set up the type at night. But where do we store it during the day? Anyone can pull a chase out of the page stackers."

"At the close of each shift every galley and chase must be moved by lift to the Chairman's offices," Ellison said.

"By the way," Harry said, "these narks you're moving in —non-union labour, I presume?"

"Yes," Ellison said.

"Then keep them out of sight."

"Jesus Christ, if we don't get this stuff off the presses do you realize there won't be any unions in this country!"

"Bill . . ." Jordan said softly.

"Don't Bill me. We're all rational men and it's time we saw beyond the end of our pet noses. I've been a member of my union for twenty-five years and I've even been an FOC in my time. When the previous proprietor here tried to fire three journalists because they had protested about working conditions, I personally led the whole Chapel out on strike. And I'd do it again. But for shit's sake get it into your heads that we're less than two weeks away from fascism!"

Again there was silence. Ellison had turned, pale and shaking, to the window. Ramsay Jordan glanced round the room: the response was good. There was no hostility. Only sympathy.

The Hour Before Midnight was on its way.

At 6.30 Jordan, Ellison and Smallhouse took the lift to the tenth floor. Sleek and glowing with the prospect of revenge, the Chairman offered them brandy and cigars. Hands in pockets, Gowers strode up and down his wall-to-wall Penthouse-Supreme carpet, chuckling with delight.

"This will take the *Monitor* up from 1.5 to 2 million, no doubt about it. The *Dispatch* is presently taking in £225,000 a week in ad. revenue. Make no mistake, we'll cream off £100,000 of it. I'd like to see Jacobs's face when the *Monitor* hits the news-stands." He glanced at Ellison warmly. "My dear Bill, you look to be on your last legs."

"I've got a spare pair in the bank."

Gowers laughed heartily and refilled Ellison's glass. "Now, Bill, let's have the story."

Ellison was waiting for this. "I haven't written it yet."

"Presumably you know what you're going to write."

"Chairman," Ramsay Jordan said soothingly, "I'm in the

dark myself, and even Magnus, I gather, doesn't know it all. Bill never discusses what he's going to write."

Gowers's face darkened. "That's real money I'm throwing away on that Kuwait supplement, Jordan. In any case, the article will have to be vetted by my lawyer."

"That's out of the question," Ellison said.

"Now wait a minute . . ." But Gowers's protest died on his lips. He knew the ultimatum Ellison would present: either the *Monitor* did it his way . . . or the *Dispatch* would get the story.

Throughout Friday, long Leyland 442 trucks rolled up from the East End warehouse towards Gowers House, each truck carrying 17 reels of newsprint, each reel 64 inches wide, 33,000 feet long, and weighing three-quarters of a ton. A normal run of the 72-page *Monitor* would consume 28 million feet of newsprint, enough to extend from Fleet Street to San Francisco. *The Hour Before Midnight* alone, restricted to the final edition, would consume 3 million feet, or 94 reels, enough to stretch from Fleet Street to John O' Groat's.

At 9.30 on the Friday morning, an Anvil armoured security van, flanked by four support cars carrying twenty men, transported a dozen deposit boxes from three London banks to the tenth floor of Gowers House. For every document thus removed, a duplicate was left in the bank vaults. This little exercise cost Gowers £500.

At 11 in the morning Ellison bedded down in a cot in the Chairman's office, behind a door jealously guarded by Cherry. All incoming calls for Lord Gowers were being rerouted by the switchboard to a smaller office on the ninth floor. Cherry woke her boss, as instructed, at 4 in the afternoon with a cup of coffee and a cheese omelette. Then he took a shower.

The huge teak desk had been stripped of all vanity-fanning bric-à-brac. The gleaming teak surface carried only a single object.

Ellison stared at the typewriter.

"Would now suit you?" he murmured.

By 6 pm on Monday Ellison had got through a hundred and fifty cigarettes, thirty cups of coffee, and three changes of underwear. On the desk before him lay a hundred and twenty pages of A4 copy paper, much of it written in first draft during the preceding weeks, but all of it re-shaped with Magnus's help during the past seventy-two hours.

"Well?"

Ramsay Jordan, sunk in one of Gowers's deep leather armchairs, laid down the final page.

"It hangs together. I'm convinced. Almost."

"It's shit. No one will believe a word of it."

"There are a couple of gaps in the evidence, perhaps."

Ellison leaned his elbows on the desk and cupped his hands over his face. "I'm waiting for that evidence." Then he nodded to Magnus. "OK, beautiful, let's start all over again."

Magnus gazed back at him out of a deep, tormented gloom.

Tuesday, 11 pm. Stan Gilbert stood in front of the huge teak desk. Ellison and Massey sat slumped in their chairs, soaked in sweat, numb with fatigue.

"Stan, we haven't got it right yet. But the first twenty thousand words will pass. Take 'em away, Stan."

The phone rang. Magnus snatched at it. Ellison lifted an extension.

She was sobbing, incoherent, distraught, agonized. Twice she screamed. "Bill, Magnus, Magnus, Magnus, please, please, please . . ." Then a voice, a man's voice, cold, clinical, precise, spoke.

"Your colleague is strapped to a chair, naked. Electrodes touch her nipples and genitals every ten seconds. She has eaten nothing for the past two days—we do, however, encourage her to consume her own excrement. She is suffering, of course, from acute dehydration and delirium. She has told us a very great deal, possibly all she knows, but we are not satisfied. We wish to know more. In short, everything you have discovered. We are sending you through the post a photograph of her present condition—several. We are, frankly, surprised by your lack of loyalty to her. She is even more surprised: her faith in you both is almost extinguished. To whom else can she appeal? No one. Tomorrow, if you persist in your stubborn silence, more serious and lasting mutilations will begin. We will keep you abreast of them by post. Have you heard me and understood, Ellison?"

"Perfectly."

"And what is your reply?"

"We'll discuss it. Ring me back in ten minutes."

"Agreed." The phone went dead.

The two men stared into space.

"Magnus, a few days ago you told me there was a way to get her back. Since Friday I've seen less of you than I would have liked. I assumed you were trying to help Judy, God knows how. Well?"

Magnus was pacing the room like a caged animal, banging his clenched fist into his palm. Time and again he searched for words, for an explanation, but each time they stuck in his throat.

Then the phone rang. Magnus took it.

"Ten minutes have passed," said the same cold, clinical, precise voice.

"Listen," Magnus said, "call us at the same time tomorrow night and we'll tell you all we know. On one condition. That in the interval you let her eat and sleep and molest her in no way. She must be able to talk to us coherently when you call."

"Agreed," the voice said immediately. "But if this is merely a strategy, a playing for time, you will regret it. *She* will regret it even more. Understood?"

A heartrending scream was followed by choking sobs and desperate pleas for mercy. "Bill, Magnus, Magnus, Magnus! Please!"

Both men held on to their extensions grimly until the phone went dead.

Twenty-one

Magnus was desperate on behalf of Judy.

The Press room of the Dorchester Hotel, lavishly equipped with typewriters, free telephones, Telex machines, Turkish coffee and sweetmeats, was barred to correspondents of the *Monitor* and the *Dispatch*. Agents of the ISP and Baghdad Squad 9 bodyguards prowled the perimeter of the Arab Mission's hotel in search of "Zionist agents". Magnus's telescope into the Dorchester was his friend Bernie Holzheimer, of the London bureau of the *New York Times*. Reared in Brooklyn, Bernie was less than a devout Moslem; the funerals of Moshe Levene and Maurice Cohn had brought out a mean streak in him.

Holzheimer's sources in the State Department had alerted him to the nature of the danger facing Britain before Ellison himself had become fully aware of it. Bernie had been the first person to mention Al-Ittihad's existence to the Searchlight team. But the White House, fearing a new Arab oil embargo, had chosen to turn a blind eye, vetoing any form of effective intervention on behalf of the beleaguered democratic forces in Britain. Bitterly frustrated and depressed during the past months, Holzheimer now recognized that Ellison and Massey were closing for the kill. He wanted to help any way he could.

Working on telephoned tip-offs from Bernie, Magnus had concentrated on the movements of two Arab women, Samar Saleh Yacoub and Nuriya Yacoub, wife and daughter of

Yusuf Hashim Yacoub, the killer of Baghdad, the man who had stage-managed the public hangings of Jews in Revolution Square. Ranked number three in the Mission, Yacoub was also known to Ellison and Massey as Zamil Kadhimiya of Al-Ittihad.

Floating about London in their chauffeured Cadillac, from Harrod's to Fortnum and Mason's, from Liberty's to Carrington's, the Yacoub women spent money like water. But their spending habits had hitherto brought Magnus no closer to the break he desperately needed. And now, on this Wednesday morning, with Judy's torturers demanding a complete account of Searchlight's investigations within twelve hours, he once again shadowed them from the Dorchester, sick with despair.

In Liberty's the Yacoub women merely trifled with the small change in their purses: £852 on a gold peridot ring, £685 on a Regency sofa table inlaid in Pollard oak and crossbanded with laburnum. And then, dumping a few parcels in the Cadillac, they abruptly dismissed both car and chauffeur. He argued excitedly but they were adamant. Within a minute they had merged into the crowd and were heading for Oxford Street, the great shopping emporium of the common man.

A hundred yards east of Oxford Circus, Magnus struck.

A Leica M3, fitted with a Leitz Tele-Elmant 90mm lens attachment, focused at sixty feet, clicked rapidly through half a dozen frames of Kodak TriX black and white film. As it did so the two women, one dressed in the traditional black abba, but unveiled, the other wearing a smart trouser-suit, entered a large store through one of its eleven pairs of glass double-doors. The 90mm lens simultaneously caught the gilded lettering, some twenty feet above the heads of the two women, which extended thirty feet across the store:

MARKS & SPENCER.

He crossed the street.

Once inside the store, the Yacoub women went mad, grabbing tricot knitwear overtops, denim jump-suits, cotton beach towels, a dozen pairs of Polyester cotton "boxer" undershorts, half a dozen "extra firm control" highline girdles, a cluster of nylon and Lycra bras, and—Nuriya's pet indulgence—a clutch of mauve and apricot garter bikinis in nylon polyamide.

He prayed: don't steal. They didn't.

When their purchases were finally assembled at the packaging counter, the bill totted up to a modest £209.14. Nuriya reached into her handbag and counted out twenty-one crisp £10 notes.

Magnus had once overheard a director of Marks & Spencer remark at a party, with an enigmatic smile, "a hundred pounds is worth a pair of scissors". The meaning of the quip now became clear as the Yacoub women, demanding two pairs of scissors, began brazenly to snip the "St Michael" brand labels off all their purchases. This done, they issued instructions that the goods be wrapped in plain brown paper.

As they emerged from the store's Poland Street side-exit, staggering under their parcels, the Leica caught the blend of satisfaction and mild apprehension on their faces. They were looking for a taxi.

"Good morning, ladies."

At the sight of the clutch of cameras hanging across the chest of the tall photographer both women froze in alarm.

"The readers of my paper will be delighted to learn that the wife and daughter of Yusuf Hashim Yacoub have been shopping in a store principally owned by Jews."

The mother understood very little English. The daughter talked rapidly to her in Arabic.

Hailing a taxi, Magnus bundled the two women into the back seat. They were too paralysed to resist.

"Just drive," he told the driver, perching himself on the jump seat opposite the Arab women.

"Who do you work for?" Nuriya said.

"My agency services all the main daily papers. And the *Jewish Chronicle*."

"£100 for the film in your cameras."

Magnus took out a notebook, wrote a message in block capitals, tore off the page, and handed it to the daughter. "Tell your father to be waiting at this place at 3 pm this afternoon."

"£500. In cash. Now."

"And tell him to come alone. Alone, understand? I don't want Aziz or Kazzar or any other Baghdad meat-cutters on the scene."

"£1,000. In cash. Take us to the bank."

He reached out and grabbed her wrist. "Use your head. These pictures are a death sentence. Understand? A death sentence. You'll find your father at the Ministry of Defence."

He halted the cab, gave further instructions to the driver, thrust a fiver into his hand, and vanished—a tall young man wearing a corduroy cap, dark glasses, and a black beard.

Ellison reached his bank in Fenchurch Street at 10.40 and was immediately shown into the manager's office.

"Good morning, David."

"You look tired, Bill."

"Lend me an office and a telephone for half an hour?"

His old friend from Oxford days nodded and led him along a private corridor to a small room which contained nothing but a table and a black telephone.

"It's all yours."

"Thanks."

Ellison turned the key in the door, lit a cigarette, then removed the message from his pocket. It consisted solely of digits: 10487435281411 0021. The last two digits represented a signature—two squares forward, one to the side: Knight.

Jack had worked on Sergei Tretiakov, Second Secretary in the Soviet Embassy and agent of the KGB.

Ellison lifted the receiver and dialled 104.

"Any delays on calls to Moscow?"

"The line is clear at the moment."

"Thanks."

He lit a new cigarette from the stub of the old one and stared out of the window at a montage of anonymous roof-tops, elevations and fire-escapes. Periodically he checked his watch and Knight's coded message. Date, today, the 14th; time, 1100 GMT. He snatched at the receiver and once again dialled 104.

"I want Moscow 874 3528."

"Your number, please?"

Presently he heard the voice of a Russian girl operator on the line; his own operator broke into halting Russian. A long pause followed before he heard the dialling tone. Almost immediately a man answered, in Russian. The girl operator said a few words.

"Hullo," said the man.

"Philby?" said Ellison.

"Yes."

"Ellison speaking."

"Really? When your daughter Faith was one year old and living in Beirut, she picked up something nasty. What was it?"

"A deadly snake resembling a black shoelace."

"How are you, Bill?"

"I need your help."

"That's nice."

Ellison mentioned a man's name. "Was he, at that time, straight or bent?"

"Judged from your own narrow line of vision?—the Empire over which the sun was never to set?"

"If you like."

"Bent."

"Local wind?"

"It looked local then."

"He confided in you?"

"I never depended on people confiding in me. No."

"What about the Canal Zone affair?"

"It was a minor job and foolish by professional standards.

You have to appreciate that it has always been a matter of conviction, of passion even, running from father to son. The money less important."

"How the hell did he get into the FO with that stain on his record?"

"He didn't."

"But he did."

"Not first time round. He sat the exam in '54. Passed with flying colours, I'm told. But the security vetting was negative."

"Yet four years later he was in."

"Well, you know how it was, after Suez, morale was shaken, they needed Arabists."

"But someone had to pull a string pretty hard to get him in?"

"Could be."

"Who pulled it?"

"Very bad line, this."

Ellison raised his voice. "I assume you're saying that the KGB got him into the FO to hasten the break-up of British influence in the Middle East?"

"Dear Bill, the more you shout, the worse the line gets."

"Did you know the Al-Ittihad people when you were in Beirut?"

"I've never been a recluse. In those days, of course, Al-Ittihad wasn't much. Nasser had almost killed the thing off."

"When did he first meet Al-Rashib?"

"Late fifties."

"And Yacoub?"

"Later: mid-sixties."

"And Nashat Al-Khatib?"

"The same."

"And Shukhairy?"

"The same. Interesting list that. I've been wondering how long it would take you to sort it all out. But what's *his* position?"

"At the top."

"Impossible. It would have to be an Arab. Sorry, I follow you now—in Britain, you mean?"

"Yes, that's where I'm standing—just."

Philby laughed quietly. "I gather you're in the firing line, Bill."

"I keep away from windows."

"What you tell me about him does make sense, I suppose. It's my guess that he was always more dedicated, more single-minded, than the others. He always had a long-term view. Very important, that."

"You should know."

"Detect a hint of asperity in your comment."

"Anything sexual in his record?"

"My own father suffered floggings in the Saudi desert, you know. And his father admired T. E. Lawrence, who was also flogged. It all goes with the sandstorms."

"Are you saying he's queer?"

"Not exactly. Neutered would be a better word. He once told me he'd rather be flogged to death than have intercourse with a woman."

"He said that!"

Philby laughed. "You always were a very straight fellow, Bill."

"One thing puzzles me. How did his father evade British Intelligence once he had committed himself to the Axis?"

"He didn't. His father died in a British prison camp in Egypt after protracted interrogation. The old boy wouldn't talk; there's no doubt he was tortured to death."

"Thanks, Kim."

"Always happy to be of service to your country."

The phone went down in Moscow.

He didn't expect Yacoub to come alone, despite his clear warning. It wasn't in the nature of the beast.

Magnus had practised this form of blind-date technique

before, but never with a character so dangerous, so powerful, as Yusuf Hashim Yacoub.

On the South Bank of the Thames, the Royal Festival Hall, the Queen Elizabeth Hall, the National Film Theatre, and the National Theatre—each designed in severely cubist contours—are joined on six vertical levels by a maze of open terraces, esplanades, catwalks, bridges and spiral staircases.

The National Film Theatre squats directly under the pillar-supported land extension of Waterloo Bridge. The note Magnus had written in the taxi and handed to Nuriya Yacoub had instructed her father to place himself, alone, at the front entrance to the NFT at 3 pm.

At 2.51 Magnus took two paces off the south-west end of the bridge, along a concrete walkway. And stopped. This vantage-point offered him five possible lines of retreat: (1) across the bridge, north; (2) off the bridge, south; (3) down a spiral staircase to the sunken car-park fronting the NFT; (4) along the walkway at the rear of the Hayward Gallery, then down into the esplanade separating the NFT from the Festival Hall; (5) along the same walkway, but turning up a staircase leading to a footbridge running across the top level of Queen Elizabeth Hall, and then down to the river esplanade. It also afforded him a clear view of the NFT entrance sixty yards away and fifty feet below.

But what particularly recommended this vantage-point to Magnus above all other considerations was the presence on the bridge, only five yards away, of a bus stop. A man standing and looking always becomes conspicuous—particularly when others are looking for him. A bus stop is a place where people stand and wait without attracting attention.

At 2.56 a black Mercedes 450 SEL glided into the almost empty sunken car-park in front of the NFT. The car manoeuvred slowly into a turn and came to rest close to the exit, facing it.

It was now that Magnus, running his eye along the rim of the bridge itself, noticed a man half-leaning over the parapet, apparently reading a newspaper. A narrow newspaper column requires only the slightest inflection of the eyes, but this man's gaze was swivelling theatrically across the page—and from right to left.

At 3.01 a taxi drew up outside the NFT entrance. An Arab dressed in a smart grey suit climbed out. Yusuf Hashim Yacoub stood motionless, waiting. Magnus walked away, towards Waterloo Station, and hailed a taxi. "Want £10?"

"If you've got it, mate, I want it."

Magnus extracted an envelope from his pocket. The letter inside was already written.

"Drive to the entrance of the NFT. You'll find an Arab standing there, middle-aged and wearing a smart grey suit. Give him this letter. When he's read it, he may take your cab. If he does, drive him to Ravenscourt Park tube station but on no account tell him where you're going."

The taxi-driver shrugged warily. "I don't want no trouble with any Arabs, mate."

Magnus offered him another £10 note. The cabbie grinned. "You've convinced me."

Magnus regained his vantage-point just as the taxi-driver drew up beside Yacoub in front of the NFT and handed him the letter. Yacoub read it carefully, shrugged, then gestured towards the Spectrum Mercedes in the car-park. It was an angry, dismissive gesture. As the taxi clattered away with Yacoub in the back, the Mercedes remained motionless, like a crippled scorpion.

Walking rapidly off the bridge towards the alley behind Waterloo Station where his Aston Martin was parked, Magnus noticed that the Arab with the newspaper was now closing on him from behind. At his peak, before Claire Boothroyd and Kicky Rapp had taught him how to prosper by standing still, Magnus had covered 100 metres of the Crystal Palace track in 10.7 seconds. Accelerating fast, he heard the first dull "phutt" behind him of a revolver fitted with a silencer—like the bursting of a paperbag only half full of air. Seeing the brickwork splinter on a wall ahead of him, he weaved, zigzagged, heard two more shots in rapid succession, sensed the passage of a bullet within inches of his head, turned a corner, sliced through dense traffic, and was finally clear.

Yacoub was standing in front of Ravenscourt Park tube station, alone and lost. Magnus waited five minutes, climbed out of his car, and signalled the Arab to follow him, leading him into the park and gesturing towards an empty bench under some trees. Yacoub sat down but Magnus didn't; he remained standing directly behind the Arab.

Yacoub studied the prints of his wife and daughter entering Marks & Spencer, scooping up handfuls of nylon garter bikinis, testing the stretch of girdles, and leaving the store. His sharp face was a study in rage and fear. Again and again he swore in Arabic.

"So. So. Who you are, what you want?"

"Many papers," said Magnus slowly, "publish these tomorrow. Many papers, yes? Unless. Unless."

"Unless what? What you want from Yacoub?"

"I want Judy Rossiter, alive and well—by midnight."

Yacoub's eyes swivelled rapidly. "You Ellison, eh?"

Massey was leaning over him now, from behind. "You'll swing from a gibbet in Revolution Square, Yacoub, just like those poor Jews did." Yacoub didn't like being leant over, he didn't like being stranded in this unknown park, he didn't like the prints in his hand. Yusuf Hashim Yacoub was used to controlling situations. He began to complain in broken English and he swore, frequently, in unbroken Arabic. The *Monitor* would cheat him, the *Monitor* held the negatives and would print the photographs anyway, personally he had nothing against Jews, only Zionists, and he knew nothing about public hangings in Baghdad.

He offered Magnus £100,000 silence money, to be paid in twenty monthly instalments. Massey walked round to the front of the bench and slapped Yacoub across the face half a dozen times. Gasping and struggling to rise, the Arab caught a sharper blow and sprawled back across the bench, nursing a bleeding lip. A group of small boys who had been kicking a football stopped to watch, fascinated and amazed, as if their favourite television serial had suddenly popped up in the wrong place.

"Yes, yes," the Arab groaned, "Yacoub fix it."

Reaching King Street, Magnus hailed a taxi, bundled Yacoub into it and slammed the door, but not before he had plucked the photographs from Yacoub's numbed hands and given a last, stinging swipe across the face to "Zamil Kadhimiya".

"Wait a minute!" yelled the cab driver.

"Take this dog to the Dorchester Hotel," Magnus said.

Twenty-two

Wednesday, 3.30 pm. Ellison groaned, swore and pushed the typewriter away from him across the huge teak desk. Cherry stood waiting while he read the Press Association tear-off she had just brought him.

Prime Minister Murdoch told the Commons at question time that the present system of government had failed the nation and required a drastic overhaul. Murdoch proposed a Ministry of All the Talents to represent the national interest as a whole. Pressed by Jeremy Bentley, MP, Murdoch declined to speculate when Parliament would be dissolved. The Sovereign, he said, had consented on his advice to return to London over the weekend.

In response to a question by Marshall Durban, MP, Secretary for War Giles Burnett declined to comment on reports that armoured infantry units had been put on stand-by alert in the Salisbury Plain area. When Durban asked him what Operation Talent was, Burnett denied all knowledge of it.

Home Secretary Martindale declined to comment on rumours that the size of the ISP had recently been doubled to 12,000. He denied that all police leave had been cancelled as from tomorrow.

"Well, darling, this is it. Have you tried Vandyke again?"
"I've tried six times."
"Seven is a magic number."

Arnold Byatt, a proof-reader for the *Sunday Monitor*, had two nagging problems: a mortgage on a house he could not afford, and heavy alimony payments to his first wife. At 4.00 pm he packed his briefcase at the end of the day shift, left Gowers House and proceeded straight to the crypt of St Bride's Church.

In ISP Control, Whitehall, Byatt's progress was monitored on one of twenty-four computer-controlled television screens scanning critical areas of London. In a second saturation-surveillance room, thirty ISP agents wearing large ear-phones sat in front of tape-recorders monitoring telephone conversations made by men who figured on the Operation Talent blacklist.

Fifteen minutes after Byatt had entered St Bride's, a new set of galley-proofs pulled from the *Sunday Monitor*'s galleys of type were spread across the desk of Superintendent Stanley Leech. He studied them intently, then flicked the intercom linking him to the man from whom the entire Home Office, including Home Secretary Martindale, took its orders.

"There's a milky political obituary for Fullerton, sir," Leech reported. "Otherwise nothing except general warnings, bleat, bleat . . ."

"I'm not impressed," Under Secretary Geoffrey Ozanne said. "Ellison is well aware that there will be no more Sundays in his calendar. For him, it's now or never."

"Yes, sir. We'll increase surveillance, sir."

"How many sources do you now have inside Gowers House?"

"Byatt, the proof-reader, plus two compositors on the stone. Jones works the edition shift and Powell the day shift. Jones reports that when he knocked off at midnight last night he noticed something unusual."

"What?"

"A half dozen linotype operators and four or five time-hands were clocking in. That's abnormal; the *Monitor*'s presses don't print a daily paper."

"Interesting."

Ozanne then picked up a No Access phone and dialled a

number known to only five men in Britain. A hundred yards down Whitehall Under Secretary Kenneth Lynedoch lifted his No Access phone.

Ozanne outlined the situation. "I also have a report just in that Zamil Kadhimiya is in some kind of trouble."

"Yacoub? What kind of trouble?"

"It's not clear yet. His security guards suspect that he has been got at or blackmailed. In any case, he's disappeared."

Lynedoch cursed in Arabic. Slowly his eye came to rest on a large photograph hanging on the wall. It depicted the great mosque-palace of Al-Alhambra.

Wednesday, 11.50 pm, ten minutes to midnight. Ellison and Massey sat paralysed, unable to work, staring at the phone. Nothing. No Judy, no phone-call.

"There's a power struggle in progress within Al-Ittihad," Ellison said.

"Let's hope Yacoub wins it."

Thursday, 11.30. Walter Vandyke and Marshall Durban breezed in to the tenth-floor office.

"Bill, I gather you're anxious that I should correct the proofs of my article."

Ellison sighed and stretched. "Walter, you're just marvellous, so clean and spruce and gleaming, custom-built for Number 10. And why did Murdoch fire Fullerton but not you? Perhaps he trembles at the prospect of a final confrontation with the Sir Lancelot of the People."

"Bill, you look tired," Vandyke said.

Ellison abruptly leant forward across the huge teak desk. "When did you last visit Steinberg for a sitting?"

"How the hell do you know about that?"

"*When*, Walter?"

"Three days ago. Why?"

"And was there a new model girl in residence?"

285

"Since you ask, yes."

"As attractive as the last one, Walter?"

"I don't think I noticed," Vandyke said stiffly. "Is all this really your concern?"

Slowly Ellison opened the desk drawer and extracted a sheaf of prints. Methodically he laid them on the desk. Vandyke stared at the pictures, horrified.

"My God! But that's . . ."

"Yes, Walter, that's my colleague Judy Rossiter and that's what Steinberg's friends have done to her. Your friend Ulf was also Maurice Cohn's friend Ulf. And that's why you haven't been fired yet; they were waiting for a picture the *Star* could carry on its front page. And now, Walter, a humble journalist is going to tell you what you're going to do—provided you make him a Dame in your first New Year's Honours List."

When the call came through at 12.30 pm, Magnus was alone in the office. A woman was on the line.

"May I speak to Mr Ellison or Mr Massey?"

"Massey speaking."

"This is the Charing Cross Hospital," the woman said in a practised, soothing tone. "We have a young lady here who was brought in this morning by private ambulance and——"

"What's her name?"

"Well, actually we're not quite sure. She was carrying no identification and was heavily sedated. She seems reluctant to give her name but she did, finally, ask to see you or Mr Ellison."

"Is she . . . I mean, is she . . ."

"I can't give you a diagnosis until the consultant has completed his examination and tests. He's with her now."

"I'm on my way." He dropped the receiver and grabbed his leather coat.

At the Charing Cross Hospital in Fulham Palace Road they kept him waiting for three hours before a young nurse finally led him up to a private room off the female casualty ward.

"You do look worried. She's quite all right, really, I mean you may get a bit of a shock at first, superficial injuries, you know, oh you do look pale, would you like a cup of tea first?"

At the entrance to the casualty ward, the sister in charge, a stout, brusque woman in starched cotton, intercepted them.

"Mr Massey, the patient still refuses to divulge her name. She's suffering from acute shock, but not amnesia. She seems terrified. We believe the police should be called. A private ambulance brought her in to the casualty entrance this morning, carried her out on a stretcher, then immediately drove away without a word of explanation."

The consultant appeared.

"Mr Massey, in view of the nature of this young woman's injuries, I feel I must ask you a few questions before I let you see her. Funny things can happen in hospitals."

"Of course."

"I take it you know who she is?"

"Her name is Judith Rossiter. She and I are colleagues on the *Sunday Monitor*."

"She's a journalist, then?"

"Correct."

"She has been severely maltreated. You knew that?"

"Yes. She was kidnapped and tortured."

The consultant nodded to the sister. "As I thought. You'd better call the police in, Sister."

"No," Magnus said.

"Now look, Mr Massey, in cases of this kind we have no option. We're under a clear obligation——"

"This isn't an ordinary criminal case, Doctor. It's political. Which means it's nastier than you might imagine. I don't know if you've ever had dealings with the Internal Security Police."

"No. Merely their victims."

"Well now you've got another one."

The consultant nodded grimly. "What do you suggest?"

"Let her recover and then discharge her into my care. In

the meantime don't let anyone else visit her. Not anyone."

"I must inform her next of kin."

Magnus wrote down Mrs Laura Box's name and address, taking care to get the address slightly wrong.

The consultant led him into the casualty ward and opened a glass-panelled door, motioning to Magnus to wait. A moment later he reappeared and nodded.

"Take it easy," he said.

For a moment Magnus didn't recognize her. The top half of her head, propped against a bank of starched white pillows, was swathed in bandages. Her arms, which lay weakly on the covers, were bandaged round the wrists and hands. Slowly her eyes focused on him.

"Magnus."

He knelt down by the bed. There was no part of her he dared touch. He was aware of the consultant and sister hovering behind him.

"Hullo, Judy."

"Magnus!" Her eyes filled with tears. "Magnus, Magnus, those people, they'll come——"

He hushed and soothed her, suppressing his own fear of the ultimate nightmare now only five days away. In five days' time there would be no refuge, no sanctuary, anywhere.

Friday, 11.45 pm. Stan Gilbert came up to the tenth floor.

"Final corrections then, Bill. You look all in, you know."

Ellison pushed a sheaf of heavily amended galley-proofs across the desk. "Stan, I would consider it a great honour if you could persuade all the boys on the job to come up here for a spot of the Chairman's whisky before they start work tonight."

"I'll put it to them." Stan Gilbert winked.

They came up, fifteen men, linotype operators, time-hands, case-hands, process department operatives, and gazed in awe at the lavishness of the Chairman's office suite.

"Well now we know how the other half lives!"

"I apply for the job!"

"You know something, Bill," said Harry, the Imperial Father of the NGA Chapels. "Until now most of us thought you was nothing but a pretty face!"

When the banter and laughter had subsided, Ellison cleared his throat. "I want to thank you gentlemen."

"It's a pleasure," Stan Gilbert said, drawing a slightly embarrassed murmur of assent.

"One small thing," Ellison said. "Tomorrow night things may get tough for the two hundred operatives and eighty journalists who work here. If it does, let's show those mother-fuckers what we're made of."

Ellison offered his hand to Stan Gilbert, and then to each of the fifteen operatives. And every hand-clasp he received was warm, tight, firm.

He slept surprisingly well and was only awakened, at 6.30, when the security guards brought the finalized eight formes, iron chases filled with lead type and picture plates, up from the composing room. He gazed at them: there it all was—back to front, inside out.

"OK, Stan?"

"OK."

"Lock them away then. Off you go to bed."

Stan Gilbert grinned. "I'll sleep tomorrow. In prison."

Ellison looked down from the high window at the hoists lifting the great reels of newsprint off the long Leyland trucks into the first-floor storerooms. On the nine floors below him Gowers House began to rumble and pulse like an ocean liner putting to sea. It was Saturday, the great day in the life of a Sunday newspaper.

At 11.10 am two private aircraft lifted off from Heathrow in rapid succession. The first was a £1.5 million Hawker Siddeley HS 125/700 business jet, with Garrett turbofan engines, the most expensive of the seven hundred privately registered business aircraft in Britain. On board as guests of its owner, Lord Gowers, were Walter Vandyke, whose dismissal as a Minister of the Crown had finally been announced from Number 10 the previous evening, his right-hand man Marshall Durban, and two Middle East experts known for their democratic sympathies. Stanford Christie had only recently regained access to his own Middle East Institute in Oxford after a long and bitter occupation. Prompted by a warm recommendation from Ellison, Vandyke had offered Christie a senior advisory position on foreign affairs when the future Vandyke administration was formed. The second expert had been smuggled out of his North London hideout and brought on board under a false passport. His name was Solomon Rupin.

The plane which followed the Hawker Siddeley into the air was an American Grumman Gulfstream 2 belonging to Sheikh Abdul Al-Abdullah Al-Jalah, Deputy Ruler of Kuwait and titular head of the Arab Mission to Britain. On board were the Sheikh himself, his closest personal adviser, and a suitably large domestic staff.

The two aircraft touched down, ninety minutes later, at an airfield near Brest in Brittany. There a fleet of cars was waiting to drive them to the port, where they were taken on board Lord Gowers's 1,500-ton yacht *Enterprise*.

An hour later the *Enterprise* was moving out into the Atlantic at 15 knots.

Saturday, 2.30 pm. Cherry came through on the intercom.

"The *Enterprise* is now heading out of Brest."

"No hitches?"

"None. Mr Smallhouse is on the line."

"Yes, Richard?"

"There's a fire in paper storehouse 5."

"Here we go."

Smallhouse was back on the intercom twenty minutes later.

"The fire's out. We lost half a dozen reels."

"That's no problem, then."

"Three of the Nohab-Ampress presses have failed on the first test run. The engineers have found clear evidence of sabotage."

"How long will they take to mend?"

"A week."

"Can we carry it?"

"Only if there are no normal breakdowns."

The next message from Smallhouse came through at 3.50.

"There's serious trouble in the foundry. Two of the three casters in use have suffered metal floods. The flongs are jammed in and casting has stopped."

"Mould another flong and use the third caster."

"I'd thought of that." Clearly the strain was beginning to tell on Richard Smallhouse. "Life was never so eventful at the *Dispatch*," he added.

"It will be this evening."

"Meaning?"

"Keep your chin up, Richard."

Saturday, 5.30. Smallhouse came through on the intercom.

"The foul-up in the foundry is resolved. We have the twelve required presses functioning on a trial run, and two reserves in working order. It's all systems go. We start to run at 6.30."

Ellison wandered to Gowers's Chubb TDR safe and unlocked it. The eight metal formes of *The Hour Before Midnight* lay there, inert and expressionless—dynamite. Slowly he ran his finger over the lead type and then smiled to himself: he had just broken the most sacred of union rules. No journalist must ever touch the type.

The door opened. It was Magnus.

And Judy.

As Ellison's arms enfolded her she buried her face in his shoulder, halfway to tears. "Hullo, Bill. I didn't want to miss the fun. Don't look at me too hard, will you."

Almost choking with his own emotion, Ellison strode out of the room and hauled Cherry in by the hand. "Cherry, this is Judy . . ."

"Hullo, Judy," Cherry said softly, taking the younger woman's head in both her hands and kissing her. "You're a very brave girl."

"Thank you." Both women were on the verge of tears.

"Hey, wait a minute," Ellison said to Judy, "don't you want to read what you've written." He pushed her into a chair while Cherry brought coffee, and thrust the galley-proofs under her nose. "At least you'll have something to distract you during the next few hours."

"Thanks for the by-line," Judy whispered, digging in her bag for a handkerchief.

"Easy, easy," Magnus murmured, holding her shoulders. But he too was moved by the 24-point bold by-line:

By Bill Ellison, Magnus Massey, Judith Rossiter and the late Joe O'Neill. A Searchlight Investigation.

Saturday, 6.30. Ramsay Jordan on the intercom.

"I want to run now. Any thoughts?"

"None. Good luck, Ramsay."

"We have five Leech Squad cars stationed round the building, one at each exit from the chutes."

"We expected that."

At 6.32 the twelve giant Nohab-Ampress machines, with sixteen stereo-plates locked into position on the cylinder of each unit, began to turn, slowly at first, until the minders had finally reached the speed of 55,000 units, or over 150,000 complete papers, an hour. While the huge sheets of paper sped out of the presses, slitters descended faster than the speed of an eye to cut the web and kites automatically folded the sheets. When the complete, folded copies began to move up the igranic wires to the publishing room overhead, agents of the Leech Squad reached out and plucked a copy from each wire. As the copies reached the publishing room the automated counter-stackers twirled quires of twenty-five copies into stacks of four, then despatched each bundle along a conveyor belt to the hand-applied brown paper and printed labels of destination. At the end of the belt the quires were automatically bound in yellow twine, then shot out towards the chutes where twenty vans were parked, with twenty others waiting in line.

Saturday, 7.18 pm. Ellison had joined Ramsay Jordan in the Editor's office. As Smallhouse's assistant brought them the first copies of the *Dispatch*, smuggled out of the rival paper's machine-room, the whole Fleet Street area was suddenly reverberating with the sinister swish-swish of Leech Squad sirens.

Ramsay Jordan closed his eyes. "They're coming this way. I suppose this is it."

Ellison looked down out of the window. Packs of Triumph 2500 Mk 2s, with beacons and headlights flashing, were converging on Tudor Street.

The phone rang. Jordan grabbed it. "Jordan," he said.

"Powerstock here. You'd better know that the *Dispatch* has been hit. They have a warrant signed by Martindale under the Public Information Act to seize and seal. They're moving up to this office now. I count on you to report this in your next edition."

"Will do," said Jordan. "My sympathies, Tim——"

But the phone at the other end had already gone dead.

Jordan flicked his intercom. "Give me the News Editor. Alec? The *Dispatch* has been hit. Put not less than three reporters on to it. I want this in by 8.30 for the Midlands and Wales."

Ellison was calmly leafing through his copy of the *Dispatch*. "But why, why?" Jordan said.

"Here's your answer." Ellison pointed to a two-page Powerstock spread entitled *The Coming Coup d'Etat*. Jordan bent over it, his eye skimming rapidly, professionally, down the columns.

"But eighty per cent of this is a facsimile reprint of *Operation Talent* itself! Powerstock must have been mad to think he could get away with that in his first edition."

"Irresistible, though."

"And how the hell did he get hold of a copy of *Operation Talent*?"

Ellison was smiling.

"My God, Bill, you didn't . . ."

"It was the least I could do for an esteemed colleague."

"Bill, you are an absolute bastard! That must be the lowest trick pulled in the whole history of Fleet Street! It's despicable. You're fired!"

Ramsay Jordan was beaming from ear to ear.

Saturday, 10.15 pm. Ellison had rejoined Magnus and Judy on the tenth floor. Smallhouse came through on the intercom.

"Second edition's running. We have eight hundred words on the *Dispatch* close-down. The Editor and Powerstock have been arrested, incidentally."

"Sorry about that."

"We ourselves are down to three ISP cars now."

"Glad about that."

Slowly, slowly, the hour hand crept round the clock.

At 11.20 Stan Gilbert appeared, followed by five security guards. He gestured towards the safe.

"With your kind permission, Mr Ellison, the moulding presses are ready."

Ellison unlocked the safe. The eight heavy metal chases were gently lifted out on to trolleys and wheeled away.

"Stan, I don't suppose I could come down and——"

"That's all we need! A maniac prowling around."

Saturday, 11.50 pm. The intercom buzzed.

"Richard here, Bill. They're off the moulding presses. The flongs are moving into the foundry now."

"Any sign of interest among the operatives?"

"Some. And they can all read a flong or a stereo-plate back to front—if they choose to."

Sunday, 0.34 am. Smallhouse again.

"The stereo-plates are locked into three presses. We also made an extra set just in case. The second edition has now stopped running. So it's up to Ramsay and you now."

"Leech Squad?"

"Down to two cars, eight men."

A moment later Jordan came through. "We ought to go now, Bill."

"Not with eight goons in situ."

"Offer them money? We've budgeted £10,000 for that purpose."

"Eight is too risky. One of them might be ambitious. Start running the final edition unchanged."

"Is that wise?"

"Run for fifteen minutes, Ramsay."

"It's your baby."

Sunday, 1.03. Jordan to Ellison.

"We've been running for thirteen minutes. The ISP seem satisfied that the final edition contains only minor changes. One squad car has departed. The four agents remaining are boozing in their Triumph. If they do lurch in later, we could probably pay them off. But it's your decision."

"Then run *The Hour Before Midnight*."

"There'll be a twenty-minute hold-up, of course."

"I've been waiting for over a year. I daresay I can endure another twenty minutes."

Twenty-three

At 1.25 am, *The Hour Before Midnight* began to roar off the *Monitor*'s presses. At 1.29, as the first bundles came out of the chutes, a taxi was guided in ahead of the vans to chute 9.

Twenty-five minutes later the taxi drew up outside a house in Church Row, Hampstead. While one security guard remained at the wheel, the other carried a package wrapped in brown paper to the door and rang the bell in three short jabs, paused, then jabbed twice more. The door was immediately opened and the package taken from him.

The Leech Squad Triumph parked outside Sir Jack Armstrong's home duly reported the event to Control, just as it had earlier reported the arrival, in ones and twos, of over a dozen senior BBC executives known to be loyal to the Director-General.

Ozanne had remained convinced throughout the evening that the executives intended to resign en bloc, as a gesture of solidarity with Armstrong, and were hammering out a ringing joint statement. But now a grain of doubt settled in his mind: the package described by the ISP agent resembled in size a couple of quires of a Sunday newspaper.

Between 1.50 and 2.05 five small vans parked in quiet side streets in central London and switched off their engines. Each van carried a radio link with Gowers House, and each

296

also carried the names and addresses of a hundred and fifty prominent citizens living within a specific postal area. Delivery was not scheduled to begin until 4.45—unless Gowers House was hit earlier.

At 2.45 Bernie Holzheimer, waiting in New Printing House Square, received a coded message from Ellison authorizing him to begin transmission of the text to the *New York Times*'s head office at 229 West 43rd Street, New York City. Holzheimer set three Telex operators to work. Almost simultaneously the London offices of *Le Monde*, *Die Welt*, the *Washington Post*, *La Stampa* and *Ha'aretz* received clearance to transmit by private line.

But no texts had as yet been passed to the wire agencies.

At 2.55 an inebriated ISP agent climbed shakily out of the lone Triumph parked outside the *Monitor*'s chutes, lurched into the building, and was immediately confronted by Richard Smallhouse.

"You can't come in here in that condition."

"Who . . . th' hell . . . d'yer . . . think . . ."

"Why don't you go home, eh?"

"Out of my way, you shit . . . or . . . !"

Smallhouse reached into his pocket and counted £500 into the agent's hand.

The News Desk of the Press Association, at 85 Fleet Street, the birthplace of Samuel Pepys, was a very quiet spot indeed at 3.45 on a Sunday morning. As often as not, the lonely desk officer was counting all the girls he might have slept with if he'd only used a different after-shave. The final editions of the Sunday papers reached him by a slow-moving, professional messenger service. When the final edition of the *Sunday Monitor* had dropped on to his desk at 3.15, he had glanced through it, found nothing new, and pushed it away. Half an hour later another copy came up.

"I've already seen this."

"You'll find changes," the messenger said.

"Someone's just won a boxing match in Hawaii?"

The messenger shrugged and left. Sighing deeply, the desk officer wearily began to leaf through the seventy-two pages. Then he sat up, bolt upright.

It took him ten minutes to absorb the gist of *The Hour Before Midnight*, focusing his attention on headlines, subheadings and picture captions. Then he headed for the wire room.

But on his way certain emotional forces beyond his control diverted him into the men's toilet where he sat, for fully twenty minutes, apparently beset by chronic constipation. He hated the Murdoch Government.

It was not until 4.25 that the night duty officers in ISP Control began to tear off the tapes coming over the PA wire-machine and rush them to the offices of Stanley Leech and Geoffrey Ozanne.

By that hour the great majority of ISP squad crews had dispersed and gone to bed. Leech had ten cars immediately available.

"Close the *Monitor*!" he screamed.

Sunday, 4.45 am. Jordan to Ellison.

"They're closing in on us now."

"We must have got over half a million copies out."

"Yep. We made it."

"Good luck, Ramsay."

"I'll need it."

While his Editor stayed to face the music, Ellison led Magnus and Judy up to the helicopter pad on the roof of Gowers House. The Chairman's personal Westland lifted off, high above the flashing beacons and the hissing sirens in Carmelite Street, and headed for Hurn airport, north of Bournemouth. Less than an hour later they were aboard Gowers's Hawker Siddeley HS 125/700, carrying two crates of documents and photographs, and four quires of the final edition.

Ellison took Judy's hand. "A girl your age shouldn't be up this late."

She smiled faintly, laid her head on Magnus's shoulder, and fell asleep.

Ellison went forward to the cockpit.

"Tune into Radios 4 and 2, will you?"

The flight engineer glanced at his watch: it was now 5.45. "You won't get anything out of Radio 2 on a Sunday until 6.00, and nothing out of Radio 4 until 7.15."

"Try it and see, eh?"

Ellison returned to his seat and put on his headphones, gesturing to Magnus to do the same. Almost immediately the crackle on the medium-wave ether was broken by a news-reader's clear, clipped, objective voice. Ellison and Massey turned to one another, thumbs up.

Jack Armstrong had come good.

As the Hawker Siddeley headed towards Brest, cruising below power at 300 mph on Ellison's instructions, the news reports on Radios 2 and 4 were increasingly interspersed by telephone-link interviews with prominent democratic MPs, trade unionists, professional men and intellectuals. Initial reactions, based on the copies pushed through their letter-boxes at 4.45, followed by an emphatic ring on the doorbell, were cautious. But by the time the Hawker Siddeley began to shed altitude over Brittany, there were signs of a general stampede to jump on the bandwagon.

"Why the hell don't they send the Leech Squad into Broadcasting House?" Magnus said.

"They were caught napping. And the longer they wait, the harder it becomes. Hold on . . ."

Both men put on their earphones.

". . . ten minutes ago," the announcer was saying, "the Prime Minister issued the following statement from 10 Downing Street. 'The *Sunday Monitor*, to my great grief and regret, has seen fit to print the most outrageous tissue of lies, libel, disinformation and Zionist propaganda that it has ever been my misfortune to read. This is nothing less than an act of moral terrorism against the unity of our people. What we have here is yet another example of the continuing abuse of a free Press which has brought my Government to a reluctant conclusion. But it is an inescapable conclusion, and the conclusion is this: that henceforward the Press in this country must put the national interest first. And if it won't, any responsible government must take steps to ensure that it does.' That is the end of the Prime Minister's statement."

Three minutes later the Hawker Siddeley touched down outside Brest. It was almost 7 am.

The *Enterprise* was now at anchor only a quarter of a mile off the port. A cutter carried them out to the yacht.

"Magnus, get Judy to bed."

"Will do."

Lord Gowers was up and awake, dressed in a smart blue and white uniform, and beaming. He clasped Ellison by the hand.

"We made it then, Bill?"

"You've been listening to the radio?"

"Of course."

"And the others?"

"No one has stirred. Still asleep."

"Let's put out to sea, Chairman, and tell your wireless-operator to close down on all indications of our position."

At 8 o'clock a steward carrying a silver breakfast tray knocked on each cabin door in turn, entered, and aroused the Chairman's guest with the words, "Breakfast and the *Sunday Monitor* with His Lordship's compliments." Then he closed the door.

Picking up speed to 20 knots, the *Enterprise* headed due west into the Atlantic.

At 10.30, Ellison was summoned to the state-room. He found Gowers already in conference with Vandyke and Sheikh

300

Abdul Al-Abdullah Al-Jalah. The Deputy Ruler of Kuwait rose stiffly, proudly, as Ellison entered, but pointedly did not offer his hand.

"Mr Ellison, this is no time for old friendships or first names. If you are right, my hand would befoul yours. If you are wrong, your hand would befoul mine."

"I'm right."

"I'm very much afraid you may be. Your evidence and the logic which binds it is overwhelming. I fear that my brother and I have gravely underestimated the rise of Al-Ittihad. But in my country and yours no man is convicted until he has been given an opportunity to defend himself."

Vandyke turned to Ellison. "You're happy with that, Bill?"

"Of course."

By 11.30 all of Lord Gowers's overnight guests had been conducted to the state-room, together with Ellison, Magnus and Judy.

Silence. A long, enduring silence. As the *Enterprise* bucked and rolled in the Atlantic waves, a mounting tension pervaded the state-room; a mood compounded of anger, doubt, fear—and shock. Ellison sat back in his chair idly tapping his fingers on the armrest; he was in no hurry.

"Bill," Vandyke said, breaking the silence, "I realize you have written it all down and that your job is done, in the narrow professional sense. But please remember that what is familiar ground to you, what has become self-evident to you through weeks of concentrated investigation, is partly new territory to us." There was a murmur of assent round the room. "We haven't assimilated it all yet. You must help us."

Bill Ellison smiled wearily.

Twenty-four

"Very well," Ellison began, pacing the state-room with his hands thrust into the trouser pockets of his crumpled suit, "the onus is on me. So let us begin at the beginning, in those early summer months when we began to suspect that Arab economic and religious penetration of Britain had assumed a sinister aspect.

"Every intelligent person understood that if the Arab Mission was to bail us out of our chronic economic crisis, we would have to pay a price. But what price? And what power group did the Mission represent?

"The pro-Arab policy of our Foreign Office didn't surprise me; nor did the flood of Arab money into Islamic propaganda projects. What alarmed me was the rising anti-semitism and the succession of sexual and financial disasters experienced by MPs and media people of known liberal outlook. Why did the inside story always get to the *Star*? Why were the semi-fascist Saviours of the Nation being allowed a free hand to terrorize local communities?

"In other words, who were the Englishmen working hand in glove with certain Arab interests to subvert our liberties and our independence?

"Ninety per cent of the Arab business interests we probed came out clean: they were run by men whose behaviour conformed to the highest traditions of Arab honour. But the more we looked at Arabair, Samarkand and Howles,

Cramp and Roope, the less we liked them; and they, in turn, confirmed our suspicions by attempting to intimidate us. The private terrorist-gangster outfit they were subsidizing suddenly surfaced in my life: Spectrum Security.

"Our investigations also disturbed some very respectable English gentlemen. Acute business pressures were brought to bear on my Chairman. I was called to 10 Downing Street and instructed to cool it. And that was the only day, incidentally, when the Spectrum Mercedes dropped out of sight. I don't mean at the corner of Downing Street, which would have been understandable; I mean from the time I left my home at 7.30 in the morning. Now why? How did Spectrum learn that the Prime Minister had summoned me?

"Murdoch, as I have said, asked me to cool it. I refused to give any such pledge. So they tried to kill me. And they succeeded in murdering Moshe Levene.

"This little sequence of events led us to wonder how deeply certain elements in the Government were involved. So, too, did the trap set for me in Czechoslovakia, which I evaded thanks solely to Judy Rossiter—all the evidence pointed to collusion between the British and Czech Governments. But at this stage I continually underestimated the scale of the conspiracy, attributing the sinister growth of the ISP to the Martindale–Ozanne–Leech clique in the Home Office working hand in glove with the Lynedoch faction in the Foreign Office. I imagined that Murdoch and most of his colleagues, together with the Opposition front bench, were being dragged along, half-blind, in the hope of saving the nation from ruin. I was wrong. But so was everyone else.

"Then we achieved our first break-through, the Irving documents. A can of worms. These papers, and the investigations they inspired, demonstrated that the Arabair group was pouring money into the FSCR for the production of Islamic propaganda programmes which were being flogged to the BBC, now controlled by the Lucas–Strachan clique. Clearly the same crowd were also responsible for framing BBC Jews and liberals, in collusion with the *Star*, which in turn was controlled by Swinburne and the trustees of the FSCR, Lynedoch, Ozanne, Lucas and Strachan.

"One of these men, furthermore—or some other man as yet unsuspected—was referred to in a Swinburne memorandum as 'the highest authority', coordinating the whole operation, selecting the victims, authorizing massive subsidies which passed from the Trans-Arabian Bank of Tripoli through the Arabair group to the FSCR, the Guardians of Decency, the Saviours of the Nation, and Spectrum Security. To which I shall, in a moment, add one other crucial organization.

"It was now that Solomon Rupin tossed the name Al-Ittihad into my lap. I didn't require much convincing, so sure was I that Al-Ittihad was the name which had died on Moshe Levene's lips.

"So who were the leaders of Al-Ittihad in Britain? Nashat Al-Khatib and Mamoun Abdul Shukhairy, for certain. Clearly they had made massive inroads into the British Establishment, and equally clearly they could have pulled this off only with the collaboration of Englishmen drawn into the conspiracy at the highest level. Ozanne and Lynedoch were obvious suspects, Arabists and by rumour Moslems, commanding an extensive network of personal contacts in the Middle East. And why, otherwise, should two civil servants of the second rank attend meetings of the Inner Cabinet from which even the Leader of the Commons was excluded?

"Now I come to the other organization I promised to mention. By a systematic approach to the victims of the frame-ups, we discovered a disguised prostitution racket called Relief, Ltd, whose directors, F. Eltenbridge and F. Cain, had registered phony residential addresses in Companies House. Who were they really? And whom did they serve? Al-Ittihad? Certainly—but *how?*

"My journey to Wales to interview General Winstanley exploded the last of my illusions. The conspiracy to destroy our democracy was far more extensive, and far more menacing, than I had imagined. A mess of pottage called the

Ministry of All the Talents, spiced with generous Arabair handouts, had easily seduced greedy men of fascist spirit and limitless personal ambition."

Ellison shot a glance towards Lord Gowers, who had turned crimson and was suddenly gazing out of the porthole.

"Clearly the Supreme Executive Council of three, granted dictatorial powers in Operation Talent, was to be filled by the leaders of Al-Ittihad. Again Lynedoch and Ozanne were obvious candidates: why, otherwise, had they not been allocated portfolios in the Ministry of All the Talents? But who was the third member, and who was to be Leader?

"We were soon able to eliminate Ozanne as a contender for this post. In *The Hour Before Midnight* you will have read of the circumstances in which Ozanne confided to Judy Rossiter that the supreme leader, Zamil Al-Alhambra, was someone else."

The men gathered in the state-room carefully averted their gaze from the one woman present. But Judy, Ellison noticed, remained serenely composed.

"It was now a race against time. As soon as I had *Operation Talent* in my possession, the kid gloves came off and the State showed its hand: the ISP emerged into the open, the arrests multiplied, Joe O'Neill was murdered, my family was threatened, and repressive legislation was passed to gag all dissent.

"Why, then, didn't I go to press before the Arab Mission arrived? Because the spider at the heart of the web continued to elude me, I couldn't prove the whole of my case. If I had sold the story then I would have sold it short and the State of Emergency would have been rushed into immediate operation.

"I had to find Zamil Al-Alhambra, the man who sits among you now—Stanford Christie."

At this moment every pair of eyes in the room was focused on the Oxford don. But Christie seemed calm enough; when Ellison named him he merely pulled a lock of black hair off his forehead, shrugged sardonically, and folded his hands.

Abruptly Ellison sank into a chair, exhausted—but more than exhausted; deeply pained that he could have for so many years trusted and admired a man of so vicious and criminal a character.

"We begin with inferences," Ellison said. "Inferences are not evidence, of course, they merely suggest lines of inquiry. As you know, Christie was present at the Oxford and Cambridge Club dinner when Moshe Levene was called away and murdered at the moment he was about to reveal something of importance. The timing could have been a coincidence, but I doubted it. The most plausible explanation, to my mind, was that a transmitter had been planted in one of my guests' clothing without his knowledge. Yet I couldn't rule out an uglier version.

"The Irving documents, as I have said, contained references to 'the highest authority', a man who evidently knew Maurice Cohn well enough to assess his character and vulnerability. Christie fitted. But so did many other people.

"Later I asked Christie what the FSCR was. After a momentary hesitation he gave me the answer, adding that Swinburne had been hunting his scalp since 1970, when Christie became Director of the Middle East Institute. Afterwards I told Joe to check Swinburne's public utterances in the press-cuttings library; it turned out that Swinburne's vilification of Christie had not begun until 1975, when the FSCR was launched. I wondered why, and I wondered whether Christie's memory had really been at fault.

"It always seemed to me that Christie knew rather less about his former Foreign Office colleagues, Lynedoch and Ozanne, then he should have done. I tried a shot in the dark, suggesting that Lynedoch had a touch of the tar brush. This phrase provoked in my friend, a man of remarkably mild manner, the darkest of rages. I wondered why. Where had I struck home?

"The walls of Christie's Park Town study contain a splendid collection of photographs and drawings, most of them undesignated. I had often been impressed by a large pen-and-ink drawing of a vast palace-mosque set round adjoining courtyards. Of course I was tempted to ask Christie what it was, but didn't—sixth sense, if you like. My interest in such things was sharpened by the revelation that the Zamils of Al-Ittihad are customarily named after Arab-Islamic buildings of historical and geographical significance, but I had nothing specific to chew on until Ozanne blurted out to Judy that the supreme leader of Al-Ittihad in Britain was known as Zamil Al-Alhambra.

"This took me to the library, where I discovered that the drawing on Christie's study wall was indeed of the Al-Alhambra mosque in Granada—a symbol of Islamic penetration of the West. Well, Christie was an Arabist, it didn't prove anything. However, on a later visit to Park Town I noticed that the drawing had vanished and been replaced by a quite different picture. Why? Ben-Dor was staying in the house. Things were hotting up. Christie was taking no chances.

"Did I have a case against Christie? None. Here was a man with a lifelong record not merely as a friend of the Arabs, but also of Israel, a man who worked in collaboration with the Hebrew University to bring Jews and Palestinians together in a civilized dialogue. I kept telling myself I was round the bend.

"Until, that is, we achieved our decisive breakthrough inside Relief. I say 'we', though the credit belongs entirely to Magnus and Judy. We learnt that Eltenbridge and Cain were in reality the racketeers Elizabeth Lyons and Frank Young, imprisoned in 1969 and married in 1975. Eltenbridge took Judy to work for Ulf Steinberg who, you will recall, had been involved in compromising Maurice Cohn on the instructions of 'the highest authority'. Steinberg mentioned to Judy that his first love was theatre design—which was very helpful of him because it led us to discover that in the 1960s he had been involved with Lyons and Young, in procuring for immoral purposes. And so, too, had his mistress Rose Weber, the stage name of Elizabeth Lyons's sister, born Margaret Rose Lyons.

"On arrival in Steinberg's studio Judy was inspected by a lady closely resembling Eltenbridge in appearance, a lady who was distinctly calling the tune. Rose Weber? Was she the intermediary who transmitted instructions to Steinberg from 'the highest authority'? If so, did she not equally transmit instructions to Relief and Spectrum through her sister and her sister's husband, the boss of Spectrum?

"An old parking ticket held the clue. Judy found it in Steinberg's bedroom, in a drawer full of women's stuff. I traced the registration number: the car, a white Porsche, was registered under the name of Rose Weber at a phony address.

"But where did that lead me?

"It led me to Stanford Christie's wife Margaret, a lady in her middle forties who dabbled in amateur theatricals as a costume designer and who spent a large amount of her time in London. Margaret Christie and Rose Weber were the same woman, born Margaret Rose Lyons. You look sceptical, as well you might.

"The parking ticket was dated June 12 and was for an offence committed in Beaumont Street, Oxford. On that day I had visited Oxford to talk to Christie and Rupin, and hoping to call in on the OUDS dress rehearsal of *Hamlet*, featuring the remarkable Faith Ellison as Ophelia. After exchanging a few pleasantries, Margaret Christie had driven off to the Playhouse Theatre for a final afternoon costume fitting.

"The Playhouse is in Beaumont Street.

"I heard her car leave its garage—unmistakably a sports car, though I didn't see it. But later, after Christie's car and mine were burnt out at the Middle East Institute, I had a pretext for casually suggesting to Christie that he would have to use his wife's Porsche. He confirmed that it was a Porsche.

"But wait, you say, consider all the contrary evidence. Christie, an unworldly don, might be in ignorance of his wife's activities, And why did his name appear on the Operation Talent blacklist? Why was his beloved Institute occupied by a mob? Why was he chased off the platform and vilified as a Zionist in the Press? Why did ISP agents pursue us as we walked across the Meadows? Why had a transmitter been planted in his shoe? Why had a Relief girl called Teresa been planted in his house?"

"Yes, why?" Solomon Rupin exploded.

"Bluff, my dear Solomon. Dust in our eyes. The whole scenario was masterminded by Christie himself.

"As you remember, the principal revelation of that walk in the Meadows concerned an English agent of Al-Ittihad called Sheikh Abdul Issa Attiqi, a masked man with a palace and a vast oil royalty in Qatar. For me the significance of that story was greater than you and Ben-Dor could realize: Ozanne had already revealed to Judy that Zamil Al-Alhambra's mother was an Arab, but the Arab world is immense—I could now focus on one tiny dot, the blob of oil and sand called Qatar. Christie, you may recall, had listened to Ben-Dor's disclosure calmly enough, but on the way home his nerve broke."

"The story about Lynedoch!" Rupin exclaimed.

"Exactly. It was a smokescreen designed at that late hour to focus suspicion on Lynedoch. But why hadn't Christie told us about Lynedoch before? Besides, no one familiar with the history of Qatar could swallow so implausible a tale. Fifty years ago Qatar was a primitive desert with only thirty thousand inhabitants, a nomadic ruling family that lived in tents, no oil at all, and a strict puritan code imposed by a fanatical Islamic sect called the Wahhabis. A foreign infidel like Lynedoch's father would never have set eyes on a Qatari woman of the ruling family, and the idea of such a woman being allowed to leave for England to have a baby and then returning home to a warm family welcome is simply preposterous. Right?"

Rupin nodded gloomily, Ellison allowed himself a hint of a smile.

309

"The birth certificates of both Lynedoch and Ozanne had been inexplicably lost in the Register of Births. Yet the index showed that their births had been registered in Canterbury and Andover. Were Arab mothers giving birth to future diplomats all over southern England fifty years ago? Unlikely. No, the certificates had been removed in order to focus any possible suspicion on them. It was bluff.

"The index for England and Wales, you see, yielded no mention of Christie's own birth. Nor, incidentally, of his marriage. It was he who had something to hide.

"And let me add one other item of evidence from that memorable visit to Oxford. After the walk, Christie lent us dry shoes of his own. Suspecting that they too must be bugged, Ben-Dor slit them open during the journey home. He found nothing. Curious: you don't bug just one pair of a victim's shoes, you take care to bug every pair he might wear. But Christie, of course, was a fake victim."

"Damn, damn, damn!" yelled Solomon Rupin, thumping his fist on the arm of his chair. "It should have been so obvious!"

"Later," Ellison continued, "Ha-Mossad's source in Qatar, young Badr Nureddin, was murdered. You will recall, Solomon, that his name was mentioned only after the transmitter had been neutralized by immersion. Thus it was not heard by the two Leech Squad agents—only by the man who commands every one of the twelve thousand ISP agents in Britain. It was for that reason that I deliberately divined Ha-Mossad's source in Qatar, which you were anxious to protect. Christie, of course, knew your source; but unless I knew it too, I wouldn't be able to interpret subsequent events, events that I regarded as inevitable."

Rupin gestured angrily. "You could have saved Badr Nureddin's life. You made no effort to prevent his murder!"

"Yes. And the same may be true of Joe O'Neill's murder. We have been in a shooting war: there are always casualties. The problem confronting me now was to prove that Christie's version of his own biography was a fake; to prove that his mother was not an American, as he claimed, but a Qatari woman of royal blood."

"Wait a minute, Bill," Vandyke interposed. "Only a moment ago you were telling us that fifty years ago no such Qatari woman could have had sexual relations with an Englishman."

"Not with an Englishman professing the Christian faith and on a temporary business visit. I wasn't talking about an Englishman living in permanent exile, estranged from his native land, converted to Islam, and able to cultivate a close friendship with the Ruler. Such a man might well have been presented with a Qatari wife of royal blood—and the legitimate offspring would be born in Qatar."

"Presumably you checked the Register of Births under Qatar," Vandyke said.

"No. Tempting but fatal. In that room on the seventh floor of St Catherine's House the search has to be made by an attendant. Even if the incriminating page of the Qatar file had not been excised, I was in no doubt that my inquiry would have reached Christie's ears within the hour. In which case an extremely unpleasant sequence of events would have been set in motion. I had to bluff; I had to pretend that I suspected Lynedoch—which was why I addressed him as Zamil Al-Alhambra at the airport. When Jack Knight later asked me, on behalf of the ISP, why I had done so, I had to bluff again.

"That was how, by the skin of our teeth, we got *The Hour Before Midnight* to press.

"If you look up Christie in *Who's Who* or any other biographical directory, you may be struck by a curious omission. Most Englishmen are proud of their schools, even if, and particularly if, they hated them. Yet the first educational institution listed under Christie's name is New College, Oxford.

"Many years ago Christie told me that his public school had been Ardingly. I checked with Ardingly. I drew a blank.

"And that seemed to be that. I had come to the proverbial

dead end. It was then that the prodigious Ellison memory justified its ratings. Nearly twenty years ago, in Beirut, Pru, Christie and I had taken ourselves off to see Chaplin's film, *The Gold Rush*. Coming out of the cinema, Stanford mentioned that the last time he'd seen that film, as a small boy, he had secretly caught a bus into Petersfield and played truant. Alas, a master who was also a Chaplin fan had spotted him and he had been soundly thrashed."

Dark clouds of rage now dominated Christie's olive-skinned features. Ellison threw a quick glance at Magnus who rose casually from his chair, as if his long limbs could stand the containment no longer, and began to pace about the room.

"There's only one private prep school near Petersfield. And it was there—roughly speaking, I have to protect this source, you understand—that the truth spilt out: a Qatari mother with the family name of Attiqi; a wretched, unhappy life at school for a boy who muttered in Arabic in his dreams; a father who never worked for the Iraq Petroleum Company but, on the contrary, had spent the last twenty-five years of his life in exile, attempting to subvert British rule in the Middle East and joining up with the Axis in the process. A rabid anti-semite. Young Christie himself had never attended Ardingly or any other secondary school in England; he had spent the war years in Qatar, under the protection of the ruling family."

"Rubbish," snarled Christie. "You're lying! What are your sources? The reason you don't reveal them is that they don't and can't exist!"

"Because you had your own uncle murdered, you mean? You overlooked another source. Careless."

Massey was now working his way behind Christie's chair. Solomon Rupin, Ha-Mossad agent, had also picked up the signals.

"Then I looked into the Canal Zone episode. Now Christie has disguised his past but his National Service with the Medway Regiment he could not conceal—there are too many old comrades about who might bump into him in the street or the club with an embarrassing greeting. Or bump into someone like Ellison. I had long ago known that something fishy occurred when the Medways were serving at the southern end of the Canal Zone. So I took myself off to Howe Barracks, Canterbury. Sorry, once again the source cannot be named. I came away with the name of the fish.

"It was then that Magnus brought me a little gift, a gift which confirmed my sanity, by that time much in doubt. Shadowing Nashat Al-Khatib's Cadillac out of Swinburne's mansion, he finally caught the sardine in his tin. On its way back to London, the Cadillac stopped first in Park Town, Oxford—where Stanford Christie got out.

"Yet I was still puzzled how a man with Christie's record—as I now knew it—had broken into the Foreign Office. So we come to my final source, Kim Philby."

"Ha!" Christie snarled. "A KGB agent, a traitor—some source!"

"The devil is not without his uses," Ellison said quietly. "From Philby I learnt that Christie's original application to join the FO had been turned down after a negative security vetting. Four years later, following the Suez fiasco, KGB agents within the FO had brought in several pro-Arab Arabists, with the aim of hastening the demise of Western influence in the Middle East. Philby, of course, knew it; he was also aware of Christie's contacts with Al-Rashib, Yacoub, Nashat Al-Khatib and Shukhairy, the future leaders of a powerful Al-Ittihad.

"Phiiby told me one other thing: that Christie's father had been captured during the war by our people, interrogated . . . and allowed to die."

"Murdered!" Christie screamed.

A stunned silence filled the room.

"Thank you, Stanford," Ellison said quietly. "And since you are now in a mood to put information at our disposal, you will no doubt confirm my analysis of how you came to achieve your pre-eminence within Al-Ittihad.

"We know your motives: hatred of Britain, hatred of Israel, hatred of everything which humiliated you as a child. That was your great advantage: an inflexible resolve. You bided your time; you cultivated your contacts within Al-Ittihad, simultaneously burrowing deep into the womb of British democratic life. That was why you left the FO and became an academic: not merely to build a liberal image, not merely to befriend a wide range of future victims, but also to give yourself freedom to penetrate the most dangerous obstacle in your path—the Israeli intelligence agency known as Ha-Mossad. While Lynedoch and Ozanne, each handicapped by having two English parents, clambered up the conventional ladders of political influence, exposing themselves to suspicion and odium, you designed for yourself a streamlined machine, entirely at your command, for the subversion of British democracy. If Al-Ittihad wanted to take over Britain, they had to do it your way: through the FSCR, through Spectrum, through Relief—they merely footed the bill whenever you nodded.

"How delicately you must have scanned the criminal underworld to fasten on Rose Weber as a wife. The fact that Elizabeth Lyons and Frank Young were then languishing in prison suited you very well; demoralized, out of action, on ice, they were perfectly receptive to the offer of undreamt-of wealth you filtered into their prison cells. And you could afford to wait—until the flow of Arab oil dictated your moment.

"Nor were you anxious to sever your wife's long established affair with Steinberg. Venal, corrupt, half-Jewish, and on good terms with prominent people, he suited you very well. Jealousy? I don't think so, Stanford. I doubt very much whether your 'marriage' was ever consummated, for was it not you who once said to Philby, with passionate feeling, 'I would rather be flogged to death than have intercourse with a woman'?"

Magnus's long arms descended forcefully as Christie, with a vicious, semi-human snarl, sprang towards Ellison. Rupin moved at the same moment.

"You Jew-shit scum," Christie snarled, "one day the gas chambers will return!"

"That's the spirit," Ellison said as a blow from Solomon Rupin across the vital nerve of the neck sent Christie crumpling to the floor. Involuntarily, Ellison turned away.

Twenty-five

Yet still the iron heel of Al-Ittihad held Britain down.

At 4 in the afternoon Walter Vandyke and the Sheikh, who had been in closed-session conclave for several hours, summoned Ellison to the state-room.

"Bill, we've been talking to Christie. We pointed out to him that his position is now hopeless, but he's immune to reason."

"Mad," growled the Sheikh, "a mad dog."

"You asked him to radio the Government in London and call the whole thing off?"

"Exactly."

"And he laughed in your face?"

"He asked us whether we intended to circle the Atlantic for the rest of our lives."

"Good question." Ellison smiled.

"In the meantime His Excellency has been in the ship's wireless-room launching a major diplomatic blitzkrieg to undermine the Mission."

"We Arabs are a proud race," the Sheikh said. "It is not easy for us to denounce our own brethren as criminals. Yet pride, and honour also, dictate that we now do so."

"Now, Bill," Vandyke resumed somewhat uneasily. "Up to this point we have given Christie ultimata. We haven't attempted to bargain with him."

Ellison nodded but said nothing.

"That may become necessary," Vandyke continued,

"assuming that the Government in London keeps its nerve and holds out."

"What kind of a deal did you have in mind?"

"A free passage back to Qatar. Of course we might commence extradition proceedings at a later date . . ."

Slowly Ellison produced a spiral-backed notebook from his inner pocket, then a pen. Vandyke watched him, aghast.

"What the hell are you doing?"

"I'm a reporter."

"Now look, Bill, there is such a thing as the national interest, you know. I realize how you feel about Christie, but I have to consider the matter in a wider context. Of course I'm not in a position to make any formal deal with Christie, I'm merely a backbench MP now. What His Excellency and I had in mind was some form of 'escape' by Christie as soon as we put into port. After all, we have no formal powers to detain him."

Ellison wrote steadily in his notebook. "Anything else, gentlemen?"

"You don't intend to quote or print what I've just told you in the strictest confidence!"

"Why not?"

"But I thought . . . Now, look Bill, we'd better get one thing straight. I intend to form an administration and I want to know here and now whether I can count on your support. If not . . ."

"Yes?"

Vandyke subsided, seething with anger. "Fuck you, Bill."

"That I needn't quote."

"I gather," the Sheikh said with dignity, "that you are opposed to any such . . . arrangement, Bill."

"Yes."

"What would you suggest?"

"Christie goes on trial at the Old Bailey on a charge of multiple murder—with his henchmen. No cover ups."

"Splendid, splendid!" Vandyke shouted. "I suppose all we need is a pair of handcuffs!"

Sunday, 10 pm. BBC Radio 4 News:

"Twenty minutes ago the Arab Mission left Britain for the Middle East, although the leader of the Mission, Sheikh Abdul Al-Abdullah Al-Jalah, was not among those boarding the chartered Boeing 747.

"According to our diplomatic correspondent, the Sheikh's movements during the past day-and-a-half remain uncertain. Reports coming in from our Middle East staff strongly indicate that the Sheikh himself has denounced the Arab Mission as a conspiracy to subvert British democracy. Statements condemning the role of Al-Ittihad have been issued during the past few hours by the Foreign Ministers of Kuwait, Egypt, Saudi Arabia, Jordan, Lebanon, Tunisia, Syria, Morocco, Algeria and the United Arab Emirates. No statements have been issued in Iraq, Libya, or Qatar.

"On leaving London, the Mission declined all comment and refused to speak to reporters.

"The Cabinet has been in session since early today. No further statements have been issued.

"Speculation continues concerning the present where-abouts of a number of prominent personalities named by the *Sunday Monitor*, notably the Oxford don Stanford Christie and his wife Mrs Margaret Christie.

"Bill Ellison, principal author of the *Sunday Monitor*'s sensational report, *The Hour Before Midnight*, is believed to have left Gowers House last night with two colleagues, shortly before the building was surrounded and sealed by the Internal Security Police.

"As reported earlier, the paper's Editor, Mr Ramsay Jordan, has been held in detention under the Public Information Act. No formal charges have yet been brought against him. This followed similar action against the Editor of the *Sunday Dispatch* and Mr Timothy Powerstock, of the same paper.

"According to a survey made by BBC reporters, the Internal Security Police succeeded last night in seizing some 65,000 out of 555,000 copies of *The Hour Before Midnight* printed. Early editions of tomorrow's newspapers report the story prominently and describe how the publication of the supplement in the final edition was planned and carried out in conditions of strict secrecy.

"The story also figured prominently in this morning's *New York Times* and other foreign newspapers. Radio Kol Israel, Tel Aviv, has broadcast news bulletins round the clock on the crisis in Britain.

"A State Department spokesman declined to comment. Diplomatic sources, however, confirm that the *Monitor*'s story is widely believed in official circles in Washington, and that the situation in Britain is viewed with the gravest concern.

"The noted *Washington Post* columnist James White has described Bill Ellison's story as 'the most brilliant and courageous piece of investigative reporting' that he had witnessed in his lifetime.

"We have just heard that Mr Walter Vandyke is now on board the yacht *Enterprise* which is at sea in the eastern Atlantic. In a statement issued a few minutes ago, Mr Vandyke described the British Government as 'a criminal conspiracy controlled by a foreign power'. He called for the Government's immediate resignation.

"According to Mr Vandyke, on board the same yacht are Sheikh Abdul Al-Abdullah Al-Jalah and Mr Stanford Christie. Mr Vandyke reports that during a tape-recorded conversation this morning Mr Christie confessed that the Ellison report was accurate and exclaimed, 'You Jew-shit scum, one day the gas chambers will return.' Mr Vandyke added that he had indignantly rejected Mr Christie's offer of a deal involving Mr Christie's escape to Qatar.

"A report just in indicates that sixteen hours ago, at dawn this morning, a Special Branch unit commanded by Superintendent Edgar Bradlaw arrested Mrs Margaret Christie, her sister Miss Florence Eltenbridge, and Mr Ulf Steinberg, the sculptor, at Mr Steinberg's house in north London. According to Superintendent Bradlaw, all three have signed sworn statements describing themselves as victims of blackmail and intimidation by Mr Christie.

"Disturbances are reported among military units converging on London from Salisbury Plain. A spokesman at the Ministry of Defence declined to confirm or deny that junior officers and other ranks have refused to obey mobilization orders.

"We now go over to our reporter at London airport: 'This is Hugh Johns, at Heathrow. During the past two hours a number of personalities named by the *Sunday Monitor* have passed through immigration control on their way to planes leaving for the Continent, South America, and the Middle East. Among those boarding aircraft were Professor Hugh Swinburne, Mr Bert Hoyle, Sir Philip Lucas, Mr Nashat Al-Khatib, Mr Mamoun Abdul Shukhairy and Mr Frank Cain. Back now to Broadcasting House.'

"Here is a news flash from 10 Downing Street. The Government has resigned."

Tuesday, 2.00 pm. A great roar went up from both sides of the aisle as Walter Vandyke entered the packed Chamber of the House of Commons. Glancing at the empty front benches on both sides of the House, Vandyke strode to his place on the back benches and sat down.

He didn't need to catch the Speaker's eye. The Speaker caught his.

Tall, handsome, polished and gleaming, Vandyke rose, watched by a crowded Press Gallery, by public galleries almost overflowing (a queue had formed outside St Stephen's entrance a mile long), and by the Sheikh and his retinue seated in the Distinguished Strangers' Gallery.

Vandyke's statement was brief. The nation was emerging from a great crisis, a profound, shattering moral collapse, but the British people were never greater than with their backs to the wall. In offering himself to the nation, Vandyke pledged himself to hold an early general election, to dismantle the Internal Security Police, to free all political prisoners, to restore habeas corpus and the rule of law, to guarantee true freedom of expression to the Press and the BBC, and to bring all criminals to justice, sparing no one.

"And now, Mr Speaker, I must mention the acute economic crisis facing this nation. As we all know, the hopes of many desperate people were focused on the promises of immediate relief, aid, investment, loans and export orders made by the Arab Mission. The previous Government warned us time and again that unless we abandoned our cherished liberties, this package would be snatched away from us like naughty children.

"Mr Speaker, it has, thank God, been snatched away. Let us, then, stand on our own feet, but let us not be too proud to accept generous help while we are once again learning to do so." Vandyke turned and, with a gracious gesture, acknowledged His Excellency in the gallery above. "I am therefore pleased to inform you, Mr Speaker, and I am sure every honourable member will join me in a sentiment of profound gratitude, that the Government of Kuwait and its friends have guaranteed any Government I may be called on to form loans and credits of £4,500 million."

An immense cheer rose from the well of the Chamber. There was pandemonium in the Press Gallery as reporters scrambled out in search of telephones. His Excellency inclined his head serenely.

As Bill Ellison, Magnus Massey and Judy Rossiter left St Stephen's entrance, a cluster of forty newsmen, British and foreign, pursued them with machine-gun questions.

"Ellison, are you satisfied with Vandyke's statement?"

"Ellison, do you regard this as another sell-out?"

"Ellison, can you confirm reports that Vandyke will offer you a senior post in the Government?"

But Ellison walked on, square-shouldered, cold-eyed, tight-lipped, his hands thrust deep in his pockets.

Tuesday, 4.00 pm. A Government saloon carrying Walter Vandyke edged through an immense, cheering crowd massed outside Buckingham Palace.

Tuesday, 16.30 GMT, Ben Gurion Airport, Tel Aviv. As Pru, Faith and Christopher Ellison were ushered on board an El Al Boeing bound for London, a large party of Israeli women showered them with flowers and smiles.

"Shalom, shalom, shalom, shalom . . ."

Christopher Ellison waved like a small king from the open doorway of the airplane, framed by two radiant stewardesses.

"Shalom!" he called.

Tuesday, 4.30 pm. Ellison, Massey and Rossiter sat with Ramsay Jordan in Ellison's office. Several floors below them, in the *Monitor*'s machine rooms, copies of *The Hour Before Midnight* were roaring off the giant presses at the rate of 60,000 an hour. The target was 7.5 million copies, to be sold at 50p a copy. At last Lord Gowers was reaping his reward.

"Well," Jordan said, "I suppose you boys and girls had better take a holiday."

"Why are we all so gloomy?" Magnus said. "I don't think I've ever felt so damned flat in my life."

"It's called post-natal depression," Judy said.

"You know," Jordan mused, "I don't think I'm a vain man, but I do wish Vandyke had mentioned us just once during his speech to the Commons."

"Seek your reward in Heaven," Ellison said.

He drove her back to Bonham Terrace in Pru's Ford Escort. Though mending rapidly, Judy still didn't feel up to driving through London traffic.

"Well," he said, "I can hardly believe it, but here I am parking right outside your front door."

"And no Leech Squad Triumph. Want to come up?"

"Yes."

"Come on, then, I'll make you an omelette."

"No."

Gently she put her hand on his. "Oh, Bill, I'm sorry. You're finding it hard, aren't you?"

"There are times."

She folded her arms round his neck and lightly brushed his mouth with hers.

"Bill, relax. You're a very attractive man."

"I'd rather you went on working for me."

"Do they have to be alternatives?"

"In practice, yes."

She smiled faintly. "There aren't many like you, Bill. Thank God."

The call from the new Prime Minister came through to Chester Place two days later. It was Christopher who picked up the phone.

"Hey, Dad, it's VD himself!"

Ellison clipped his son across the ear and took the receiver from him.

"Good morning, Prime Minister."

"Bill, I've been talking to Jack Armstrong. As you know, he's nearing retirement age and he feels exhausted, physically and mentally, by recent events. He and I are both agreed that the next Director-General should come from outside the Corporation, to clean up the mess. Jack is happy to retire immediately on one condition, and I endorse it. You must take his place."

"I'm honoured, Prime Minister."

"And I'm delighted, Bill. I have no doubt that the new Board of Governors will recognize that you're the man for the job."

"I can't think of any job I'd rather have—other than my own."

"Now, Bill, you must put the national interest——"

"Sorry, Walter."

"Bill, you disappoint me."

"That's my vocation."

"What is?"

"Disappointing Prime Ministers."

The phone went down in 10 Downing Street.

Ellison grinned and winked at his son. "Strip down, Zatopek, we're going for a run in the park."